D1519523

1

Fauxmance

L.H. COSWAY

"No matter how long I live, I shall live longer than you will love me."

— Alexandre Dumas fils, *La Dame Aux Camélias.*

One
Julian

I was obsessed with the woman from the coffee shop.

She always sat at the same table, and her stories were *everything*.

Each Tuesday at ten-thirty in the morning, she'd meet her friend with some new piece of scandal or adventure to tell. I normally arrived early, ordered my latte and sat down to wait for the latest episode of Elodie's eventful love life.

On this particular Tuesday, I watched her walk into the Polka Dot Café with a blue scarf wrapped around her neck. She ordered a drink, then took a seat at the table close to mine where her friend was waiting. Elodie was medium height, with long, silky red hair and captivating green eyes. Her makeup was immaculate; red lips, smoky eyeshadow, and her clothes were edgy and sexy. She was also never without a pair of sky-high heels.

Her friend, whose name was Suze, was Asian and wore funky designer clothing from head to toe. Think Moschino with a touch of Vivienne Westwood. Visually, she was more striking than Elodie, but she didn't have her friend's adventurous soul, her *joie de vivre*.

I feigned preoccupation with my phone while they exchanged greetings.

"Gosh, my Kenneth just won't stop going on about getting me a boob job," Suze complained. She was also a source of entertaining anecdotes, though she had nothing on Elodie.

Elodie made a face. "Your boobs are fine. What does he want you to end up like? A blow-up doll?"

Suze chuckled. "Probably. Most men prefer silence and submission, right?"

"I'm not so sure about that. The guy I was out with on Saturday definitely enjoyed my vocalisations."

A cackle from Suze. "Oh, do tell! How did you meet this one?"

Elodie took a sip of her coffee and made a face. I'd adjusted my seat so that I could watch her covertly from the corner of my eye. "On Tinder. He invited me for dinner at the Ivy and then we decided to hell with it and booked a hotel room."

"I swear you invented the philosophy of YOLO," Suze said with envy.

"I just want to enjoy myself while I'm young."

"So, are you going to see him again?"

"Hmmm, maybe. He said he manages a gym. If things go well, I could get a free membership."

"You're too much," Suze tittered.

"Anyway," Elodie continued, "he had nothing on the guy I went to dinner with last Thursday. He was a pilot, even showed up wearing his uniform. I just about died and went to heaven."

"Seriously? How do you find all these amazing men?"

Elodie grinned. "I won't lie, it's a skill."

"Sometimes I wish I wasn't married so that we could go out together and paint the town red every night."

"Hey! It's more like every second night," she chided playfully, and I smirked before taking a sip of coffee. She was a woman after my own heart and I loved it.

Suze sighed. "Ugh, I'm so jealous. What happened with the pilot?"

"He was sort of kinky, wanted to tie me up."

Suze slammed her hand down on the table. "No way!"

"And get this, he brought a pair of handcuffs. Fur lined to avoid chafing, of course." She raised a saucy brow.

"Of course," said Suze.

"It was all going great until we started doing the deed and he made these loud, high-pitched sex noises. I was like, okay, this is weird. But you know, he was good in bed, so I gave him a pass on the girly moans."

Suze laughed so hard she almost spit out her coffee. "Oh, man. That's too funny. You should write a newspaper column. More people need to hear these stories."

There was a pause before Elodie replied, "Now where would I find the time for that? I'm too busy going out and enjoying myself."

"Well, that's true," Suze agreed.

I listened to the rest of Elodie's account of her night with the pilot and wondered if I should introduce myself someday. After all, I felt like I knew them both better than some of my real-life friends at this stage, such was the extent of my eavesdropping. I could be the third member of their group. Just one of the girls. Strangely, I'd always gotten along better with women than with men.

My bestie, Rose, could attest to that.

One of my few male friends, David, says it's because I'm a lesbian trapped in a straight man's body. I like to talk to women about their feelings and I also like to have sex with them. I happen to think that simply makes me an evolved modern gentleman rather than a lesbian, but what do I know?

David, aka, David Jonathan, was a pop star in the eighties. He achieved a grand total of three Top Ten singles and a platinum record before fading into obscurity. Now he worked as a wedding photographer. To his annoyance, I often enjoyed reminding him of two things. One, the lyrics of his biggest hit, "Naughty", and two, the fact I was a mere toddler when it released in 1987.

Speak of the devil, a few minutes after Elodie and Suze departed, in walked David. He wore his usual faded jeans and jumper combo, ever-present black-rimmed spectacles in place. Sometimes he wore a suit and contact lenses, but only if he was going somewhere fancy. David was attractive in that 'grey at the temples, retired male model' sort of way. You could tell he was once stunning, but now his looks were more distinguished.

"Thought I'd find you here. Do they put crack in the lattes or something?"

"If you must know, I come for the ambiance."

"The ambiance or the entertainment?" David asked, glancing around. He was aware of my obsession with Elodie and Suze, but none of Elodie's stories seemed to shock him. That was probably because he'd experienced so many outrageous hijinks in the eighties. He was too jaded to be shocked.

"Both."

He pulled out a chair and sat down, calling to the barista that he'd take a cappuccino. "So, what was this week's escapade? Did she fly to Amsterdam and take in a live sex show? Perhaps hire a stripper to give her a private dance?"

I shook my head. "She had a one-night stand with a kinky pilot who made sex noises like a lady."

David chuckled. "Oh, really."

"I think she's fabulous. If only the rest of the world were so free with their sexuality."

"Yes, if only. We'd all be walking around with chlamydia. What a wonderful world it would be."

"Don't be such a pessimist. It's quite possible to have an active and varied love life free of STDs so long as you're careful. I can attest to that."

"Hmmm," David mused just as the barista came and set his drink in front of him. "Can you remind me, what does Elodie look like again?"

I shot him a narrow-eyed glance. "You know what she looks like. I've told you numerous times."

"Ah right. Now I remember, scarlet hair, eyes like emeralds. Who does that remind me of?"

"Don't be smug, David dear, it doesn't become you."

"All I'm saying is, she does bear a striking resemblance to a certain Hollywood starlet. One Alicia Davidson, the only woman who ever came close to stealing that closely guarded heart of yours."

"All right," I allowed. "I'll admit she does look a little like Alicia, but that's where the similarities end." My tryst with the American actress was brief and intense. I was prepared to give her everything and she cast me aside. It hurt at the time, but that was two years ago. I was over it now.

"She's also a sexpot. I rest my case," David continued.

I rolled my eyes. "Your case is far from rested."

"Why don't you give her a call? I read in the tabloids just last week that she's still single."

Now I pursed my lips. "She made herself very clear she wasn't interested. A call would be pointless. Besides, I barely think about Alicia these days. I've moved on."

"To a lookalike."

"Don't start."

"One you haven't even spoken to yet."

"I'll introduce myself when the time is right."

"The time was right weeks ago. You're practically stalking the poor woman."

"I'm not stalking her. I've never tried to follow her home. I only ever see her here."

"It's still a second cousin to stalking. Soon you'll go all Robert John Bardo on me. I can see it happening. Before we know it, you'll be slapped with a restraining order. Better to introduce yourself now before things get out of hand," he chided teasingly.

I folded my arms. "I'll introduce myself when I'm good and ready. And I do not appreciate being compared with a murderer, thank you very much."

David grinned. "Thought you might be too young for that reference."

"I'm not just a pretty face, you know."

He chuckled and shook his head before lifting his cup for a sip. After a moment, his expression grew earnest. He studied me in that close way of his, checking for cracks.

"How have you been?" He clasped his hands together.

Just recently, I'd expressed to him my feelings of weariness. How I was growing tired of my routine, how something deep inside of me yearned for a change. I just didn't know what it was yet.

"I've been fine," I answered.

"Are you still feeling restless?"

"It comes and goes. I'm just in a bit of a slump. I'll get out of it eventually. I always do."

David was quiet a moment, then said, "I wonder if you've developed this Elodie fixation to distract yourself."

I lifted a shoulder. "I don't think so. Elodie reminds me of myself. That's why I find her so interesting."

"That may be the first sign of narcissism," David arched a speculative eyebrow. "And I think Elodie reminds you of a past version of yourself. A version, as you've said, you're growing weary of. I think your fixation is you refusing to move on."

I stiffened, not too keen on his assessment, probably because a part of me knew it echoed certain truths. And moving on was not an easy feat. "Somebody's been watching too much Dr. Phil."

David smirked. "Well, I do work odd hours. Daytime television and I are in a committed relationship."

Later that day, I was still pondering my conversation with David as I got ready for work. Tonight, I was meeting with a newly divorced divorce lawyer. The irony was not lost. Her name was Cathy and we'd spoken on the phone several times before I agreed to take her as a client.

My work as an escort spread through word of mouth. I never advertised, never had business cards printed up. If a lady enjoyed my company, she was inclined to recommend me to a friend, and so on.

I first got into the business because I was young, desperate, and needed the money. Now I did it because people fascinated me, women in particular. If I could indulge that fascination while also making a living, then who was I to say no?

Everybody was a little bit of a weirdo once you got to know them, and I relished discovering the weirdness inside each new client. Enjoyed facilitating them to live out their peculiarities with me.

"That's a nice shirt," Rose commented when I came out of my bedroom. Both she and her significant other, Damon, were in town for work, and they always stayed with me when they were in the city. Rose was a dance choreographer and Damon an actor. They divided their time between London and Damon's cottage on the Isle of

Skye in Scotland. I'd visited them there once or twice. It was a beautiful spot, but far too isolated for my liking.

I needed to be around people or I went insane. My mind required constant stimulation and I preferred to be busy. Rose and Damon were the opposite. They liked the city well enough, but whiling away their days in the peaceful island life was their favourite.

"Thanks," I replied, noting she had her head buried in a book yet again. Rose was currently obsessed with the popular *Sasha Orlando* series. It was a set of novels based on the trials and tribulations of Sasha, an investigative newspaper journalist who wrote about love and relationships. There were already seven books in the series and Rose loved to regale me with Sasha's latest adventures.

I much preferred eavesdropping on Elodie at the Polka Dot Café, but to each their own.

Rose eyed me speculatively. "Are you meeting someone?"

"Yes."

"Work or pleasure?"

I shot her a crooked smile. "Why can't it be both?"

She shook her head. "Sometimes I think you could be a character in one of these books."

"Oh? Does Sasha cross paths with a handsome male escort who shows her a night she'll never forget?" I teased.

Rose placed a finger to her lips. "She actually wrote an expose about escorts in book one. Maybe I should email the author and suggest she revisit the storyline."

I dropped down onto the couch beside her and plucked the paperback from her hands. Skimming the page, I smirked when I saw she'd gotten to a sexy bit.

"Give me that," she complained and grabbed for the book, but I held it out of reach.

"Maybe these stories do have something going for them," I grinned and recited a paragraph. *"Sasha's cheeks suffused with warmth as Sebastian stripped, revealing toned, tanned muscles. He was a sight to make any woman's underwear melt, and hers was currently ablaze. It was too bad this encounter was to help her write a column about male strippers, because she could've gone for a night alone with Seb, just the two of them, a hotel room and several hours to spend as they wished."*

I chuckled as I handed the book back to Rose and she scowled at me in annoyance. "Why Rose, I do believe your cheeks are "suffused with warmth" right now."

"You're cruel."

"I just love making you blush." I stood to put on my tie, straightened it out in the mirror then ran my fingers through my hair. I went to grab my coat when Rose said, "You should read the series yourself. I think you'd find a lot in Sasha that you can relate to."

"Maybe I'll save them for when I come to visit you and Damon on the island. I love a good romance novel when I'm on holiday."

***

A week later I was back at the Polka Dot Café, never one to miss an episode of my favourite real-life soap opera. Suze arrived regular as clockwork, followed by Elodie a few minutes later. She swished into the place on a gust of cold London air, ordered her usual, and took a seat across from Suze.

"How've you been, hon?" Elodie asked as they exchanged kisses on each cheek.

"I'm having a 'mare of a week, babes, and it's only Tuesday. Two of the models for our show this weekend have come down with the flu. I'm in a mad scramble to replace them."

As far as I'd gathered, Suze was an up-and-coming fashion designer, which explained her distinctive dress sense. Elodie worked in finance, but she didn't discuss it very often. She was much more inclined to chat about her colourful love life, and I for one was grateful. I mean, it was fantastic that she had a good job and all, but finance interested me about as much as retiring to the countryside.

"I'm sorry to hear that. Do you think you'll have enough time to find replacements?"

Suze sighed. "I mean, I hope so, but it's Fashion Week. Every model worth his salt has been booked out months in advance."

Usually, I was as subtle and discreet as you could get. I'd been listening to these two for weeks and I was pretty sure neither of them ever noticed me sitting here. Being invisible was a skill one acquired having grown up in a tumultuous household.

Most weeks, I sat one table away from Elodie and Suze, but today I'd daringly opted to sit at the table right next to theirs. I lifted my cup to take a sip, and as I lowered it back down, I missed the mark and brown liquid splattered over my table and halfway across theirs.

Suze let out a gasp as I apologised. "I'm so sorry."

I grabbed some napkins to wipe up the spilled coffee from their table, inwardly cursing my sudden clumsiness. Awkward was not a word anyone would use to describe me. I didn't have a clumsy bone in my body. I guess it served me right for paying too much attention on listening and not enough on what I was doing with my hands.

Suze looked me up and down with marked interest. Her pretty eyes went wide as they travelled from my feet all the way up to my face. "Don't apologise. I can't believe I didn't see you sitting there."

I gave her a charming smile. "Well, I am sorry for splattering coffee all over your table. Please allow me to pay for both of your drinks." My eyes briefly went to Elodie, but she stared intently at the table. Her shoulders were rigid and her mouth a straight, tense line. That was odd.

"I hope you don't mind me saying, but you're simply beautiful. Have you ever modelled before?" Suze asked.

"I haven't, but thank you very much for the compliment."

"Are you a fast learner?"

"Pardon?"

She stuck out her hand. "I'm Suzanna Lee. I have a collection showing at London Fashion Week and I'd be forever in your debt if you agreed to model for me this weekend. Two of my guys have come down with the flu."

I shook her hand. "Julian Fairchild, and I'm afraid I have to decline."

Her frown encompassed her entire face. "I'll pay you handsomely, and I'll be especially grateful if you happen to have a twin brother."

I gave a soft laugh. "Unfortunately, I'm an only child." I glanced at Elodie again and this time managed to catch her eye. Hers got big and fluttery, like she was nervous or frightened, which confused me. I frowned as I returned my attention to Suze, feeling bad for turning her down so quickly. She really did seem desperate, and perhaps this was my chance to ingratiate myself with the two of them, get to know Elodie better by doing a favour for her friend.

"I guess if you really need the help I could throw on some clothes and strut down a catwalk," I told her, and she smiled wide.

"Oh em gee, thank you so much! And do you have any friends who look like you? Handsome men run in packs, right?" she joked.

"I have one, but he's older."

"How old?"

"Fifty-one, I think, but if asked he'll tell you he's not a day over forty-five."

Suze laughed. "Well, it's a gentleman's prerogative to shave off a few years. Do you think he'd be up for a bit of modelling?"

"I'll run it by him," I replied and pulled out my phone to text David. I still couldn't believe how quiet Elodie was being, and I was more than a little disappointed that she hadn't taken the opportunity to flirt. Like Suze said, I was a handsome, well-groomed specimen of a man. She should be all over me.

Or maybe my ego had lost the run of itself. It wasn't like every woman I met fell at my feet. I'd been rejected my fair share of times just like everyone else. Still, the idea of being rejected by Elodie bothered me. Having listened to all her stories, I felt a kinship towards her.

Didn't she realise we were soul mates? At the very least two peas in a pod.

I focused on texting David and his reply was prompt.

David: *Sure, I'll do it, so long as there'll be champagne and models to ogle.*

I grinned at his message and typed back.

Julian: *Models young enough to be your daughter, yes, there'll be plenty.*

David: *Great. Thanks for ruining it for me.*

I looked to Suze. "He says he'll do it."

"Fantastic! Here, let's exchange emails and I'll send you everything you need."

As Suze was emailing me all the information, I turned to Elodie and held out my hand. "Hello, I'm Julian. It's a pleasure to meet you."

She stared at my hand like it had a venereal disease, then lifted her eyes to mine. Now that I was looking at her up close, there was something strange about her irises that I couldn't quite put my finger on.

"Elodie," she mumbled, not taking my hand.

"Is everything all right?" Suze asked as she slid her phone back into her handbag.

"Yes, perfectly fine. I was just introducing myself to your very beautiful friend here." Elodie's cheeks went bright red, *suffused with warmth* as Rose's book would describe it, and I couldn't get my head around why she was being so incredibly awkward.

"Oh, do you hear that, Elodie. This beautiful man thinks you're beautiful, too. Isn't that something?" Suze chimed with a wink.

Elodie stood from her seat and gathered her things. "Uh, I've just remembered I have a meeting at work. I have to go."

Quick as a flash she fled the café, leaving Suze and I frowning in her wake.

"I'm sorry. She's not usually so abrupt," Suze said.

I waved her away. "No worries. I guess I'll see you this weekend."

"Yes, and I look forward to meeting your friend. Please do send me a couple of pictures and his measurements so I can decide what outfits to put him in."

"Will do. Do you need mine as well?"

She grinned and ran her eyes down my body. "No need. I already sized you up the moment you spilled your coffee."

I chuckled at that. Quite like Elodie, Suze was my type of lady. At least, I'd thought Elodie was my type. Suze went, and I sat back down, wondering about Elodie's sudden departure and personality one-eighty. Did I smell bad? Was it something I said? Did I remind her of a cheating ex? Really, it could've been anything, but disappointment still filled me. I thought that once we finally met, we'd get along like a house on fire.

Instead, she'd fled the house running and screaming.

Oh, well. Perhaps she'd turn up for Suze's show this weekend. That would give me a second chance to win her over. I'd be my most charming self, and if all went to plan, she'd be mine before the night was through.

Two
Ellen

I'd never seen a more beautiful man in my life.

He was so pretty he could've been a girl, and I was a tongue-tied, sweaty, anxious mess the moment he introduced himself. What on earth was wrong with me?

Okay, there were many answers to that question. One of which was that on Tuesday mornings I put on a disguise and pretended to be someone I wasn't. You know, the usual.

I was in a strange sort of denial. A part of me knew what I was doing was wrong, but I just couldn't seem to give up my friendship with Suze. She looked up to me like I was a goddess, an expert man tamer who could have anyone I wanted. Little did she know, I was about as adept at flirting as a shark on dry land.

I was, however, an expert fantasist. I could make up a story like you wouldn't believe, which was why Suze had no idea her pal Elodie was a fraud.

I never should've let things get this far, but I was addicted to the admiration. I'd always felt more at ease pretending to be someone else, but up until about six months ago, it had only ever been in the safety of my own mind.

I'd attended Gay Pride with my boss, Bernice, and her partner, Felicity. Bernice owned the Zigzag Bookshop, where I worked part-time. She invited me along and we went to see a drag show. There was a competition at the end for a makeover, and lo and behold, I won.

One of the most convincing female impersonators I ever saw remade me. I was transformed from a caterpillar into a beautiful butterfly when I stepped out of that dressing room with long red hair, green eyes, and clothing that fit tight to every inch of my body.

Weirdly, I'd never felt more myself.

Bernice and Felicity went home, while I went to a bar. I wasn't the type to go drinking alone, but in my disguise, I felt confident, fearless. If I didn't have to be me, then I could be anyone. I didn't have to fear rejection or worry about embarrassing myself.

At the bar was where I met Suze. She sat next to me, waiting for her husband to get out of a business meeting for their date night. At first, I was struck by how cool she was. She wore a leopard print miniskirt, a paisley top, and neon pink heels. Miraculously, she managed to pull off the mismatched look. Suze was one of those people who could wear a thrift shop outfit and make it look expensive.

She introduced herself and I shook her hand. I opened my mouth, and somehow, Elodie just flowed out of me. Even the way I spoke was different. I turned into a wise-talking, take no prisoners man-eater who was about as far away from the real me as you could get.

Who knew a wig, contact lenses, makeup, and a new outfit could achieve such miracles?

Or maybe I was developing some sort of personality disorder. Since I spent most of my days alone, I wouldn't be surprised. Isolation could do strange things to people.

I thought it was harmless enough to lie, since we weren't going to see each other again. But then she offered to exchange numbers. Before long we became Tuesday morning coffee buddies. It turned out Suze's studio was only a ten-minute walk from my house, though thankfully she'd never asked to come visit. I was lucky she was always busy with work.

Still, I hated that I'd let things get this far, but I wasn't ready to give her up yet. Having grown up in a house full of men, a female friend was a luxury I didn't take for granted.

Then Mr. Tall, Dark, and Beautiful had to go spill his coffee on our table and I behaved like a speechless, inarticulate schoolgirl. All this time I'd been acting like men were putty in my hands. No wonder Suze was perplexed. And to top it all off, she offered for him to model at her fashion show. I'd been so looking forward to attending. I was going to step up my game and try to be Elodie in a larger social setting, but no way could I go now, not if he was going to be there.

There was something about him that flustered me, like if he looked too long, he'd see past my disguise. And I had a feeling not even a ridiculously expensive, handmade, human hair wig would fool him.

I dropped my keys on the entry table then wandered into the kitchen to say hello to my lovebirds, Skittles and Rainbow. I opened the window to let some fresh air in, then put the kettle on for tea. While it was boiling, I popped upstairs to remove my wig and makeup. Little by little my true self was revealed; light brown hair, big ole tortoiseshell glasses, pale freckled skin, brown eyes.

I invite you to meet Ellen Grant: hermit, tomboy, make-believe artist.

I grabbed a T-shirt and some leggings, relieved to get out of my super fashionable Elodie ensemble. Sure, it looked amazing, but it was about as comfortable as a straitjacket. I enjoyed the reaction I got when I wore sexy clothes, but I also adored the comfort of going casual. If I had to choose, I wasn't sure I could give that up, even if I got to be magically transformed into Elodie for real.

When I went back down to the kitchen, I made myself a cup of peppermint tea and sat at my computer to check my emails. Working from home was the best, but it was also the worst.

It was the best because I didn't have to deal with people, and that was also the reason why it was the worst. Isolation became a self-perpetuating cycle. The more you had of it, the more you needed it, and the less equipped you were to deal with normal, everyday interactions that others took in stride. That was why I forced myself to keep my part-time job at the bookshop. I certainly didn't need the money, but I needed to practice my people skills.

I ignored several nagging emails about things I wasn't ready to deal with yet and opened one from my brother, Nick. He and my other brother, Cameron, were twins, but they were as opposite as you could get. Nick was happy, charming, and generally pleasant to be around, while Cameron was grumpy, mistrustful, and often rude. He was one of those people who liked to claim they were always honest, but that was just an excuse for being mean. Anyway, I didn't get to see either of them often since they lived back in my hometown of Torquay.

Nickg2012@gmail.com   to Ellengrant11@gmail.com

Subject: A visit from your marvellous brother ;-)

Hey Ellen!

I hope you're doing good :-) Dad's been asking for you. He says you better visit us soon or he'll come to London and drag you home himself. Speaking of visits, Cameron's going to be in the city for work next month and he was wondering if he could stay in your spare room? Give him a call and let him know.

Say hello to Skittles and Rainbow for me!

Love,

Nick

I sighed when I finished reading the email. From the subject line, I had hoped he was going to tell me *he* was coming to visit. Obviously, the "marvellous" part was sarcastic. He knew just as much as I did what a cranky bastard Cameron could be. Unfortunately, I didn't have it in me to refuse him. I did have a very nice spare bedroom and I rarely had visitors. I should put it to use, even if my guest was my lesser preferred brother.

I typed out a reply.

Ellengrant11@gmail.com   to Nickg2012@gmail.com

Subject: RE: A visit from your marvellous brother ;-)

Dearest Nick,

You know as well as I do that Cameron is far from marvellous, but alas, he is my brother, so I won't leave him to sleep on the streets. You can tell him I said yes. I'm not in the mood for a phone call with King Grump.

Skittles and Rainbow say they miss you.

Ellen <3

P.S. How's everything been with Cruella Deville?

Cruella was our secret nickname for my dad's girlfriend, Shayla. She was originally from London, but they started dating last year after she moved to Torquay for work. We called her Cruella because she was a bit of an ice-queen. She also had a real fox fur coat she wore in the winter that gave me the heebie-jeebies.

It didn't take long for Nick's reply.

Nickg2012@gmail.com   to Ellengrant11@gmail.com

Subject: RE: RE: A visit from your marvellous brother ;-)

She's been upping her game big-time. I popped over to the house last week to borrow Dad's lawnmower and there were some suspicious noises coming from upstairs. At midday on a Tuesday no less! Definitely wants him to put a ring on it.

P.S. By suspicious noises I mean sex noises.

Lovely. Trust Nick to put me off my peppermint tea. I closed out my emails and started on some work I needed to get done, trying to put the image of my dad having sex out of my head.

The thought that I had to make up an excuse not to attend Suze's fashion show hung heavy on my mind. Later on, I contemplated the screen of my phone as I whipped up some chicken and pasta for dinner. Chewing my lip, I picked it up and opened my messages to compose a text.

Elodie: *Bad news. I have to work this weekend on a large project that's due Monday. I'm not going to be able to see your show :-(*

Suze: *Noooo! Is there any way you can get out of it? The show doesn't start until 7 pm, so you could still work during the day. Please, please, please. You're my lucky charm, Elodie. I need you there. xxx.*

Her reply made me feel bad, and guilt ate at me. I had to stop lying to her. Either Elodie needed to ghost her, or Ellen needed to come clean. The problem was, I was flattered she considered me her lucky charm. It was definitely a good feeling to be valued by someone like Suze, even if she didn't know the truth.

I mulled things over for a second. Maybe I could go and simply avoid Julian Fairchild, beautiful specimen and thief of words. After a couple of minutes, I determined I had to go for Suze. Her friendship meant a lot to me, and yes, I was aware how messed up that was, but it was the truth.

Elodie: *Let me see what I can do. I really don't want to miss your show <3*

Suze: *YES! You're the best. xxx.*

The weekend rolled in too quickly. Before I knew it, I was donning my wig and contacts, squeezing myself into a forest green contour dress and slipping my feet into four-inch heels. They brought my measly five foot four up to an elegant five eight. I was short, but I wasn't small or dainty in any way. I carried an extra fifteen pounds or so thanks to my sedentary lifestyle and love of sugar. Luckily, the fashion industry saw fit to invent Spanx, which allowed me to mould my shape into something akin to curvaceous.

Whatever that meant.

I mean, we all had curves. It wasn't like skinny people had square bottoms.

When I was all set, I called a cab to take me to the show. It was a little overwhelming when I stepped out into the media frenzy covering the event. A lot of buzz had been generated around Suze after a well-known actress started wearing her clothes and posting pictures to Instagram. I was excited for her.

I was also excited to be here as Elodie. Maybe I'd summon up the courage to flirt with a man.

I clutched my bag tightly, palms sweaty as I gave my name to the lady at the door with the guest list.

"Oh, you can go through this way," she said, gesturing to a side entrance. "Mrs. Lee said to direct you to the backstage area. She wants to see you before the show starts."

I swallowed tightly. "Great, thank you."

I walked down the crowded corridor, full of half-dressed models and frazzled looking assistants. When I found Suze, she was handing a shirt to a topless middle-aged male model. He was handsome and in good shape for his age, with black hair and salt and pepper stubble. I wondered if maybe I should try to flirt with him later. An older model might be less intimidating than the young ones, right?

As soon as Suze spotted me, her eyes lit up and a smile spread across her face.

"Elodie, you're here! I'm so happy you came." She threw her arms around my shoulders and hugged me tight.

"I couldn't miss your show," I told her, returning her smile.

"Come, let me introduce you to David. He's Julian's friend. Remember the guy from the coffee shop? I really lucked out stumbling upon him, let me tell you."

Words got stuck in my throat as she ushered me over.

"David, I'd like you to meet my good friend, Elodie."

His gaze found mine as he slid a tie around his neck, warmth in his eyes like he already knew me. It was odd. "Oh yes, Elodie, Julian told me about you."

He did?

What was there to tell about a fifteen second, fumbling introduction?

"It's a p-pleasure to meet you," I said and shook his hand, just as one of Suze's assistants scurried over.

"Mrs. Lee, you're needed by the stage. The show starts in five minutes."

"So soon!" she exclaimed, then looked to me. "I can't believe this is finally happening. Come find me after, won't you?"

"Of course, and good luck," I replied as she rushed off.

David cleared his throat and I brought my attention back to him. Again, the knowledge in his gaze flustered me. "Elodie, could you do me a favour and straighten this tie? I can't seem to get it right."

My throat dried. "Sure."

I reached out and quietly fixed his tie—something I'd done countless times for my brothers—only now I was a lot more nervous. David's focus seared me.

"Have we met before?" I asked, not meeting his gaze. The intense way he studied me was off-putting.

"No, but don't worry, a lot of people ask me that. I've got one of those faces," he replied, like there was some inside joke I wasn't aware of.

"That's not it," I mumbled.

"No?"

"There you go. Straight as a whistle," I said.

His brow furrowed at my odd turn of phrase. "That's not the saying."

I was already moving away. "A whistle is straight, isn't it? Anyway, it was great to meet you, but I better go find my seat. Break a leg out there," I rambled and left before he could say anything else. I had that panicked, spiders crawling down the spine feeling of everyone being on to me. For a moment, I felt like the word 'fraud' was stamped across my forehead, but then I found my seat and managed to take several calming breaths.

David didn't know anything. I was being paranoid.

After a minute or two, the lights dimmed, and music started up. I got lost in the show, marvelling at how Suze managed to design such stunning outfits for both men and women. Her style was colourful and quirky, but somehow chic at the same time.

When Julian walked out, wearing a pastel shirt and funky print slacks, my jaw dropped. He really was stunning, and I wondered what he did for a living. I remembered him declining Suze's offer at first, so he couldn't have been an actual model, though he certainly had the looks for it.

The next time he walked out, he wore a long, tailored wool coat. As he neared the end of the catwalk, he removed the coat to show off the outfit underneath; a fitted jumper and stylish trousers. He also wore brown leather shoes with no socks. I noticed this was a real trend lately, but I wasn't a fan. It just made me think of how sweaty your bare feet would be against the leather.

Yuck.

At least there was one part of him that wasn't perfect. It helped break the spell his beauty cast over me.

I startled when I lifted my gaze and he was looking right at me. Our eyes locked and held for a split second before he turned around and another model took his place.

For the rest of the show, I had tingles.

Who was this guy? And why did I find him so intriguing/scary/mesmerising?

When it was over, Suze walked out to meet her audience and I stood to give her a round of applause. Her husband, Kenneth, who I'd only ever seen in photographs, came and handed her a huge bouquet of flowers.

I made my way backstage and found her swarmed by people congratulating and showering her with praise. I hung back to wait until she was done, swiping a glass of champagne from a table of refreshments.

"So, what did you think?" came a voice from over my shoulder.

I turned, and Julian Fairchild stood a mere foot away. He'd changed back into his own clothes, which, no offence to Suze, suited him much better. His dark grey shirt highlighted the colour of his hazel eyes, while his slacks hugged his hips perfectly. He wasn't overly muscular. In fact, there was something about him that was quite feminine. He reminded me of Louis from the Anne Rice vampire novels. Well, a modern version at least.

He had a sexy, masculine aura, but he was too beautiful to be described as manly.

Androgynous was the word.

I swallowed a gulp of champagne for courage, then replied, "I'm no fashion expert, but I thought you all looked great."

Julian moved closer until we stood shoulder to shoulder. "I hope I lived up to Suzanna's expectations. I've never done a catwalk before."

"You seemed fine to me," I said, my voice neutral. I couldn't seem to muster any warmth or flirtation, such was his effect on me.

I wasn't looking at him, instead keeping my eyes trained on Suze and her bevvy of admirers, but I could hear the humour in his tone when he replied, "Just fine? You really know how to boost a man's confidence."

I flicked my eyes to him briefly, words coming out before I could think to censor them. "Surely, your confidence doesn't need boosting."

"It does when the lady I'm trying to chat up is as disinterested as you are," he said with a wry smile.

I frowned. He was trying to chat me up? *Me?* I almost forgot I was Elodie tonight, not Ellen. Of course, he was trying to chat me up. My dress left very little to the imagination.

Okay, this was my chance to flirt with a real live human. *Don't screw it up, Ellen.*

I mean, Elodie.

Damn, this was confusing.

I mustered a smile in return, a real one. "Who says I'm disinterested?"

Julian's laugh was just as attractive as the rest of him. "Oh, you're not?"

"I asked my question first." I tried to keep my voice sweet and flirtatious, lighthearted. That's what Elodie would do.

He pursed his lips, considering me. I hoped my layers of makeup kept my rosy cheeks from view. "Hmm, your body language for a start. It screams 'leave me alone'. Then there's your tone of voice, your facial expressions. They all tell a story."

The way he spoke intrigued me. There was something different about him, something unlike most men. I'd grown up with two brothers and a widowed father, so I knew what I was talking about. Julian paid a lot more attention than the average male.

When I lived at home, I could've walked into a room with blue hair and green skin and my brothers wouldn't have batted an eyelid.

"Am I so transparent?" I asked, because I wanted to hear more. He ensnared me.

Julian's gaze wandered from the top of my forehead, lingering on my eyes and nose, then my mouth. "I wouldn't say that."

Heat filled me from the way he took me in so completely. This man. This stranger. He was unlike anyone I'd ever met.

Or maybe it was all down to Elodie. She attracted men in a way the real me never could. Sure, I could stand to wear more makeup, dress a little sexier, but there was something about a disguise that felt so freeing.

"Elodie! There you are!" Suze approached arm in arm with her husband, smiling widely. "I wanted to introduce you to my Kenneth. I can't believe you two haven't met yet."

I felt Julian's keen attention as I stepped forward and shook hands with Kenneth. "It's great to meet you."

"You too," he replied. "Suze has told me so much about you, and I see she wasn't lying. You're just as gorgeous as she described."

"Oh, I like you already," I chirped, going into full Elodie mode. Usually, I was a pro at becoming her, but Julian somehow managed to break past the mask. He was a chink in my armour.

"We're having a few people back to our place, if you'd like to come," Suze went on then glanced at Julian. A small smirk graced her lips as she took in the two of us. I knew what she was thinking. *Typical Elodie snagging the most attractive man in the room.* She had no idea how befuddled I was on the inside. "You and David are welcome to join us, too, Julian."

"We wouldn't miss it," he replied graciously.

"Great. Well, we'll grab a couple of cabs in a little while, but for now, enjoy the champers," Suze winked as she and Kenneth went to do the rest of their rounds.

A moment of silence fell between Julian and me. I took a sip and looked around the room, at a loss for what to say.

"You've never met her husband before?" he asked curiously.

"No, this is the first time."

"How long have you two been friends?"

I shrugged and wondered why he was asking so many questions. "A couple of months."

"That's surprising."

"It is?"

"You seem like you've known each other all your lives."

"When we met it was like kismet, we just clicked," I replied.

His friend, David, approached. He too had changed back into his own clothes; a wool jumper with a collared shirt underneath, jeans and black-rimmed glasses. He seemed a lot more approachable now, like your friend's hot dad, or an attractive college professor.

"I see you two are getting acquainted," he said, eyeing Julian a moment before his attention fell on me. "I didn't get a chance to thank you earlier for fixing my tie. You rushed off so suddenly."

"Oh well, a lady has places to be," I replied sweetly. It was a lot easier to act as Elodie now that he was dressed down.

David smiled. "I'm sure she does. Are you going to the after party?"

"I am if you are."

His smile grew wider, a twinkle in his eye. "Well, now I have to go."

I gave a flirty laugh and Julian cleared his throat. "Looks like we're all going then." His tone showed a hint of irritation. *Was he jealous?* My inner Elodie preened at being pursued by two men at once.

Unfortunately, all that changed when two of Suze's female models shared a cab with us. They were stylish and beautiful, and I was disappointed that they'd drawn David's attention. It wasn't that I fancied him more than Julian. He was just easier to talk to. This was my first proper foray in the world as Elodie, and David was perfect for Beginner's Level flirting. Julian was Big Boss Level and I definitely wasn't ready for that yet.

"Nice part of town," he commented, his voice husky in my ear as we drew up to Suze's building. He sat right next to me, his citrusy cologne invading my senses.

"Kenneth runs *Cabello's* in Soho. It's a Michelin star restaurant," I replied.

"Oh, really? I ate there once. Hard place to get a reservation."

I nodded. "That's why he earns the big bucks."

"And do you live close by?"

I shook my head. "My place is just down the street from the Polka Dot." Why had I answered honestly? It was incredibly difficult to lie to this man. Staying in character was impossible, which again was why I wished David wasn't so preoccupied with Suze's models.

We left the cab and headed inside the fancy apartment complex. Julian didn't let up on his questioning.

"What a coincidence. I live near there, too. I can't believe we've never run into one another before. I haven't seen you around the area."

"I work a lot," I replied stiffly.

"Oh? What do you do?"

"Finance. I'm an accountant." The lie sat heavy on my tongue.

"Impressive. So, you must have a good head for numbers."

"You could say that. What do you do?" I queried, turning the tables on him before he asked more questions I couldn't answer.

He eyed me, seeming hesitant, then replied, "I'm in hospitality."

I wanted to ask specifics, but a moment later we were inside Suze's apartment. Erasure's "A Little Respect" blared from the expensive sound system. The place was modern and spacious, the décor pared back with a few nods to Suze's quirky style here and there. She came at us, eyes shining with merriment, as she gave me yet another hug.

"Welcome to my humble abode, drinks are in the kitchen. Make yourselves comfortable." She glanced at David, pursing her lips drunkenly. "Do you know what? I feel like I know you from somewhere. It's been bugging me all night."

David gave her a charming smile. "I get that a lot. I just have one of those faces."

It was the same thing he'd said to me earlier in the evening, and it made me curious.

"Oh, don't listen to him. He's being modest," Julian chided. "David was a heartthrob in his day. Ever heard the song "Naughty"?"

Suze's eyes widened, as did mine. He hadn't looked familiar to me, but maybe I just wasn't looking properly. Now I could see it clear as day. David Jonathan. I'd seen enough TV shows and documentaries about the music industry in the eighties to know it was him.

"Oh, my goodness! I can't believe I didn't realise," Suze exclaimed. "How does the song go again? *I want your mind...*" She trailed off, trying to remember the lyrics.

Julian was quick to remind her. "*And I want your body. Come on, babe, let's do it naughty.* A classic for the ages," he teased. David gave an exasperated sigh.

"How you enjoy torturing me."

"But it's a great song. You should be proud. You're up there with likes of Boy George and George Michael," Suze enthused.

"A pity you didn't pick David George as your stage name," Julian continued to tease. "They could've called you The Three Georges."

"That's a regret I'll just have to live with," David deadpanned.

"Do you know what? I think I might have your song on my karaoke machine," Suze exclaimed. "You should sing it for us!"

"I think I'll have to very respectfully decline," David said politely. He looked like he'd rather eat the legs off a spider than serenade us with his classic hit.

"Oh, come on. How long's it been since you performed?" Julian cajoled.

David narrowed his gaze at his friend. "Not long enough." His lack of enthusiasm didn't put Suze off though, because she grabbed his arm and led him further into the apartment. I kind of felt bad for the guy, but at least this was a private setting.

Well, so long as no one recorded it on their phones, which, okay, was highly unlikely.

I went into the kitchen to grab a drink. To my delight, there was a whole selection of wines and spirits set out on the island, including two trays of tasty looking finger foods. I helped myself to a tiny pastry with onion chutney, and a cracker with cheese and salami, chomping away before I realised I had company. Julian grabbed a bottle of red wine and a glass.

Had he been here the whole time?

A tinge of embarrassment pinched me as I swallowed the final bite.

"Care for a glass?" Julian offered, his eyes warm with affection. It still felt surreal that this perfect specimen was showing me so much interest.

"Yes, thank you."

He poured the wine for me while outside I heard the intro to David's song start up. "You're cruel to your friend."

Julian's mouth twitched. "I prefer to think of it as good-natured ribbing."

"You do realise videos of him singing his own song on karaoke are going be on YouTube by the morning, right?"

"We all require a little something to keep us humble. No fifty-one-year-old man deserves to look as good as he does. Believe me, he needs to be brought back down to earth every once in a while," Julian replied, mouth lifting at one end.

"And what if it backfires? The video could go viral and start a revival of his music." I countered. "Just look how it happened for Craig David."

Julian grinned and handed me the glass. "Ah, now that would be poetic."

I took a sip of wine, absently noting that he hadn't poured any for himself, and moved to walk by him. "I guess we should go out and witness his humiliation."

He caught me softly by the elbow. "Stay and talk with me."

I looked up into his eyes. "Why?"

He moved a tiny bit closer, holding my gaze with his hand still at my elbow. I was hyperaware of the contact, since it was the first time a man had touched me in who knew how long.

His reply was confident. "Because I find you incredibly sexy and interesting, and I'd very much like to get to know you better."

I inhaled deeply. He was so...straight forward. I'd never been hit on like this before. And yes, okay, I could count the number of times I'd been flirted with on one hand, but still. There was something about Julian that drew me in.

He had stories behind those eyes.

I slowly moved away from him and sat down on a stool. "Well then, what would you like to talk about?"

Julian grabbed a bottle of water from the countertop, twisted open the lid and took a sip. "Where did you grow up?"

"In Devon."

His brows rose. "I didn't peg you for a country girl."

"Seaside town, actually. I've been living in London for the last six years. I like to think all signs of my humble upbringing have been erased by now."

"There's no shame in humble beginnings. Some of the most incredible people in the world started with nothing."

"Well, I didn't exactly start with nothing. I had a normal middle-class childhood, no deprivation or anything quite so dramatic," I replied. I couldn't believe I was answering all of his questions honestly. With Suze, I made most things up. But Julian might as well have the lasso of truth wrapped around my neck.

"And did you have any brothers or sisters?"

"Two brothers. They're twins."

"Older or younger?"

"Older in age, younger in maturity."

Julian gave a soft chuckle and I inwardly delighted at making him laugh. "How old are you, if you don't mind me asking?"

"I don't mind. I turn thirty in a couple of months."

"That's a big birthday. Got anything special planned?"

I leaned forward and rested my elbows on the countertop. "I've been thinking of taking a trip to Italy, doing some vineyard tours, taking in the history."

"Sounds a treat."

"And how old are you?" I asked.

He tutted. "A gentleman never reveals his age."

I laughed. "I think that was my line."

"How old do you think I am?"

I studied him. "I'm not sure. You seem sort of ageless."

"I hope that's a compliment."

"It is," I assured. "You've got that whole immortal vampire thing going on. Like you've lived several lifetimes but haven't aged a day."

My candidness surprised me, and something about what I said gave Julian pause. "Very perceptive. Unfortunately, I'm quite mortal. I just turned thirty-two."

I drank some more wine and fiddled with the stem of my glass. Thirty-two was a good age. Not too young and immature, but also not too old either. When I looked up, Julian was staring right at me.

"Has anyone ever told you you've got the most unusual coloured eyes? They're so green."

I sat back, my entire body tensing. If he kept looking at me this closely, he'd soon realise the truth. That what's unusual about them is that they're completely fake.

"I um, I'm sorry, but I'm not feeling very well. Please excuse me." I stumbled off the stool ungracefully and headed for the living room.

"Hold on, let me help…"

I didn't catch the end of his sentence because I was already at the front door of the apartment. When I managed to flag a taxi and climb inside, I realised I'd lost an earring. It was expensive too, made of real diamonds. I considered going back in, but my reserves of confidence had run dry. Instead I texted Suze, apologizing for leaving early and requesting she search for the lost earring.

I slid my phone back in my bag and dropped my head into my hands.

What a disaster.

Three
Julian

David: *Someone posted this video on YouTube. You owe me big time.*

I grinned as I clicked the link and up popped footage of David at Suze's apartment, reluctantly serenading the room with his dulcet tones. Elodie's prediction had been right, though honestly, I didn't understand why David was mad. He looked good and his singing was on point. He definitely hadn't lost his voice over the years. When I scrolled down, the majority of comments were positive, mostly ladies expressing how they'd very much like to 'get naughty' with him.

Sure, there were one or two twats who posted insulting comments, but this was the internet. It was par for the course.

Julian: *Read the comments. You should be thanking me. They're calling you a DILF. And besides, today's news is tomorrow's loo roll.*

David: *I'd need to have actual children to be a DILF. Someone said I look desperate. This is why I don't accept any of those offers to take part in nostalgia tours.*

Julian: *Whoever called you desperate is jealous and probably lives in their parent's basement. You look and sound great. Own it.*

I put my phone away when my date for the evening, Cathy, arrived. She walked into the bar looking a little unsure of herself, though I suspected it was because this experience was still new to her. She was a recently divorced thirty-eight-year-old. However, from our casual first meeting last week, I could tell she knew what she wanted from our arrangement. Cathy's reason for hiring me was simple. She wanted to enjoy some male company without any obligations for a relationship. Most of her time was dedicated to her work, and though she did want to find love again someday, right now, she was only in the market for some no strings fun.

That's where I came in.

And before you ask, no, I didn't always sleep with my clients. But yes, I did sleep with a lot of them. I laid out my rules very clearly. There's a set charge for the date, which does not include sex. Sex requires a second charge, but I only allow that to happen if both parties are feeling it and things progress naturally.

I know it sounded very clinical, but believe me, it wasn't.

I'd done clinical in my early days as an escort. I would show up to a flat or hotel room, with an instruction to let myself in. When I went inside the woman would be waiting somewhere, scantily clad or not at all, with the expectation of getting straight down to business.

After a year of those sorts of jobs, I said no more.

Now I dealt in intimate, one-on-one experiences. Yes, I was being paid, but I genuinely enjoyed getting to know these women in a deep and meaningful way. I wasn't only intrigued by those who were beautiful or sexy. Past experiences desensitised me to any disgust in the multitude of variations in the human form. I could just as happily make love to a woman society deemed "pretty" as I could to another deemed "ugly".

I was mostly fascinated by how people could transform in your eyes after you heard them speak. A person's voice, mannerisms, and beliefs revealed the truth about them, and all were a huge factor in determining their attractiveness.

After all, a plain person could open their mouth and become the most beautiful person you've ever met, and a beautiful person could speak and turn ugly.

It wasn't just an empty saying. I truly believed that beauty was in the eye of the beholder. It didn't live on the surface of our skin, but rather deep inside the depths of our hearts.

If I clicked with clients on a personal level, then looks were irrelevant. And believe me, coming from someone who had always been considered attractive, I knew it could be a curse just as much as a blessing.

The women I took on dates were vetted in advance via phone calls. I also did background checks, since you could never be too careful. I once had a journalist masquerading as a lovelorn singleton try to hire me, but with a little sleuthing I discovered her real identity. I wasn't interested in being the topic of a magazine article for strangers to read and judge.

I had endured enough shame during my teens and early twenties.

What I did with my life now was nobody's business but mine.

Cathy was slim but pear-shaped. She wore a pencil dress under a wool coat and had straight brown hair. Her eyes were blue and her nose pert, her upper lip thinner than her bottom. She was neither striking nor unattractive, but there was a light behind her eyes that interested me. It spoke of hidden depths and secret passions.

It was good to feel that interest, that spark, small as it may be. Like I'd confessed to David, I'd slowly been losing the joy in my work, slowly yearning for something else. Something different. Perhaps Cathy would be the one to re-inspire me.

"Julian," she said as I stood to greet her.

"It's a pleasure to see you again, Cathy." We hugged briefly, then sat. I already ordered her a glass of pinot grigio, as she'd mentioned it was her usual tipple.

"I think you get more handsome each time I see you," she blurted.

I gave a pleased smile for the compliment. "That's very kind of you to say. I hope you don't mind that I ordered you a drink."

She lifted the glass. "I never say no to a glass of wine. I'll admit I'm a little nervous this time."

"Why be nervous?" I asked and leaned forward so that we were close. "You set the pace. Whatever you'd enjoy doing tonight, I'm your willing participant."

She swallowed nervously and glanced to the side. "Can I be honest?"

"Of course, always."

"Well, what I'd really like to do is go dancing."

I smiled wide. "I love to dance."

"I didn't know if you'd be up for something like that, or if tonight was all about…" she trailed off bashfully.

"Sex?"

"Well, yes."

"Like I said, this can be whatever you want it to be. We're simply here to enjoy the pleasure of each other's company."

My words seemed to ease her stress as she swallowed a gulp of wine. "There's a Latin night not too far from here."

"Well then, that settles it. I dance a mean *Paso Doble*."

The relieved anticipation in her smile was exactly what I'd been hoping for. "Thank you," she whispered. I reached out to give her hand a brief, gentle squeeze.

"No thanks necessary. We're going to have a fantastic night, I promise."

***

It was Tuesday again and this time I had a reason to go see Elodie at the Polka Dot Café. I was in possession of a small diamond earring that belonged to the object of my obsession. I saw it on the floor after she pulled her disappearing act, twinkling under the light of the bulb overhead. I still didn't understand why she had left so suddenly. Even I, who had many years' experience getting up close and personal with the opposite sex, was at a loss to explain her behaviour.

When I arrived, both she and Suze were sitting at their usual table, deep in chat. I stepped up behind Elodie and carefully placed the earring down in front of her. "I believe this belongs to you," I purred flirtatiously. She blinked at the earring then looked up at me.

"Oh. Thank you," she breathed.

"I searched my entire apartment for that earring and you had it all along," Suze commented with a slantways grin.

"Afraid so," I said, eyes on Elodie. "I would've called to let you know I had it, but alas, I don't have your number."

"Well," said Suze, smiling widely at her friend. "I'm sure we can remedy that. Give him your number, Elodie."

Elodie took a sip of her coffee as though to delay answering. She seemed to be gathering her nerve before she glanced up at me, a twinkle in her eye. "I don't go handing out my number to just anyone."

Ah, there's my girl. This was the first time I got to experience the real Elodie, the one I'd been watching for weeks, the one who oozed confidence and self-possession.

I pulled out a chair and sat. "I'll have to work on not being just anyone to you then, won't I?"

Suze laughed and eyed Elodie. "Oh, he's smooth."

"Smooth can sometimes be slippery," Elodie murmured into her mug.

"And sometimes it's velvety soft," I countered, seductive. I hoped the dark look I gave her translated.

Suze fanned herself. "You two. It's like watching the start of a porno. One with great production values."

I chuckled. Elodie appeared to flush and I studied her, puzzled. Surely, a woman of her experience wouldn't be embarrassed at a little bit of harmless flirting. The other night at Suze's, there'd been a moment when I thought I had her, but then I lost her just as quickly. Maybe I should just leave her alone. She really didn't seem to be very interested. And from the stories I'd spent weeks listening to, when Elodie was interested in a man, he knew about it.

I cleared my throat. "Well, I'll leave you both to it. I just wanted to come and return the missing earring."

"Nonsense! Stay and chat with us," Suze argued, placing a hand on my arm. "I was so impressed with how well you and David did on the catwalk, especially given neither of you have experience."

"True, but we both had our peacock phases, so we're well adept at showing off."

Elodie gave a small smile and I was glad to see I'd amused her. If she wasn't interested in me romantically, then maybe we could be friends.

"Looking how you do, I'm not surprised," Suze said. "I sometimes wonder what it's like to be a devastatingly handsome man. Women must fall at your feet, and men for that matter."

"Not always," I said, casting a quick look at Elodie before I brought my attention back to her friend. "And besides, you're a beautiful woman. It's not so different for you, I'm sure."

"A beautiful woman who's married," Suze sighed. "Come on, I'm trying to live vicariously here."

"Well, I can't really say whether or not people treat me differently, because I've always had this face. However, sometimes people let you get away with more simply because you're pretty to look at."

"How very interesting," Suze said, fingering the rim of her cup.

Elodie frowned. "Does that mean you use your looks to trick people?"

"Not at all. Just that you sometimes you're forgiven more easily for poor behaviour. For instance, you could be in a bad mood, or say something surly, and nobody would call you on it. Little things like that. I don't agree with it, but it definitely happens."

"So, you live in 'the bubble'," she stated, miming bunny ears before folding her arms. All of a sudden, I felt like I was being interrogated. Where had that steely look come from?

"Don't you? Surely men are rendered babbling fools in the face of your beauty all the time."

"That's different. I never use my looks to get what I want."

I leaned forward, resting my elbows on the table. "Nor do I."

"That's not what you just insinuated."

"Hey! What's put a bee in your bonnet?" Suze interjected, shooting Elodie a baffled look. "Has that pilot not returned your calls?"

Elodie blinked, then frowned, then worried her lip. I got the sense she hadn't meant to challenge me like that. She shook her head, her expression apologetic. "I'm sorry. I'm feeling a little catty today. And no, I never called the pilot. If you must know, I've moved on."

"To?" Suze asked, grinning now. I could see she was hoping for a story. Truth be told, so was I. Elodie's stories never failed to entertain.

"Actually," she said, glancing between the two of us. There was an odd sort of calculation on her face before she continued. "I've started seeing a male stripper."

"What?!" Suze exclaimed. "Okay, tell us everything."

Elodie emitted a theatrical sigh. "I've just been a little insecure reconciling the reality of his job with the fact that I have feelings for him. He strips in front of women every night for money, gives lap dances. It makes me unreasonably jealous, but then, the sex is incredible and he's such a sweet person."

"What's his name?" Suze asked.

Elodie cast me a quick, speculative glance before replying. "Sebastian. He's from Northern Spain."

"Oh, what a sexy name!" Suze enthused. "I bet he's gorgeous. Do you have any pics?"

Elodie shook her head. "No, but I'll bring one to show you next time. You're going to die when you see him."

"I already can't wait."

Something about Elodie's story niggled at me, but I couldn't put my finger on it.

Still, the idea that she was insecure about dating a stripper made me certain she wouldn't be able to handle going out with me. It was definitely best that I look at her as a friend and nothing more.

Elodie was regaling us with details of her last date with Sebastian when my phone rang. I saw it was Rose, so I stood to answer.

"I'm just going to take this outside," I said and headed for the exit.

I emerged into the mild London morning and hit 'answer'. "Hello, darling."

"Julian, I thought you'd be at the flat. Where are you?"

"Just having a coffee with some friends."

"Oh, well, I was hoping we could go for lunch. I also wanted to pay a visit to the bookstore. Damon's filming until late and it's my day off so…"

"So, you were hoping for some company. Not a problem. I'll meet you at the flat when I'm done here. We'll do Greek for lunch then go to the bookstore after, how does that sound?"

I heard the smile in her voice. "Perfect. See you soon."

I'd just hung up when the door to the café opened and Elodie walked out. I stood off to the side, so she didn't see me as she buttoned up her coat and headed down the street. An odd urge struck me to follow her. My feet started moving before I could stop myself. I had no clue why I didn't call out to her, but then, maybe I did.

There was just something about Elodie that didn't add up. I'd sensed it the first time we spoke, and the more time I spent with her, the more I suspected something wasn't quite right.

It was just a feeling I couldn't seem to shake.

I walked a good distance behind her for about five minutes, then she turned and went inside a small, independent bookshop. I couldn't see too clearly, but it looked like she retrieved a key from her bag to unlock the door. When I got closer, I saw her flip the sign from 'Closed' to 'Open' then disappear inside the shop.

Huh.

Did she work there? I distinctly remembered her telling me she was an accountant. Plus, she'd mentioned it several times during the conversations I'd listened in on. Was she lying about her job?

I didn't go inside, not wanting her to know I'd followed her, and instead continued on to my flat. I'd walked by that bookshop a million times but never thought to go inside. Rose normally shopped at the larger chain stores because they had a bigger selection, but I was struck with the urge to bring her here after our lunch.

I rejected the idea. Elodie's business was none of mine, and if she was lying about her job, well, it was hardly my place to out her.

"My goodness, I'm stuffed," Rose groaned as we walked arm in arm out of the tube station. We'd shared a delightful lunch in Soho, before heading back home. I'd managed to convince her to check out the bookshop Elodie had gone inside earlier.

I know, I was despicable, but my curiosity about this woman just wouldn't let up.

She was a mystery I had the unfathomably strong urge to solve.

"You were right, this place is adorable," Rose enthused when we arrived at the Zigzag Bookshop. A middle-aged woman with short blonde hair sat by the till, her head buried in a dog-eared copy of *Don Quixote*. She glanced up as we entered, giving a polite nod before returning her attention to her book.

I looked around, but there was no sign of Elodie. Perhaps her shift ended earlier. Or maybe she was the owner? She wore the type of clothes you could only afford if you had money, so that would make sense.

There was a little reading nook by the window with lots of zigzag furnishings, and the walls were papered with a similar zigzag design. If you stared too long, you'd get a headache. Rose headed down a narrow aisle, already lost scanning the spines of possible purchases. I frowned, and I had to admit I was disappointed Elodie wasn't around. Not because I wanted to confront her with her lies, but merely because I yearned to see her again.

Why was it that we humans always wanted the person that didn't want us in return?

I wandered past Rose, going further down the aisle, then turned a corner to head into the next one.

I paused, because a woman knelt on the floor, arranging books on one of the lower shelves. She had long curly brown hair and her hand went to her chest like I'd startled her, which I probably had since the shop was so quiet back here.

"Oh, excuse me," I said with a smile. "I didn't mean to startle you."

Her hair curtained most of her face, alongside a pair of thick, tortoiseshell glasses. She blinked several times then murmured, "No worries," before shifting out of the way so I could get by in the narrow space.

"Tight squeeze in here, isn't it," I commented, and she nodded shyly without reply.

I continued on to explore the rest of the shop. It really was a quaint little place, an oasis of quiet, nestled amid the hustle and bustle of the city.

But no Elodie in sight.

When I returned to Rose, she had three paperbacks under her arm and was considering a fourth. I enjoyed reading, but my best friend went through novels at a record-breaking speed.

We approached the lady at the till and Rose handed over her purchases. "You don't happen to have the newest *Sasha Orlando* book in stock by any chance?" she asked.

"Not at present," the woman replied. "That one doesn't release until the weekend, but we'll definitely have it then if you want to pop back on Saturday."

"Oh yes, I will," Rose enthused. "I've been dying for it to come out. I thought maybe you might have a few early copies available."

The woman rubbed her chin, seemingly charmed by Rose brazenly trying to snag a copy of a book that hadn't released yet. "I don't think the delivery has arrived but let me just check with Ellen. She usually handles stock intake." She left her stool and went to call out to the woman I'd bumped into at the back of the shop. "Ellen! The new *Sasha Orlando* book. Has the shipment arrived yet?"

There was a pause, a clearing of a throat and then an oh so quiet, "No, it doesn't arrive until Friday."

The woman gave Rose an apologetic look. "Sorry about that."

She gave a sheepish look in return. "No worries! I was being cheeky asking anyway. I'll just have to wait like everybody else."

"My partner, Felicity, loves that series, too. She gets really excited when a new book comes out."

"It's the best," Rose agreed.

"Might I ask a question?" I interrupted, unable to help myself.

The woman's attention came to me. "Of course. Were you looking for a particular book?"

55

I shook my head. "No, actually, I was wondering if you have an employee here named Elodie? Red hair? She might be the owner."

She frowned. "Afraid not. My name's Bernice and I'm the owner here. It's just Ellen and I, and Felicity pitches in from time to time."

Rose shot me a questioning look. She knew all about Elodie but was obviously confused by me thinking she worked here.

"Oh, I must be mistaken. Perhaps I was thinking of another place."

If this woman owned the shop and had never heard of Elodie, then how the hell did she have a key? Too many questions filled my head. A loud clatter sounded from the back, jolting me from my thoughts. I turned to see the shy woman, Ellen, had dropped a stack of books. Looking frazzled, she hurried to pick them back up. She tucked her thick hair behind her ear and I got my first proper view of her face.

Elodie!

She looked exactly like her, except her eyes and hair were brown and she was significantly shorter. I left Rose to continue chatting with Bernice and walked down the aisle. When she saw me approach, she froze, her doe eyes widening.

"Hello again," I said. "I hope you don't mind me asking, but do you happen to have a sister?"

Four
Ellen

Panic set in.

I was a deer caught in the headlights. An imposter about to be unmasked. Blinking several times, I stared at Julian, words failing me. Fortunately, he didn't look suspicious or angry, only intrigued. My throat ran dry as I endeavoured to speak.

"P-pardon?"

Julian took a step closer, eyes wandering over my features keenly. I knew what he saw: a bookish version of Elodie, her complete opposite with the same face.

"I was wondering if you have a sister?"

Looking past him, Bernice was chatting casually with the woman Julian had come in with. I'd been stacking books, but as soon as I heard his voice, I panicked. How the hell had he found me? I ran back through my memories of the morning. Feeling too nervous to keep up the act, I made my excuses to Suze and left the café before Julian returned from his phone call. He'd gone outside, so he must've seen me leaving. Had he followed me?

Why on earth would he follow me?

And to top things off, the woman he came with had asked for the latest *Sasha Orlando* book.

My book.

My career as an author wasn't something I advertised, mainly because I was a hermit and too socially phobic to do appearances. My dad and brothers were the only people who knew I was a writer.

I had a pen name, and nobody knew what E.S. Grant looked like. Funnily enough, it seemed to add mystery and increase book sales. And conspiracy theories. Lots of people thought that Sasha was a real person, the books more fact than fiction. If you looked on the internet, you could find speculation galore, which made me wonder if Julian was one of those people.

He'd never told me his profession.

It was very possible that he was a journalist himself, or a blogger out to seek the truth.

Too panicked to think straight, I answered, "Yes, I do have a sister. W-why?"

He took a step forward. "Her name wouldn't happen to be Elodie?"

I took a step back. "Do you know her?"

To Julian, I must've sounded edgy and mistrustful. On the inside, I was scrambling for a way to get out of this mess. I knew there were only two viable options: come clean about everything, or, lie and pretend I was Elodie's sister. Obviously, being me, I took the coward's route.

I could wriggle my way out of it...eventually. If he came looking for Elodie again, I'd tell him she died in a helicopter crash. Or got struck by lightning. Or was inducted into a religious cult. Fell down a well.

Julian's eyes danced, as though he were thoroughly amused by the thought of Elodie having a sister who was so unlike her.

"We're acquainted, yes. It's a pleasure to meet you...Ellen, wasn't it?"

"Uh huh." I tugged at the sleeve of my shirt. I needed this interaction to end *now*. "Well, I'll let Elodie know I bumped into you, but I have to get back to work, so..."

"Julian. Tell her you bumped into Julian."

"Okay."

"Are you twins?"

I arched an eyebrow. "Do we look like twins?"

"You could be fraternal twins, but really, the resemblance in your facial features is uncanny."

"We're not twins. I'm her younger sister," I blurted, my deep-seated addiction for making up stories tumbling out. I should just shut up and let him leave, but there was something alluring about Julian. The sparkly light behind his eyes pulled me in.

"Ah, I see. Yes, you do strike me as the younger sister, but funnily, I recall her telling me she only had two brothers."

Oh crap, I had said that, hadn't I?

I needed to start keeping better track of my stories. Elodie's stories. That was the problem with being a dirty deceiver. Eventually, you started to drown under all the lies.

I forced a casual tone. "Right. She doesn't like to tell people about me. We don't exactly get along very well."

"Oh, and why is that?" Julian asked, his lips forming a scandalised pout. "Did you sleep with her teenage boyfriend? You seem like the type."

His teasing surprised a laugh out of me. "I also stole her signed poster of The Backstreet Boys, so we're basically enemies for life now."

His answering smile was beautiful, and I was internally impressed with myself for managing to conduct this conversation without swooning and/or fainting.

"Ems for life, huh? Sounds serious. Now I'm glad I don't have any siblings."

"Yep, you're pretty lucky," I said, nodding awkwardly.

"Julian, are you coming?" his friend called from where she stood at the front of the shop. I was fairly sure she wasn't his girlfriend, since he'd been coming on pretty strong with Elodie at Suze's apartment.

He glanced in her direction then brought his mesmerising gaze back to me. "Looks like I'm wanted. It was great meeting you, Ellen. Try not to sleep with any more of your sister's boyfriends. Actually, strike that. If I ever manage to convince her to date me, feel free to work your seductive charms." He waggled his brows and again, I laughed. I knew he wasn't flirting with me. He was being friendly because he wanted to get with Elodie, my alter ego, and now, fake sister.

"Right, I'll keep that in mind."

With one last parting grin, he went and linked his friend's arm, then left the shop. I slumped back against a bookshelf and tried to catch my breath. The panic that had been racing through my body made me feel like I'd just run a marathon.

But then it transformed into something else, something that zinged through me, a heady rush.

I felt...oddly powerful.

I'd gotten away with it, albeit fumblingly. I'd pulled off a ruse. Mastered some trickery. Convinced Julian I wasn't some weirdo girl with a complicated and very deeply thought out alter ego. Elodie was a glove that fit perfectly to my hand, but perhaps Ellen wasn't such a bad actress either. Or maybe my supreme timidity clouded the fact that I was a fake. After all, anyone as awkward as me couldn't possibly have the confidence to pull off a con.

Either way, in my somewhat uneventful life, this gave me a thrill.

When I arrived home that evening, I ran my hand along the familiar hallway wall, painted in a mural of climbing roses. Something I haven't mentioned yet, my house was sort of unique, or well, visually striking was probably a better description. It was my haven, the place where I spent most of my time, and I'd put a lot of effort into making it special. Sometimes it felt more like a work of art in progress than a house.

My kitchen was a jungle of lovingly cared for potted plants, with Rainbow's and Skittles' antique birdcage the focal point. Behind it, I'd painted a mural of a cherry blossom tree in full bloom, so that it spanned out around their cage in all its soft pink glory. Painting was a hobby I indulged in whenever I wasn't writing.

When I was about eleven, I discovered the joy of writing fiction. I also loved to draw, so I'd create illustrations to accompany my stories. It was how I released all my unspent, creative energy. My stories no longer required pictures, so now my house was my canvas.

My brother, Nick, said my paintings were an outward expression of my inner self. My other brother, Cameron, said all the colours gave him a headache.

I told you he was the cranky one.

Anyway, Nick liked to psycho-analyse people. Some folks in our hometown called him the Shrink Barista, though he wasn't exactly qualified. He dropped out of his Psycho-therapy degree in year two and now worked in a coffee shop full-time. His take on me was that since I was so socially phobic, I channelled all my unused social energy into art. I tended to agree with him, since up until the age of five I had what they termed 'selective mutism'. I would only speak around a select group of people. In my case, that was my immediate family. With anyone else, I was completely silent.

At school, my teachers tried to lure me out of my shell by giving me special treatment, letting me sit right by their desk or draw pictures while the other kids did maths. My memories of that time were hazy, but somewhere between the age of five and six, I started talking. I was still unbearably shy, but I was no longer totally mute. My dad thinks my mutism was a form of post-traumatic stress from Mum dying. But I was only two when she passed and even now I barely remembered her.

Others (Nick) thought it was anxiety. That social situations made me so anxious as a kid I couldn't bring myself to speak. I was more inclined to believe this theory, since I still suffered from the dreaded social phobia. However, I wasn't nearly as bad as I used to be. Ever since I created Elodie, I was coming on in leaps and bounds.

She freed me from the oppression of choking every time I had to talk to an unfamiliar human being.

Cases in point, Julian and Suze.

Before Elodie, I never would've had the courage to befriend a woman like Suze. Nor would I be ballsy enough to lie to a man like Julian.

Was it ethical? No. But it was helping me, so I had to convince myself the pros outweighed the cons.

I heated up some leftover stir-fry for dinner and opened my email. My agent, Daniel, had sent another message with requests to book public appearances, but there was no way I could do a book signing. Not unless I went as Elodie, and she looked so much like my character, Sasha, that it would only back up the theories she was a real person.

Still…

The idea set my deceptive, black heart aflutter. To be Elodie and revel in the adoration of hundreds of fans would be a thrill ride like no other. Maybe I could…

I clicked on 'reply' and started to type.

esgrantauthor@gmail.com to danielfranks@franksliteraryagency.com

RE: Book Signing Offer (I'm not above begging)

Let me think about it.

P.S. I'm making no promises.

His response came minutes later.

danielfranks@franksliteraryagency.com to esgrantauthor@gmail.com

RE: RE: Book Signing Offer (I'm not above begging)

Anything I can do to convince you? A holiday in the Caribbean? A case of Dom Perignon? Foot rub? Just say the word and it's done. I did say I wasn't above begging ;-)

I chuckled. I was fond of Daniel, even though we'd never met in person. We spoke on the phone every once in a while, and aside from Bernice and Felicity, he was the one other human connection I'd made here in London. Some days I felt so down, so lonely, especially when I went a full day or two without talking to another human being. The fact that I could pick up the phone and talk to Daniel was a big relief.

esgrantauthor@gmail.com to danielfranks@franksliteraryagency.com

No bribery needed. Just...give me time.

I closed out my email, made short work of my dinner, then opened my newest manuscript. I was only two chapters into the latest Sasha novel, but it was an important one because it was to be the last in the series. It was bittersweet, and although I adored this world and the characters I'd created, I knew it was time to say goodbye. I already had several ideas for a new series, but for now, I was going to enjoy taking Sasha on one final adventure.

Two days later, I was a few hours into my shift at the bookshop when the bell over the door rang, signalling someone's entrance. I sat by the counter, reading the Agony Aunt section of a celebrity gossip magazine. I enjoyed the stories because they were always so ludicrous and clearly made up. It was a relief to know I wasn't the only out there who enjoyed weaving fantasies.

I glanced up to check who entered, and my breath caught when I saw Julian. What was he doing here again?

"H-hello," I greeted, palms growing sweaty. "Can I help you?"

He wore that lazy, sparkly-eyed smile that seemed to be his signature. "Reading magazines during your shift, eh? I should report you to Bernice."

He was joking, but he wasn't too far off the mark. Bernice was a firm believer that if people were going to read, it should be literature, not trashy gossip.

I made a concerted effort to look him in the eye. "Do you need something?"

Julian placed both hands on the counter in front of me. "I was wondering if your sister was around?"

"No, Elodie doesn't really come here much."

"But I saw her use a key to get in the other day," he countered.

So, he *had* followed me. Hmm. My suspicions went into overdrive. *Was* he a journalist? He didn't look like one. Then again, I had no idea what he looked like. I'd never met someone like Julian before. I frowned, certain it created a deep indent between my eyebrows.

"She was doing me a favour. I asked if she'd look after the shop while I went to my dentist appointment," I responded.

"That was very kind of her, especially given you two don't get along so well," he mused.

"She owed me one."

Julian didn't take his eyes off me and it was unnerving to say the least. A moment of silence fell, and my heart started doing a thrumming anxious beat inside my chest. Imagine the drums from Phil Collins 'In The Air Tonight' in super speed.

Julian looked like he was settling in to stay a while, which was the exact opposite of what I wanted him to do, dammit!

"So, Ellen, what does a girl like you enjoy doing in her free time?"

Okay, if my suspicions went into overdrive a minute ago, now they were on red alert. I narrowed my gaze. "Why do you ask?"

Julian shrugged. "Just making conversation."

I exhaled a heavy sigh. "If you're looking for a book, you're welcome to check out our shelves. Other than that, I can't help you." I brought my attention back to my magazine, hoping he'd take the hint and leave.

But of course, he didn't. "Actually, come to think of it, there is a book I'm looking for. I gifted my copy of *La Dame Aux Camelias* to a friend and have been meaning to replace it. It's a favourite of mine."

I remembered reading that book in Uni. It was about a French courtesan who ended up dying tragically young. An odd choice to be a favourite book for a man in his thirties. Then again, there was nothing about Julian that struck me as typical.

"I'm pretty sure we don't have that one in stock."

"Can you check anyway?"

Pursing my lips, I placed my magazine down, then got up and walked around the counter. Julian smiled as though he'd won the battle to wear me down. I led him over to a shelf, scanning titles as he stood next to me.

"Have you ever seen *Black Books*?" he asked. "You remind me of the main character."

Unwittingly, I scowled, because I had seen that show and the character he was referring to was a wine-swilling, cranky old bookshop owner who treated every customer like a burden. I didn't bother to justify his question with an answer.

"My first assumption was correct. We don't have it. Sorry about that."

He pursed his lips. "Too bad. I'll have to search elsewhere. By the way, I do believe your top is on inside out."

I followed his gaze as it lowered over me and he was right. Embarrassment filled me.

The stitching on my green T-shirt was on the outside instead of the inside. I couldn't believe I hadn't noticed. I needed to start getting up earlier, so I had more time to get ready. Last night I'd stayed up until the wee hours writing. The muse had been upon me. *Thanks, Muse!*

Julian laughed softly. "You hadn't noticed?"

"I was in a rush this morning," I mumbled and walked back to the counter.

He glanced at his fancy wristwatch. "It's almost half past two. You haven't looked in a mirror all day?"

"It's not really a priority for me."

"No? If I had a face as interesting as yours, I'd be looking in the mirror all the time."

Wariness trickled through me. "What's your game?"

He gave a puzzled look. "My game?"

"Yes, your game. Why are you here talking to me? If you…" I inhaled a nervous breath. "If you think it'll win you points with Elodie by cosying up to her sister, then you're dead wrong. I told you, we don't get along. Besides, I'm pretty sure she's already seeing someone."

"Of course, the stripper. She's mentioned him," Julian said, studying me even more closely now. "And I'm not here to win points with Elodie. Believe it or not, I pass by this shop most days. I saw you sitting there and came in on a whim. Yes, I like your sister, but I also happen to think you're adorable."

Pfft. Whatever. "Sure, you do. What's your profession?"

My question seemed to give him pause, which only furthered my suspicion that he was a journalist. The fact that *La Dame Aux Camelias* was his favourite book pointed towards arts journalism. I'd bet my last penny he was a book critic.

"My profession is something I don't like to advertise."

"Why?"

"Because if I tell you, you may not wish to get to know me. Usually, if people get to know me first, then discover my profession, they're more accepting. They've already found out for themselves that I'm a good person, and what I do for a living doesn't cloud their judgement."

Okay, I had no idea what he was talking about now. "Are you a journalist?"

He affected a confused look. At least, I imagined he was affecting it to throw me off the scent. "Why ever would you think that?"

"Just a hunch."

"I'm not a journalist."

"Sure, you aren't. Listen, I think you should go now. You're not going to find any story here."

Julian opened his mouth to say something when the bell rang, and Bernice walked in to relieve me from my shift. She glanced from Julian to me. "Hello again. Are you back to look for the new *Sasha Orlando* book for your friend? It's still two more days before it goes on sale."

Julian scratched his head. "No, I, uh, was just passing through." He looked back to me, a conflict on his face. "It was a pleasure seeing you again, Ellen. Bernice."

With that, he left. I played back our conversation in my head, but it only made me more confused than ever.

Five
Julian

I walked back to my flat, perplexed by my conversation with Elodie's sister, Ellen. Perhaps it was the fact that they didn't have a good relationship that made her frosty. But then, she'd acted weirdly suspicious, thinking I was a journalist out to find a story. What was that all about?

Again, something simply wasn't adding up.

When I'd discovered Elodie had a sister, I was amused and intrigued by the resemblance. They had different coloured hair and eyes, but their facial features were identical.

Ellen reminded me of Elodie insofar as they had the same face, practically the same voice, but that was where the similarities ended. Ellen wore jeans and T-shirts, no makeup, and had a smattering of freckles across her cheeks that were adorable.

I liked to imagine myself as a scholar of women. All of their variations and idiosyncrasies fascinated me, so to discover two sisters who were so different in temperament made me feel like an archaeologist who'd just stumbled upon a rare fossil.

One more thing they had in common: neither sister was interested in me, which was perfectly fine. I'd long since accepted I was not the sort of man women chose to date or settle down with. I was the sort they enjoyed a thrilling, sexually adventurous affair with for a few weeks before moving on, and that was okay. Sure, more and more often these days, I wondered what it would be like to be loved completely and unconditionally by someone, but I would never ask a single woman to accept what I did for a living. It just wouldn't be fair.

I reminded myself that life was too short to spend it with any one person. With my particular profession, I got to enjoy all the colours, shapes, sizes, and souls that God had seen fit to create.

Rose was packing when I arrived home. Tomorrow was Damon's last day of filming, so they were off back to the island on Sunday. Since they were the only real family I had, I'd be sad to see them go.

My mother had been admitted into a psychiatric hospital when I was in my late teens and I'd never met my father. Now Mum lived in an assisted living facility. I went to visit her a few times a year, but it was never certain if she'd be happy to see me. Sometimes she'd greet me with a smile, maybe even a hug. Other times she'd be cold and withdrawn, too much inside her own head.

She suffered from an extreme form of bipolar depression. It was one of the many things she passed on to me. However, unlike Mum, I was able to manage my moods with medication and self-care. When her past lover, Elijah, with whom she'd been having a polyamorous relationship including two other women, chose one of the other women over her, Mum suffered a manic break. It was one of the most tumultuous periods of my life, and in the end, I had to make the hard decision to admit Mum into a facility. It was a choice I lived to regret somewhat, because now she didn't want to leave. She was institutionalised, and the idea of re-entering the outside world terrified her.

"Penny for your thoughts?" Rose asked as I flopped down onto the bed. She knelt on the floor, carefully folding clothes and placing them in her suitcase.

I made a dramatic frown. "I don't want you to go."

Her expression softened. "Why don't you come with us? You could do with a break from the city. Do some meditation. Read a few books. It'll be good for you."

I considered it. The idea of getting away from all the hustle and bustle was appealing, but then I thought of my current preoccupation with Elodie and Ellen. I was too intrigued by them to leave right now. There was just something about them that I needed to get to the bottom of.

"It's not a good time for me to go away."

"Oh? Does this have to do with a client?" Rose asked, curious.

"No, for once this has nothing to do with a client. You know Elodie?"

Her expression turned knowing. "Ah, right. The sexpot from the coffee shop."

I smiled at her phrasing. "Well, do you remember Ellen, from the bookshop the other day?"

"I thought her name was Bernice?"

"No, that was the owner. I'm talking about the shop girl in the back."

Rose twisted her mouth to the side, trying to recall. "Vaguely."

"Well, it turns out she's Elodie's sister."

"Really? Small world."

"I know, but there's something about them that doesn't add up."

"Like what?"

"I don't know. Both are immune to my charms, for one."

"That old chestnut. You want what you can't have."

"It's not that. I've had my advances rejected before, as you well know. It's just that they both seem...overly suspicious of me. Like they don't trust my intentions even though they don't even know me."

"Huh. Maybe they're just bitches," Rose suggested. I picked up a pair of rolled up socks and threw them at her head.

"They're not bitches. Well, at least I don't get that impression."

"Then what?"

"That's the problem. I have no idea."

"So, you're going to be consumed with finding out what their deal is for the foreseeable future and that's why you can't come to Scotland?"

"Pretty much."

She exhaled a breath. "You're always wrapped up in some new person or other, so I'm just going to leave you to it. You better come in the summer though. I miss you when you're not around."

"Aw, and there was me thinking I was the third wheel to yours and Damon's epic love life."

Rose scoffed. "Shut up."

"Are you still going to the bookshop tomorrow to pick up that new novel you wanted?"

She nodded excitedly. "Of course. I've been counting down the days."

"Mind if I tag along?"

"So that you might bump into Elodie's sister again?"

I smiled wide. "Perchance."

***

I considered the idea that Ellen was simply shy, and her standoffishness was a form of armour. But then, what was Elodie's problem with me? She certainly wasn't shy. At least, that was the impression I got from the weeks I spent listening to her conversations with Suze.

It sounded pretty bad when I put it like that, didn't it?

Oh well, I never claimed to be some noble, trustworthy prince.

I was surprised to find the bookshop crowded with people when Rose and I arrived on Saturday afternoon. A large display featuring the latest *Sasha Orlando* release, *The Games We Play*, had been set up in the middle of the store and people were queueing up to get their copies.

"This is so exciting," Rose exclaimed as she grabbed a paperback and joined the queue. I looked around for Ellen, but there was no sign of her. Bernice stood by the counter, ringing up purchases. I felt a measure of disappointment and wondered if maybe she was in the storeroom out back. Rose had her nose buried in the book, already several pages in by the time we reached the counter.

Bernice gave a friendly smile when she saw us. "You came back."

"I have a trip tomorrow, so I need my reading material," Rose replied with a wide grin.

"Well, I'll thank you for your custom."

"Is Ellen working today?" I asked. "I was hoping to speak with her."

Bernice gave a sad look. "She was, but she went home about an hour ago. Poor thing suffers terrible anxiety in crowds. Normally it's just one or two customers in here at a time, but when there's a big book release, we get a lot more people in."

Huh. Was that the reason for how she acted around me? I suddenly felt horrible for forcing conversation on her. She must've been nervous as hell having a stranger come up to her like that.

"That's awful," Rose said.

Bernice nodded. "She was in such a rush to get out of here that she left her ticket behind. It's for tonight's show of *Hamilton*. A friend of mine works at the theatre and managed to snag a seat for Ellen. I'm hoping to get a chance to drop it over to her at some point today, but I've been rushed off my feet."

"Does she live close by?" I asked.

"Yes, she's just over on Esther Crescent."

"Rose and I can slot the ticket in her letterbox, if you like? We're walking that direction anyway."

Rose gave me a questioning look, while Bernice eyed me with playful suspicion. "Are you certain you aren't trying to snag the ticket for yourself?"

I winked at her. "I promise you my intentions are honourable."

She chewed her lip. "Well, since the show starts in a few hours it's important she gets it." A pause as she seemed to conclude that she could trust us. "Her house is number 119." She pulled a small envelope out from behind the counter.

"Perfect. We'll have it to her in no time."

I was certain that if Rose, my blue-eyed, innocent and kind looking best friend weren't with me, Bernice wouldn't be quite so willing to trust me with the prized ticket. We walked out of the shop, waving goodbye to Bernice. Once we were around the corner, Rose stopped me in my tracks.

"Perhaps it's not such a good idea for you to go over there. If she suffers from anxiety, then having someone like you show up will only make it worse."

I arched a brow and put a hand on my hip. "Someone like me?"

"Don't play dumb. You're well aware of the effect you have on women. You fluster them. I've witnessed it plenty of times."

"I'm just going to slot the ticket in her letterbox, no euphemism intended," I winked. "There won't be any flustering."

"Do you promise?"

I swept a finger over the left side of my chest. "Cross my heart."

Rose eyed me. "Okay, good, because I have to go meet Damon for lunch."

"Hold on. You're not coming with me?"

"I can't. I already told you I have plans."

"Fine, go. I'll see you back at the flat later."

"And remember, drop off the ticket and leave. Don't knock on the door, don't hedge to be invited in. In summation, don't try to work your devilish charms in any way."

"Heard and registered. No door knocking, hedging, or devilish charming shall occur. You have my word."

I saluted her, and Rose shook her head. We exchanged a hug and then she walked in the direction of the nearest Tube station. I headed toward the address Bernice gave, the long street lined with period homes. They didn't appear to be split up into flats either, which meant Ellen lived in one of these all by herself. How on earth did someone who worked in a bookshop afford a place like this?

But then, I remembered Elodie mentioning she lived in this area, too. Did they live together? No, that didn't make sense, especially considering they supposedly weren't close. Perhaps it was some kind of house share.

I climbed the steps leading to the front door of 119, eyed the letterbox, then hesitated. Rose *had* warned me against it, but what harm could it do to knock and present her with the ticket in person? Some part of me yearned to see her, check if she was okay. Surely, it wasn't a good sign for a few extra people in the bookshop to freak her out so much.

Feeling spontaneous, I lifted the knocker. A moment passed. No one answered. I glanced at the window and saw the curtains twitch. Ellen peeked her head out for a second then ducked out of view.

I knocked again, and again there was no answer.

"Ellen, I came with your ticket for the show tonight. Bernice said you left it behind at the bookshop," I called out.

More silence.

"I know you're in there, darling. I saw you peek out just now."

Still nothing. She must've been embarrassed. After another moment or two, I decided to slot it through the letterbox like originally planned, but then I heard the lock flick over. The door opened, and Ellen stood before me. She hid most of her body behind the door, and her face was slightly blotchy. Had she been crying? My heart clenched at the thought.

I knew what anxiety felt like, since I'd experienced enough of it as a kid. Mum was always up and down, always with a new boyfriend, some of them nice, others not so nice. When you lived in an unpredictable world with no security, anxiety was your ally. It warned you of coming danger. But like I said, with the help of medication, I'd since learned to manage it. If the look of Ellen was anything to go by, she was deep in the midst.

"Hi," she said, reaching a hand out for her ticket.

"Are you okay?" I asked as I handed it over, my question edged with sympathy.

"I'm fine. Thanks for bringing this." She sniffed, then made to close the door.

"You don't look fine. Is there someone I can call for you? Elodie? Maybe one of your brothers?"

She must've heard the genuine concern in my voice because she lost some of her guardedness. "No, thank you. I'll be o-okay."

The quaver in her voice broke my heart, and I felt the strongest urge to comfort her. I placed my hand on the door to keep her from closing it in my face.

"My mum used to get the same thing. When I was a kid, she was pretty nervous in crowds. She self-medicated though, and that just made things worse," I blurted, frowning at myself. I hadn't meant to share that.

Ellen opened the door a little more. "Your mum?"

"I don't get to see her very often anymore," I said sadly.

She stared at me, and I tensed. Her big brown eyes seemed to have this way of looking right into your soul. I hadn't felt that with Elodie. With Elodie, I'd gotten the sense that she was looking past me for a better option. But Ellen truly looked at you, gave you her full attention. She appeared to come to some conclusion when she said, "I'm sorry for being rude to you the other day. I wasn't myself."

"No apology needed. I understand."

She shook her head. "No, you don't."

"Then explain it to me," I urged.

I had no idea why I felt such a strong draw to her. Maybe because I'd spent so many hours studying her sister, who looked so much like her, I felt a connection, like I already knew her somehow.

Ellen was quiet for a long moment, her head tilted up to study me. "I'm probably going to regret this, but would you like to come inside for a cup of tea?"

I gave her a soft smile, something unfurling in my chest at the offer. She was clearly going out of her way to be kind to me, when all she probably wanted to do was close herself inside her house and wish the world away.

"I'd love to."

She opened the door so I could step in by her, and I was instantly met with a beautiful hand-painted mural of climbing roses. It started at the door and meandered up the antique staircase.

"Do you live here on your own?" I asked.

She seemed hesitant to answer. "Yes, I, uh, inherited the place from my Grandma."

"It's a beautiful building."

She nodded. "I'm very lucky."

Ellen led me into an even more impressive kitchen. It had a large modern window that looked out into a fairy forest of a back garden. There were hanging lights and twisty vines climbing the walls, overgrown plants, and wildflowers all over. The forest theme seemed to extend into the kitchen as there were plants everywhere. Another mural encapsulated the back wall, this one of a cherry blossom tree. I wondered who the artist was. The painting fanned out around a large, intricate brass cage, inside of which were two exotic looking birds.

Seriously, who lived in a house like this? The Grandma story aside, Ellen was hiding something.

I walked up to the birdcage to admire her stunning creatures. "Hello there."

"Their names are Skittles and Rainbow," Ellen said quietly. "They're lovebirds."

I tilted my head to her. "Is it true that they mate for life?"

"Most of them do, yes."

"Why lovebirds?" I turned to give her my full attention now. It was strange that I'd thought Elodie was the interesting one because I was starting to suspect her sister had hidden depths.

She glanced at the floor, lifted a shoulder, then said, "They make such strong bonds. They're happy to sit side by side, day in and day out. There's something lovely yet heartbreaking about it."

I took a step closer to her. "Heartbreaking?"

When she spoke, her voice was still so quiet, like she wasn't used to having long conversations. "If one of them dies, they mourn just like humans mourn loved ones."

"That is heartbreaking," I said in agreement. The tip of her nose was red from crying, and again, I had a strong urge to comfort her, give her a hug. I knew how it felt to be overwhelmed by the world. I resisted though. Ellen was a little like a bird herself. I felt if I got too close she'd fly away.

"And the monogamy?"

"I guess if humans could be as simple as lovebirds, there'd be a lot less broken hearts in the world."

At this, I warmed to her, because she was so like Rose. My best friend believed firmly in monogamy, in having sex with someone you were in love with, and though I disagreed, I could appreciate the romanticism of the concept. I personally thought sex could be amazing so long as there was mutual respect. Love didn't have to come into it. You could meet someone, have an incredible night, then never see them again. There didn't always have to be strings.

Ellen turned and went to put the kettle on. She wore a baggy jumper and leggings, her hair piled up in a bun. I took a seat at her table and clasped my hands together.

"What happened today to upset you?" I asked gently.

I had no business asking such a sensitive question. But like I said, I felt I knew her even though I didn't. She had Elodie's face and a heart like Rose.

Her cheeks coloured, and she appeared embarrassed. "Nothing. I'm not upset."

I held her gaze, my eyes telling her I saw through the lie. "When I was a teenager, I caught an ex-girlfriend out on a date with someone I considered a close friend. I was so upset I went home and cried my eyes out. We all do it. Even men."

Some of her embarrassment faded. "I've always hated large groups of people. I feel like I can't breathe."

My voice held affection. "You picked the worst city to live in."

She sniffed and looked up at the ceiling. "When I decided to move here, I thought it would be better, that I could be whoever I wanted, leave the old me behind. Pretty silly since I didn't change one bit. Most days I don't even leave the house." Her eyes flared, like she hadn't meant to admit that. If she spent most of her time alone in this big house, then her fear and suspicion of me made even more sense.

"Don't worry. There's very little you can say that would shock me."

"You've seen it all, huh?" she practically whispered.

"And then some. A lot I wish I could unsee."

We stared at one another, a moment of understanding passing between us, even though our experiences in life were probably far different. She finished making the tea and set a cup down in front of me.

"I've been making a lot of selfish choices lately," Ellen revealed, then shook her head at her herself. "I don't know why I'm even telling you this. You have a pull, do you know that?"

I placed my hands around the cup. "I've been told I'm easy to talk to because I don't judge."

"Well, whatever it is, I don't usually talk to strangers, not as…never mind. The point is, I like talking to you, even though I know I shouldn't."

"Why shouldn't you?"

"Because it frightens me. You're a stranger, too. I shouldn't have let you in here. It's reckless."

"Yes, it is reckless. Luckily, I mean you no harm. Besides, we should always do the things that frighten us, Ellen. Except for jumping off cliffs."

She gave a tiny laugh, and it pleased me to see her smile, even if it was only a small one. "Indeed. I can't believe Bernice gave you my ticket. Like I said, you're a complete stranger. What was she thinking?"

"My friend Rose was with me at the time. She has a very trustworthy face."

Ellen arched a brow. "Not you?"

"Nope. I have the face of a rapscallion."

Her tinkering laugh was light and airy, the laugh of someone relieved not to be feeling so anxious anymore. It felt good to put her at ease. "Do you know what, you do! I really don't know why I let you into my house. I need to get my head checked."

"Looks perfectly fine to me."

"You haven't seen inside it."

"Oh?"

"It's a mess in here."

"I like messes. They're interesting."

"Has anyone ever told you you've got an answer for everything?"

"It's my party trick. So, you and Elodie grew up in Devon. What was that like?"

She looked away, took a sip of her tea. I wondered at the shutters that suddenly closed behind her eyes. "It was quiet. Peaceful. Too quiet sometimes."

"I can understand that. Rose lives most of the year on a remote Scottish Island. When I visit it's so quiet, I have trouble getting to sleep. I'm used to the constant buzz of city noise."

She appeared interested by this. "You don't find it stressful? I mean, I hate too much quiet, but the noise can be just as bad."

My expression sobered. "I guess I sometimes prefer the noise because then I don't have to listen to my thoughts."

She leaned closer, her brown eyes unfathomably big. "What kinds of thoughts?"

I met her gaze levelly. "Bad thoughts."

A beat of silence fell. We both startled when there was a ding on her doorbell. Ellen stood. "I better go get that."

She left, and I looked around her kitchen, a feeling of discomfort in my chest. Ellen wasn't the only one who felt a pull, because I'd revealed more to her than I did to most people. There was an innocence about her, an openness that felt safe.

I heard the front door open and indistinct voices. I got up and went over to admire Ellen's lovebirds again, smiling to myself. Unlike most, I didn't judge others for having different beliefs to mine. In fact, I respected people more when they believed in something fiercely. Monogamy was an idea almost as old as my profession. It was something I'd always struggled with personally, and for years I berated myself for not being able to conform, to simply pick a woman and settle down. That sense of shame was something I had to disconnect from if I didn't want to drown in it.

Now I allowed myself the freedom to live in a way that felt right for me. It was the only way I knew how. Still, the simplicity and innocence of the idea of searching for one true love, for a soul mate, was something that always made my chest ache.

It was like believing in angels. You wanted them to be real so badly, but your common sense wouldn't allow you to indulge in the folly.

I wished love at first sight, soul mates, and being destined for one single person was real, because it was a romantic, idealistic fairy tale. And I envied Ellen for her ability to believe.

But I, well, I'd had my eyes opened too many times in this life to still believe in fairy tales.

The front door closed, and I went out to check on Ellen. It appeared she'd had a delivery because there were several large, heavy-looking boxes on the floor.

"Need some help?" I asked, and she blew out a breath, hands on her hips.

"Please, if it's not too much trouble, could you help me carry these upstairs?"

"No trouble at all," I said and went to pick up a box. I was right, it was heavy. "What's in here?" I asked as I climbed the stairs.

"Just, um, some new bits of furniture I ordered online," she said, sounding oddly sheepish.

I left one box on the landing, then went down to get the next. When I'd brought all three boxes upstairs, I turned to go back down, and my gaze caught on something in one of the bedrooms. The door was ajar and carefully placed on a stand on the dressing table was a wig—a red-haired wig to be exact. I frowned, because it was practically identical to Elodie's hair. I froze on the step, staring at it, mind racing.

"What's wrong?" Ellen asked, traversing several steps. She frowned as she followed the direction of my gaze. I heard her sharp intake of breath when she realised what I was looking at.

I turned to her in confusion.

"Elodie?"

Six
Ellen

Crap, crap, crap!

As soon as Julian uttered the name "Elodie" I started to shake. My throat ran dry and the ability to speak evaded me. I'd been caught. Embarrassment and shame threatened to fill me whole.

"You're Elodie, aren't you?" he said, closing the distance between us. He didn't appear angry, which was a good sign, but he did look incredibly confused, and a tiny bit…well, intrigued.

Who the hell was this guy? And why on earth did I invite him into my house? Ever since I invented Elodie, I'd been having these strange, catastrophic urges, destined to lead to dire consequences. It was like I'd spent so long living this quiet, hermit life that something in my subconscious yearned for the thrill of disaster.

I turned and walked back down the stairs, reached for the front door and pulled it open. I ducked my head when I whispered, "Please go."

He walked down the final few steps. I felt his gaze burn into me, but I was too mortified to look him in the eye.

"Ellen, you can talk to me. I told you, I don't judge." His voice was soft, understanding, but that just made it so much worse. I wished for him to be mean so that I could feel justified in kicking him out, but he had to go and be nice about it. Ugh!

I kept my voice firm. "I said leave."

For a second, he didn't move. I sensed a struggle in him before he finally walked to the door. Unable to resist, perhaps because I was a glutton for punishment, I lifted my gaze to his. All I saw was sympathy and my face grew hot. He felt sorry for me, probably thought I was some sad loser who got her kicks from pretending to be someone she wasn't. And let's face it, that was the truth.

"If you ever need someone to talk to, you know where to find me."

Yes, I did know where to find him. Tuesday mornings at the Polka Dot Café. A sense of loss filled me to realise I couldn't ever go there again, not as Elodie anyway. The jig was up, and Julian was certain to tell Suze all about his discovery.

Suze!

A feeling of grief clutched me. I didn't want to lose her.

Julian left and I slammed the door shut, lowered myself to the floor and dropped my head into my hands. What a mess. That tense, awful feeling of chagrin trickled its way through me. It seared my insides, leaving humiliation in its wake. Julian was one of the most fascinating men I'd ever met. No, he was *the* most fascinating man I'd ever met, and now he saw me for what I really was.

A fraud.

I needed to get my shit together, quit pretending, finish writing my book, and be a responsible adult again. I needed to throw away my fanciful ideas about Elodie, quit lying to people and get back to being the socially inept hermit that was in my DNA.

Being myself was safe, and safe was what I needed to be.

So why did I feel like I'd lost a vital part of myself?

I got a text later that evening from Bernice, asking if Julian and Rose had dropped my ticket off. I didn't tell her that it was just Julian, nor did I complain to her about giving my personal property to two virtual strangers. Sure, it was only a ticket, but still!

All day Sunday I wallowed and tried to get over the intense feeling of mortification. Of being *exposed*. To have someone know you pretended, to know you dreamt up this fantasy and tried to make it real, was worse than being discovered as a fake.

On Monday I had an early shift at the bookshop. I opened up and a number of customers came and went. At around eleven thirty, I was stacking shelves when the door chimed open. My gut dropped, and the small hairs on my arms stood on end. Julian walked in wearing dark slacks, a forest green shirt with several buttons undone, and a black velvet blazer. He had this sort of grown-up Peter Pan style going on (ironic, I know). I was certain it wouldn't work for anyone else on this planet other than him.

Why hadn't he given up on me yet? It made no sense. Upon further consideration, I'd decided Julian most likely wasn't a book critic seeking to "out" me. On Saturday, three boxes of books had arrived at my house and he'd barely given them a second glance as he carried them upstairs. If he were trying to discover my true identity, he would've taken the opportunity to peruse the sender details, since my publisher's name and address was right there on the boxes.

But if he wasn't on a secret investigation, then why was he so interested? Why did he continue seeking me out? It certainly wasn't for my glowing personality, and now that he knew Elodie didn't exist, it most definitely wasn't for my good looks.

On instinct, I ducked down behind the bookshelf and hid, hoping he'd leave. I spied on him through a crack between the books and watched as he placed two takeaway coffee cups down on the counter. The edge of his mouth curved in a smile when he said, "I can see you hiding over there."

Great. As if I needed anything else to be embarrassed about with this man. Inhaling a deep breath, I mustered some self-respect, rose and dusted my hands off on my jeans.

"What are you doing here?"

"Bringing coffee to my new friend. You take it with milk, no sugar, yes?"

I narrowed my gaze and walked around him to the counter. He'd gotten takeout from the Polka Dot, and their coffee was my favourite. The rich aroma invaded my nostrils and it was *so* hard not to pick it up and down it.

"Thank you, but I've already had my coffee for today."

"Go wild, have another," he encouraged with an impish grin.

"I can't. Too much caffeine gives me heart palpitations."

"Ellen, if you don't drink it, I'm going to have to throw it away, and wasting coffee is a sin even a degenerate such as myself refuses to commit."

Gah! Why did he have to be so amiable? The glint in his eye was impossible to resist.

"Fine," I allowed. "But only because I wouldn't want that sin weighing on your conscience."

I lifted the cup and Julian took the other, still grinning at me as he brought it to his mouth. Okay, so he was an inordinately sexy person. This was something I noticed about him from the beginning. He exuded sex appeal in a subtle way that had nothing to do with his clothes or his looks. It was an energy that surrounded him. It was a freedom and comfort in his own skin few were lucky enough to possess. Maybe that was why I felt such a draw to him. He was everything I wished I could be. Everything I was pretending to be as Elodie.

We drank our coffee in silence and the shop door opened. A middle-aged man walked in and didn't spare us a second glance as he headed for the History section.

"Can we talk about the elephant in the room?" Julian ventured, and I blinked at him, bristling.

"No, I'd actually rather not."

"Why though? I'm honestly fascinated."

"What am I? Some sort of sideshow? Do you take pleasure in ridiculing crazy people?"

"I'm not ridiculing you, not at all. And besides, if anyone here is crazy, it's me."

I eyed him speculatively and chewed on my lip. "What do you mean?"

"My mother has been living in an assisted care facility for the last thirteen years. I also suffer from the same illness, however I manage to function in the outside world far better than she."

Mental illness? Was that why he was here trying to befriend me when anyone else would've run a mile? I wanted to question him, but I didn't have it in me. Despite the fact he'd shared the information, it still felt too personal.

"You're very candid," I said and placed my cup down on the counter.

"I try to be."

Hmm, perhaps I should take a leaf out of his book. "Why are you so interested in me?"

His eyes held mine captive. "Don't sell yourself short, Ellen. You're a very unusual person. Not at all what most would imagine at first glance. That's why I'm here. I like interesting people and that is what I find you to be. Besides, we live close to one another, frequent the same coffee establishment. It'd be a shame not to become friends."

I gave him a look. "You only want to be my friend because of Elodie. If you saw me on the street, the real me," I gestured to myself, "you wouldn't give me a second glance."

"There are plenty of people I wouldn't give a second glance. That doesn't mean they aren't worthy of friendship. It simply means we're all too busy with our own lives to stop and say hello. How lucky we are that through Elodie we're now aware of one another's existence." He gestured between us with his hands and smiled.

Damn, he really had a way with words. I forced myself to look him in the eye.

"Cards on the table, Elodie is...*was* a total glitch. I am the most boring person you'll ever meet, and I have every intention of going back to being as boring as possible."

He leaned close to whisper, "I don't believe you."

Tingles skittered down my spine at the warm look he gave me. I glanced at the man who'd come into the shop, just to make sure he wasn't trying to steal anything. He had his head buried in a thick hardback, not paying Julian or I any attention.

The shop door opened again and a group of five or six tourists walked in. Judging from their accents, they were American. They spoke excitedly about going to see the house from *Notting Hill* and visiting the markets. I watched them wander down the aisles, oohing and aahing about how quaint the shop was.

I looked to Julian and noticed he was watching me watch them.

"What?" I mouthed.

He looked like he was about to say something, then thought better of it. "How are Skittles and Rainbow today?"

I was surprised he remembered their names. "Skittles was being feisty this morning. Rainbow is the well behaved one. Skittles sometimes bullies him."

"Do they require a lot of care?"

"Yes, you need to handle them every day to keep them tame. My grandmother had a pair when I was little, Toto and Leaf. I loved those two birds so much I decided to get two of my own."

"I've never had a pet," Julian confessed, and I widened my eyes at him.

"Not even when you were a kid?"

He shook his head. "Mum didn't like animals in the house, which was ironic since that was the word I'd use to describe many of her boyfriends."

I frowned, not knowing how to respond to that, nor understanding how he could so casually reference personal subjects. "Well, um, you should consider getting one. If you live alone, they're great company. Skittles and Rainbow always get so excited when I come home. Rainbow likes to sit right on top of my head, and Skittles bites on my hair." I gave a soft laugh. Most people didn't realise what characters birds could be. They each had their own personality. Even though Skittles and Rainbow were practically identical, with their green, yellow, and peach feathers, I could always tell them apart.

Before Julian could reply, several of the tourists walked up to the counter. "This place is just adorable," one of the women exclaimed and I smiled politely.

"Yes," another added. "I was just saying I could spend hours looking through your shelves."

I forced another smile as I started to clam up, drumming my fingers on the countertop. It wasn't that they were being in any way scary or intimidating. Quite the opposite, in fact, they were nothing but friendly. *I* was the problem. When I had to speak to more than two or three people at a time, I choked. Heat built up inside me and I just couldn't get the words out. School had been a nightmare. Whenever a teacher called on me to speak or answer a question, I became mute, even when I knew the answer.

Hence, why being Elodie was so liberating.

"Are you the owner?" a man asked. All six of them had gathered around the counter now, including Julian. I hadn't spoken to this many people all at once in years. Normally, Bernice was around to converse with customers, but today she had a doctor's appointment.

My cheeks grew warm and my lips dry. I opened my mouth but only an inarticulate, "Erm…no I…" came out.

"She's not the owner," Julian volunteered, eyeing me.

"Oh, well, we really love this place. It's so cute," the first woman said.

"Do you stock the *Harry Potter* books?" the other woman asked. "I told my son I'd bring him back the British version of book one. Apparently, the title is different over here."

I swallowed a deep breath and forced myself to reply. "Y-yes. I'll go grab you a copy." Fetching the book was the escape I needed. It was one thing talking to Julian alone, but another entirely having a dozen or more sets of unfamiliar eyes on me.

I found the book too quickly, and when I returned, Julian was chatting with the tourists.

"If you're looking for good vegetarian food, I highly recommend Mildred's in Soho. There's also Tibit's in Mayfair if you're interested in something quick. They do an amazing quinoa bowl," he said. I envied his ability to converse with such confident ease. Then again, most people didn't react to social situations in the same way I did.

Why couldn't I just be normal?

"Here it is," I whispered as I presented the book to the woman.

"Fantastic! I'll take it," she replied, and I rang up the purchase.

A minute later they left, and I felt like I could breathe again. The man in the History section was still perusing books and didn't look like he'd be leaving any time soon.

"So, is that why you pretend to be Elodie?" Julian surmised when we were alone.

My brow furrowed. "Pardon?"

"Those tourists. You looked like you were about to have a panic attack when they spoke to you."

I'd say he was perceptive, but anyone with a pair of eyeballs could see something wasn't right. I swallowed and replied, "I typically clam up when I have to talk to more than one or two people. One on one is fine, two on one is okay. Anything over and above that, I tend to freak out a little. But it's all right. It's just something I have to deal with."

Julian's face grew thoughtful. "Why do you think that is?"

I shrugged, not really wanting to talk about it. "I don't know. I've just always been this way."

He was silent for a moment, studying me. "You're shy."

State the obvious, why don't you. My throat grew heavy because for some reason it upset me when people pointed it out. But really, this never felt like simple shyness. It was an invisible disability that everyone could see. I know that didn't make sense, but it was the only way I could think to describe it. And it didn't even really deserve to be compared to a disability, because there were people out there with problems much worse than not being able to talk sometimes. It was an inconvenience. I just had to struggle through it.

I refused to feel sorry for myself, or at least, I refused to acknowledge my selfish woe-is-me feelings of self-pity.

"So, can I ask where Elodie came from?" Julian rested an elbow on the counter, giving me his full attention.

I tugged on the hem of my top, that familiar sense of embarrassment creeping in. I decided to just bite the bullet and tell him. "She's a…a character I made up. When I'm her, I don't feel shy or self-conscious. For the most part."

"Ah. So, she helps you deal with being around people, making friends," Julian guessed.

I nodded. "It's weird, I know. I'm a weirdo."

"Not at all," he was quick to counter. "I think it's genius. You created a persona, whereby you can go out, have fun, interact with people and not have to worry about being self-conscious. For Elodie, there are no consequences, because she's not real. For Ellen, there are, because she is real."

I felt exposed when he summed me up in such a perfect nutshell.

"Um, yes, that's…that's pretty much why I do it."

Julian's eyes glittered as he slowly shook his head from side to side. "Amazing."

Having him look at me like that while wistfully uttering the word 'amazing' was *quite* the feeling. My heartbeat sped up.

Then, a worrying thought hit me. "Are you going to tell Suze?"

One eyebrow rose slightly. "Suze doesn't know?"

"I met her as Elodie. That's who she thinks I am."

"My, my, you must be a good actress."

"Too good," I said, suddenly relieved to be able to talk about all this with someone. Julian wasn't judging me. If anything, he appeared impressed by my oddness. I felt, I don't know, justified somehow.

Another silence fell, and I saw cogs turning over in his brain. He stared at me, gaze alight.

"What?" I asked, far too curious as to what he was thinking.

"Why don't I help you?" he suggested.

"Help me how?"

"If you wish to explore more possibilities as Elodie, I can take you out, introduce you to people. You can pretend to be her at parties and soirees and such. I get invited to a lot of those sorts of things. You could be my plus one."

"What are you, some sort of socialite?"

"In a sense, yes."

Hmm, that would explain his fancy dress sense and the fact that he was swanning around town mid-morning with seemingly no job to answer to. I wondered if he was a trust fund baby or the heir to some big business. Perhaps his surname was Dyson.

"What's your surname?" I asked with interest.

"Fairchild, why?"

That did sound fancy, but I didn't recognise it. "Just wondering."

"Are you going to Google me? You won't find much. I don't have any social media accounts."

"Neither do I." Aside from my author accounts, but those didn't have any pictures.

Julian smiled. "We're birds of a feather. So, what do you say, Ellen? Would you like to explore the world as Elodie with me as your guide? I have to say, I'd be honoured if you said yes."

I tensed, but I couldn't deny the idea was tempting. It was actually more than tempting, it was also scary. I had no idea if being Elodie would even work with anyone other than Suze. "I don't even know you."

"And I don't know you. Finding out is half the fun."

"So, you want to be my what? My fairy godmother? Or wait, fairy godfather?"

Julian smiled, a dimple deepening in his left cheek. "Since I believe gender is non-binary, fairy godmother will do. I definitely have one lurking inside of me somewhere," he joked and gave a soft chuckle, gazing down at me. "My little Cinderella, I intend to prepare you to be the bell of every ball."

I gulped, having a feeling I was in for something far removed from my normal, quiet little life. Ellen was quaking in her boots, but Elodie could hardly wait.

Seven
Julian

Fairy godmother.

I smiled to myself, quite liking the sound of that. When I got home after sharing coffee with Ellen at the bookshop, I thumbed through my diary, searching for an appropriate social engagement I could invite her to. Aside from meeting with clients, I prided myself on maintaining a full and varied social calendar. Over the years living in London, I'd made many friends and acquaintances spanning an array of social classes.

I kept all my upcoming events listed in my diary, mainly because I preferred hard copy over soft. I didn't like to leave any sort of electronic trail in regard to my work. Sure, I used the internet from time to time, but I never saved any important information on my laptop.

I scanned the coming weekend and found I was invited to the birthday party of Branson Sutton. Branson was a successful and very wealthy race car driver whose wife frequented the same nail salon as I did. Yes, I got manicures and pedicures once a month just like any self-respecting metrosexual. Besides, keeping my appearance in optimum condition was technically a work expense.

That's what my accountant said anyway. My official job title was "Freelance Alternative Therapist". Go on, laugh, I know you want to. But nobody could deny that my work was both alternative *and* therapeutic for the women who hired me.

Anyway, Branson's wife, Krystyna, was a blonde Polish beauty who thought I was an absolute hoot. Every time I saw her, she invited me to some new social event or other. The party would be a great opportunity for Ellen to spread her wings. She would be a complete stranger on the arm of an enigma. I was a known face in these circles, but few knew what I did for a living, unless they were a past or present client.

I pulled out my phone to send a text. Ellen and I had exchanged numbers before I left the bookshop.

Julian: *Be ready this Saturday at 8 pm. I'll pick you up from your place. Dress code is black tie.*

Her response came several minutes later.

Ellen: *Can I ask where you're taking me?*

Julian: *To a party. Trust me, Elodie will love it ;-)*

She didn't text back after that, which I interpreted as acceptance. These days, I was a little jaded when it came to parties. They didn't possess the same allure, and the women I met at them rarely interested me sexually. So yes, I was somewhat jaded in that respect, too. But the idea of going with Elodie, pretending with her, excited me. I enjoyed the prospect of being her escort, showing her a world she's never experienced before. Opening her up to the possibilities.

If my estimation of Ellen was correct, she hadn't done much socialising in her life. It would all be new to her, and I got to experience that newness through her eyes.

On Saturday, I pulled out my finest Hugo Boss suit, showered, spritzed on some Paco Rabanne, and I was ready to go. I arrived in a cab outside Ellen's house at 8 pm and got out to knock on the door. It opened a little too quickly, like she'd been pacing the entryway, waiting for me.

There was a flash of red hair, my eyes catching on the black silk evening gown she wore. It had been a while since I'd seen Elodie. I'd almost forgotten how differently she dressed compared to Ellen. Every inch of the dress hugged the curves Ellen normally kept hidden under baggy T-shirts and jeans.

She ran her hands down her sides. "Is this okay? I ordered it online, so I wasn't sure how it would fit."

I held a hand out to her and she took it. "First of all, the dress looks incredible. And second, Elodie is not the sort of woman to second-guess what she's wearing."

She let out a nervous breath. "Right. I forgot. Sorry."

I arched a brow and gave a tut. "Would Elodie apologise?"

Ellen blinked, inhaled a deep breath, then said, "No, she wouldn't. Elodie knows she looks fantastic no matter what she wears."

I smiled my approval. "Exactly."

I helped her climb into the waiting cab, my gaze idling on the impressive diamante encrusted heels she had on. They gave her an extra five or six inches of height, and I realised that was why I thought Elodie was taller. She always wore heels, no matter what.

"Nice shoes."

She glanced down a moment, then back to me. "Yes, I like them, too."

"Are they new?"

"No, but this is the first time I've worn them…out."

My lips twitched. "Does that mean you wear them around the house?"

She gave a sultry look that was pure Elodie. "Maybe I do."

"They must've cost a pretty penny."

Now she smirked. "A lady never reveals the price of her possessions."

Again, I wondered how she could afford such fancy things.

Not that her possible wealth changed my opinion about her. I was a firm believer that people got to decide who they wanted to be in life, no matter their beginnings. Having been born the son of a poor, single mother with alcohol and mental health issues, not to mention little education, I shouldn't speak, act or dress the way I do. However, this was how I chose to portray myself to the world.

I refused to let my start in life define me, and I thought that if more people did the same, there would be a lot less misery out there.

"So, are you going to tell me where we're going, or shall it remain a mystery?" Elodie asked. I'd call her Elodie now, since most traces of Ellen had vanished. Gone was the uncertain girl who'd answered the door so hastily. Now she held her chin high in a haughty fashion, taking on the air of a woman who took what she wanted from life and apologised for nothing. I relished her immersing herself in her role.

"We're going to Branson Sutton's birthday party at the Savoy," I replied, and she blinked at me.

"The race car driver?"

"The one and only."

She took a moment to absorb this, then flashed me a sassy smile. "Great. Maybe I can bag myself a rich racer boy."

"You aren't seeing the stripper anymore?" I questioned, playing along.

Elodie shook her head and levelled me with a coy look. "No, when it comes to matters of the bedroom, I don't like to share. Strange women had their eyes all over him every night. I didn't like it."

Something about the statement made my chest burn. Perhaps because there were certain similarities between my work and that of a stripper. I brushed it aside. It wasn't like I was doing any of this to romance her. I was doing this out of sheer enjoyment and mischief. I quite liked the prospect of fooling all the rick folks at this party into believing Elodie was real. My fatigued soul needed a change to make parties exciting again, and Elodie was the perfect recipe to provide it.

I returned my attention to her and winked. "In that case, let's find you a racer boy."

When we arrived at the hotel, a bellhop came to open our door. I got out first, then assisted Elodie. I offered her my arm and we strode into the party. We were two people aware of our attractiveness, intending to use it to our full advantage.

"Is that Elton John?" Elodie leaned close to whisper, awe trickling into her voice.

"I do believe it is. Old bastard borrowed my Alexander McQueen scarf last month and never gave it back."

Elodie laughed. "Good one."

"I'm not lying."

Her eyes widened. "Well, in that case, why don't you go ask for it back?"

"Later. Right now, I have some people I'd like to introduce you to."

"Why can't you introduce me to Elton?"

"Because he'll only bore us with tales of how he slept with Cher in the seventies."

Now she gasped. "He did?"

I chuckled and led her further into the party. I snagged a glass of champagne from a server and handed it to her. "Here you go."

She took it and brought it to her mouth. "Mmm, that's good champagne. Why aren't you having any?"

"I don't drink."

"Oh." She frowned, then asked. "Any reason?"

I answered honestly. "It was a problem for me in the past."

Her expression sobered. "Right. Understood."

I was surprised that she simply accepted my explanation without wanting to know more. Usually, when it came to my past addictions, people were nosy, but not Elodie.

"Julian," came a sweet accented voice and I turned to see Krystyna walk toward us. She and her husband were arm in arm, looking the picture of youthful, wealthy elegance.

"Krystyna, you look wonderful. And Branson, I'd never guess you just turned forty," I teased.

The handsome, dark-haired man gave an amused laugh. "Thirty-seven, actually."

"Ah, right. My apologies," I winked and he shook his head.

"And who is your lovely date?" Krystyna asked, eyeing Elodie with interest. I'd heard through the grapevine that Krystyna and Branson hosted swingers' parties from time to time. Alas, I'd never been invited, since I was too much of a wild card. Celebrities typically only let loose at small private gatherings consisting of other celebrities. Everyone had to have something to lose, and I didn't.

"Elodie Grant," Elodie replied with a practiced smile as she held out her hand. "It's a pleasure to meet you both."

"And you," Krystyna said, coming forward to give her a kiss on either cheek. Branson did the same, and I was surprised at how Ellen took it all in stride, not once breaking the act.

"Well, please enjoy the party, and hopefully we'll see you again before the end of the night," Krystyna went on and the two turned to mingle with more guests.

I led Elodie away. "That went well."

"He's even better looking in real life," she exclaimed. "And his wife, my God, she's one of the most beautiful women I've ever met in person."

"She is quite something. I think she liked you, too."

Elodie preened at this. "You do?"

"I do. Maybe they'll invite us to one of their partner swaps."

She blinked and almost spat out the mouthful of champagne she just swallowed. "Their what?"

"Branson and Krystyna have an open relationship. They host uber-exclusive swingers' parties at their house in Hampstead."

"Oh." Colour rose in her cheeks, a glimpse of Ellen trickling in. She cleared her throat. "Have you, uh, ever gone to one?"

I shook my head. "I've never been invited, I'm afraid. I'm not in the circle of trust, though I get the feeling Krystyna is planning to vet me."

She took a long gulp of champagne. "Vetting? They really take this stuff seriously."

"Wouldn't you?"

"I guess so. How does it all even work? Do they put their keys in a bowl or something?"

"Not quite. Like I said, I've never been, but I have been to other such parties. Normally people partner off as they so please."

"That sounds…interesting."

"It is. If you're into that sort of thing."

She eyed me now, all curiosity. "Are *you* into that sort of thing?"

"I was, for a while."

She went quiet and I could see her thinking, turning it all over in her head. When she looked at me, I found myself frustrated at the green contacts covering her naturally brown eyes. No wonder I'd thought them so odd before. Now that I knew they were fake, it was hard to believe I'd ever been fooled by them. Even her wig, that was clearly expensive and expertly made, seamless to the untrained eye, seemed obviously false.

"The other day," Elodie ventured, breaking me from my thoughts. "You said you believe gender is non-binary."

"True."

"Does that mean you're bisexual?"

Hmm, how to answer such a tricky question. I took a deep breath. "I believe gender is non-binary because I've never felt like a typical male, or well, I've never possessed typical male attributes. When I was a little boy, lots of people mistook me for a girl. As I grew older, I couldn't relate to boys in the same way I related to girls, but I wasn't gay, so I fell into this odd, nondefinable category. I also don't consider myself bisexual, but I admit I've been with men in the past when I was still discovering myself. It wasn't unpleasant, and I certainly enjoyed it, but it's not something I seek out. Those instances, well, they happened organically. Even though I consider myself straight, I'm a firm believer in allowing moments with other human beings to progress naturally. If sex happens, great, but if it doesn't, that's fine, too. Does that make sense?"

She stared at me in fascination. "Yes, actually, it does."

I chuckled. "I guess you could call me experimental. I don't typically have sexual feelings towards men, only women, but there have been occasions in my life when I've—"

"Experimented?" Elodie put in.

I smiled down at her. "Yes."

She went thoughtful again. "I guess women do that sort of thing all the time."

"Kiss girls?"

A soft laugh. "It's just more of a taboo for men though, I suppose."

"Well, I've never been one to let taboos stop me from doing what feels good."

"I need to take a leaf out of your book," she murmured.

I clinked my glass of orange juice to her glass of champagne. "And I'm more than happy to teach you."

We shared a moment, locked in each other's eyes before we were interrupted by a suave, slimy, and annoyingly familiar voice. I grimaced, wishing him away.

"Hello, Julian."

"Warren, what a nice surprise to see you here," I said, mustering a pleasant tone as I met the gaze of the six foot five blond Adonis in an Armani suit. Warren Gold and I had known each other for years, but we weren't what you'd call friends. We shared a profession; however, our methods of operation were far different. Warren had a website, social media accounts, the whole shebang. He posted oiled up, topless pictures of himself sunbathing on exotic beaches to Instagram, which seemed to work a treat in attracting customers.

I operated on nothing more than word of mouth.

The dark-haired woman on his arm was not a stranger. She was an ex-client of mine named Marie. We'd amicably parted ways about a year ago. Clearly, she'd decided to move on to new pastures. I didn't hold it against her, even if her taste in escorts left a lot to be desired.

"I was just saying the same thing to Marie," Warren replied. "It's been what? A year?"

"Too long," I lied and turned to his date. "Marie, you look well."

She lifted her glass, a face on her like the cat that got the cream. "Thanks. You don't look so bad yourself."

"And who is this beautiful little thing?" Warren asked, casting his serpentine gaze on Elodie. His quaffed, shoulder-length hair was worthy of a shampoo advert.

"This is Elodie, she's a close friend of mine," I said, lying again, and belatedly realised my error. I should not have introduced her as a close friend, because that only made her more of a prize to Warren. He had an ongoing vendetta against me. A couple of years ago, one of his clients dumped him and hired me instead. Ever since, he made it his mission to return the favour, which was clearly the case with Marie.

He'd also tried to seduce Rose a while back, but luckily my best friend was too wise to fall for it. She'd had the same upbringing as I did. I feared Elodie might not be so discerning as Rose when it came to men, and Warren had a way of dazzling people, so they couldn't see the tarnish beneath the false shine.

He stepped forward, took her hand, and brought it to his mouth for a kiss. Everything inside of me recoiled at the action. I wasn't sure why, because I hardly knew her, but I felt protective of Ellen.

"Hello, it's nice to meet you," she said, gazing up at him, clearly dazzled.

He smiled his practiced in the mirror, overly white smile and murmured, "The pleasure is all mine."

Marie cleared her throat, the ghost of irritation flashing across her face. It was gone in an instant, but I caught it all the same. "So, Julian, how have you been?"

"I can't complain. And you?"

She looked to Warren, her expression turning smug. "Oh, just wonderful. Warren's been taking very good care of me."

I didn't take the bait. "So, I see."

"Marie and I are off to Majorca for a little break tomorrow," Warren put in, sliding his arm around my ex-client's waist. "I can't wait to get some sun. London can be so dreary."

"True. There's not many occasions for sun worshipping in this city, and I do know you're fond of a sunbathing selfie." *Stick that in your pipe and smoke it, Mr. Gold.*

His only sign of irritation was a slight twitch in his left eyebrow. "Well, we can't all be off the grid like you, Julian. Nobody would ever be able to find us." He laughed boisterously, and Marie joined in. Elodie glanced at me with a raised eyebrow, and I was glad she didn't indulge Warren with a fake laugh like Marie had.

"I think we all should take a break from social media from time to time," Elodie said. "It does the soul good."

Warren gazed down at her. "Does it now? Perhaps I'll give it a try sometime."

Up on the stage, a well-known rock band took their instruments and started to play their latest hit. I couldn't remember their name, but I knew they'd been in the charts a lot lately because their song was on every radio station.

"Oh, my goodness, is that actually them? I love this band," Elodie exclaimed, showing her greenness. Instantly,

Warren knew she was innocent and ripe for manipulation, which was his specialty.

Couples were taking to the dance floor, and calculation shone in Warren's eyes. "Do you know what? Me, too. Care to join me for a dance?"

Elodie hesitated only a moment, glancing to me as though for permission. Grudgingly, I gave her a look that said *go ahead*, while inside I'd rather pull teeth than have her dance with Warren. His surname always reminded me of the proverb, *all that glitters is not gold*.

I watched as he took her hand and guided her to the dance floor. Marie folded her arms and stood beside me, annoyance written all over her face.

"You would have to be here with some irresistibly sexy redhead on your arm," she griped. "Do you know how long it took me to get an appointment with Warren?"

"Oh Marie, fret not, you'll have him back by the end of the song," I said, finding her jealousy tiresome. Marie was the type of client who fooled you into thinking she was fine with the arrangement, but who secretly thought she had some kind of claim over you. She wasn't necessarily a bad person, but she was rich enough to think that meant she could simply buy whatever man she wanted.

"I better," she hissed, swiping a glass of champagne from a passing server and taking an angry sip.

My gaze followed Warren and Elodie's movements. Thankfully, it wasn't a slow song, so he didn't have cause to put his hands on her. That didn't stop him from shimmying close. Too close. I swallowed, putting my feelings of jealousy down to the fact that I disliked Warren and his methods immensely. He was the proverbial thorn in my side. It wasn't because I felt something for Ellen. I mean, *Elodie*.

Not at all.

Eight
Ellen

Wow, this man was *tall*.

If I weren't wearing heels, I was pretty sure I'd look like his kid standing next to him, which was a weird thought. His blond hair was shinier than any person's I'd ever seen, and he was built like a superhero.

If Thor were a supermodel, he'd look like Warren Gold.

Still, there was something too perfect about him. Something in his eyes I found unappealing. But maybe I was being too judgemental. Incredibly good-looking men were very intimidating, after all. Not to Elodie, of course, but to Ellen they were mythical creatures to be gazed at and never spoken to.

It was a good thing I was here as my alter ego tonight.

"So, Elodie, how did you and Julian meet?" he asked as we danced. It was hard to hear him over the music, which was probably why he leaned close to speak in my ear. His hot breath danced across my skin.

"We live close by and met at our local coffee shop," I replied, answering as honestly as I could in case he happened to ask Julian the same question. I sensed an uneasy vibe between them and suspected Warren's date, Marie, might be an ex of Julian's. The woman practically eaten Julian up with her eyes, even though she was on the arm of the most attractive man in the room.

"How quaint. I thought you might've been a client of his."

A client? I realised I still hadn't asked Julian what he did for a living. When we spoke, I always got so distracted, fascinated by every word that came out of his mouth. I didn't want to give anything away, so I simply replied, "No, I've never been his client."

Something I said piqued Warren's interest. "Well, if you're ever interested, I'd be more than happy to take you on."

"Oh? You're in the same business?"

"We are. Just ask Marie if you'd like a reference."

Okay, now I was confused. Luckily, the song ended and Julian swooped in. "My apologies, but I have to steal Elodie away. There's someone I'd like her to meet."

"Of course," Warren replied, taking my hand and kissing it in farewell, a seductive glint in his eye. "Until we meet again, beautiful Elodie."

I linked arms with Julian and he led me away. "Wow, he's intense."

Julian gave an amused laugh. "That's one way of putting it."

"How do you know him anyway? Is Marie an ex of yours?"

He arched an eyebrow. "What makes you think that?"

I shrugged. "The way she looked at you." A pause as I glanced at him. "The way you looked at her."

He seemed hesitant to answer, not meeting my gaze. "I guess you could call her something of an ex, though we were never in a relationship."

"So, she was a hookup?"

"Along those lines, yes."

"And you don't like Warren because she's with him now?"

We walked by a table of hors d'oeuvres and I swiped a little cracker with salmon and cream cheese. I'd been so nervous for tonight that I'd barely eaten all day and hunger was starting to creep up on me. Julian exhaled deeply and guided me further through the fancy room.

"There are many reasons why I dislike Warren, but none of them have to do with his current relationship with Marie."

I popped the cracker in my mouth and chewed. "Okay, so tell me one of them."

"Has anyone ever told you it's impolite to speak with your mouth full?"

"Elodie never claimed to be a lady. Now spill. I want to hear why you hate Thor, Supermodel Edition."

Julian laughed at this. "Hate is a very strong word. But one of my main gripes with Warren is that he tried to seduce Rose a few years ago, with every intention of discarding her afterward."

Huh. Rose was the woman who'd come with him to the bookshop. "Were you and Rose together at the time?"

He shook his head. "Rose is my closest friend. We've known each other since we were children and our mothers entered into a polyamorous relationship with one another. In fact, she's more like a sister."

"A polyamorous *what*?" I gaped at him. If I hadn't already swallowed, I might've choked.

"Polyamory is when you enter into a relationship with more than one person. Unlike me, my mother was bisexual, though she had a preference for men. Anyway, the point is, Rose and I have been through a lot together, and I was not going to allow Warren to hurt her. Luckily, she was wise enough to see through him." He eyed me meaningfully.

"Don't worry. I can see through him, too. There's something not right about his eyes."

Julian appeared relieved. "I'm glad to hear it. Warren will love you and leave you, Ellen...I mean, Elodie."

"Well, it's a good thing *Elodie* isn't looking for a relationship right now."

"And what about Ellen?" he questioned, seemingly interested.

"Ellen will be happy enough just to get by without having a panic attack every time a stranger tries to talk to her."

Julian tutted. "That's no life for a pretty girl like Ellen."

He thought I was pretty? Colour stained my cheeks as I whispered, "We can't always have it all."

He turned to face me now, his face full of sincerity and warmth. "My dear, you can have anything you set your mind to."

A silence fell as I looked around the room. These celebrities lived in a whole other world, and I certainly understood the ordinary person's fascination. It was a world where everyone appeared to be living their best life. Julian didn't seem to be a part of it, but rather, on the fringes. A welcome guest but not a fully-fledged member. I glanced at him and found him studying me.

"What are you thinking about?"

"About you," I answered honestly. "You have quite an interesting life."

His eyes held a sparkle. "Oh Elodie, you don't know the half of it."

I was locked in his gaze again. If I wasn't careful, I could get lost there. I looked away, scanning the room. "So, who was it you wanted to introduce me to?"

His tone was playful. "Are you familiar with the work of J.K. Rowling?"

My mouth fell all the way open. "Shut up! She's here?"

Julian motioned me forward. "Come along. We met while I was holidaying in Fiji last year. The woman is a delight."

***

By the time the night was through, Julian had introduced me to so many celebrities my head was fit to burst. I was on a buzz as we climbed into a cab to head home. I'd be high off the adrenaline of that party for months. And the fact that they all believed Elodie was a real person? *So* exhilarating.

It was a victimless crime. Well, except for Suze. I was still trying to figure out what to do about her. Maybe it would be best if Elodie just ghosted her, but the idea of letting her go hurt. I'd come to like Suze a lot.

When we arrived at my house, I turned to Julian. "Do you want to come in for a little while?"

His smile was teasing. "I never sleep over on the first date."

I swiped him on the shoulder. "Not what I meant! I just…I still feel too excited to sleep. Tonight's been amazing."

His expression was tender. "It was certainly a lot of fun painting the town red together."

I opened the door to the cab. "So…"

Julian pulled out some money to pay the driver. "Fine, I'll come in for a little while, but I'm warning you, if you get handsy I'm gone."

The cab driver chuckled quietly in the front. I rolled my eyes. "Trust me, your virginal body is safe with me."

We stepped out of the cab and Julian gave a loud hoot. "This body hasn't been virginal since the Monica Lewinsky scandal."

I slotted my key in the door, chuckling. I wasn't tipsy since I'd only had two drinks. I'd been too busy taking it all in. The party. The people. The thrill of pretending.

Rainbow and Skittles chirped in their cage when I came in. "Hello, my babies!" I greeted jovially, high on life. Julian walked into the kitchen behind me as I opened their cage. Skittles flew out and perched on a wood beam close to the ceiling, while Rainbow came to sit on my shoulder, fascinated by my wig.

"Vocal little things, aren't they," Julian commented as he took a seat by the table.

"Yep. This house wouldn't be a home without them."

"How long have you had them?"

"Almost six years. I got them soon after I moved to London. But lovebirds can live for up to fifteen years, so they'll be around for another few years yet."

"Will you be sad when they die?"

"Of course! It's like losing any pet. They're my best friends."

Julian's expression softened, and I realised how sad that sounded. My closest friends in the entire world were my pet birds. I grimaced.

"It's not as pathetic as it sounds, I promise."

"I don't think it sounds pathetic at all. Look at this beautiful house and those wonderful birds. You've got it made."

"Yes, well, I could stand to try for a little more human interaction."

"You're already doing it. Tonight, you were charming celebrities like you'd been doing it your whole life."

I held up a finger. "Correction. Elodie charmed them. Ellen would've hidden under a table and waited for it all to be over."

"You do realise that you are Elodie. She's right there inside of you. You just need to dress up in order to let her free."

I petted Rainbow's head and placed him back in the cage before he decided to poop on my wig. It was often a hazard of letting your pet birds sit on your shoulder.

"Yes, but I don't think I'll ever be able to be like her while I'm...me. This is going to sound confusing, but when I'm Elodie, I'm more myself than when I'm actually being myself."

Julian was quiet a moment, thinking. I pulled two bottles of water out of the fridge and handed him one. He took it and silently unscrewed the cap. "What if you try a slow progression? You could keep being Elodie until one day you feel comfortable not to wear high heels. Then, maybe a couple of weeks later you'll wear jeans instead of a dress, and so on."

I exhaled. "You're making it sound simpler than it is. This is a psychological block. It's not so easily overcome."

"Well then, you just keep going out as Elodie and see where it leads. What's the worst that could happen?"

"I could suffer the ultimate mortification of being found out. Oh, wait, that's already happened," I deadpanned.

Julian smiled. "Exactly. And did the world come to an end? No, it didn't. If pretending to be Elodie makes you happy, then you keep on pretending. Lots of people have alter egos, just look at drag queens. You're no different."

I pointed my water bottle at him. "It's funny you should say that. Elodie actually began when I won a makeover at a drag show I went to with Bernice and Felicity."

Julian slammed his hand down on the table. "Shut up! I love that. So, you got made over and just decided to keep doing it?"

I nodded as I swallowed a gulp of water. "I met Suze that same night. I think I was just so excited that someone like her wanted to be my friend that I kept up the ruse. Now I'm in too deep."

"Not necessarily. You can always come clean when you feel ready. I'm sure Suze will understand. Besides, you're more comfortable to be yourself as Elodie, so Suze still knows you, Ellen. She just knows you with more makeup and different hair."

I worried my lip. "Yes, but…I've lied to her about so many things. All the stories I've told her about my adventurous love life, they're all fake."

His expression sobered. "If Suze isn't willing to forgive you for lying, then there isn't much you can do about it. You made a mistake, but you'll move on from it."

My chest deflated at the idea of losing Suze. "I guess you're right."

Julian levelled me with a sincere look. "My philosophy in life is to do what makes you happy. So long as you're not hurting anyone else, there's no reason to feel shame."

"More people should have that philosophy."

"That's what I say but who listens to me?"

"I do."

A flash of affection. "Well, you're special."

Something in his tone made my heart beat faster. I drank more water then finally asked a question that had been nagging at me. "Julian, what do you do for a living?"

His face clouded. "Why do you ask?"

"Tonight, when I was dancing with Warren, he said you two were in the same business. I realised I still haven't asked what you do."

Julian stared at the table, then his magnetic eyes flicked up. "Do you promise my answer won't change our friendship?"

"Of course it won't."

He still seemed unsure. Nonetheless, he held my gaze as he answered. "I'm a male escort."

Nine
Ellen

"I'm a male escort."

I blinked at him, not sure if I heard correctly. He's a…a male escort? At the back of my mind, I'd worried he might be a drug dealer or some sort of criminal. There was just something a little bit sinister about Warren Gold. He was too glossy, too polished, like he was trying to hide something. When he told me he and Julian did the same thing, it set off warning bells, but prostitution didn't even enter my mind.

Perhaps I was jumping the gun. Being a male escort didn't necessarily mean he was being paid for sex. He would've said he was a gigolo if that were the case, and okay, yes, that was wishful thinking because 'escort' was merely a fancy term for a gigolo but…

"You're freaking out," Julian said.

"No, I'm just…a little shocked."

"Shock is expected. It's not a commonplace profession. At least, I doubt you've met someone such as myself before."

"I haven't. It's a lot to take in."

"Have I scared you off?"

I shook my head. "Of course not. It'd be rich of me to judge you for what you do when you haven't judged me."

His tone was teasing. "I may have judged you, just a little."

I gave a quiet laugh. "Well, I still refuse to judge you back. Your job is something I know nothing about, so how can I make assumptions?"

"Do you have questions?"

"Yes, but you don't have to—"

"Nonsense. Ask me whatever you like. I'm impervious to offence." He paused then added, "Mostly."

I screwed the cap back onto my almost empty water bottle. This conversation had given me a case of perennial thirst. "Well, in that case, what's the difference between a male escort and a...a—"

"A prostitute?"

I cleared my throat, cheeks heating. "Yes."

"There isn't necessarily a difference, though what I provide is more a holistic experience than just offering sex. I entertain my clients, take them out and do the things that they want to do. I get to know them on a personal level. Sometimes that leads to sex, sometimes it doesn't."

Huh. That all sounded very civilised, and he spoke about it so casually, like it was any normal job. I still wanted to know more though. When it came down to it, Julian had sex for money. I had a real-life male escort sitting at my kitchen table, ready to answer any questions I had for him. All of a sudden, I felt like my fictional character, Sasha, conducting an interview for journalistic research. It was like a scene right out of the first book in my series. Reality mirroring fiction.

"And how do people hire you?" I went on.

Julian smirked. "Are you interested?"

"No," I sputtered, then blushed. Even though I was still dressed as Elodie, I'd shaken off the act. Talking with Julian right now was too enthralling to pretend to be anyone other than Ellen. "I just mean, like, how does it all work? Do they find you online? Fill out a form? Or do you have an agency that manages everything for you?"

"I don't have an agency. I operate on word of mouth, friends passing recommendations on to friends and such. I vet all potential clients myself before agreeing to a date."

"You vet them? Like a detective?"

His lips twitched. "Something like that. I have to ensure they are who they say they are, but also decide if we're compatible. Some women are not emotionally stable enough to handle the experience of dating an escort."

"You mean, they might develop feelings?"

"Or imagine that what we are doing is a real relationship. Don't get me wrong, I feel something for every client I take on. We develop a connection, but it's not the same as a real-life coupling. I look at myself as a stepping stone. I provide comfort and company until a client is ready to move on and find a real relationship. Sometimes a woman might be lacking in confidence, so I build her up. Other times she's simply too busy and I am a convenient way to experience physical contact without a long-term commitment."

But what about you? I wondered. Did the sex affect him psychologically? I met his gaze. "So, you can separate your emotions from the actual sex act?"

Julian shook his head. "That's something I used to tell myself when I was younger. The truth is, I fall a little bit in love with every person I sleep with. Or at least, something akin to falling in love. I know that sounds very fanciful and romantic, but it's a finite sort of love."

A finite love. But that sounded so depressing. Then again, maybe Julian didn't feel sad because when one love ended, another began.

"It's an odd way to put it, I know, but it's the only way I can think to describe what I share with the women who hire me. I enjoy guiding people, bringing them out of their shell or helping them discover new things about themselves. I also value making connections with people, understanding them. It's a big source of fulfilment in my life."

Was that what he was doing with me? Well, perhaps not, since I didn't get the sense he wanted to sleep with me. Even though he was one of the most beautiful men I'd ever met, this thing between us definitely felt platonic. I guess Julian didn't need to pursue me sexually, since sex was so plentiful for him. Maybe a platonic friendship was something he needed.

"You sound like some sort of hippy guru," I teased.

"Well, it took a long time for me to get here. My work wasn't always so fulfilling. When I started out I was young and desperate, taking any job that would put food on the table. I didn't have a choice and selling myself was a last resort. Now it's morphed into a lifestyle I enjoy and love."

Thinking of a young Julian in that position, with no other choice but to sell his body, made me immeasurably sad. And like anybody would, I wondered if there was a little bit of bluster in his speech. I wondered if being an escort really made him as happy as he was trying to make out. But maybe that was just the cynic in me. Popular culture teaches us that anyone who resorts to prostitution does it because they're at their lowest ebb. That nobody would choose such a life. But like many things, that could be wrong. Maybe Julian truly did find fulfilment in his work.

"You don't look convinced," he said, like he'd read my mind.

"It's just a lot to get my head around."

"And...?"

I took a deep breath. "And I like spending time with you. What you do for a living doesn't change that. So, I'd like for us to continue being friends, if you do too, that is."

He reached across the table and took my hand. "Ellen, I would be absolutely honoured to continue my friendship with both you and Elodie, and for us to keep on tricking celebrities and socialites at fancy, upscale events."

I laughed. "Sounds like a plan."

***

Late on Sunday evening, there was a knock on my front door. I frowned and went to the window, wondering who it was. I didn't normally have visitors at this hour, or any hour for that matter. When I spotted my brother, Cameron, standing on the doorstep, I grimaced and remembered I'd agreed to let him stay with me this week.

Wonderful.

Now I got to listen to his grumpy ranting about how awful London was every evening when he got home from work. I opened the door and plastered on a brittle smile.

"Cameron, hi."

"What took you so long?" he complained as he stepped in by me. As usual, his gaze wandered to my wall mural and he shook his head, like a school teacher might shake their head at a fanciful child.

"How was your train journey?" I asked quietly and followed him into the kitchen. He didn't ask permission when he opened the fridge and pulled out a can of iced coffee.

"Awful. I was sitting behind a family with three children under five. They didn't stop yapping for the entire trip."

"Well, at least you're here now."

"Did you buy a new mattress for your guest bedroom yet? The last time I visited I barely got a wink of sleep on that springy old thing."

"Yes, I got a new mattress," I said, then murmured under my breath. "Wouldn't want his majesty suffering any discomfort."

"What was that?"

"Nothing."

"Anyway, I'm going to take a shower. I'm convinced one of those children on the train had a cold. I need to wash off the germs."

"Sure, go ahead," I replied.

As soon as he left the room, I turned to Rainbow and Skittles and rolled my eyes. They'd met Cameron before, so they knew the drill. My brother was only thirty-two, but he had the personality and tolerance of somebody much older. He was like a cranky old grandad in a young man's body. He had a way of dragging down your mood. Perhaps that was why Nick was so happy and cheerful. He needed to counteract Cameron's gloominess.

I went about putting together a meal, since I knew he'd be hungry and would complain if there wasn't anything to eat. He'd call my dad to gripe about what a terrible host I was.

No wonder he was still single.

Cameron wasn't a bad looking guy. In fact, some might even consider him handsome, before he opened his mouth. Any girlfriends he's had have eventually gotten tired of his ways and left him. You'd think he'd take the hint and try to lighten up a little, but no, that never happened.

As I put together a cheese and ham omelette, my mind wandered to Julian. His revelation last night still had me reeling. I felt this pang in my chest for him and I didn't know why. I was glad he found fulfilment in what he did, but to me, there was just something terribly empty about having sex with woman after woman after woman.

Of course, that was my own sheltered experience of life colouring my judgement. I'd only had sex with one person, and that barely even counted. I'd been eighteen and steaming drunk. I lost my virginity to John Simpson, one of Nick's close friends, something he still didn't know about to this day. It had been messy and fumbling and my memories of the night were vague. I drank an entire bottle of wine and came onto him during Nick's twentieth birthday party at our house. I had a crush on him for years, but I was pretty sure John barely noticed me up until that night.

So yeah, when it came to sex, I knew very little. All the love scenes in my books were 'closed door'. People enjoyed the stories because they were fun and entertaining. Sasha lived a fast-paced life, had great banter and was always on the hunt for a new article. I could write scenes of flirting and sexual tension for days, but when it came to actual sex, I left that to the reader's imagination. Mainly because my own imagination didn't have any real-life experience to draw from.

I was mostly okay with it. Sure, deep in my heart I yearned for a partner, someone to spend my life with. It had just always been so hard for me to put myself out there. When I considered going out and trying to meet people, it was like there was this invisible forcefield preventing me. One time, I'd decided to go for a drink at a pub down the road. For a full twenty minutes I stood outside, willing myself to open the door, sounds of chatter and joviality coming from within. When a man approached, about to go into the pub, and asked if I'd like to join him for a drink, I'd mumbled some incoherent excuse and ran home.

Cameron walked into the kitchen, his hair damp and wearing a T-shirt and lounge pants.

Normally, we didn't talk about personal stuff, but I was feeling raw and he was the only one around. That might've been why I blurted, "Cam, do you think there's something wrong with me?"

He didn't miss a beat as he took the omelette I'd just plated up and carried it over to the table without so much as a thank you. "You've always been in your own little world," he said past a bite.

"I'm not in my own little world. I'm very much in touch with reality. I suffer from social phobia. There's a difference. I was just wondering if you have any theories on why I'm like this?"

He blinked, shifted uncomfortably in his seat. "You're not on your period, are you?"

Ugh, he was horrible. "No, I'm not on my period. And just as a piece of advice, please don't ever ask any woman that question again. I just want to know your opinion. You've known me my whole life. Do you think there's something that's made me this way, or do you think I was born like this?"

Cameron shrugged and continued chewing. He was silent a long while, looking tense and vaguely irritated before he said, "When you were little you didn't talk to anyone expect me, Dad and Nick."

"Yes, I had selective mutism."

"Sounds like something you'd be born with."

"What about Mum dying? Maybe that affected me somehow."

He frowned hard, his jaw working. "You were only two years old. It hardly affected you."

"Even babies are affected by their circumstances. Like, if they're not held enough and stuff, it can affect them later in life."

Cameron scoffed. "Who told you that?"

"I read it in a book."

"Babies are a lot more resilient than people think. Most likely, losing mum didn't affect you."

"So, you think I was born this way?"

"Maybe." He was quiet a moment, then said, "Everyone in our family is a little weird."

I placed a hand on my hip. "Okay, explain."

Cameron exhaled an annoyed breath, like he'd much rather sit in silence than be having this conversation. "Nick's a perennial teenager. It's like he's stuck at nineteen, working in that café, dating women far too young for him. Dad's obviously going through some sort of mid-life crisis with Shayla, and I'm…" he trailed off, grimaced, then didn't continue.

"And you?" I probed, interested to hear his own theory on himself.

He put down his knife and fork and rubbed his jaw. "I'm a workaholic, anti-social misanthropist who would rather be pulling out my own fingernails right now than having this conversation."

I shook my head, though it was interesting to note that Cameron was self-aware. "Lovely."

He stood and carried his empty plate to the sink. "I'm tired. I'm going to bed."

"Okay. Do you want Chinese takeaway for dinner tomorrow evening?" I asked, knowing the local Chinese restaurant was one of the few things he liked about London.

There was a beat before he replied gruffly, "Sure."

I listened to his footsteps going up the stairs, distracted when my phone buzzed with a text.

Julian: *What are you doing next weekend?*

My heart skipped a beat. He wanted to see me again, or well, Elodie. The prospect of joining him for another night out excited me.

Ellen: *I'm free next weekend. What do you have in mind?"*

Julian: *Want to crash a wedding with me?*

I smiled, anticipation already whirling in my belly.

Ellen: *I'd love to :-)*

Ten
Julian

"So, where is she?" David asked as he snapped pictures of the wedding guests arriving at the church. He'd mentioned he was hired for a wedding this weekend and I thought, what better place for Elodie and I to have some fun? Since the happy couple said he could bring along a guest or two, I decided to invite myself.

"She said she'd meet me here," I replied, staring up at the building. When I was little, Mum had never followed any religion, but looking at everyone gathering inside the church, I could sort of understand the appeal. There was a community here, a safety, a sense of belonging.

David arched a brow as he peered through the camera lens. "You think she got cold feet?"

"We're not the ones getting married. She'll be here."

I hadn't told David about Elodie's true identity. In fact, I hadn't told anyone, not even Rose. I didn't want her to feel uncomfortable with people knowing her secret. It was hers to reveal should she make that decision. When I'd finally told her what I did for a living, Ellen hadn't shown any judgement or misgiving. Instead, she'd been curious and open, asking questions, eager to learn.

I hadn't even realised how badly I wanted her to accept me. When she did, a tension in me released.

"I've been invited to audition for a part on the West End," David said casually.

I brought my attention back to him. "You have? That's fantastic. Which role?"

He scratched his chin, took another snap. "Seems that the YouTube video raised my profile a little. They want me for the part of Judge Turpin in *Sweeney Todd*. They like that I'm a bass vocalist."

"You'd be perfect for that role. I can see you now, all evil and brooding. Are you going to go for it?"

David shrugged, but I saw the edge of his mouth curve. He was definitely flattered, and I often got the sense he missed performing. "I'm definitely considering it," he replied.

A taxi pulled up outside the church and Elodie stepped out. My gaze wandered up her shapely legs, resting on the curve of her thighs. She wore a stunning peach dress that complimented her pale skin, matching peach heels, her scarlet hair pinned to one side. I tried to figure out how she managed it with the wig, then realised this was a whole other wig. Did she have a collection? She really had gotten invested in her character.

Ellen must've spent a good deal of time practicing to walk in heels because her stride was effortless. She approached and David snapped a picture. The sun glinted off her green contact lenses, making them look even more striking.

"Hello, Julian and David," she greeted and gave a little curtsey.

"Look at you! Rita Hayworth," I said, smiling.

She gave a pleased look. "Oh, stop."

"Hi, Elodie, it's great to see you again," David said, before returning his attention to his camera.

I took her hand and pulled her close so that I could whisper in her ear. "Seriously, where do you find all these amazing outfits?"

130

She laughed, though I did notice a few goose bumps grace her skin. Why did that please me? "I might have a bit of an online shopping addiction."

"Well, the addiction pays off. You look incredible."

A small, barely visible flush claimed her cheeks as she turned to take in the arriving guests. "So, who's getting married?"

"Barry Stevens and Una Mann. I have a feeling Una's side of the family are going to be entertaining when they get drunk at the reception."

Her gaze followed a middle-aged couple as they walked inside. "Hmm, they do have that stick up the bum look about them. Maybe some alcohol will loosen them up."

I grinned. "That's what I'm counting on."

"The bride should be arriving any minute," David interrupted. "If you two want to snag a seat at the back of the church, go ahead."

I held out my arm and Elodie took it. I enjoyed how easily we fit together and how she smelled like coconut. "The question is, do we sit on the side of the bride or the groom?"

"We definitely don't have sticks up our bums, best go with the groom," she replied, and I chuckled. We took a seat at the very back. The church was almost full, and I thought this couple must've had some cash to splash with the number of wedding guests they'd invited. The church was also in an affluent neighbourhood and David mentioned earlier that they were local.

"Aren't you Judy's nephew? Alan?" the elderly woman I'd sat next to asked. I plastered on a charming smile. If Ellen could be Elodie for the day, then perhaps I could be Alan.

131

"Yes, how are you…"

"Margaret Adams. You probably don't remember me. My, my, the last time I saw you was at Wendy Jones' funeral. You must've only been a teenager."

I made a sad face. "Wendy was such a nice lady."

"Yes, I do think about her sometimes. I must say, you've grown up to be a handsome young man. I'll have to tell Judy I bumped into you when she gets out of the hospital."

"Of course, poor aunt Jude. You should go visit her. I'm sure she'd love to see you."

"Do you know what? Maybe I will." She paused and gestured me closer. I bent down, aware of Elodie listening in amusement to the exchange. "Did you hear that the bride used to date the best man?"

I affected a scandalised expression. "I did not. When did they date?"

"Oh, years ago, I think. Still, can you imagine? I wouldn't like to be in her shoes right now."

I arched an eyebrow. "Me neither."

Up by the alter, the groom stood next to his best man. He looked the tiniest bit nervous when the string quartet started their rendition of *Ave Maria*. I glanced at Elodie and found her enthralled by the ceremony. The bridesmaids, wearing lavender, Grecian style dresses, made their way up the aisle and my companion watched them with keen interest. She must've noticed my studying her when she glanced to the side and whispered, "I've never been to a wedding before."

This surprised me. "Not even when you were a child?"

"My dad hated going to weddings. I think since Mum passed they made him sad."

"That's understandable."

"It's amazing though. The amount of effort people put in. This must've taken almost a year to organise."

"Probably. But I'm sure it's worth it when the couple finally gets to have their day."

"Yes, I suppose," she murmured and turned her attention to the altar. I marvelled at her wonder, a part of me wishing I could be so excited about the little things again, even if just for a day. For a while now I'd felt this expanding emptiness, but seeing the world through Elodie was a pleasant distraction.

Later on, we arrived at the hotel where the reception was being held. The room was lavishly decorated in ivory ribbons and white roses. Elodie peered at the cage of doves. She walked up and trailed her hand over the bars, whispering a quiet, "Hello."

Her fascination with birds interested me. Most people chose dogs or cats for pets, but birds, and lovebirds in particular, was an unusual choice.

"I apologise in advance, but the bride caught wind that we're all single and has seated us at the singles' table," David said regretfully as he approached.

"Don't apologise. The singles table has all the best characters," I replied and placed my hand to Elodie's lower back as we walked through the room. She tensed for a second, then relaxed into it.

"Yes, that's what I'm afraid of," David sighed and led us to a table where three women and two men were already seated. Both men's eyes lit up when they saw Elodie and I told myself it was a good sign, even though, admittedly, it made me a tiny bit irritated. I was becoming possessive of her. It was something that happened every once in a while. I could become attached to clients just the same as they could become attached to me. It was like a temporary love affair. Intense for a while, but eventually, it fizzled out.

Not that Elodie was a client. She was...something new entirely. I couldn't deny there were similarities between our friendship and the sort of relationship I had with clients. A part of me wished to help her, bring her out of her shell. Another part was simply interested in her unique psychology and enjoyed spending time with her. Also, I wasn't getting paid, so this was not a business arrangement.

I'd almost forgotten what it was like to make a new friend. So many of the ones I already had I'd known for years.

"Hi, I'm Keith, and this is Steve," said the dark-haired man, giving Elodie his full attention. His gaze wandered from her tight dress all the way down to her sexy heels. Something in my throat tightened. I didn't like the way he looked at her.

I did my best to shake off the feeling. I wasn't here to be possessive of Elodie. I was here to help her develop her social skills and meet people—*and* enjoy myself in the process.

Elodie smiled at Keith. "Hello, I'm Elodie." They shook hands and I watched as his hand lingered. He definitely planned on trying to sleep with her tonight.

"Beautiful name, and beautiful eyes," he said. She tittered girlishly. I was amused at her act, now that I knew it was an act. Ellen didn't even realise it, but she was adept at flirting. She'd lower her gaze, look away then look back. Sometimes she'd subtly touch a man's elbow. I'd witnessed it at Branson Sutton's birthday party, and I was witnessing it again now. I thought I was the best flirt I knew, but Ellen, when she was being Elodie, was a complete natural.

The blonde I sat next to turned and offered her hand, distracting me from my study of Elodie. "This is a good table," she said. "One of the best I've had the pleasure of sitting at, and I've been to a *lot* of weddings."

I smirked at her assessment. "And how do you evaluate a good or bad table?"

She tipped her wine glass to her lips, took a sip, then said, "I evaluate it based on the attractiveness of its occupants."

"How very mercenary."

"I call it how I see it. I'm Val, by the way."

"Julian. Nice to meet you."

"So, is the redhead your sister?"

"Why do you ask?"

"I figure two people as attractive as you are have to be related if you're not together."

"I disagree. And we're just friends."

Val didn't look too convinced, but I only arched an elusive eyebrow. I enjoyed people who started talking to you like they already knew you. It was a ballsy way to introduce oneself.

Elodie, who sat on the other side of me, was looking around the party now, taking it all in. The bride and groom had just arrived, and everyone clapped. My phone started ringing, distracting Elodie from absorbing the scene. She was a watcher, took people in, focused on the little details. I'd caught her doing it several times now.

She looked at me and laughed, her face lighting up. It took me a second to realise what she was laughing at. My ringtone was 'Roxanne' by The Police. I shot her a conspiratorial grin and glanced at the screen, seeing it was my client, Cathy.

These days, I only tended to see one client at a time. More than one and I grew distracted. I stepped away to take the call, lifting it to my ear as I approached the bar and signalled to the bartender for a cranberry juice.

"Cathy, what a pleasant surprise," I purred into the phone.

"Julian, hello. How are you?"

"All the better after hearing your voice," I replied, lower now, seductive.

She made a breathy noise in the back of her throat. "I was wondering if you're free tonight."

From her tone, I suspected she was ready to take things to the next level. We'd been on several dates, but the right moment hadn't come for us yet. My gaze went across the room to Elodie. She was laughing at something Keith said, and a fiery, burning sensation travelled up my oesophagus. I needed to get a handle on this jealousy I was feeling. It was counterproductive.

"I'm busy tonight, but how about tomorrow? I've been looking forward to seeing you again."

"You have?" Cathy asked. I could hear the genuine surprise in her voice. It was one of the things I liked about her. She didn't have an ego, didn't take your interest for granted.

"Of course. That dress you wore the other night, I haven't been able to stop thinking about it."

"Julian," she breathed, and I grinned as I got the reaction I'd been hoping for.

"Tomorrow night at eight. Wear something nice. I'll text you the details of where to meet." I hung up and slid my phone in my pocket, returning to find Elodie telling an anecdote. She had the entire table's attention.

"We were at this bar for my brother's thirtieth birthday. All of a sudden, the fire alarm goes off, the sprinklers come on, and we're soaked to the skin. As expected, people panic and start pushing to get outside. I trip, fall, and bang my head on the edge of a table. When I come to, the most handsome face I've ever seen is directly in front of me. He asks if I'm okay. I say, I am now." Laughter comes from those at the table. "He asks if I feel any dizziness. I tell him I think I might need mouth to mouth." More laughter. My lips twitch in amusement. I think of how skilled she is at making up stories off the cuff, when the anecdote starts to sound familiar.

"I'm telling you, he was the sexiest fireman I've ever seen. I had to take a chance. So, I asked him if he'd like to get a drink after his shift. I expected him to brush me off, but miraculously, he said yes! I soon realised why. When he left me sitting in an ambulance to be checked out by paramedics, I looked down and saw that my white blouse was completely transparent, thanks to those pesky sprinklers. And I was wearing a fuchsia pink bra to boot!"

Our table mates burst into more laughter, while I narrowed my gaze. I'd heard that exact story from Rose. When she was reading, if she got to a particularly funny or exciting part, she'd tell me about it, and that story was straight out of the latest *Sasha Orlando* book. Rose had regaled me with it during our phone call a few nights ago.

I thought of her story about dating the stripper, Sebastian, and realised that that too was from the same series of books. Elodie was stealing her stories from fiction. I didn't know how to feel about it. Part of my fascination with her was how she managed to make all these crazy, adventurous tales seemingly out of thin air.

Now that I knew she was plagiarizing, it took away some of the shine.

Eleven
Ellen

Julian was looking at me funny.

His features were flat and serious, and I couldn't tell why. Was I talking too much? Was he annoyed that I was hogging all the attention? That couldn't be it, because the last time we went out, he'd been delighted when I'd regaled people with fake Elodie stories.

"Are you okay?" I asked quietly. Food was being served and a fancy salad with quail eggs was placed in front of me.

Julian blinked, then plastered on a pleasant smile that somehow appeared forced. "I'm perfectly fine," he replied, lifting his fork and taking a bite of his starter.

I lost some of my confidence after that, too busy wondering what I'd done wrong. His change in demeanour baffled me, but then, I hardly knew him. Maybe this was just how he acted sometimes.

David was busy across the table, chatting with a pretty brunette, while Julian focused his attention on the blonde next to him. I was a little disappointed that he and I weren't working as a team like we had at the last party. Now he seemed to be doing his best to ignore me.

"You've gone quiet," Keith commented. He sat on the other side of me and I got the vibe he was interested. In fact, he definitely wanted to have sex with me/Elodie. It was problematic, mainly because sex wasn't really my goal. I derived pleasure from the admiration and compliments Elodie received, the interactions she had, but I didn't have any urge to take things further. At least, I hadn't explored it yet.

Maybe that made me a tease. All I knew was, going home with someone wouldn't exactly be easy. What if my wig came off midway through the act? Or what if one of my contact lenses fell out? I knew lots of women cosmetically enhanced themselves to look better with false lashes, chicken fillets, etc, but the costume was my safety net. If I took it off, I was just Ellen again.

I glanced at Keith and mustered a smile. "I'm just a little tired."

"I'll have to figure out a way to wake you up then."

I knew he was flirting, but something about the statement fell flat. It didn't make me feel good, not like when…never mind.

To be honest, I was just feeling off because Julian was acting funny.

I needed to sort myself out. He wasn't obliged to make me the centre of his attention all the time. He probably didn't even realise he was ignoring me since he was chatting with an attractive woman. My selfish side wanted him all for myself, but I knew I had to quit feeling that way. We were friends. I didn't have any claim over him.

Across the room, an argument had broken out at one of the tables. It seemed Julian was right. The bride's side of the family were good for some drama. A middle-aged woman stood, gesticulating wildly at a man who I guessed was her husband.

"That's it! I've had enough of you leering at every bridesmaid who walks by. It's humiliating!"

The man, who looked bleary-eyed and wobbly on his feet, reached for her but she pushed him away. "I wasn't leering," he said. "I was just looking!"

"Same thing," she yelled and reached for her shoe. She pulled it off and threw it at his head. Thankfully, she missed and several people came and separated them. Scandalised whispers spread amid the other wedding guests.

"I heard he cheats on her all the time," the woman Julian had been talking to said. I think I heard him call her Val. "Guess she finally lost it."

Suddenly, I was no longer amused by the scene. I just felt bad for the woman who'd thrown her shoe at her husband. Obviously, her outburst would be the subject of gossip for many weeks to come.

"How does everyone feel about getting out of here? We can go back to my place," Julian suggested. Val's eyes lit up at the offer, as did Keith's.

"I have to stay and take a few more shots, but you go ahead if you like," David replied.

I didn't particularly want to go back with Keith, but I was curious to see Julian's flat. I knew he lived in my neighbourhood, but I hadn't yet been invited over to his place. A few minutes later, Julian, Val, Keith, and I huddled into the back of a black cab.

I sat on one of the fold-out seats, mainly to keep my distance from Keith. He seemed like a nice guy, but I didn't want to lead him on any more than I already had. I was directly across from Julian. He caught my eye and mouthed a question.

You okay with this?

I nodded, trying to appear casual and not wanting to come across prudish. I knew he must've invited people back to his flat all the time. It wasn't a big deal to him like it was to me.

When we arrived at Julian's building, I stepped out into the cool night air and inhaled deeply for courage. Julian was obviously going to have sex with Val. I might witness some of their foreplay. I'd never seen two people do sexual things in real life before. I couldn't tell if that was why I was nervous, or merely because…

Because a part of me wished to be Val right now.

The realisation was sobering, but not very shocking. Julian was beautiful, charming, and kind. He was the first person to try to befriend me in a really long time. Obviously, I was attracted to him, but I wasn't under any illusions that my attraction was reciprocated.

Sure, he'd fancied Elodie at first. But now he knew the real me, and I was certain he didn't still feel that way.

We climbed several flights of stairs to his flat on the top floor. It was an older building, so there wasn't a lift. I had to stop midway to take off my shoes. Keith, who was directly behind me—and I was pretty sure checking my arse the entire time—said, "I can carry you the rest of the way if you want." His voice was low with a hint of flirtation. Again, I wasn't feeling it. Being Elodie in a public setting was a whole lot different to being her in private. It was too close. No escape routes.

"That's okay," I replied in a sassy voice. "I'm an independent woman, I can carry myself."

Julian's chuckle sounded from up ahead, clearly having heard Keith's offer and finding my refusal amusing. I chanced a peek at Keith and he appeared a tad chagrined.

When we reached Julian's flat, he opened the door into a spacious yet cosy space. The walls were covered in various artworks and photographs. Lots of memories. I noticed several pictures of him with his friend, Rose. There was a large bookshelf loaded with paperbacks. For a second, I froze, heart beating fast as I scanned for any copies of my own books. His friend read them, after all. Perhaps Julian did, too.

The idea of him reading my stuff was nerve-wracking, mainly because many of Elodie's anecdotes were stories from my novels. Sure, some of them I made up on the spot, but the more detailed stories came directly from *Sasha*. If Julian ever put two and two together…

Well, I wasn't sure how I'd feel about it. I'd never had to explain my profession to anyone before, because I kept it to myself. Although it wasn't hard to keep secrets when the only people I ever really spoke to were my pet birds. Sure, there was my boss, Bernice, but though we were friendly, we weren't close. Most people thought I only worked in the bookshop. No one expected someone as quiet and unimpressive as Ellen Grant to be an international bestselling author.

I was relieved not to find any of my books in his collection. They were mostly classics. I did smile when I saw he owned all of the *Fifty Shades* books, plus a few Jackie Collins. Julian read romance?

He caught me looking and came to whisper in my ear, "Those belong to Rose."

I smirked. "Sure, they do."

His eyes sparkled at my teasing. "Christian Grey is admittedly dreamy."

I laughed louder than expected, garnering the attention of Val and Keith.

"What are you two snickering about?"

"The allure of bondage," Julian answered, not missing a beat as he turned to her. "Would you care for a drink?"

Val preened. "I'd love one."

I was surprised when Julian produced a bottle of expensive wine, given the fact he didn't drink alcohol. It reinforced the idea that he entertained people here often.

I took a seat on the plush love seat, only realising my mistake when Keith lowered to sit beside me. He threw his arm over the back and I stiffened. It seemed being Elodie gave me confidence only so far as talking to people. Physical contact was a whole other ball game.

Julian came and offered me a glass. I took it gratefully, needing some Dutch courage. He went and sat next to Val on the larger couch as she asked him questions about the artwork he owned.

I decided I needed to make an effort with Keith. It was rude to come back here and not even talk to him. "Do you live in London?" I asked.

"No, I'm from Nottingham," he replied. "The groom is my cousin, so I came down for the weekend to attend the wedding."

The fact he didn't live close was a relief. At least there wasn't much of a chance I'd see him again. Maybe I should take advantage of this situation and practice my non-existent seduction skills. He was a good-looking guy, so it shouldn't be too difficult.

"Well, Julian and I are wedding crashers. We don't even know the couple."

Keith grinned down at me, took a sip of wine and said, "Little rebel, are you?"

"Yes, very rebellious." *What are you saying?*

Keith arched an eyebrow and moved a tiny bit closer, lowering his voice to a whisper, "Care to show me *how* rebellious?"

I smiled my best Elodie smile, it was all puckered lips and flirty eyes. "Maybe," I whispered back, then forced myself to be spontaneous. I pressed my lips to his. He tasted like wine, smelled like generic cologne. The kiss was pleasant, but it didn't make me feel much of anything. He pressed closer, his lips coaxing mine to open. He slid his tongue into my mouth and I instantly broke away. I stood and looked around. Julian was too busy chatting with Val. He didn't even see the kiss.

"I need to use the bathroom," I said, then turned and hurried down a hallway. I opened the first door I saw and stepped inside. Unfortunately, it wasn't the bathroom, but Julian's bedroom. The sheets were mussed, as though he'd just decided to leave them that way, and there was a gigantic painting of a naked woman over his bed.

I was taken aback for a second. It was just so sensual, so unexpected. It looked like an original, too. The woman lay in bed, a dark silk sheet strewn across her torso, her breasts and bottom half exposed. My cheeks heated just looking at it.

I stepped closer to study the painting better, still trying to catch my breath after the kiss. To anyone else, a kiss like that would be nothing. But to me, it was a very big deal. I didn't kiss people, not ever. The last time had been when I was a teenager, and that memory was so old it hardly felt real anymore.

I sat down on Julian's bed, the familiar smell of him soothing my nerves, and stared up at the large painting. Whoever the artist was, they were more skilled than me. I mostly painted flowers, sometimes scenery, but I wasn't great with people. I didn't have the technical skill to get their proportions right. Any time I tried, I'd always make their legs too short, or their torso too long. Not this artist though. The naked woman in the picture was so well executed you felt like you could reach out and touch her skin.

I jumped when the door opened, and Julian walked in. "Is everything all right?"

"Yes, I just...I needed a moment."

He studied me. "Everything okay with Keith?"

I glanced away. "Not really. I kissed him, then freaked out and came in here."

Julian rubbed his jaw and came to sit down beside me. "I saw."

He did? I thought he'd been too busy with Val to notice. A measure of embarrassment trickled in. "I'm not sure if Elodie is meant for kissing."

Julian reached out and touched a tendril of hair on my wig. "Of course, she is," he murmured. "She just needs some practice."

"I don't know. Maybe I'm just not attracted enough to Keith. I'm not sure how to handle advances when I don't like the other person."

"Oh darling, you're talking to the master of handling unwanted advances. Come, let me show you." He patted the space beside him and gestured me closer. I shimmied over, wondering what he had in mind. "Pretend I'm a woman," he said.

Well, that wouldn't be too hard, since he was prettier than most girls anyway.

"Okay, I'm pretending you're a woman. Now what?"

His gaze was unwavering. "You're the man. You're interested. Come on to me."

"I...um..."

"Chat me up. Touch me. Try to kiss me. Whatever you want."

I swallowed thickly, not sure this was helping me so much as making me more nervous. Still, sitting here with Julian, being this close to him, was intoxicating in a way it definitely hadn't been with Keith.

I readied myself, then placed a hand on his knee. "Hi, uh, what's your name?"

Julian fluttered his lashes, and that action alone made me tongue-tied. His expression was sultry, but there was strength behind it. "I'm Tiffany. Please be a dear and take your hand off my knee." His voice was sweet and coaxing. It charmed even while it rejected.

I instantly removed my hand. "Right. Sorry."

Julian laughed. "We're role-playing. You don't need to apologise. Besides," he waggled his brows. "I don't mind your hand on my knee."

I cleared my throat, feeling shy now. "What should I do next?"

His look was mischievous. "Try to kiss me."

I blinked and leaned forward. Intoxicated by the smell of him, I licked my lips. His eyes lingered on the movement, and my entire body flushed. Was it just me, or was this room getting hotter?

I thought I heard him inhale ever so slightly when I moved to press my mouth to his. Right before our lips met, he turned his head to the side, and my mouth collided with his cheek. Even a sweet, chaste kiss on the cheek felt naughty with Julian Fairchild.

He placed a finger to my shoulder and drew away. "If I want to kiss you, I'll make the first move," he said, again in that sweet, unassuming voice.

"O-okay," I stammered, still reeling from the feel of his skin on my lips.

"You see," he gestured between the two of us. "It's not difficult to decline advances, so long as you do it in a certain way. Sometimes, people like a challenge. It's their problem if they're foolish enough to believe they're going to get anywhere with you."

"I feel like you have a lot of practice with this."

"Women can be just as forward as men, you know. Just the same as there are be shy men out there, inexperienced with flirting."

"Like me," I said, chagrined.

"There's nothing wrong with shyness, and there's nothing wrong with confidence, either. We all act how we feel. People tell themselves they need to be a certain way. But really, all we need to be is ourselves."

"You do realise you're talking to a woman in a costume right now? I wouldn't know how to be myself if it slapped me right in the face."

He fiddled with a strand of my wig again. "I already told you. If Elodie comes from within you, then she is you, Ellen."

I stared into his eyes, lost for a moment, when suddenly the bedroom door opened. "What are you two doing hiding in here?" Val questioned, looking between us in suspicion.

I stood from the bed and ran my hands down my dress. "I'm going to order a taxi."

Julian turned to me. "You don't have to go."

"I'm tired. I think I'm done for the night."

He seemed sad that I was leaving, but I'd reached my stimuli limit for the day. Kissing Keith was one thing, but that whole role-playing with Julian set my heart racing. Getting close to him excited me. I'd wanted to kiss him. When he gave me his cheek, deep inside I was disappointed.

Funny how I'd thought our friendship was platonic, because for me it definitely wasn't.

Thanks to the miracle of phone apps, my taxi arrived in less than five minutes. Keith suggested he escort me back to my place, but I wasn't silly enough to fall for that. Julian hugged me before I went, placing a soft kiss on my cheek, just shy of my ear. It was almost the same place I kissed him, and it made me tingle all over.

I couldn't stop thinking about him during the short journey to my house. Even as I went inside and greeted Skittles and Rainbow, I was distracted. The fact of the matter was, I wanted to explore things with Julian. I wanted to know what it would be like with him, but with his profession, I didn't even know if he dated people.

Maybe I should just hire him.

The thought startled me. I couldn't believe I was even considering it, but it made logical sense. Whatever he charged, I had more than enough money to pay him. And eventually, I did want to have a relationship, find a man and fall in love, get married, have babies.

Right now, Julian was the only man who made me feel comfortable. He was the only man I was attracted to. I was far too inexperienced to go out there and meet someone. I needed training wheels first before I could learn to cycle on my own.

Hell, even thinking about broaching the topic with him made me break out in hives.

But then, any time I'd been embarrassed around Julian, he'd never judged me. Never made me feel small.

These thoughts pitter-pattered around inside my brain all through the night and following morning. I'd just added two thousand words to my manuscript and was getting ready to take a break when my phone rang. It was Dad.

I picked up, my voice cheery. "Hi, Dad. How is everything?"

"Everything's good down here. How are you? Nick and I have been hoping you'll come visit soon."

"I'm well. And I'm going to visit. I just need to finish this book I'm writing and then I'm coming to Torquay for a weekend. We can go have dinner at Lily's, my treat."

"I do love their steaks. Sounds like a plan. How did everything go with Cameron? He stayed with you last week, didn't he?"

"He was fine. His usual self."

Dad chuckled. "I wouldn't describe Cam's usual self as fine, but okay. I actually called because I have some big news."

"You do?" I questioned, hoping it was good big news and not bad big news.

"Shayla and I are getting married. I popped the question last night and she said yes!"

My chest deflated. "You did? That's great, Dad." I tried to muster as much enthusiasm into my voice as I could. It wasn't that I thought Shayla was a bad person, she just wasn't *my* sort of person. And maybe I'd gotten so used to having Dad all to myself since I was a kid that I'd become selfish and possessive. He deserved a bit of happiness. Even if that happiness came in the form of Shayla.

"We've decided on a spring wedding, so make sure to keep the last week in April free."

"Wow, that's soon."

"When you get to my age, you don't have time to wait around," said Dad.

"No, I guess you don't. Congratulations."

His voice gentled. "Thank you, sweetheart. Your blessing means a lot to me."

I hadn't exactly given him my blessing, but then, how could I refuse it? He was a sixty-one-year-old man. If he wanted to get married, then that was his decision.

Only a couple minutes after I hung up with Dad I got a text from Julian inviting me to a charity event the following night. It was the distraction I needed, and I responded right away that Elodie would be there.

***

The charity event was just as fancy as the birthday party at the Savoy. There was so much money in the air you could almost smell it. I often donated to charity, but I guess it took much deeper pockets and a certain type of ego to do it in such a public way.

"How were you even invited here? Are you secretly rich?" I asked Julian as we walked arm in arm about the room.

"I'm comfortable, but by no means rich. Besides," he said and eyed me, "I'm not the one who owns an entire house in a fancy part of London. But to answer your question, I was invited by an ex-client. She's the wife of a member of Parliament."

I ignored his comment about my house because I'd already given him the Grandma story. Instead I asked, "Which member of Parliament?"

"That I can't divulge. She's no longer a client, but we're still friends. She invites me to events like this from time to time. I think she imagines I'll find high-profile clients by attending."

"I have no doubt you would. I've already spotted several women cast their covetous gaze on you."

"This is why I like you. You say stuff like 'covetous gaze'. I thought I was the only one who indulged in wordiness."

"I just…read a lot," I said.

He smiled and gestured to a table of drinks. "Want one?"

"I think I've drank more champagne since I met you than I have in my entire life."

His smile turned impish. "I'll take that as a yes."

He handed me a glass, his eyes sweeping the room. I wondered if he was searching for possible clients. I also wondered if he was seeing anyone at the moment. The thought made my chest burn. Then I thought of my crazy plan to hire him. I'd never have the balls to do it, but even imagining it gave me a thrill. I wanted to so badly.

A few moments of quiet passed before I spoke. "The painting in your bedroom, who's the woman?"

He glanced at me. "What makes you think I know her?"

"I don't…I just, there's something about it that feels personal."

Julian took a second to answer. "The woman in the picture is another ex-client of mine, actually."

"Oh?" I was even more curious now.

His face turned thoughtful, like he was remembering. "It was a few years ago. Her name was Zara. When she first came to me, she was terrified of being naked with a man. I taught her that nakedness was nothing to be afraid of. When she finally conquered her fear, I asked an artist friend of mine to paint her. When it was complete, I offered it to her as a gift. She declined and instead requested that I hang it in my room. She felt liberated to know her naked form was out there in the world. Being admired by all the lovers who passed through my bed."

"Wow, that's…incredible." *And exactly how many lovers passed through his bed?* I coughed, not brave enough to ask the question. "I mean, it's a big fear to help someone get over. You must be good." It also reinforced my idea that Julian might be able to help me, too.

His gaze darkened, the look in his eye making my stomach flip. "Better than you know," he said huskily.

I looked away. There was too much intensity in him now. I wondered if he did it intentionally, if he wanted me to feel this way, or if it was simply natural. Some people didn't have to try to seduce. They just did. It was as easy as breathing.

"So, how did everything go with Val after I left the other night?"

He nudged my shoulder. "Why Elodie, are you fishing for sexy details?"

I grinned, while on the inside the small bit of jealousy I felt expanded. "I might be."

"Well, I wish I had a story to tell. Unfortunately, she left soon after you. I suspect she might've gone back to Keith's hotel with him."

Why did this news relieve me so much? Oh right, because I fancied the pants off Julian.

I sighed. "How easily some people's affections are swayed."

"Quite," Julian agreed. "Now I better start introducing you to people before the bidding begins."

He swept me through the room, and just like last time I made the acquaintance of dozens of important and wealthy people. Some of them I recognised from television. It was oddly sobering to see them in a non-airbrushed reality. Plus, with Elodie as my mask, I wasn't intimidated.

I recognised Branson and Krystyna Sutton when they approached. Krystyna wore a long, colourful sequins dress that gave the effect of stained glass. It was one of the most unique gowns I'd ever seen. She approached gracefully, her smile practiced and demure.

"Elodie," she greeted, then turned to my companion. "Julian. What a wonderful pleasure to see you both again."

"Likewise. Elodie and I had a wonderful time at your party last week."

"Indeed. I was sad we didn't get to spend more time together," Krystyna went on, her husband silent and watchful by her side. Now that I studied him, there was something intense about Branson. He didn't say much, but he watched you like a hawk. I wasn't sure if it made him intriguing or scary. I guess it took a unique sort of person to be a race car driver.

"I was actually hoping to see you here," Krystyna said. "I have an invitation for you. We're throwing a party at our house next weekend and I'd love for you both to come."

A party at their house? Did she mean one of their sex parties? Nerves fluttered in my belly while Julian politely accepted the invitation. "We wouldn't miss it."

Wait, what? I couldn't go to a party like that. I just...the very idea had me completely flustered and coming out in hives.

She removed a small envelope from her purse and slid it into the pocket of his suit jacket. "See you soon," she purred before she and her husband moved on.

A beat of silence passed as I blinked at their retreating forms. "Well," I breathed.

Julian let out a quiet chuckle and turned to face me, his voice low. "Can you effing believe that?"

I shook my head, flabbergasted. "Did we just get invited to a celebrity swingers party?"

His smile was so wide, so handsome. "You bet your arse we did."

"Fuck." It was a rare occasion that I swore, but this certainly called for it.

Julian gave my shoulder a squeeze. "Fuck indeed, my dear Elodie. Fuck indeed."

Twelve
Julian

"You're quiet tonight," Cathy commented.

We were at a rooftop bar, sipping cocktails, or well, mocktails in my case. I'd chosen the location specifically because there was a hotel below and I knew Cathy felt ready to take the next step with me. The problem was, *I* didn't feel ready, or perhaps 'ready' wasn't the right word. I just wasn't my usual self. On our previous dates, I'd enjoyed her company, and she was as lovely as always.

The issue lay solely on my doorstep. I couldn't stop thinking about Ellen. She was in my thoughts, and when I was fixated on one woman, it was difficult to put my all into another.

"I apologise," I said, turning to my date. "I've been distracted."

She lightly touched my wrist, shifting closer in her seat. "Something on your mind?"

Not something, *someone*.

I sipped my drink. "You could say that."

Her thumb brushed lightly back and forth. "Feel free to unload on me. I'm a divorce lawyer," she gave a soft laugh. "I often have to double as a client's therapist."

I shook my head. "This date is for you. If anything, you should be unloading on me."

"Well, I deleted my Facebook account several weeks ago, so I can no longer spy on my ex-husband and stress about all the floozies he posts photos with, which means I don't have much to complain about these days."

I blew out a breath. It would be unprofessional of me to talk about Ellen while I was working. But I really could use some perspective and Cathy was a wise lady. I glanced at her, her understated beauty, soft and feminine, her eyes kind and warm.

I should want to peel back her layers, see how she looked when she came, hear the noises she made. Unfortunately, my curiosity was all for someone else. That growing emptiness I'd felt before I met Ellen had started to shrink. Her presence in my life filled it.

"I made a new friend and I've been thinking about her a lot," I confessed.

Cathy studied me, eyes gentle, but I did see a flicker of disappointment. It was understandable. You didn't want the person you were with to be preoccupied with another. "You like her," she surmised.

"Yes, but there's more. She's not at all what I first imagined her to be."

She sat back and fiddled with her delicate gold bracelet. "Sometimes people can surprise us. One of my closest friends, when I first met her, I thought she was a right cow. It was only later that I realised what a great person she was. It's those sorts of people, the ones who blindside us, who are unexpected, that often turn out to have the greatest impact on our lives."

"I'm not accustomed to being so…consumed by someone."

Cathy eyed me and lifted her glass. "No, I imagine it's others who become consumed by you."

I gave a soft smile. "You overestimate my charms."

She shook her head. "I disagree. You're one of a kind, Julian. If this woman doesn't see that, then she doesn't deserve you."

Was that what I wanted? To be with Ellen romantically? It was a new sensation for me to feel a paternal protectiveness for someone, while at the same time finding them captivating, both spiritually and physically. Normally, it was one or the other. I wanted to protect someone platonically, like I did with Rose, or I wanted to sleep with them, get lost in a sexual affair.

Better that than ever be alone with my own thoughts.

With Ellen, it was a new mixture of both. I wanted to protect her as she discovered the world as Elodie, but I also wanted to shag her senseless.

Later on, Cathy and I parted ways. There was no sense trying to force things when they didn't feel natural. Besides, we could try again once I got out of my Ellen fixation.

The weekend rolled in quickly and I was to escort her to the Suttons' house party. I read the invitation for the umpteenth time.

You are cordially invited to the residence of
Branson and Krystyna Sutton for midnight supper.
Please arrive at 11:30 pm sharp.
No mobile phones or recording devices permitted.

I chuckled and decided I needed to add "midnight supper" to my repertoire of euphemisms. I was still trying to get my head around how we were even invited. Invites were reserved solely for celebrities, people in the public eye, and their companions. Elodie and I were neither, which begged the question, why had we been welcomed into the circle of trust?

I thought perhaps their group was getting a little stale, too many of the same people. What better way to spice things up than with two attractive and interesting strangers? When Elodie and I were together, we attracted attention. We were a potent combination. Krystyna had obviously seen that and wanted to get to know us better, as it were.

I wondered if Ellen was still meeting Suze on Tuesday mornings, but I'd purposely stayed away. She was worried about her true identity being discovered, and I didn't want to make her nervous by showing up.

I texted her the details for the night ahead and got a response not long after.

Ellen: *It starts at 11:30 pm? Why can't people do things at normal hours anymore?*

A smile curved my lips as I typed a reply.

Julian: *You can't very well have midnight supper at 7 pm, now can you?*

Ellen: *I still think it's ridiculous. Who has the energy for a sex party at that time of night?*

Ellen: *Also, I don't know what to wear.*

Julian: *Surprise me.*

Ellen: *Okay, I think I have a couple of dresses that might work.*

A few minutes later I received another text.

Ellen: *Awkward question but...are you planning on having sex with anyone at this party?*

I paused, my finger hovering over the screen as I considered my answer. The only person I was interested in having sex with these days was her, but I couldn't very well say that. Instead, I replied evasively.

Julian: *I believe that's the point.*

Ellen: *Okay.*

Julian: *Would you prefer it if I didn't?*

Ellen: *I just won't know what to do if you go off with someone. I'll be standing there like a spare tit.*

Julian: *In that case, I'll make you a promise. I won't "go off with someone" unless you are already otherwise engaged. Wouldn't want to make a tit of you ;-)*

Ellen: *You should've heard the snort I just made.*

I grinned and put my phone away. When I arrived to pick her up, she answered the door in a long, flower print dressing gown, the sort an octogenarian might wear. Her makeup was done, but other than that she wasn't anywhere near ready.

"I need your help. I'm freaking out a little," she admitted as I followed her upstairs to her bedroom. Laid out on the bed were several outfits. I knew as soon as I clapped eyes on the deep purple dress that it was the one she should wear tonight. It would look perfect against her creamy skin.

I lifted the dress and handed it to her. "This one."

Her mouth opened. "How did you know what I was going to ask?"

"It wasn't too hard to guess, what with you being in that very handsome dressing gown," I teased.

She scowled, lips twitching as she replied, "It might not be very sexy but it's the most comfortable thing I own, so I don't care if you're judging me right now."

I only smirked in reply and her expression turned anxious again. "Julian?"

"Yes, Ellen?"

She worried her lip. "I've been wondering if maybe I shouldn't go to this party."

"Why not?" I frowned.

"Well, I know nothing about these sorts of things. I'm going to be completely out of my depth," she explained, her voice growing shaky.

I came forward and took both her hands in mine, my voice low and soothing. "I promise I won't let anything happen that you're not comfortable with."

She took a deep breath, her eyes moving back and forth between mine as though deciding if she should trust me. "Okay," she finally whispered.

I gave a tender smile. "Just think of me as your chaperone. If any gentlemen are too forward, I'll intervene with my very best disapproving schoolmarm glare."

Now she chuckled. "I know you're joking, but it would actually make me feel so much better if you did."

My expression was gentle as I squeezed her hands before letting them go. "You have nothing to worry about tonight. I'll be right there with you the whole time."

Ellen appeared relieved. She had no clue that *I* was the one she should be wary of, what with these lustful feelings I'd been having.

She took the dress and went inside the bathroom to change. On a shelf, I noticed several dog-eared copies of the *Sasha Orlando* books. They had colour coded tabs and sticky notes protruding from the spine. *Well, there you had it.* My theory that she was stealing anecdotes from the books was correct. I tried not to be too crestfallen.

When she emerged, I forgot all about her plagiarism, because my breath left me. The dress was like a second skin. It moulded to every inch of her body, the curves of her hips, the swell of her breasts. Her bra must've been thin because I was certain I could see a hint of her pert nipples peeking through. She hadn't put her green contacts in, nor was she wearing her wig. Her golden-brown curls hung long around her shoulders, her brown eyes big and fathomless.

"How do I look? I'm not wearing my glasses, so I can't see your expression. Your face is just a blur right now."

Without thinking, I stepped forward, placed a hand on her delicate shoulder and ran it down her arm. Her skin was

161

cool and soft. For a second, I had an urge to throw her down on the bed, tear off that sexy dress and have my way with her.

But I resisted. After her bout of nerves just a few minutes ago, she might have a panic attack of epic proportions if I did that.

"You're breathtaking," I whispered and her eyes grew larger. A small, surprised breath escaped her and she blinked.

"I was aiming for passable, but breathtaking works t-too," she said, seeming nervous at my proximity. Her attention lingered on my throat before rising to meet my eyes. I gazed down at her, battling an inner struggle to kiss her. In a short time, we'd grown close, but it felt longer to me since I'd spent weeks watching her pretend to be Elodie at the café.

I now realised that it wasn't just the outlandishness of Elodie that drew me in, it was Ellen herself. It was the aura that surrounded her.

My mouth hovered mere inches above hers before I blinked myself out of the swell of desire.

"You should probably finish getting ready if we don't want to be late," I said, my voice croaky.

Ellen nodded hastily and stepped away. "Yes, I'll be as quick as I can."

I felt out of sorts, and that was not usual for me. I wasn't the type of person who flustered easily, but Ellen (not Elodie) was getting under my skin.

She was everything I never sought in a partner, and yet, getting to know her, peeling away her unexpected layers, was my new obsession. She'd pulled me in with the ruse of Elodie, who embodied the sort of woman I normally chased. Then the curtain fell to reveal something far more enthralling beneath.

By the time she was ready, I'd just about gotten my perplexing feelings under control. As our taxi approached the large, period home in Hampstead Heath that belonged to the Suttons, I studied Ellen's reaction. She was in full costume, but I couldn't seem to see her as Elodie anymore. She was just...her. For me, Elodie and Ellen were one and the same. A kaleidoscope of a single fascinating person.

"Big house," she commented quietly.

"Lots of bedrooms, I imagine."

She appeared to swallow, and I suspected her nerves were again getting the best of her. This was by far the most intimidating party we'd attended yet, and we hadn't even gone inside. When the car pulled to a stop, I paid the driver and got out, going around to Ellen's side and taking her hand. She held on tight.

We were welcomed by a butler and two maids. I leaned close to Ellen and whispered, "It's just like *Downton Abbey*, except you get body searched before you can come inside." The butler checked Ellen's bag for any recording devices, then one of the maids searched her body, while I underwent the same treatment.

She gave a soft laugh. "I'm pretty sure whatever we're about to walk into isn't going to be anything like *Downton Abbey*."

"The X-rated version perhaps?"

She shook her head at me as the butler took our coats and handed us each a lacy, Venetian style mask. I put mine on then helped Ellen with hers before we were led into a large dining room. There must've already been twenty people there. They all wore half masks, too, but even so, I recognised some famous personalities. Ellen seemed a little awestruck as she took it all in.

"I always tried to tell myself that behind the glitz and glamour, celebrities probably live boring, jaded lives, but I'm starting to think that isn't true," she whispered.

"Depends on the celebrity."

"Have you ever slept with a famous person?" she went on, still whispering.

I glanced down at her, my expression wry. "One or two."

"Really? Who?"

I suspected she was trying to distract herself from her nerves, so I indulged her this once. "Have you heard of Alicia Davidson?"

She stared at me, mouth agape. "Are you freaking serious? She's like, one of the most beautiful women in the world."

"Yes well, everybody poops."

She scrunched up her face at my response and I chuckled. "You'll no longer be in awe of beauty if you imagine the person taking a dump. It's a scientific fact."

"I don't want to imagine any of these people doing a number two, thank you very much," Ellen replied before Krystyna approached.

"Elodie, Julian, so lovely to see you both," she said, her smile somewhat predatory. I understood why when she walked up to Ellen, placed a hand on each of her shoulders, then kissed her right on the mouth—with tongue. Ellen blinked in shock and I couldn't help my grin.

It was certainly one way to initiate her into the party.

I knew I'd promised her I wouldn't let any men make untoward advances, but I hadn't anticipated it would be a lady I had to look out for.

Krystyna turned to me and gave me the exact same kiss on the mouth. I wasn't quite as shell-shocked as Ellen, as I'd been expecting it. I imagined that's what thrilled Krystyna, the fact she could shock people with her sexuality. I'd gone through a similar phase during my twenties.

"You two are our guests of honour tonight. Come and let me introduce you to everyone."

"Sure," Ellen finally spoke, but she still seemed a little out of it. Was that the first time she'd kissed a woman? The colour in her cheeks, and the way her chest rose and fell, sent a swell of desire directly to my groin.

This party was certainly going to be *interesting*. Though I had a feeling my attention would be all for my lovely date and not for any of the other attendees. And at a swingers party no less. How very ironic.

First Krystyna introduced us to a well-known TV actress who'd recently won a Bafta, and her husband, who was a strikingly handsome executive. He took Ellen's hand and kissed it, and I noticed her swallow nervously, her nostrils flare. Again, I enjoyed her reaction, though a part of me wished to be the one eliciting it.

"Elodie, I hope I'll see more of you later," he murmured into the kiss.

Normally, I was all about the free love, but tonight my possessive streak was coming out. It was coming out more and more around Ellen.

We were introduced to several more couples before my eyes landed on a familiar face. I just couldn't seem to shake Warren Gold these days. He approached us, a different lady on his arm tonight. Thankfully, she wasn't an ex-client, but a famous singer. She looked young. Too young for him. I

165

knew for a fact Warren was pushing forty, even though he'd been telling everyone he was thirty-five for years.

"Julian, we have to stop meeting like this," he said, all white teeth and bronze tan.

"I can see you've been enjoying the Majorca sun," I replied.

"I just got back a few days ago. I miss it already, though London does have its charms," he said, casting his gaze on Ellen. He took her hand, kissing it just like her previous admirer. "I'm so pleased to see you again, beautiful Elodie, and in such an opportune setting."

I wanted to punch him. The only saving grace was that the singer on his arm was eyeing me appreciatively. Warren noticed, too. I could tell by the slight twitch of his jaw that it bothered him. Still, I slid my arm around Ellen's waist and pulled her to me, just to make my point clear. Warren would not be putting his hands on her tonight. Or ever.

She gasped quietly at how tight I held her. I turned my attention to Warren's date.

"I'm Julian."

I held out my hand and she took it, giggling when she replied, "Rebecca."

We shook hands, but before I could say anything more, there was the clink of silverware on glass. Branson Sutton stood at the head of the long dining table. He wore a dark shirt, the first few buttons undone.

"I'd like to welcome you all to our humble home tonight. The chef will be serving a menu of grilled figs, veal, and for dessert, well, I'm sure we would all prefer to indulge in other pleasures."

There was some low laughter before he continued, "I see some old faces and some new. I hope tonight lives up to every one of your expectations, for there is no higher

166

pleasure in life than to seek the ultimate divinity of our flesh."

I leaned in to whisper in Ellen's ear. "Somebody thinks they're in *Eyes Wide Shut*."

I saw her try to stifle her laughter, and I inhaled her sweet scent. Coconut. Always coconut. "Does seem a little much," she whispered back.

"I can't wait to watch him have sex. I bet he makes sure there's always a mirror nearby."

She let out a small titter then clasped her hand over her mouth. We took seats side by side at the dining table, and I endeavoured not to grit my teeth when Warren pulled out a chair on the other side of Ellen.

Just like in a period drama, a line of servers came and placed our fig starter down in front of us. I had to admit, I appreciated the pomp and ceremony. There was nothing worse than showing up to an orgy that turned out to be in a grotty bedsit, a bottle of cheap, week-old sauvignon blanc the only available refreshment.

I may have come from impoverished beginnings, but as soon as I started to earn money, I'd acquainted myself with the finer things in life.

"My favourite," Warren said in a silky voice as he leered at Ellen, picked up a fig and popped it in his cartoonishly handsome mouth. I absently wondered if he used lip fillers.

"Fresh figs are always a treat," I agreed, plucking one from Ellen's plate and holding it to her mouth. She took my flirtation in stride, making eye contact as her soft lips met my fingers. She ate it right out of my hand, sending a jolt of arousal directly to my cock.

I flicked my gaze to Warren, my expression steely. It all worked to communicate a blaringly loud *she's mine* without any need to say the words.

All through the starter and main course, Warren tried to ingratiate himself with Ellen, and I successfully cockblocked him at every turn. Ellen didn't appear interested in him, and it pleased me that she saw through his act. Irritated that he couldn't get anywhere with my date, Warren turned his glacial gaze to me.

"How is Rose doing these days, Julian? I was always fond of her."

She's happily engaged to a movie star and living on a remote Scottish island, far away from you.

"She's well," I replied congenially, not providing any details.

"Please tell her I was asking for her," he went on, sipping smugly on his wine.

I didn't know why he felt smug, since he'd never actually gotten anywhere with Rose. It was a typical Warren style head game. I held my tongue and ate a slice of veal. The food was delicious, but I would've enjoyed it more in better company. As people finished their meals, they started to leave the dining room, partnering off in search of private nooks around the house.

I rose from my chair and held my hand out to Ellen. Relief flashed in her eyes. I knew she feared being approached by another attendee and propositioned. Like I said, Ellen was a people watcher. I sensed she wanted to be here to observe how the attendees interacted, witness how the whole thing played out.

It would take time before she felt comfortable taking part. These sorts of sexual exploits were something one worked up to. You didn't just go from ordinary, everyday sex to swinging. It was a gradual process, which was why I wouldn't allow her to do anything tonight that she wasn't comfortable with.

There was also the fact I felt possessive of her, but that was something I tried not to delve into too much.

I led her to a cushioned window box just off the dining room. We sat down, and from our vantage point, you could see directly into the study, where a man and two women were entering into foreplay. The man kissed one woman's neck, while the other woman started to unbutton his shirt. When Ellen saw what I was seeing, her eyes got big and she glanced away.

"Are we supposed to be watching this?"

"They would've closed the door if they hadn't been hoping for an audience," I replied, studying her reaction. Her breathing quickened as she bit her lip. "Voyeurism is a large part of all this. In fact, some people like to watch and nothing more."

"Oh. That's...interesting."

I enjoyed the physical responses she gave off. She continued to bite her lip, eyes flicking to the scene in front of us and then away. Despite her persona as Elodie, she was a fish out of water.

The man, shirtless now, spread one woman out on the desk. He pushed up her skirt, pulled down her underwear and proceeded to eat her out. Ellen emitted a quiet, startled noise, but her gaze never left the scene. She shifted in place, squeezed her thighs together and let out a long, shaky breath.

I wanted to touch her.

Without thinking, I reached out and pushed her hair over her shoulder, revealing her smooth neck. The urge to kiss her right in that hollow curve was maddening. I leaned close, then whispered in her ear, "Do you like watching them?"

She didn't respond right away, goose bumps rising on her skin, then said, "I think so."

I sat back. "Then we'll stay."

She appeared disappointed when I didn't touch her again, which was expected. Watching the threesome, she was aroused. She wanted someone to soothe her aches, but I didn't trust myself to stop once I started.

The other woman let her dress drop to the floor, her eyes on the two as she removed her underwear. She sat down on a velvet armchair, spread her legs wide and began stroking herself.

"Oh, my God," Ellen whispered.

My pants tightened, which wasn't surprising, though I wasn't very interested in the threesome. It was how Ellen reacted that turned me on. A flush rose on her chest, the dress revealing a healthy dose of cleavage that I could hardly take my eyes off.

The woman pleasuring herself produced a dildo from a nearby handbag and plunged it inside herself. The man tongued the other woman's clit and her moans of ecstasy trickled out into the hallway. She opened her eyes, saw that Ellen and I were watching, and smiled in pleasure. She'd definitely hoped for an audience.

Ellen's voice was croaky when she spoke. "Have you seen anyone you like?"

Only you.

I levelled my gaze on her, hoping she got my meaning. "Perhaps."

Her nostrils flared. "Who?"

I grinned coyly and wagged my finger. "Now that would be telling."

As though a force was pulling on her, she looked back to the threesome. How I wished I could feel what she was feeling right now. When I was young and new to sex, I was like a kid in a candy shop. It became an addiction, just like most things for me, and I couldn't get enough. Over time, it took more and more to excite me.

But Ellen wasn't jaded like I was. She was looking at it all with fresh eyes and I absorbed her experience like a man drowning of thirst.

The woman pleasuring herself came loudly. I loved how intently focused Ellen was, like she'd never seen someone bring themselves to orgasm before. The man turned his attention to her, stripping off his pants to reveal a large, throbbing erection. He fisted himself, pumped up and down, then climbed atop the woman and shoved himself inside her.

Ellen sighed.

I wanted to swallow it. I wanted to absorb every little thing she felt. I wanted to push inside her, make her sigh with my cock.

The man fucked the woman hard and fast. The other woman, who was lying on the desk, fingered herself now, pinching one nipple and then the other.

Ellen exhaled heavily. "I think we should probably leave."

My mouth curved. "Why? They've just gotten started."

She rubbed the goose pimples on her arm. "It just feels…"

"Lewd? Naughty? Arousing?" I provided.

She frowned, cheeks rosy, then said, "Invasive, too."

"I already told you, they want to be watched."

"Yes, but, it's a little frustrating."

I arched an eyebrow. "Would you like to join them?"

"No!" she blurted, then lowered her voice to a whisper again, "I'm just a bit conflicted."

Now I grinned. "You mean horny?"

Her face showed embarrassment. "Okay, yes. I'm horny," she said in the quietest voice imaginable.

Impulsively, I took her hand and pulled her up. "Come with me."

I led her upstairs, peeking in several rooms (where lots of sex was happening) before I found an empty bathroom. I closed the door behind us then lifted her up onto the counter by the sink.

"What are you doing?"

"Open your legs."

"Julian!"

My voice held a low edge as I spoke in her ear. "I just want to help you, Ellen."

She swallowed at my use of her real name and I palmed her thighs, gently pushing them apart so I could stand between them. I took her hand in mine, then lowered it to the fabric of her underwear. "Are you wet?" I asked, my voice soft, intimate.

She closed her eyes, throat bobbing as she swallowed, then nodded.

"I can't hear you," I prodded and bit gently on her earlobe.

"Y-yes," she breathed.

"Feel yourself," I urged, guiding her fingers past the elastic of her underwear. She didn't resist, but I felt her hand shake a little. I was rapt, taking all of her in. I saw her uncertainty and endeavoured to reassure her.

"Make yourself feel good."

My hand was over her knickers, coaxing her fingers to move. I knew the moment she properly touched herself because a small whimper escaped her. The tiny sound thrilled me. I moved my hand, pressed it tight to her. I was going to come in my pants when she moved her fingers in circles over her clit.

"That's it," I whispered, frustrated by her closed eyelids. I wanted to see what she looked like when she orgasmed.

She moaned and buried her face in my neck. I relished the feel of her lips when they brushed my skin, but I couldn't tell if it was intentional or if she was simply lost in the moment.

My hand yearned to join hers, but that wasn't what this was about. Her pleasure was my pleasure. "Julian," she said, voice strangled. Her hand stilled as several tremors shook her body. She gripped my shirt as she came, her hot breath on my neck, her thighs clenching around my hips. I was hard as a rock, but I wasn't frustrated. Delayed gratification was a heady thing.

When she finally drew away from me, her eyes were round as saucers. A million thoughts flickered across her face, like she was talking herself around in circles in her head.

"Feel better?" I asked. She looked away, flushed.

She stared at a bar of fancy soap by the sink, then spoke quietly, "I want to hire you."

I blinked at her, frowned, then replied, "You want to what?"

She seemed to steel herself. "As an escort. I want to pay you to have sex with me."

173

Thirteen
Ellen

As soon as I saw his expression, I knew I shouldn't have said it. Julian looked stunned at first, then offended, then he just seemed pissed.

I hopped down off the bathroom counter and spoke in a nervous ramble. "Um, forget I said that. I didn't mean it. It was a moment of temporary insanity."

I walked out of the room and headed downstairs, not waiting for him to respond. Fumbling in my bag, I searched for my phone to call a taxi, then I remembered I'd left it at home. Stupid no mobile phones rule.

I was almost to the front door when I walked headfirst into a hard chest. I slowly looked up to find Warren Gold staring down at me. He looked like a cat that just sweet-talked its way into a canary's cage.

"Elodie, just the person I've been looking for," he said, all sultry. He was the last person I wanted to see right now. In fact, he'd bothered me all through the meal with his inane attempts to flirt.

"Excuse me, please," I replied and moved to walk past him.

He caught my elbow, his grip a little hard. "I just want to get to know you better."

"I'm in a hurry."

"Oh, come on, stay awhile," he cajoled.

Footsteps sounded down the stairs before Julian ground out, "Take your hand off her."

Warren's expression darkened as he dropped his hand and stepped back. Julian traversed the final few steps, slid his arm through mine and led me to the front door.

"Bloody vulture," he whispered under his breath.

"Thank you," I said, glad he'd come to my rescue even after I'd offended him.

Julian didn't say anything as he led me to the door where the butler from earlier was waiting. "Leaving so soon?" he queried.

"Unfortunately, we have an early start in the morning. Please let Mr. and Mrs. Branson know we had a wonderful time tonight."

"Of course," the butler replied.

Outside, there were a number of cars waiting. Julian guided me to one, opened the door and gestured for me to get in. I slid into the back seat, expecting him to join me, but he only closed the door and went to speak with the driver. My stomach dropped when he walked to the second car and got inside. He must've told the driver my address because a second later we were on the move.

I'd royally screwed up tonight.

Sure, our friendship was unconventional, but it was still a friendship. You didn't ask your friend to have sex with you for money. You just didn't. Even if was their job. Even if they'd just given you the most powerful orgasm of your life without even really touching you.

That was clearly what scrambled my brain. I'd come so hard I wasn't thinking straight. And it had escalated so quickly. Julian caught me in a web of lust and I was helpless to resist.

The way he looked at me with such desire and heat, it was a new and addictive feeling.

A sense of grief gripped me. What if he never talked to me again? What if I'd inadvertently broken some golden rule?

By the time the car stopped outside my house, I'd worried myself into a tizzy. Feeling desperate, I sent him a text.

Ellen: *I'm so sorry. Forgive me?*

No response. My mind ran back over the night's events. I could hardly believe where I found myself, smack dab in the middle of a celebrity swingers party. It was surreal, to say the least. I'd felt edgy, nervous, like someone would point at me and declare, *this one doesn't belong here!* All day I'd gone back and forth over whether or not to cancel, but in the end, I forced myself to be brave. Do something outside of my comfort zone—way, *way* outside of my comfort zone.

Now I wondered if maybe I should've just stayed home, that way nothing would've happened between Julian and I and we'd still be friends.

I barely slept a wink that night, endlessly staring at the screen of my phone, hoping for a message. There was none, and I didn't have the guts to send another.

Two days went by and I still heard nothing from him. On Tuesday, I went to meet Suze at the café, hoping Julian might show up. For the last three weeks, I'd told her I was travelling for work. After having my true identity discovered, I'd been too scared to go see her. It felt like my lies were fraying at the edges, on the verge of coming apart completely.

But I missed her a lot, which was why I forced myself to be brave, don my costume and go see my friend.

Sometimes I wondered what it would be like to be a normal person.

Suze arrived a few minutes after me. I sat at our usual table, nursing a macchiato, when she walked in, a big smile on her face, arms outstretched for a hug. I stood and she threw her arms around me, squeezing tight.

"Oh em gee, I've missed you! A week just isn't the same without my Elodie fix."

I laughed. "I've missed you, too. Travelling for work has been such a bore."

"Let's not talk about work. I want to hear how you've been doing. Are you still seeing the stripper?"

I opened my mouth, hesitated, then decided to be honest for once. "Actually, no. I've been seeing Julian."

Her eyes grew big with excitement. "Seriously? Lucky you! He's beautiful as sin."

I sighed and rested my chin on my hand. "I know, but I think I may have screwed things up with him."

Her brow furrowed. "Oh no, what happened?"

"I think I offended him. You know I have a big mouth sometimes. I say what's in my head. Anyway, I haven't heard from him in two days, so I think he's done with me."

Suze's expression was sympathetic as she reached across the table to squeeze my hand. "Oh well, I'm sure someone else will come along. It's his loss."

If only she knew that nobody else would come along, and certainly not someone like Julian. He was one of a kind, the first man to ever make me feel like I could just…be myself. At the party, he'd called me Ellen, and I couldn't help loving how that felt

"Maybe," I replied, forlorn.

"How about you come to my next fashion show at the end of the month? It's for my men's clothing line, so there'll be lots of delicious, single models."

I mustered a smile. "Sure, sounds like fun."

"By the way, I know I said we shouldn't talk about work, but I was wondering if I could ask a favour. I've fallen out with my usual accountant and I was hoping you might have time to look at my accounts for last year? I'd owe you big-time."

I froze. Finally, the lies I'd told her were coming back to haunt me. Why hadn't I made up a more unskilled job? Accountant had just sounded so professional at the time when it fell out of my mouth.

"I'm really busy at the moment. I don't think I'll have time to fit you in."

"Not even on the weekend?" she hedged. I hated to say no to her, but I had no other choice. I knew about as much about accounting as I did about astrophysics.

I opened my mouth, brain fumbling for an excuse, when my blessed phone started ringing. I pulled it from my bag, took a look at the screen and saw it was my agent, Daniel. I sent Suze a look of apology.

"This is work. I actually have to get back to the office. Do you mind if we cut today short?"

She smiled kindly and waved me away. "Not at all. I'll see you next week." She stood to place a quick kiss on my cheek and I hurried outside to answer the call.

"Daniel, hi," I breathed. He had no idea how grateful I was that he'd called when he did.

"Hello, Ellen, how are you today?" he replied, his voice warm and friendly. Sometimes I suspected he treated me with kid gloves because I was so skittish. I was one of his highest selling authors and he didn't want to scare me off. I wished I didn't give off that vibe. It was something I needed to work on.

"I'm well. Was there a reason you called?"

"Just the weekly call to nag you about doing a signing," he said on a chuckle. "And don't worry, I've already prepped myself for rejection."

I really did feel bad about saying no to him all the time. The man had the patience of a saint. "I just worry I'll disappoint people. I feel like I'll screw it all up. Trust me, I'm better off remaining an enigma. It sells more books."

"I don't believe you. Your readers would love to meet you, Ellen. They already worship the ground you walk on. All you have to do is show up and smile and they'll be over the moon."

I continued walking toward my house, scratching my neck. This conversation always made me break out in a rash. "The idea still freaks me out."

Daniel was quiet on the other end, then said, "How about we meet up for coffee, somewhere quiet? I'll talk you through the whole thing and then you can decide. If it's still no, then I promise never to ask you again."

"I don't know, Daniel…"

"One coffee. I'll pay. What's the worst that could happen?"

His friendly, playful voice managed to draw me out of my shell. I stopped walking and looked down at myself. I was still dressed as Elodie: leopard print blouse, leather effect jeggings, Louboutin heels. Maybe I could do this.

I cleared my throat. "Okay. One coffee. Where do you want to meet?"

There was stunned silence on the other end before he leapt into action. He obviously thought I was going to decline, just like I always did. I could hear him moving around his desk, probably grabbing his things so could run out of the office.

"I'll text you the address. See you there in thirty minutes?"

"See you in thirty minutes," I confirmed and hung up.

My hand shook as I placed my phone back in my bag. When I arrived at the large, open plan coffeehouse, I spotted Daniel right away. I knew what he looked like because there was a photo of him on the agency's website. It didn't really do him justice, because he was a lot better looking in real life. He had light brown hair and smiling blue eyes. He looked like the boy next door, the one any girl would be proud to bring home to meet her parents.

The exact opposite of Julian, my brain added.

As soon as I thought of him, my heart gave a heavy pang. I tried to ignore it and plastered on a friendly smile as I approached the booth.

"Hello, Daniel," I greeted, and he looked up from his tablet.

He stared at me for a full five seconds, blinked, then stood up fumblingly. "Ellen?" he questioned in disbelief. His gaze went from my red hair to my green eyes, then travelled all the way down my body. He pushed his black-rimmed glasses back against his nose and held out his hand. "Wow, it's a pleasure to finally meet you."

"And you," I replied, shaking his hand then taking a seat. "It's weird, but I feel like I know you already. We've spoken so much on the phone."

He ran a hand through his hair and sat back down. "Yes, me too, though you're nothing at all like what I expected."

I smiled at this, channelling Elodie. "What did you expect?"

He coughed, flushing slightly. "Well, um, authors who look like you don't generally shy away from signings."

"I'll take that as a compliment."

He nodded profusely. "You should." Pausing, he clasped his hands together. "So, what do I need to say to convince you?"

"Tell me it won't turn out to be an absolute disaster?"

Daniel chuckled. "Has anyone ever told you you've got a very catastrophic way of thinking? Rarely do book signings end in disaster. I'd say you're more likely to walk out onto the street and get struck down by a flying Doberman pinscher."

"That's a very weird analogy, Daniel."

"Yes, it is. What I'm trying to say is, I'll be there to hold your hand the whole time. I'll even give you a back massage while you sign if you like, uh, in a strictly non-sexual harassment way, that is."

"Back massages are always a plus, so long as they're consensual," I replied, because he seemed to be getting flustered. I couldn't believe I was having this effect on him. Well, not *me* me, but me in my current guise.

"Okay, great," his eyes flickered back and forth between mine, uncertain. "So, will you do it?"

I pursed my lips. "Exactly how much time will I have to prepare?"

He thought on it a moment. "We can arrange a signing here in London in about a month? That'll give you enough time to make a dent in your WIP and maybe read an excerpt before you sign?"

"Look at you, trying to get as much bang for your buck as possible." Plus, a month was pretty soon.

He smirked at me, and wow, it was sort of sexy. He definitely wasn't *all* boy next door, that was for certain. "There's a reason why I run my own agency at thirty-five years of age, Ellen."

181

I pushed aside my reservations and forced myself to do something brave. "You drive a hard bargain, but you've done so much for me over the years, I guess I owe you."

He beamed at me. "Seriously? You'll do it?"

What was happening?

I mustered a confident, Elodie-like smile. "Yes, Daniel, I'll do your beloved book signing."

He slammed his hand down on the table. "This calls for a celebratory round of lattes. My treat."

I sat back and laughed. "I'll take a mocha, with whipped cream on top."

He saluted me. "Coming right up."

***

I took a cab back from my coffee date with Daniel. My shoes weren't designed for traversing the streets of London. I smiled to myself because our meeting had gone so well. Daniel felt like a friend, someone I could trust.

I stepped out of the cab, my mind racing. Perhaps I should just dress as Elodie all the time, that way I'd never have to feel socially anxious ever again.

My mood changed instantly when I found Julian sitting on the steps leading up to my front door. He wore a long grey coat, a navy shirt underneath, and faded jeans. His hair hung forward around his eyes and he stared at me with both sadness and affection.

He stood to greet me. "Someone's been out and about. I tried to call you five times, but you didn't answer. Thought you were ignoring me."

I pulled out my phone and saw he was telling the truth. There were a bunch of missed calls, but I'd put my phone on silent when I went to meet Daniel. "I wasn't ignoring you. I was out with my…um, what are you doing here?"

Julian glanced down the street then back to me. "Guess I'm a glutton for punishment."

I frowned, heaving a guilty sigh. "When I said what I did, I never meant to offend you or hurt you in any way. I was an insensitive idiot and I'm sorry."

Julian leaned back against the railing, considering me. "You hardly called me a whore, Ellen. And I already told you, I don't offend easily."

"Still, I shouldn't have said it. We're friends. It was wrong of me."

A moment passed, and my neighbour opened her front door. She looked between the two of us, locked her door then walked down the street. Since I never really talked to any of my neighbours, she didn't spare me or my unusual attire a second glance. Probably didn't even recognise me.

I pulled my keys from my bag and stepped up to my door. "Do you want to come inside?"

"Sure." Julian stood behind me, and I swore I could feel his heat. His presence was a potent force and there was a magnetic energy about him today, more so than normal.

We walked into my kitchen and I let Skittles and Rainbow out of their cage. Skittles bypassed me and flew right onto Julian's shoulder, nibbling on his ear. "Hey, buy me a drink first," he chuckled. It had only been two days, but I'd missed his laugh.

"Sorry, they can be a little familiar sometimes," I said and dropped my keys down on the table. I plucked Skittles off Julian's shoulder and placed her back in the cage. I didn't know what to say. I wanted to rewind the clock and go back to how we were before I ever opened my big stupid mouth.

"So, can we just—"

"I'm here because—"

I held out a hand. "You go first."

He glanced at the couch by the window. "We should sit down. I have a feeling this is going to be a long conversation."

Oh, man.

I followed him to the couch and sat. He angled his body to face me, gazing at me for a long moment. There was something about Julian's stares, like he saw all of you, even the parts you tried to keep hidden. I grew self-conscious and fiddled with the hem of my blouse.

Julian blew out a breath. "I guess I'll start by asking you this. Why do you want to hire my services?"

"I already said it was a mistake—"

He cut off my words by placing a finger to my lips. I was momentarily speechless at the feel of his skin on my mouth. He lowered his hand. "We both know you don't just blurt things out. You're a worrier, Ellen, and worriers think on things for a long time before they say them. You obviously thought about this for a while."

I lowered my gaze, feeling shameful. "Okay, you're right. I have been thinking about it, but I never planned on actually asking you. For one, it would be taking advantage, and for two, it would ruin our friendship." I paused, feeling self-conscious as I remembered the last time we were together. "Then at the party, all that *stuff* happened between us and I had a moment of insanity."

Julian's expression heated. "Darling, you couldn't take advantage of me if you tried. But back to my original question, the moment of insanity aside, why did you want to hire me?"

My old friend embarrassment crept in. "You're the first man I've ever really gotten close to, aside from my dad and brothers. I just thought, since it's your job, you could help me gain some *sexual experience*." I whispered that last bit.

Julian's eyebrows jumped. "Are you a virgin?"

"No!" I exclaimed, then added, "Not quite."

"What does 'not quite' mean?"

"It means my experience is limited, *very* limited."

"I see."

I studied him. "Do you?"

Julian sat back, appearing to mull everything over, then asked, "How many men have you been with?"

I tensed up. "That's neither here nor there."

"I wouldn't ask if it weren't pertinent."

Huffing a breath, I reluctantly replied, "One."

Again, his eyebrows jumped. I wished they'd quit doing that. I already felt like enough of a loser. "Just one?"

"Yes."

Julian rubbed his jaw, looking away while he murmured to himself. "Might as well be a virgin."

I swiped him lightly on the shoulder. "Hey! You're not making me feel any better."

He looked back at me. "My apologies. This is just an unusual situation for me. Clients normally come to me through recommendations. We speak on the phone first, I vet them. It's all very official, but with you it's—"

"Complicated?"

Julian exhaled. "Yes, very complicated."

"Well, like I said, I've reconsidered and decided it's a terrible idea anyway so…"

I trailed off because what I said appeared to bother him. A deep line formed between his eyebrows. "What will you do then? Keep your body hidden away, never explore the sexuality hidden inside you? You're a beautiful woman,

185

Ellen. You deserve to know what it's like to be desired, and to desire another."

I definitely knew what it was like to desire another.

I swallowed down the words and instead replied, "Then what?"

Julian held my gaze. "I will take you on as a client."

He would?

"You will?"

He lifted a finger. "But, there will be rules, for both of us."

Was this actually happening? I had to be dreaming. My heart threatened to beat its way right out of my chest.

"Obviously, I haven't taken this decision lightly, which is clear from the fact that it took me two whole days to consider it."

Was that why he hadn't been in touch? He'd spent the entire time thinking about my offer?

I nodded soberly. "I understand."

He eyed me a moment, then blew out a breath. "Rule number one. When we're together, you'll be Ellen, not Elodie."

"But…"

"No excuses. Nothing about this arrangement will be pretend."

My throat ran dry. "I'm not sure I can do it as myself."

"Of course, you can. You're you all the time, you just need to take off the wig."

But the wig is my safety blanket, Julian, you don't understand.

"Rule number two," he went on before I could argue. "You won't discuss our arrangement with anyone."

"Not even Rainbow and Skittles?" I asked for comic effect. This conversation was getting too serious.

Julian's lips twitched. "Not even Rainbow and Skittles. Rainbow's a notorious gossip."

I let out a soft laugh. "Is there a rule number three?"

His expression sobered. "Yes, when our arrangement comes to its natural end, we might not be able to see each other again. It all depends on how things pan out, but we need to prepare ourselves for the possibility."

My gut sank. I liked having Julian as a friend. He brought me out of myself and gave me butterflies. Made me feel more alive. I didn't want to lose that.

"Some clients I've stayed in touch with, but others, well, it was for the best that we parted ways."

"Why was it for the best?"

He seemed reluctant to answer, then said, "Those clients, you could say they were the ones I had the most intense connections with."

"Like the woman in the painting over your bed?"

Julian nodded. "Yes, like the woman in the painting."

"But...I don't want to lose you as a friend."

His expression softened. "Then you need to seriously consider if this is something you want to do." I frowned. Julian must've seen the conflict on my face because he continued to speak. "You've said yourself you've had limited experience with sex. When you're with someone in that way, there are emotions involved. Sometimes people try to pretend there aren't, but they're only fooling themselves. Staying friends with someone you've had a sexual relationship with can be painful for both parties, particularly when one person moves on to someone new..." his words trailed off, his meaning sinking in.

He thought I'd be brokenhearted, and seeing the person you long for, trying to be friends, would certainly be an unbearable experience. Was I prepared to give him up if it meant gaining experience that could help forge a life for myself, one where I actually had a family of my own one day and wasn't cursed to be alone forever?

I was almost thirty years old. I couldn't keep living like a hermit, afraid of human interaction. Nor could I continue pretending to be Elodie. As much of a comfort as she was, it wasn't healthy.

Being with Julian had to be worth the risk. Heartache faded eventually, right? Even if it hurt to lose him, I wouldn't feel that way forever.

I steeled myself and met his gaze. "I understand the rules, and I'm prepared for the possibility that we won't be able to stay friends."

Something about my response seemed to pain him. When he replied, his expression was grave. "In that case, I have just one more question to ask you."

"And that is…?"

He leaned forward, fiddled with the collar of my blouse and levelled his sexy, hazel eyes on me. The hint of a smirk graced his lips when he spoke, like we were sharing an intimate secret. "When would you like to begin?"

Fourteen
Julian

Ellen Grant was now my client.

The last time I'd been so fixated on someone was two years ago, when I'd had a brief but intense affair with the actress, Alicia Davidson. I met her through Rose, who was choreographing the West End musical Alicia was headlining. I'd pursued her relentlessly, and she resisted my charms for a while. From the very beginning, she made it known that I wasn't her type. She wanted someone nice, someone reliable, someone whose profession didn't fall into a grey area of legality.

I thought she was "the one". I thought at long last I was going to give up my work as an escort, get a normal job and be monogamous to a single woman. Then she cast me aside like yesterday's newspaper. I soon learned that Alicia wasn't "the one". Nobody was. They were all just "the one" for a while until the next one came along.

This was why I wasn't so concerned about being intimate with Ellen. My obsession with her would fade, just like it did with all the others.

At first, I'd had misgivings. She knew the real me, knew where I lived. I'd always kept my personal life and my work life separate. It was a rule I set for myself a long time ago, and hence another reason why I needed a few days to consider things.

But then, the more I thought on it, the more it made sense. Ellen needed experience and I was a fine candidate for the job. I would immerse myself in our relationship, teach her that sensuality was a vital part of the human experience, then set her free into a world of new possibilities.

It had always been my calling.

Some people were meant to find one person and settle down. I was meant to help ducklings learn how to fly.

I sat at the hotel bar, waiting for Ellen. We'd arranged to meet at 7:00 pm and it was now 7:06 pm. I wondered if she'd gotten cold feet. After we discussed all the ins and outs of the arrangement, my fee and the rest of the rules, she'd become somewhat withdrawn. All of that stuff tended to negate the sexy factor, but it was a necessary evil.

I decided I'd give her until 7:30 pm and if she didn't show I'd leave.

"Would you like another sparkling water?" the bartender asked, seeing I'd drained my glass.

I looked at my watch. 7:17 pm. "No, I'm good for now."

"Hey," a soft, unsure voice cut in.

She'd finally arrived, and she was *all* Ellen, not a hint of Elodie in sight. She wore a sensible, navy-blue dress, black tights, and kitten heels. Her hair was in a loose bun, her makeup light. My eyes focused on the peach gloss coating her lips. Aside from her eyes, they were her most entrancing feature.

"Hello, stranger." I stood to kiss her cheek, just shy of her mouth. She flushed in a way that satisfied my inner possessive streak. "Can I get you anything to drink?" I went on, helping her onto a stool.

She sat and looked at the bar. "Um, I'll t-take a red wine. Whatever's good."

I motioned for the bartender's attention. "A glass of your Ripasso, please."

"Sorry, I'm late." Ellen didn't look at me as she gripped the edge of her stool. The bar was crowded, and I thought it might be adding to her nerves.

I placed a hand on her knee, hoping the touch would ground her. "You're one of the few people I'd wait for."

"Thank you," she whispered, finally giving me her eyes. She had no idea of the power she wielded.

The barman placed her wine in front of her and she downed almost half of it in one gulp. "I almost didn't come," she confessed.

"I would've been terribly disappointed if you hadn't."

She rolled her eyes. "You're just saying that."

I caught her chin between my thumb and forefinger. "I never say something unless I mean it."

"Okay." Her voice was breathy.

I allowed her to concentrate on her wine, giving her a few moments to settle. She broke the silence when she blurted, "Do you know you have the name of a Jane Austen hero?"

I glanced at her, amused. "I don't recall there being a Julian Fairchild in *Pride and Prejudice*."

"Not your actual name. What I mean is, Julian Fairchild *sounds* like a Jane Austen name. It's like, the name of a well-bred gentleman."

I smirked. "How very ironic."

"You don't think you're a gentleman?"

"Not in the traditional sense, especially since I plan on doing some very ungentlemanly things to you tonight."

She looked away bashfully, lifted her glass with a shaky hand and downed the last of it. I thought perhaps a change of scenery was in order. "Are you hungry?"

"Yes, but I'm too nervous to eat."

191

"Eating might counteract your nerves. Would you like to go to the restaurant or would you prefer room service?"

She still wouldn't look at me when she replied, "R-room service."

I smiled because it was the answer I'd been hoping for. I left some money on the bar to pay for our drinks then helped her down from the stool. I took her hand in mine, lacing our fingers together as I led her out into the lobby to the bank of lifts.

"This is so strange," she muttered quietly.

I arched an eyebrow. "It's not too late to change your mind."

Her eyes widened. "No, no. I'm definitely going through with this."

I chuckled as we stepped onto the lift and I pressed the button for the tenth floor. "You sound like you're about to have a tooth pulled at the dentist."

Ellen winced. "I do, don't I?"

Several other people got on and we stood in silence as the floors went up. I kept her hand firmly grasped in mine as I bent to whisper in her ear, "You look beautiful tonight. I can't wait to be inside you."

"Julian," she hissed, eyes widening.

My smile was playful. "Relax. Nobody heard me."

When we reached our floor, I led her down the hall to our room.

"Is this how you usually operate?" she asked. "You meet at a hotel?"

"Sometimes I go to clients' houses, but I prefer hotels. It's a neutral middle ground."

"You never bring them to your flat?"

I opened the door with my key card, gesturing for her to step inside. "No. You're the only client who's ever been to my home."

"Oh," she breathed, her expression thoughtful. "Is that problematic?"

"Not unless you plan on stalking me." Ironic, since I was the one who'd semi-stalked her not too long ago. I kept that information to myself, for now.

She gave a soft giggle. "I don't have any current or future plans to stalk you, you have my word. Besides, I'd be terrible at it."

I shot her a flirty look. "I disagree. You're a master of disguise."

She swiped my shoulder. "Shut up. Elodie's the only disguise I've mastered, and she hardly blends into the scenery."

"You're right, she stands out," I said, gently pulling on her hair tie so that her curls fell around her shoulders. "So, does Ellen," I went on quietly. Her gaze was on my hand, eyelids lowering. She blinked then stepped away, took a deep breath.

"So, room service?"

"Menu's by the bed. Order whatever you like."

She walked woodenly across the room and I knew I still had my work cut out getting her to relax. It was expected, since she'd only ever been with one person. This was all new and scary to her.

Ellen sat on the edge of the bed, the menu on her lap, her tone deceptively casual when she asked, "Have you ever slept with a virgin before?"

I sat down on the armchair by the window, crossed one leg over the other and clasped my palms together. I hadn't been with many virgins, or near-virgins, in Ellen's case, but

I had been with a few. It wasn't something I shied away from, merely a fact of life. Everyone had to have a first time at one point or another.

"Several, yes."

She still didn't look at me. "Were they clients or…"

"Most of them were clients."

Now she glanced up. "So, they hired you for the specific purpose of losing their virginity?"

"Correct."

"Well, that makes me feel a little better."

"You don't need to feel self-conscious in the slightest, Ellen. I'm fond of you exactly because of who you are, that includes your experience or lack thereof."

She ignored my compliment. "I think I'll order the chicken. Do you like chicken?"

"I love chicken."

She closed the menu, lifted the phone and made the order. She also included a bottle of wine, but I hoped she didn't plan on getting drunk. I wanted her to relax, but I also wanted her lucid. I wanted her to feel every moment of this night right along with me.

"Tell me about one of the virgins," she said, turning to face me now, all business.

Since we were in private, I indulged her request. "The most memorable was a lady in her mid-forties. She was a university professor of mathematics, had devoted her life to her studies, but she'd never had any romantic interactions with a man. She felt she'd gotten too old to put herself out there, which I disagreed with, but anyway, she hired me because it felt less intimidating than going to a bar and trying to pick up a man."

"And you did it? You took her virginity?" Ellen asked quietly, leaning forward.

"I did."

"How did she feel afterward?"

"She was happy, I think. She never hired me again, so I'm not sure if she ever went on to find someone or if she simply went back to her old ways."

"That's what I fear will happen to me," she revealed. "That I'll be alone forever."

"If you are, it will be by your own choice. You can be with someone, Ellen, you just need to be brave and overcome your fears."

"That's what I'm trying to do," she muttered.

"Come here," I said, voice soft.

Her pretty eyes flicked up and she visibly swallowed. She stood and closed the distance between us, standing before me. I placed a hand on each of her hips. "Sit on my lap."

Hesitantly, she placed one knee on the armchair, followed by the other so that she straddled me. She held her body up, and I had to press on her hips to coax her to sit.

"Hi," I said, our faces close. I touched my nose to her chin and nuzzled.

There was a moment of frantic breathing before she replied, "H-hello."

Carefully, I removed her glasses and set them on the side table. Next, I grabbed her hands and placed them on either side of my neck. Being close like this was a good start. I trailed my fingertips along the underside of her arm when I spoke low, "Is there anything else you'd like to ask me?"

She bit her lip, looked away then back. "Do you always know what your clients look like before you meet them?"

Interesting question. "No, actually. We only speak on the phone."

195

"So, you make a decision purely based on their personalities?" She appeared to find this curious.

"I do. I've had sex with all manner of women, Ellen. Big, small, young, old, beautiful, ugly. If we have a connection, looks are irrelevant."

"I don't believe you."

"Why not?"

"Because, in order to have sex with someone, you must need to at least find them a little physically attractive."

I continued to stroke the underside of her arm, enjoying her small, pleasured inhalations. "That's true for many people, but not for me."

She scrunched her brow. "Why not for you?"

I took a moment to consider how to answer. It was a deceptively complicated question. "Because I've had sex with countless people, and from a very young age. The way I think about it, how my body reacts, has evolved. To put it in simple terms, I don't become aroused by seeing a naked, beautiful body. If I see two people being intimate in porn, for example, I find it appealing but not titillating. For me, sexual arousal is a much deeper thing. It happens when I find something hidden inside my partner, something only I can see."

Her fascination appeared to override her shyness when she asked, "Have you found that in me?"

I caught her cheek in my hand, pulled her closer and replied, "I found it quite a while ago, Ellen." I angled my head and pressed my lips to hers lightly. I could feel her pulse hammering away as I bent to taste her again. Her mouth was soft, her movements unsure, but she definitely enjoyed the kiss. I continued to press my lips to hers, nibbling at her, opening her up until she submitted to me.

Her mouth finally opened fully, and my tongue swept inside.

She was so innocent, so new to all this. I savoured the way her body trembled, how she fisted the collar of my shirt, pressed her soft breasts to my chest, unable to get close enough. We kissed fast, then slow, then long and lusciously deep. I relished kissing someone new, someone who had layers I'd yet to discover. It blew my mind to have her react to every little touch, every press of my lips, every flick of my tongue.

I was lost in her, completely and totally swept away. I didn't know how long we kissed, but it must've been a while because we were interrupted by a knock on the door.

"Must be room service," I said and reluctantly broke away. Ellen's eyes were still closed, her mouth slightly open, like she hadn't fully recovered from our make-out session. I slid her off my lap and went to open the door. She sat dreamy-eyed on the armchair while our food was rolled in on a cart. After I tipped the hotel worker, she left, and I lifted the metal cover. The food looked delicious, but I'd much rather go back to kissing Ellen.

I opened the wine and poured her a glass, feeling she might need it. My gaze lingered on her reddened lips as I handed it to her. She took it in a daze.

"You look so fuckable right now."

"You're not so bad yourself," she replied without looking at me.

I laughed. "You're getting better at flirting, but you need to work on your eye contact."

I held her gaze, lifted one of the plates and brought it over. Kneeling down, I placed it on her lap, forked up some of the mushroom risotto that accompanied the chicken and held it to her mouth. She ate, doing her best not to look away. I fed her another few bites, watching her throat as she swallowed. I found it inordinately sexy.

When she seemed to have had enough, I put the plate aside, then took her wine and placed it on the coffee table. I took her hand and led her over to the bed. Without speaking, I started to undress her, slowly, sensuously. I enjoyed taking the lead with Ellen, relished how all the little ways I took charge produced a reaction in her.

I lifted her dress over her head. Underneath she wore a black lace bra and knickers, the dark colour highlighting her lovely skin. To my delight, she wasn't wearing tights but hold-up stockings. A grin tugged on my lips as I ran my fingers along the lacy edge.

"Did you wear these for me?"

"Yes," she replied breathily.

I wanted to lick and bite every inch of her. I climbed onto the bed, gazing down at her with what I imagined was sheer carnal passion. When she started to clam up, I wrapped my fingers around her ankle. She gasped at the contact as I lifted her leg and threw it over my shoulder. Then I nestled my shoulders between her thighs, bent and pressed a kiss to the lace covering her pussy.

"W-what are you doing?" she whispered breathlessly.

I didn't reply, and instead slid the fabric of her underwear to the side. She was so pretty, so wet, I couldn't resist a taste. I swept my tongue along her folds and her back arched. She gripped my shoulders and let out a sharp cry of pleasure.

"That's it, let yourself go," I urged, gazing up at her.

She was the sexiest fucking thing I'd ever seen.

Fifteen
Ellen

What was happening?

The soft, fluttery, wet sensation of Julian's tongue on my vagina was by far the best thing I'd ever felt. He was like a God below me, so practiced, so confident and sure of himself.

I was in a hotel room with a male escort, receiving oral sex for the first time in my life.

It felt like some sexy alternative reality. Definitely not something that would be happening to me.

But then Julian held my gaze, flicked his tongue around my clit, sending spikes of awareness all through my body. This was very real, no doubt about it.

"Y-yes, like that," I urged and my encouragement seemed to please him.

He smiled as he closed his eyes and sucked hard on my clit. Both his hands spanned my waist, his fingers delicate yet masculine at the same time. They weren't fingers that had done manual labour, but they were fingers that had spent a lifetime pleasuring women.

When he opened his sultry, hazel eyes, they seemed to look right into my soul. In that moment, Julian wasn't an ordinary human, he was an otherworldly, supernatural being, sent to earth purely to seduce the female population.

He was certainly too beautiful to be human sometimes.

"Tell me when you're going to come," he rasped then went straight back to work.

I nodded, my entire body flushing as I fisted his hair. It was the first time I appreciated its length. You could really grab a hold of it. For a second, I wondered about all the other women who'd done exactly the same thing but pushed the thought aside.

I wouldn't think of that tonight. Tonight was all about enjoying myself.

Speaking of, Julian started doing this fluttery thing with his tongue and I almost came. Was there a female equivalent of premature ejaculation? It was embarrassing, but it wasn't my fault. Years of nothing but masturbation and my own imagination meant the real thing was pretty fucking mind-blowing.

I arched my hips and he palmed my thighs, fingertips digging in, his eyes urging me to let go. When he dipped his mouth and slid his tongue inside me, I moaned *loud*. His tongue returned to my clit, laying on just the right amount of pressure at just the right tempo.

He really was a pro.

"Julian," I breathed as I came. My stomach muscles clenched, my spine arched further, but he didn't let up. He continued to lick until he drained every ounce of my orgasm. When it finally petered out, I fell into the pillows, boneless.

Julian removed his shirt then wrapped his arms around me, tucking me tight to his body so that we were spooning.

"That was very pretty to watch, Ellen," he purred in my ear.

I smiled, too blissed out to reply. I didn't mean to fall asleep, but there was something comforting about lying in bed with him, something peaceful.

When I woke up, it was a little chilly. I realised why when I sat up and saw the window was open. Julian sat on the ledge, shirtless and smoking a cigarette. He stared out at the city skyline, his expression thoughtful.

"I didn't know you smoked," I said, breaking the silence. I was also pretty sure smoking wasn't allowed in the hotel, but I didn't mention that.

Turning to face me, he took the last drag then flicked the butt out the window.

"I don't, not normally. Funnily, it's the one thing I never became addicted to."

"Is it a post-coital ritual?"

His mouth twitched. "Something like that. Although, technically we didn't have "coitus" yet."

I laughed and flopped back into the pillows. "Don't call it coitus, you weirdo."

"Hey, when you're as experienced I am, you have to come up with new words for sex. Keeps things interesting."

He came and hopped on the bed, holding himself up on an elbow as he gazed down at me, those eyes of his sparkling with energy. Julian was so *alive*, and he made you feel alive right along with him.

"How do you feel?"

I remembered what we did before I fell asleep and self-consciousness kicked in. "Fine. A little tired."

He feigned a sad face. "What? You aren't a changed woman? I've been told my style of cunnilingus has miraculous transformative qualities."

I chuckled at that. "Okay. You're right. I'll never be the same. You've changed me, Julian Fairchild."

He gave a devilish look. "Have I corrupted you though? Because that's my main goal."

"I'm definitely a little corrupted."

He flopped back and threw his hands above his head. "Another successful evening then."

We lay in quiet for a few minutes. I thought on what he said, about cigarettes being the one thing he hadn't become addicted to. Did that mean he used to do drugs?

I turned over to face him and ran my fingers across his chest. He closed his eyes and made a masculine noise of satisfaction, seeming to enjoy it.

"Julian?"

"Hmmm?"

"What drugs were you addicted to?"

For a second, he almost appeared to stop breathing. Then he exhaled slowly and opened his eyes. "I might've been with a lot of women in my time, but heroin was my greatest love affair and the hardest to let go of."

I was taken aback. I'd never met anyone who used heroin before. When I thought of those people, I saw skinny, unwashed, gaunt faces, dark circles under the eyes. I couldn't picture Julian like that. He was too vibrant.

"What age were you?"

He stared at the ceiling. "Seventeen when I started using. Twenty-one when Rose locked me in my room and forced me to go cold turkey. After that, there was a long period of rehabilitation."

I studied his profile, so peaceful looking. His life must've been pretty tumultuous once upon a time. "Why did you start?" I whispered.

He didn't answer right away, and I got the sense he wasn't too keen to talk about it. Still, he replied eventually. "When Rose and I met, after our mothers became polyamorous, believe it or not, that was the better part of my childhood."

"It was?"

His throat bobbed as he swallowed. "Before that, Mum had a lot of different boyfriends. I didn't know it back then, but I would one day inherit her promiscuity, though I'm far more selective who I sleep with nowadays. Mum was never selective. Several of her boyfriends were abusive. They'd beat her up then move on to me. Unsurprisingly, I became a troubled child, and predators have a way of seeing victims coming. The year she was with Charlie was the worst of my life. His abuse wasn't physical but sexual. I was only twelve years old."

He spoke in a flat voice, devoid of emotion, like the past he recalled didn't happen to him but to a stranger. He went quiet and my heart thrummed in my chest. His story was shocking, but I was also upset and angry for him. No kid should have to go through something like that.

"I had a hole in me for a long time. When I found heroin, it was a way to fill it up."

I didn't realise I had tears in my eyes until I spoke, my voice watery. "Julian, that's awful." I reached out to stroke his hair away from his face, and he seemed to appreciate my touch. "You're the strongest person I've ever met," I told him softly.

His eyes flicked open, his expression wry. "I'm not strong, I'm just stubborn. I don't give up easy."

I didn't agree, but I also didn't argue. I was still reeling from his past, and I felt honoured that he was comfortable enough to share it with me. Something in my chest unfurled, a new and unfamiliar feeling. It was an affection for Julian, but it felt bigger, stronger, more intense, and also worrisome.

I rubbed at my chest, telling myself it would subside. It was a product of spending the evening together. We'd grown closer, that was all.

I refused to accept any other explanation, no matter how it pitter-pattered on the fringes of my brain.

Sixteen
Julian

"My God, don't tell me you're reading those damn books, too," I said when I entered my flat.

Rose and Damon were in the city for a press junket for Damon's latest film, *Sunset Over Lancashire*. It was his first gangster flick. Rose said he played a crime boss with a dark past and I knew Damon would nail the edgy role.

Currently though, the actor lounged on my couch, a *Sasha Orlando* novel in hand. He couldn't be further from a brooding crime boss as he gave a sheepish look. "Rose got me into them. They're pretty addictive."

"Yes, they are."

"How do you know? She said you refuse to read them."

"I'm familiar with several of the storylines," I replied, thinking of Ellen. I wondered if she realised just how popular those books were, because if she continued to claim parts of the stories as her own, she was eventually going to come across someone who'd already read them. Since she worked in a bookshop, she must've known. Maybe she enjoyed flirting with disaster. I still hadn't confronted her about it, but perhaps it wasn't relevant anymore.

Our relationship had evolved. We'd been intimate.

For the most part, I slept with people for money. Yes, I savoured the pleasure that came along with it, the connection, the feeling of being desired, but all that was secondary. With Ellen though, the money was unimportant. I desired her in a way I hadn't desired anyone in a long time. Such arrangements were always tumultuous, but a part of me relished the drama, the heightened emotions, the insurmountable, drugging lust.

When she'd asked to hire me at the Bransons' party, I'd been conflicted. Mostly because I wanted her so badly I was prepared to go about any means of having her, and that was normally a bad sign.

For weeks she'd bewitched me as Elodie, and now I was going to get to know the deepest, darkest parts of Ellen. Going down on her at the hotel last night had been intense. I'd savoured every moment, every little shiver and sigh, the way she looked when she came. She didn't feel like a client, she felt like a lover. I frowned at the troubling realisation.

"I'm on book three," Damon said, breaking me from my thoughts. "I actually think this series would make an excellent movie franchise. Did Rose mention I've been looking to get into directing?"

"No, she didn't. You're considering those books?" I asked with interest. Damon making his directorial debut would be very big news in the entertainment world.

"I was, but I inquired about the rights and apparently the author refuses to sell them. She's very reclusive. So far nobody's been able to make an offer that she'll accept."

I gave him a conciliatory look. "That's too bad."

Rose emerged from the bathroom wrapped in a towel. "Well, if this isn't the start of a porno I don't know what is," I teased.

She laughed and shook her head. "I don't know what sort of pornography *you* watch."

I gave a saucy smile. "The kind where a fresh-faced beauty walks out of the shower and gets DP'ed by two handsome, strapping young men who just so happen to be hanging about."

"That's wrong on so many levels." Damon frowned down at his book.

"Hey, you signed up for all this when you got with Rose," I said, gesturing to myself. "We're a package deal."

Rose glanced at Damon. "Don't listen to him. He just likes to shock people."

"He's well aware of my MO by now, I'm sure." I followed Rose into the spare bedroom.

"Have you just gotten home? You were out when we arrived last night."

"Yes, I was working." *Sort of.*

"Well, we'll just be here for three days and then we'll be out of your hair."

"But I love when you're in my hair. You know I don't like to be alone."

"Speaking of which, you haven't been calling as often as usual. Is there something I should know about?"

"Or someone," I replied. She was clearly hedging for information, but I never minded indulging Rose. She was my best friend, my confidante, my sister from another mister. "I've been spending a lot of time with Ellen, actually."

"Elodie's sister?"

"Yes, we've become pals."

"What about Elodie?"

"Elodie's...complicated."

Rose moved about the room, pulling outfits from her suitcase and hanging them in the wardrobe. I admired a pretty, embroidered dress. She must've been planning to wear it to Damon's premiere.

"How is she complicated?" she asked as she studied the dress, then carefully hung it up.

I wondered if I should just tell her the truth. Rose would never reveal Ellen's secret, and besides, it would be good to get some perspective. I sat down on the bed, ran my hand over the pale duvet cover. "Well, Elodie and Ellen are actually the same person."

She paused her unpacking to look at me, one eyebrow slowly rising. "Okay, you're going to need to explain that."

I huffed a breath and fell back into the pillows. "This is going to sound crazy, and it is crazy, so bear with me. You see, Ellen has problems interacting with people. She's shy...no, that's not the right word. Think of how reclusive Damon was when you two first met and multiply it by ten. She lives in a big house all by her herself, but aside from her part-time job at the bookshop, she rarely goes out. So, she invented Elodie to overcome her social phobia."

"Wait, Elodie is what? A persona?"

"Yes."

Rose shook her head. "I swear to God, Julian, I don't know where you find these people."

"I found her at the Polka Dot Café."

"You know what I mean. Dressing up and pretending to be someone else isn't normal. She could have deeper issues."

"Yes, her deeper issue is a fear of social interaction. And I love the abnormal, you know that."

"Right, but why is she so scared of social interaction? People don't just wake up one day and fear the outside world. There's usually a reason."

"I don't think there is a reason. It's just how she is."

"Hmmm, I wouldn't be so sure about that."

What Rose said made me think. Perhaps I'd been naïve to believe Ellen didn't have some deeper internal issues. After all, my entire way of life was the result of many,

many internal issues that started out from when I was a young boy.

A few moments of quiet fell between us while Rose finished unpacking and hanging up her clothes.

"I see you've managed to hook your fiancé on those books you're so obsessed with," I commented.

She grinned, looking pleased. "Yep, and I'll get you reading them soon enough. By the way, have you any plans for dinner?"

"Nope. I'm free as a bird."

"Good. I'm making my special beef casserole and I think I might've bought too much food. You can invite David over if you like."

Her offer got me thinking. "Can I invite Ellen instead?" I didn't want to wait days to see her again, and this way she got to officially meet Rose.

She studied me, considering it. "I guess it could be helpful for me to meet her, just to make sure she isn't a complete nutcase."

"She's not a nutcase. In fact, I have a feeling you two are going to get along."

"All right, then. Invite her, but maybe give her some advance warning about Damon. People tend to get a little starstruck."

I nodded and pulled out my phone. "Good thinking, Batman."

Julian: *Are you free for dinner tonight at my place? Rose is cooking.*

Ellen: *Feeling under the weather. Think it might be a cold. I don't want to infect you.*

Hmmm, I knew a brush off when I saw one.

Julian: *I won't take no for an answer. Quit letting your fears win.*

209

Ellen: *I don't know what you're talking about. I'm sick.*

Julian: *I'll come over and get you myself.*

A few minutes went by and I could tell she was talking herself around. She was obviously worried about meeting Rose and not being in costume. When she finally replied, it was a one-word answer.

Ellen: *Fine.*

I smiled as I typed.

Julian: *That's my girl.*

Julian: *Btw, Rose's fiancé is Damon Atwood. He'll be here, too. Just wanted you to have a chance to mentally prepare.*

Ellen: *What?!*

Julian: *See you at seven ;-)*

I shut off my phone so she couldn't try to talk her way out of it. Later that evening, the flat smelled amazing. When we were teenagers and had to fend for ourselves, Rose learned how to make cheap food taste good. Over time, she'd become an amazing cook. It was one of the reasons I missed living with her.

I helped set the table while she made the finishing touches. Damon was ensconced in the window nook, his head still buried in his novel. He'd been reading all day. Maybe I *should* get into the series, see what all the fuss was about.

I got a text on my phone.

Ellen: *I'm outside.*

Julian: *Be there in a sec.*

I glanced at Rose. "Ellen's downstairs. Be nice when she comes up, okay?"

She shot me a look. "I'm always nice."

"Well then, be extra nice."

210

When I got downstairs, Ellen stood just outside the door, chewing on her thumbnail like a nervous wreck. "I'm not used to this," she confessed.

I put my arm around her shoulders and pulled her close, automatically inhaling the smell of her hair. I was breaking all my rules for this woman, but I couldn't stop now even if I tried.

"It's just dinner with friends, nothing more. You'll be fine."

"Yeah, but you had to go and drop the "Damon Atwood" bomb on me then turn off your phone. I tried calling you. That was cruel."

I squeezed her shoulders and led her inside. "Yes, well, I apologise for that, but this will be good for you. I promise. You'll love Rose and Damon. They're the most down to earth people you'll ever meet. And you definitely need practice meeting people."

"Yes, I suppose you're right," she sighed as I opened the door and motioned her inside.

Rose stood by the kitchen counter, smile in place. She wiped her hands off on a dishcloth and came toward us.

"Hi, Ellen, I'm Rose. It's lovely to properly meet you."

"And you," Ellen mumbled and perhaps for the second time I got to see just how introverted she was. I'd witnessed it once before at the bookshop, when that group of tourists had come in, and I was seeing it again now.

She stared at the floor, hands in her pockets. Rose and I shared a look. The majority of times we'd been around other people, Ellen had been dressed as Elodie. But now she had no costume to hide behind, and the results were painful to watch.

Rose cleared her throat. "Well, I hope you like beef casserole, because I've made enough to feed a small army. Have a seat. Damon, come meet Ellen," she called.

Damon rose from where he was sitting, book in hand. Ellen's eyes widened when she saw him. Like most actors, Damon was striking in person. Well over six feet tall, with dark hair and even darker eyes, he was every inch a heartthrob. Ellen saw what he was reading, and she grew even more tense. Guess she wouldn't be telling any stolen anecdotes tonight.

I put my hand to the base of her neck and gently massaged. She shivered at my touch and some of the tension left her. I thought of her face when she came on my tongue, how her lush lips fell open on a moan, how she breathed my name.

"Hi," Damon said, almost as awkward with introductions as Ellen was.

"Hello," Ellen answered so quietly she might as well not have spoken at all.

"So, Ellen, you live close by?" Rose asked, making conversation.

Damon helped her dish up the food and set it on the table. Ellen nodded but didn't speak. This was going to be a *long* evening.

I wondered at how she could manage to conduct conversations with me, but not with other people. Perhaps it had to do with the fact I'd met her as Elodie first, and I knew more about her than most.

Rose, Damon, and I chatted about Damon's latest project while we ate. Ellen remained quiet, only nodding intermittently at stuff we said.

"Did Damon tell you he's hoping to buy the film rights for the *Sasha Orlando* books?" Rose put in animatedly.

"Yes," I said, eyeing Damon. "Your directorial debut. Exciting times."

"There's this amazing dance scene in book one, *Good Girl, Bad Lady*, where Sasha goes for salsa lessons and flirts with her teacher," Rose added. "Damon says I can choreograph it if the movie ever comes to fruition."

Ellen dropped her cutlery, making a loud clatter as it fell against her plate.

"Sorry," she muttered and went back to eating.

Damon ate a bite of casserole, not looking very confident. "Well, that's if my agent can manage to convince the author's agent to sell, and that's a big if. Several movie houses have put in bids and all have been rejected. I'm hoping the author will like my vision. It'll be an indie project, so it won't have a big budget. But I think big budgets can sometimes ruin book adaptations. They use all these fancy costumes and wigs and CGI, and it all becomes a little cartoonish. I want to portray the story on screen in a way that feels real."

Ellen appeared to be listening intently, surprising everyone when she spoke, "What do you mean, in a way that feels real?"

"Well," Damon elaborated. "It's not the popular opinion, but I feel like most film adaptations of books don't work because they try to make it scene for scene the same as the novel. That's okay when it's fantasy or science fiction, that's a whole different story. But when it's contemporary, they try to make the actors look exactly like the characters, and it all just ends up feeling forced. I think that an adaptation should be just that, the story needs to be adapted to fit a different medium."

"You're right," said Ellen. "There are things that happen in books that just don't work on screen."

Damon smiled softly. "Well, I'm glad you agree. Unfortunately, I don't think my opinion will go down well. Most authors want everything in a movie to be exactly how it is in their book."

Ellen played with her fork. "You should still give it a try. You never know." Now she stood. "Excuse me, I need to use the bathroom."

She went, and Rose lifted both eyebrows. "That woman is freaking terrified of us."

"I told you she had difficulty with social interaction."

"Yes, but this is a whole other level. She's been silent since she got here."

"Not true, she spoke to Damon just now."

"I still think she should get help. Is she seeing a therapist or a councillor? It's not healthy that the only way she can cope is by putting on a disguise and pretending to be this Elodie person."

"Will you keep your voice down? She'll hear you," I hissed.

"Okay, I'm lost. What's going on?" Damon asked.

"I'll fill you in later," Rose replied.

The bathroom door opened, but I didn't hear a flush. I suspected Ellen had been freaking out in there rather than actually using the facilities. I knew she'd heard our conversation, despite our whispers, when she emerged with reddened eyes.

"I think I'm going to go home now," she said, head down as she grabbed her coat and made a beeline for the door.

"Ellen, wait," I called and went after her. She was faster than I expected, reaching the bottom of the stairs before I caught up.

"Just let me go, Julian," she begged and pushed open the door. It was raining out and I hadn't brought a jacket. I still chased her, grabbing her elbow and pulling her around.

"What's wrong with you?"

"I heard you all talking," she sniffed, raindrops running down her cheeks. "You said you wouldn't tell anyone about...about Elodie."

"It's just Rose. Rose would never—"

"That's not the point, Julian. You promised!"

My chest deflated. "I only want to help."

"Yes, well, helping me is more trouble than it's worth. You don't...you don't know everything about me."

I stepped forward and grabbed her hands. "Tell me then."

"It's not that easy," she whispered. I hardly heard her over the passing traffic and the rain sploshing onto the footpath.

"Let's go back upstairs. We can go into my room and talk in private. We'll catch our death if we stay out here."

Something in her eyes softened, and reluctantly, she nodded. "Okay."

I took her hand and led her back inside. When we reached the flat, it appeared Rose and Damon had retreated into the spare bedroom. I grabbed some towels from the airing cupboard and brought Ellen into my room. I stripped her out of her coat and wrapped the towel around her shoulders. Her hair hung in ringlets around her face and a small tremble went through her.

"You're freezing, come here." I pulled off my shirt and wrapped my arms around her, rubbing up and down to try to warm her up. She dropped her head onto my shoulder.

"I'm so tired."

"We didn't get much sleep last night."

After she woke up and found me enjoying a rare cigarette by the window, we'd talked for hours. She told me stories from her childhood, about her dad and her two brothers. I'd told her tales of Rose and I, battling against the odds to survive, two homeless teenagers in the wilds of London.

"I'm sorry if I acted like a weirdo in front of your friends."

"It's a good thing I adore weirdos."

She laughed softly and snuggled closer. "It's just that everyone seems to be reading those books and..." she trailed off. I had a hunch where this was going.

"It's okay, Ellen. I already know."

She pulled away a little, brow furrowing as she peered at me. "You do?"

"Rose talks about Sasha Orlando all the time. It wasn't too hard to figure out."

She stood, the towel falling away, wet hair hanging over her shoulder. "I don't understand."

I stood, too, and took both her hands in mine. "Ellen, I put two and two together a while ago."

Her head moved slowly from side to side, disbelieving. "But how?"

"When we went to the wedding with David, you told everyone that story about the fireman, and I realised you'd stolen it from one of those books. Rose had recounted it for me just a few nights previous. Like I said, she talks about that series all the time."

Her face showed consternation. She let go of my hands and turned around, staring at my bedroom walls when she said, "You think I've been stealing the stories."

"Ellen, it's okay. I'm not judging you."

She turned around, her expression fierce. "Julian, I never stole anything. Those stories are mine."

"They're from the books—"

"No," she interrupted. "You still don't get it. The stories are mine because I wrote them. *I'm* the author of the *Sasha Orlando* series."

Seventeen
Ellen

Julian gaped at me. I was pretty sure this was the first time I'd seen him truly shocked.

My own books seemed to be haunting me everywhere I went these days and I couldn't keep it to myself any longer. When he thought I was stealing the stories for Elodie's anecdotes, I had to tell him the truth. They were *my* books. *I'd* written them. And I was damn proud of what I'd created.

"You wrote those books?" Julian questioned. "Seriously?" He didn't sound disbelieving, but it definitely knocked him a little.

"Yes," I said, sheepish. "And I didn't inherit my house from my grandmother either."

He ran a hand through his hair, then dropped back down onto his bed. "No, I don't imagine you did."

He stared at the wall for a second, then brought his gaze to me. "So, all that time you spend alone in your house, you don't just talk to Rainbow and Skittles. You write books?"

"Uh huh."

A slow smile crept across his face. "You're an international bestselling author."

"Yes."

His smile transformed into a full-on grin. "That's incredible, Ellen." A moment of quiet fell between us before he spoke again. "But, I don't understand why you wouldn't tell anyone."

I gave a humourless laugh. "It doesn't exactly come up a lot in conversation, not that I have many casual conversations with people."

Julian stared at me in fascination, like all the puzzle pieces were finally falling into place for him. "You're amazing."

"I make stuff up for a living. I'm pretty good at it, but I wouldn't go so far as to say it's amazing."

He stood, took my face in his hands and gazed right into my eyes. "Ellen, you are the most amazing, interesting, and unexpected person I've ever met."

I swallowed. "That's…um, thanks."

His lips curved appreciatively as he whispered, "You're welcome," then he took my mouth in a deep, sensual, mind-melting kiss. My knees almost went out from under me. It was a good thing he lifted me, turned us then threw me onto the bed. I heaved a shaky breath as he crawled up my body and kissed me again just as deeply.

"Wait, wait," I breathed. "We can't."

He stroked my hair away from my face, his voice low and husky. "Why can't we?"

"B-because this isn't an arranged meeting. It's unofficial."

"Unofficial sex is the best kind," he countered and planted kisses down my neck. I moaned and threw my head back, unable to help myself. We'd only spent one night together, but I was already addicted to his kisses, his touch.

He was under my skin, in my veins.

When I closed my eyes at night, all I saw was him. He invaded my heart and soul. I couldn't stop thinking about him. This wasn't just about sex, it was about the very heart of Julian.

Ever since I met him, my life had opened up, like a rose coming into bloom.

He licked his way from my throat to my earlobe, whispering, "I hope you're ready for this, Ellen, because I'm going to fucking eat you alive."

I shivered.

Julian peeled away my shirt and unhooked my bra in a matter of seconds. The cool air hit my skin and my nipples instantly hardened. He removed my glasses then kissed his way down my chest, taking a nipple in his mouth. A whoosh of air escaped me at the soft, wet pressure of his tongue.

His eyes flicked up, and I was hooked. He was all predator and I was all willing victim.

He released my nipple with a pop. His voice was rich, dark, like expensive whiskey. "What shall I do with you now?"

My throat went dry. I lay immobile and forced myself to reply. "Do whatever you want with me."

His eyes were dazzling, his lips curving in a way that told me that was the right answer. "As you wish."

Quick as a flash he flipped me over. I felt his mouth at my calf, then it moved up to the back of my thigh. His lips whispered across the crest of my bottom and I grew wet. From behind, his fingers slipped between my legs, testing, searching. He pulled down the elastic of my knickers and kissed the spot at the very base of my spine. It sent a shimmering, tickling sensation right up my back, lingering in the curve of my neck.

I made a sound like *guh* as I pressed my face into his pillow. It smelled like him, and I was drowning, no hope of swimming to the surface.

"So soft." His hand moved further between my legs; he pulled my underwear down and threw them to the floor. Skin to skin, he touched the folds of my sex and I undulated beneath him. He slid two fingers inside me and I cried out. My body wasn't accustomed to being touched like this, so everything he did was magnified.

He bit my bottom and I let out a surprised yelp. Julian grazed his teeth along my hip, a growl emanating from deep in his throat. Breathless, I turned around to face him. His pale skin had hints of olive tones, his torso muscular but not overly so. I soaked in the sight of him. It was one of the few times I'd seen an almost naked male body up close and I was a little mesmerised.

"Can I just…look at you for a second?"

His eyes were pure sin as he repeated my own words back at me. "You can do whatever you want to me."

I let my head fall back into the pillows and just, well, *stared*. Julian rose to stand at the foot of the bed, his hands going to his trousers. He undid the fly and pushed them down. In nothing but his boxer briefs, his erection was evident and my cheeks heated. Julian held my gaze, practically reading my mind as he pushed his boxers down to reveal his throbbing cock. My eyelids fluttered, and I lowered my gaze, unable to help gawking.

Every part of him was beautiful. It was clear why women paid to sleep with him. He was the man of your fantasies, the one you had sexy dreams about. When you woke up, you willed yourself back to sleep.

He merely stood there, letting me look my fill, but the expression on his face was what captivated me most of all. He appeared fascinated by my appreciation of his naked form.

"Is it okay if I touch you?"

221

His eyes heated. "You don't have to ask permission, Ellen."

I reached out and ran my hand along the V at his hip, then up to stroke his abdomen, and higher to his pectoral. His chest rose and fell, and I wondered if he was feeling this as intensely as I was. I pressed my lips to his stomach and his muscles jumped. When I looked up to check if I'd done anything wrong, his face was a picture of male need.

He wanted me.

It was a powerful feeling, to be wanted.

"Julian?"

"Yes?" he breathed.

I swallowed, forcing myself to be brave when I said, "I want you to fuck me."

In a heartbeat he was on me, our skin flush. I adored the feel of him, his heat, his hardness against my softness. I felt his cock press against my inner thigh, his hips moving in a slow, hypnotic rhythm while he kissed and sucked at my neck.

He reached for his dresser, opened the drawer and pulled out a condom. I watched, riveted, while he tore it open and slid it on. It was something he'd probably done a thousand times before, but I didn't want to think about that. Besides, what was transpiring between us felt too important, too real. Anything that happened in the past didn't matter.

It was just us. Here. Now.

"Still okay?" he asked as he readied to push inside me.

I bit my lip and nodded, tensing up a little. Julian shook his head. "That won't do. I want you relaxed." He reached down between our bodies and fingered my clit. My eyes rolled back in my head. He nipped my chin, his voice raspy. "Come for me."

His movements sped up and I came in a quick, intense burst. He obviously had magic fingers. I was languid now, my body ready for him. He didn't give me a chance to come down from my high, instead thrusting inside of me. Involuntarily, I moaned and gripped his shoulders.

"Give me your eyes, Ellen," he coaxed.

I met his gaze and he thrust into me deep. I felt a stretch, my body expanding for him, welcoming him. He never looked away while he fucked me, and I was captured in his spell. I suspected sex with Julian wasn't like ordinary sex. It was an experience, almost a performance on his part. One where he gave you his entire self and demanded all of you in return.

I was his, completely and irrevocably.

Julian gripped my thigh, hitching it up and around his hip so that he could enter me from a deeper angle.

"Oh, my G…" I gasped, unable to finish the sentence when he swallowed my words with a kiss. His tongue plundered my mouth with abandon, his hips pounding wildly.

My inner muscles tightened around him and he groaned loudly into our kiss, his lips sliding lusciously from my mouth, across my cheek and to my ear where he whispered, "Your pussy likes me."

God, he really knew how to talk dirty. And he sounded so pleased with himself.

He bent to suck my nipple, swirling his tongue in a circle then giving it a little bite.

I whimpered. "J-Julian."

"I love how my name sounds on your sexy mouth." He laved attention on the other breast, hand reaching up to grip my neck. His fingertips dug in as his thrusts quickened. I was mesmerised.

Was he going to come?

Julian gathered my hair in his fist and gave a little tug. I emitted a startled moan, the pain he gave mixing with the pleasure. Goose bumps covered my skin when he kissed my lips, softly, sweetly, then came with a whispered, raspy, "*Fuck.*"

He fell on top of me and my body savoured his hot, sweaty weight. His smelled like pure *man.* I swore you could bottle and sell the stuff.

He rolled us so we switched and I was on top of him. He was still trying to catch his breath when he asked, "Can you go again?"

I giggled. "You're insatiable."

He smirked. "Something like that."

"Just...give me a moment."

His deep chuckle vibrated through my body as his arms came around me, hugging tight. "That good, huh?"

"Good is too tame a word," I said, suddenly shy.

His hand sunk into my hair, gently stroking. "Compliments like that are always welcome."

"I can't believe we just did that."

His ran his nose along the side of my neck. "I'm not even done with you yet."

A grin tugged at my lips. "You're aren't?"

His smile was devilish. "Not by a long shot."

"You have a very impressive sexual appetite, Mr. Fairchild."

"It's a good thing, too," he purred. "I have so much to teach you."

He flipped us again, lowered his head between my legs and proceeded to give me my second orgasm of the night, this time with his mouth.

Eighteen
Ellen

I was…changed.

In the space of a night, I'd shed some form of chrysalis. However, unlike a butterfly, it wasn't evident on the surface, but rather deep under my skin. The fact that I could share myself like that with someone, expose the most vulnerable parts of myself, felt liberating in a way nothing ever had before.

And it was all because of Julian.

I didn't leave his bed until late afternoon the next day. His hunger for me didn't seem to abate. He made love to me in all the ways I'd been missing out on these past years, and my body was completely and totally spent. It was also waking up, unfurling like a newly sprouted flower.

My feelings grew, just like I feared they would.

"Don't leave yet. I want to fuck you one last time."

Julian lay in bed, the cover coming to his midriff, his gorgeous chest and abdomen exposed.

"I can't. I have a book to write," I resisted, getting dressed. It was nice to be able to say that now. All our secrets were finally out. Absently, I wondered if Rose and Damon had heard us last night (and this morning), and colour stained my cheeks.

"What's that?" Julian asked with interest, rising from the bed to circle me. "Have you gone shy on me again?"

"No, I just…" A breathy sigh came out as he ran his hand down my spine. "I really do need to work today."

He tutted softly. "Too bad. I was looking forward to coming inside you again."

I buried my head in his shoulder, falling into him. His dirty words made me weak. "You could come over later," I suggested shyly.

"No," he said. "You come here. I've quite enjoyed having you in my bed."

I shivered and glanced at his mussed sheets, the ones we'd spent half the night shagging on. His gaze followed mine, his expression hot. Tenderly, he stroked my hair away from my face. When he looked at me like that, all melty soft eyes, it was hard to think straight.

Butterflies invaded my stomach. *He enjoyed having me in his bed?* The way he said it made me feel like he was trying to tell me something without saying the words.

You're important to me, Ellen.

I pressed a kiss to his neck and he made a pleasured sound in the back of his throat. "In that case, I'll try to get done early so I can come over."

"Rose and Damon will be attending a premiere tonight. So we won't need to stay quiet this time," he went on devilishly.

If last night was his version of quiet, then I trembled to think what he'd be like when he let loose.

He kissed me then, a promise of what was to come. It was difficult to drag myself away, but I eventually managed. On the short walk home, I wondered about our arrangement. Neither of us had brought it up, and the sex had been completely spontaneous, but was it still part of his services? It didn't feel that way. It felt private, intimate, but how was I to know if that wasn't how he was with all his clients? It was his job to make them feel special, after all.

Confused, tired, and totally spent, I changed into pyjamas as soon as I got to the house. That was the perk of working from home, you didn't need to get dressed if you didn't want to. I'd just finished making a sandwich, about to sit down and make another dent in my WIP, when my phone rang. I smiled when I saw Nick's name on the screen. My brother had made "Havana" by Camila Cabello his signature ringtone because apparently, she was his ideal woman.

So original.

"Hi, Nick, how are you?" I answered, lifting the phone to my ear and taking a bite of my sandwich.

"What are you eating? It sounds delicious."

"How can you determine deliciousness based on sound? That's nonsensical."

"It's a skill you acquire working in a café," he quipped. "Anyway, I just called to see if you're all set for the Red Wedding at the end of the month."

I chuckled. "You think it'll be that bad?"

"Shayla's opted for a red colour scheme for the reception. She wanted to go for something different since this is her second marriage. What did you think I meant?" he replied playfully. I rolled my eyes.

"Right. Well, I'm ready for it. As ready as I can be."

"Are you staying at my place or Dad's? My sofa bed's yours if you need it."

I sighed. "No, I'll stay at Dad's. Your sofa bed is a torture contraption."

"I know. Cameron always refuses to stay over because of it. It'll never be replaced."

"Now why didn't I think of that? He'd been complaining about the mattress in my guest room for ages, so I bought a new one just to satisfy him."

"That's because you, my dear Ellen, are a soft touch. You need to take a leaf out of my book."

"I'm sure there's a devious streak inside of me somewhere," I replied, pausing before I went on. "Do you think Dad's happy with her? Shayla, I mean?"

I heard him blow out a breath. "Yeah, I think he's happy. As happy as I've ever seen him. I know Shayla can come across a little vacuous, but she's actually good for him, Ellen. You don't see it because you're never here, but he smiles all the time now."

Something in my heart clenched. It was true that our Dad didn't smile very often, but I'd always considered it a part of his stoic demeanour. He was a quiet man. And I trusted Nick, so it was a relief to hear him say that Shayla was good for him. I knew we liked to joke around about her, but we weren't the ones marrying her. If she made Dad happy, then that was the main thing.

"Sometimes I can't believe she's the first person he's been with since Mum," I whispered.

"Neither of us have ever really been in love, Els. We don't know what it's like to lose the love of our lives like Dad did. That leaves a big mark on a person."

"I'm twenty-nine and you're thirty-two. Isn't it sad that we've never been in love?"

"Hey! Our day will come, you mark my words. I'm hopeful," Nick said.

"And what about Cameron? Is he still being an arsehole to every woman who tries to date him?"

"Pretty much. Sometimes I think it makes them like him even more."

"We need to go to siblings' therapy or something," I joked.

"I'm game if you are."

"Oh, man, that would be so awful."

Nick chuckled. "Right?"

I blew out a breath. "Anyway, I better go. I have work to do."

"Oh yeah? What's Sasha's final adventure going to be? Personally, I'm holding out for her to get stranded on a desert island with a sarcastic Michael Douglas type."

"That's not a bad idea. I miss that trope so much. Someone needs to bring it back."

"Yes, you!" Nick enthused, and I laughed. He always had a way of cheering me up. "Okay, go write, and I'll see you at the Red Wedding."

"You really need to stop calling it that."

"Nope, it's stuck in my head now. Sorry."

When we hung up, I checked my emails, seeing one from Daniel. I got a case of the nervous flutters when I saw it was about the book signing I'd agreed to. Now that it was so close, I was having cold feet. I looked across the room, where one of my wigs hung over the back of a chair. Somehow, it felt like a step backward to go as Elodie. Julian was pushing me to be myself more and more, and it made me feel good on the inside.

When you kept secrets, there was this constant brick in the pit of your stomach, made solely of worry and dread. It was liberating to feel that brick start to dissipate. Telling Julian that I wrote books for a living had also felt amazingly freeing. The look of respect and admiration in his eyes, knowing I'd achieved something few managed, was an addictive feeling.

Maybe being Ellen wasn't such a scary prospect after all.

***

Three weeks went by. Julian and I fell into a regular routine of sleepovers. Sometimes he came to my place, other times I went to his. Every day I fell deeper under his spell, but he

229

seemed to be just as enthralled by me. It was still a little hard to get my head around.

One day he showed up at the bookshop. I was the only one on shift. With a wolfish look, he flicked the sign on the door to 'closed', took my hand and led me to the storeroom at the back. He held my gaze and fucked me against the wall until my knees were weak.

Another day, I decided to take a chance and went over to his place. He answered the door wearing an open shirt, the fly of his jeans undone. For a second, my heart stopped beating, because he looked like he'd just been rolling around in bed with someone. However, when he saw me, his expression smouldered, and he dragged me to his bedroom. There was nobody there.

"I was just thinking about you," he confessed.

"Oh?"

His gaze darkened. "And touching myself."

Something I'd learned about Julian. He had an insatiable sexual appetite, and he'd awakened the same in me. Tiny little things could arouse me; the swish of fabric against my skin, a cool breeze tickling the back of my neck.

"Do you think of me when you touch yourself, too, Ellen?" he asked in a quiet, sensual voice. He palmed my breast over my top and I ran my hands down his bare abdomen. I loved the ripple of his muscular form, the heat that emanated from him whenever we touched.

"Yes." My whispered confession lit a spark in him and he lowered himself between my legs. Going down on me seemed to be a favourite of his. He told me it wasn't something he often did with clients, and though it reminded me that what we were doing was still a business arrangement, it did make me feel wanted.

And feeling wanted was a new sensation for me.

I'd been thinking about returning the favour for a while, but I'd never given a blow job before. I even looked up some tutorials online, but the right moment never came, and I was too nervous, worried I'd do it wrong and either embarrass myself or end up hurting him.

Julian's sexual MO seemed to be all about pleasuring the woman, which wasn't surprising given his job, but it meant I never really got a chance to explore his body like I wanted to.

The day after I showed up at his place, I found Julian on my doorstep. I'd paid a visit to the corner shop, and when I returned, there he was.

"Missed you," he said, sitting on the steps that led to my door.

I had butterflies thinking of him missing me. He pressed a kiss to my lips and I led him inside.

"I've never asked who painted your walls," Julian commented as he followed me into the kitchen.

"Oh, I painted them," I replied while I put away my purchases.

His gaze went from the mural by the birdcage to me in disbelief. "Seriously?"

I shrugged. "I've always loved to paint. It's my second favourite pastime after writing. I actually considered going to art school, but then chose English Literature at Cambridge instead. I'm a passable artist. My real talent was always writing, making up stories."

"I'd say you're a bit more than passable, Ellen," Julian said, his eyes still on the mural. "You're a woman of hidden talents. Cambridge, eh?"

"You should've seen me the day I got my acceptance letter. I don't think I'd ever been happier. It was too bad I didn't get more involved in college life. I mostly hid in my dorm room and studied, read books."

Julian's expression was playful. He came and placed his hands on my hips, gazing down at me. "If I were there, I would've lured you out."

"Oh, really. And how might you have done that?"

His hands moved down over my backside, lightly squeezing before he bent to capture my lips in a hot, languid kiss. He proceeded to show me exactly how he might've lured me out of said dorm room. I couldn't believe this was my life now, a series of sexy, seductive interludes throughout what used to be a pretty uneventful work week.

The day before my book signing arrived and I went into a bit of a meltdown. I hadn't told anyone I was doing it, not my dad or my brothers, not even Julian. If I had told Dad, he'd want to come and support me, but somehow that just felt like more pressure. Besides, I was on a knife's edge over whether or not to cancel.

But then I kept thinking about the five hundred people who'd bought tickets. I repeat, *five hundred people*! I couldn't let them down. The idea made me feel sick to my stomach. No, I would do this, even if it killed me, but I could definitely use some help.

Julian's phone rang for only a few seconds before he answered. "Hello, Ellen." When he spoke to me, his voice was always so intimate. It sent a tremor through me every time

"I need you."

His tone heated. "I'll be there in twenty minutes."

"No!" I blurted. "I mean, not like that. Well, yes like that. But right now, I need you for another reason."

Now he was all business. "Say no more. I'll be as quick as I can."

I was already pacing the hallway by the time Julian knocked on my door. I opened it quickly and he stepped inside. He wore a white T-shirt, black jeans, and a Fedora with a green feather. I loved his quirky dress sense. Ever since I created Elodie, I'd become addicted to online shopping and finding unique pieces. Julian's style was effortless.

"I'm here for whatever you need," he said.

I inhaled a deep breath, met his gaze, then exhaled. "I have a book signing tomorrow." Even saying the words made my stomach twist with dread.

His eyebrows jumped. "You do?"

I nodded, chewed on my thumbnail and led him into the living room. I sat on the couch and Julian lowered to sit beside me. "A couple of weeks ago, I impulsively went to meet with my agent, Daniel." A pause as I eyed him. "I went dressed as Elodie."

Julian absorbed what I said. "That was brave of you."

"I know. We'd only ever communicated through emails and over the phone. For years he's been trying to convince me to do an appearance. He finally wore me down."

"And now you're thinking of backing out?" he guessed.

"Well, yes, but I can't. It's being held in one of the biggest bookstores in London. There are five hundred people coming to see me. I can't disappoint them. Though I'll probably do that anyway by freaking out during the event."

Julian took both my hands in his. "Ellen, what do you want to do?"

I blinked at him. "I want to do the signing."

233

His mouth curved into a smile. "Then you'll do it."

His confidence gave me confidence, but my words still came out shaky. "I n-need to figure out what to wear."

"I like your navy dress," he suggested.

I shook my head. "No, that's not an Elodie outfit."

"I know that. I don't think you should go as Elodie. I think you should go as Ellen."

I sat back, flustered. "I've already met Daniel dressed as Elodie. I mean, he knows my name is Ellen, but aside from that—"

"So what? I'm assuming you make this Daniel a lot of money. He's not going to drop you just because you wore a wig and a sexy outfit the first time you met."

Well, when he put it like that... Daniel might look at me funny, think I was a bit of an oddball, but he wouldn't drop me as a client. Like Julian said, my books were too lucrative.

"You don't want your first public appearance to be a lie, Ellen. Then you'll just have to keep on lying, and before you know it, you'll be drowning in it." He leaned forward and pressed a chaste kiss to my cheek. "Besides, Ellen is a beautiful, intelligent, funny, and kind woman. Why wouldn't you want to be her?"

"How do you always know just the right thing to say?"

He kissed me again, this time a little less chaste. "I just know you now. We've spent a lot of time together these last few weeks and it's helped me understand you more, your motivations. I can see you want to be you, not Elodie. You don't want to hide, but you just need someone to give you that final push."

And push me he did. The next day, I tried on numerous outfits, several different hairstyles and an array of makeup choices, unable to settle on anything. Julian stayed with me the entire time for moral support. I swear he had the patience of a saint.

I flopped down onto the bed, exasperated. "That's it, I give up."

After sitting on the armchair in the corner of my room, watching me try on outfits for the better part of an hour, Julian finally stood. Without a word, he picked up a pair of jeans, a sleeveless white blouse, and a pale grey cardigan.

His instruction was simple. "Wear these."

I glanced at the offered clothes. "But they aren't very—"

"They're you. You'll be comfortable in them, they'll cover up your very beautiful body, and that's all that matters. Now go put them on."

I huffed a breath. "Dammit, you're always right."

When we arrived at the bookstore where the signing was being held, there was already a line down the street. I swallowed tightly, and Julian squeezed my hand. "You're going to be fine. I'll be right here beside you the entire time."

His reassuring words soothed me. Since nobody knew what E.S. Grant looked like, I was able to walk right into the shop without anyone batting an eyelash. I saw Daniel waiting just inside, glancing at his watch as though worried I wasn't going to show. Just like the readers outside, my agent didn't recognise me without my costume. I walked up to him, Julian at my side, and said, "Hi, Daniel."

He glanced at me. "Do I know y..." his words trailed off as he frowned, squinted, then asked, "Ellen?"

I nodded sheepishly. "Yes, I, um, dyed my hair since we last met."

His attention wandered over me, probably noting that my hair didn't look dyed, but natural. It was the only excuse I could think of.

"But your eyes—"

"I wear coloured contacts sometimes. Obviously not today, since I have my glasses on." My gut tightened. I worried he was going to reject me, say he didn't believe me and order security to take me out of there.

Instead he scratched his head, lifted an eyebrow and exhaled a breath. "I have questions, but for now we need to get you ready. Come on, there's an office out back." Daniel's gaze went to Julian, as though waiting for an introduction.

"This is my friend, Julian," I said. "He's here for moral support."

"Pleased to meet you," Julian put in.

"And you." They shook hands and Daniel led us to the office.

"Did you bring an excerpt to read?" he asked, and I nodded, my throat running dry at the thought of doing a reading, not to mention a question and answer session afterward.

"Good," Daniel went on. "You'll also notice a few members of the press out there. The book world is very excited to finally meet E.S. Grant."

"Fabulous," I deadpanned.

Daniel chuckled and patted me on the shoulder. "You're going to do just fine. Everyone's dying to see you."

I noticed Julian frowning at Daniel's hand, where it rested on my shoulder a little longer than necessary. My agent was totally oblivious, but my stomach still flipped at the possessiveness radiating from Julian.

"Okay, I'll be back in about fifteen minutes. There's a coffee machine in the corner, so help yourselves." Daniel gave me a kind parting smile and then he left.

Julian sat down on an office swivel chair. "Your agent has a crush on you. I'd think it was cute if it didn't make me so jealous."

I screwed up my face. "You're imagining things. He thinks I'm a weirdo since I've turned up looking nothing like the woman he originally met." The idea of him being jealous sent a flutter through me.

"Ellen, I know a crush when I see one. And Daniel's definitely got one," Julian replied, swinging around on the chair, deceptively casual.

I ignored him and went to make coffee, hoping the caffeine might pep me up a little. When I moved to walk by him, he caught my wrist, rubbing his thumb along the delicate inside. "Ignore me. I'm being an idiot."

"It's fine. I'm just…"

"Nervous?"

I exhaled. "Yes."

"You've got this, Ellen, and I've got you, I promise. I've had you to myself these past few weeks, and now I'll be sharing you with the five hundred people out there. It's bringing out my selfish streak."

My heart thrummed. There was so much I wanted to say, but it all got stuck in my throat. "Thank you for being here. And for everything."

Our gazes held a moment before there was a knock on the door. One of the store workers ducked her head in. She wore a green polo shirt and a name tag that read 'Michelle'. She also held a copy of *Good Girl, Bad Lady* to her chest. She looked from me to Julian shyly, finally deciding that I was the author. Julian definitely didn't look like someone who spent the majority of his time weaving tales on a laptop, though maybe it was just my glasses. There was no correlation, but they always made a person look more bookish.

"Sorry for barging in, I was just wondering if I could get you to sign my book before the event starts."

I stared at her, wide-eyed, opened my mouth, shut it again. I'd never met a fan before, so this was all new. I wasn't sure who was more nervous, her or me. Finally, Julian came to the rescue. He stood and took the book from her. "E.S. would be more than happy to sign your book." His gaze lowered to her name tag. "Would you like her to make it out to you, Michelle?"

She smiled gratefully. "Yes, please."

Julian flicked to the title page, picked a pen up off the desk and handed me the book. "Sign away."

My hand shook as I pressed the pen to paper. When I was done signing, I forced myself to walk across the room and hand it back to her. "There you go. It was l-lovely to meet you, Michelle."

She flushed bright pink. "And you! Thank you. Thank you so much."

With that, she scurried out and I looked back to Julian. His expression was smug. "Now, was that so bad? Were you struck down by the Gods?"

I shoved him in the shoulder. "Fine. You were right. *Again.*"

Twenty minutes later, the bookshop was full, everybody waiting in the large event area for me to come out. I tucked my hair behind my ear while Julian took my hand and gave it a firm squeeze, then pulled me to him. He hugged me tightly as he whispered in my ear, "Remember, everyone out there adores you, and so do I."

We broke apart and I sent him a look of gratitude. He had no idea that five hundred people adoring me mattered much less than him adoring me. I was so lost to him now, trying to turn back was futile. And I really couldn't have done any of this without him.

I mustered all the calm I had in me, running the speech I'd prepared through my head as the bookshop manager made the introduction. I spotted Daniel across the way; he smiled encouragingly and gave me two thumbs up.

"We're honoured and thrilled to have her with us here today and to be hosting her very first public appearance. Without further ado, I give you E.S. Grant."

The crowd erupted with excited applause. A lump formed in my throat, my palms dripping with sweat. Julian leaned close to murmur, "It might help if you imagine them all naked."

An involuntary chuckle escaped me, the humour exactly what I needed right then. He kissed my cheek and ushered me forward. "Go on, knock 'em dead, tiger."

I laughed again, shaking my head as I inhaled a deep breath and turned to face the audience. I could do this. These people read my books. They'd come here to see me. They were my tribe.

A small measure of calm filled me as I stepped out onto the stage. The clapping grew louder, but it still didn't drown out the sound of my heart hammering in my ears. Several cameras flashed from the press in front. I blinked, the white light momentarily blinding. Guess there was no turning back now.

An armchair and a small table were set up centre stage, the pages of my excerpt sitting on the table. I flexed my hand, something of a nervous tick, and walked toward the chair. The bookshop manager came and handed me a microphone and I held it to my mouth. My gaze scanned the crowd, hundreds of faces staring back at me; eager, excited, smiling faces.

I opened my mouth to speak, to say hello, thank them for coming, but my voice failed me. Tears sprung in my eyes and my entire body froze. My muscles felt like lead and all I wanted to do was run right off that stage.

This was it. I was choking. My worst fears became real.

Nineteen
Julian

Shit.

She was choking out there.

Ellen stood in the middle of the stage, eyes wide as saucers, microphone held to her mouth, but no words came out.

Her agent, Daniel, appeared at my side. "What's wrong with her?"

"She's never been on a stage before, and certainly not with so many people looking at her. She's freaking out."

His brow furrowed. "Should I go get her?"

He made a move, but I stayed him with a hand. "Wait, give her a minute."

Come on, Ellen. You can do this. You're strong. Find your inner strength and use it.

Several more seconds of silence fell, and I almost gave up, but then, miraculously, Ellen spoke. It was music to my ears.

"H-hello, thank you all for coming today."

I exhaled in relief. I hadn't noticed how tense I'd been. Hadn't realised just how much I wanted her to succeed.

"As you know, this is my first ever book signing, so I apologise in advance if I mess up. This is all pretty terrifying."

There were a few affectionate laughs from the audience. They loved her already, in spite of her awkwardness, or maybe because of it. Sasha Orlando, who was more or less Elodie, was a role model for these people. Maybe they all felt a little like Ellen on the inside and

241

yearned to be more like Elodie on the outside. More confident, fearless, and brave.

She cleared her throat. "So, um, I have a little exclusive excerpt to read for you. It's from *Ampersand*, the final book in the series, which will be coming out next year." There were cheers but also noises of sadness from the audience that the series was ending. Ellen lifted the papers from the table in front of her and started to read.

"Chapter One. Toby sat across the desk from me, hands clasped together, glasses resting almost on the tip of his nose..."

The more she read, the more confident she became. By the time she finished, and the manager came back out to moderate the question and answer session, she was almost taking it in stride. She fumbled her words once or twice, but she didn't choke again. When the final question was answered, and it was time for the signing part of the event, she came off stage and ran straight into my arms. With her face nestled in the crook of my neck, she sighed in relief. "I can't believe I got through that."

I pressed my lips to her hair, inhaling her scent. "I was certain you were about to do a runner at the beginning."

Her voice was bashful. "Yeah I, um, took your advice and pictured them all naked."

My smile grew as I gazed down at her. "I knew it. Just like the bend and snap, it works every time."

Her lips twitched. "I feel like I should apologize for defiling them, especially the people in the front row."

I chuckled and pulled her into a tighter hug. "I'm so proud of you."

"I couldn't have done this without you, Julian. Meeting you, it changed me. You've helped me break out of my shell."

And you've stolen my heart.

The thought knocked me for six. These past weeks, I'd grown closer and closer to Ellen. I let her in my bed, and resultingly, deep under my skin. *And I wanted her to be mine.*

When we went out socialising, I hated it when other men flirted with her. Every part of me rebelled against the idea of wanting to own someone because it went against everything I believed in regard to sex and monogamy. I believed people should be free to explore their sexualities without being confined by backward, outdated rules. But with Ellen, I wasn't interested in sharing, and funnily enough, I wasn't interested in being with anyone else either.

Was this what I'd felt was missing, what I'd been yearning for? Monogamy? One person to share my life with?

"Come with me to Devon this weekend," she said, breaking me from my thoughts.

"Devon?"

She nodded, looking up at me hopefully. "My dad's getting married. I wasn't going to bring a date, but…I don't want to go without you."

Her dad was getting married? This was the first time she'd mentioned it. I knew her mother died tragically when she was just a toddler, but I assumed her father already remarried at some point over the years.

I stroked a hand down her hair and smiled softly. "I wouldn't miss it. Now go, your loving public awaits."

I sat next to her as she signed book after book, smiled for pictures and made small talk with her readers. Sure, she had a few awkward or nervous moments, but she got through it. I felt like a proud parent, but a part of me was also sad. She might not know it yet, but Ellen was out in the world now. Soon enough, she wouldn't need me anymore.

Ironically, it now seemed that *I* needed her.

My phone buzzed with a text and I pulled it from my pocket.

Rose: *WTF!? Ellen is E.S. Grant! Why didn't you tell me?*

I chuckled to myself as I wrote a reply.

Julian: *It wasn't my secret to tell. Anyway, how do you know already? Her first appearance literally *just* happened.*

Rose: *I'm signed up for Google alerts. People are already posting pics online. Thought I spotted you in the background!*

Julian: *You really are a superfan.*

Rose: *Will you ask if she'll sign my collection the next time we come to London?*

Julian: Sure.

Rose: *Thanks! You're the best friend ever. E.S. Grant! I still can't get my head around it :-O*

* * *

The train journey to Devon was almost three hours long. Ellen had a glow about her, and I knew it was a result of her successful book signing. She sat across from me, tapping away on her laptop

"What are you staring at?" she asked, sensing my attention.

I smirked and folded my arms. "You. You're glowing."

She rolled her eyes. "Shut up."

"It's true though. Own it, girlfriend."

She laughed, her eyes on her laptop screen before they flicked to mine. Her voice was quieter now, more intimate. "If I'm glowing, then it's all your doing."

My only response was a beaming smile. She was transformed, and I adored the change in her. It was so satisfying to see her blossom.

"So," I went on. "What's the itinerary for the weekend?"

Ellen paused typing. "Um, tomorrow evening there's a dinner for friends and family. Then the wedding's all-day Saturday, then home on Sunday."

"I can't wait to meet your relatives. Do you have any embarrassing aunts or uncles I should know about?"

She thought on it a second. "My brother Cameron might be rude to you, but he's rude to everyone so don't take it personally. Also, my aunt June can get a little handsy with the younger men after she's had a few gins, just FYI. I think that's it."

"Rude brother. Handsy aunt. Got it."

Her light chuckle hit me right in the chest. I loved that sound.

When we arrived at her dad's house, Ellen used her own key to let us in. It was a quaint two-storey cottage on the edge of the seaside town of Torquay, also known as the English Riviera. Her childhood home was a short walk from the beach and the July weather made the place even more picturesque.

Growing up here must've been starkly different to my own childhood. Mum and I rented a carousel of grotty, single bedroom flats, no garden, no view. Comparing the two was like a study in opposites. No wonder Ellen wrote so many books. This was a place that fuelled the imagination.

Ellen led me into the kitchen where her dad sat reading a newspaper. He was a bespectacled, grey-haired man, with the same kind brown eyes as his daughter.

"Els! I didn't hear you come in," he said, standing to pull her into a hug. "It's so good to see you. I've missed you so much."

He squeezed her tight, and something about his affection for her gave me a pang in my chest. When I went to visit Mum, she never greeted me like this. If she were having a good day, she'd give a small smile, a bad day and all you got was a derisive nod, barely any eye contact.

"Dad, this is my, um..."

Seeing she was at a loss as to how to explain our relationship, I decided to take one for the team. And okay, perhaps I was also being a little opportunistic. "I'm Julian. Ellen's new boyfriend."

Ellen's eyes widened, and her dad appeared surprised. She obviously hadn't told him she was bringing a friend, certainly not a boyfriend. He gave me a quick once over then held his hand out for a shake. "Julian. It's good to meet you. I wish I could say my daughter has told me all about you, but well, she hasn't." He shot her an accusing look.

I laughed cordially. "That's quite all right. Ellen and I have only known each other for a few months, but I'm honoured she invited me this weekend. You have a lovely home."

"Thank you," he replied, looking back to Ellen. "Shayla is staying at the hotel tonight, and I have to run a few errands this evening, but you two get settled and order in some food."

"Sure, Dad," she replied, seeming a little shy after I introduced myself as her boyfriend. It needed to be done though. There was no way I was being friend-zoned for the weekend and sleeping on the couch.

Ellen led me upstairs and I grinned when I saw her childhood bedroom. The walls were pale yellow, flower printed bed sheets, and cornflower blue curtains. There weren't any embarrassing posters of boy bands. Instead, one entire wall was lined with bookshelves, and there was a framed movie poster of *A Room with a View*.

Ellen saw where I was looking. "It was my favourite film when I was a teenager."

I walked around her room. Directly out her window was the sea. She definitely had a room with a view.

She sat on the edge of the bed, chewing on her lip. "What are you thinking?"

"I was just thinking, I can't imagine ever having a bad day living here."

"It's pretty peaceful."

I shot her a cheeky wink. "Tell the truth. Did you ever go skinny-dipping on the beach when you were a teenager?"

She shook her head. "I was the most boring kid on the planet. When I went to the beach, I usually brought a book."

I dropped down beside her. "You never went out with your friends, drank too much cider, and snogged a boy who was no good for you?"

"Nope. I spent most weekends with my dad or my brothers."

"Well, that just won't do," I tutted and stood, holding out my hand to her.

"What's going on?"

"You're taking me out and giving me a tour of your hometown. Then we're going to have greasy fish and chips for dinner before buying a bottle of cheap cider to drink on the beach."

She didn't look convinced. "That sounds..."

"Marvellous. I know. Now, come on."

We spent an hour walking around Torquay. Ellen pointed out places of interest before we stopped at a café. "My brother, Nick, works here. We can see if he's around. He might give us free coffee."

I gestured for her to lead the way. Inside there was a guy with the same curly brown hair as Ellen, but instead of brown eyes, his were blue. He was pouring a latte when he spotted her walk in, his smile wide and confident.

"Would you look what the cat dragged in," he called out.

"Thought I'd drop in and say hello."

"Come here and give me a hug, baby sis."

She went to him, and they embraced. I was so glad she had people who loved her this much. Again, my chest itched in a way no amount of scratching would soothe.

"Who's this?" he asked, eyes coming to me.

"I'm the new boyfriend," I replied.

"This is Julian," Ellen supplied, looking a little flushed at me dropping the boyfriend bomb again.

Nick looked me up and down, somewhat impressed, then gaped at Ellen. "*Whuuut?*"

Ellen slapped him on the shoulder. "Don't sound so shocked."

"Well, what do you expect? You tell me everything, and you never once mentioned a boyfriend. Nice to meet you, Julian, by the way."

"You, too. Ellen tells me you're the nice brother."

"Yep, you'll understand once you meet Cameron."

I laughed. "I'm looking forward to it."

"Come on and sit down. What can I get you both to drink?"

We spent a half an hour chatting with Nick, who apparently dropped out of college to backpack across Asia, before returning to his hometown to work as a barista and regale customers with tales of his travels. He was a delight, and I wondered how two siblings could be so different in countenance. If Nick was an open book, then Ellen was closed tight. She was coming out of her shell, sure, but it was still interesting to note the differences.

Her arm was linked through mine as we strolled along the beach. Just as I'd promised, we stopped for fish and chips, then paid a visit to the local off-licence for a bottle of cider. When we found a suitable spot, I took off my jacket, spread it out on the sand and gestured for her to sit. We drank in quiet, passing the bottle back and forth as we watched the tide go out.

"Tell me something about you I don't know yet," I said as I admired her profile. The sun was starting to go down, the dimming golden rays falling across her face, highlighting the smattering of freckles across her nose and cheeks.

"Like what?"

"What were you like at school?"

She took a swig of cider, staring off into the distance. "I was quiet, kept to myself. I had selective mutism up until the age of six. Most of my family put it down to Mum dying, but I was only two when that happened, so I'm not sure that's true."

"You never know. Things can affect us in strange ways when we're still developing." I'd heard of selective mutism before, but I didn't think it was a very common thing. It made sense for Ellen to have it, considering how shy she was.

"I guess so. Anyway, it was my curse from there on out. Even when I started talking, I was still unbearably shy. Socialising was almost a physical pain. I don't know how to describe it."

"Did you ever see a therapist?"

She shook her head. "My dad runs his own construction company. He's a man's man, doesn't really like to talk about feelings. I guess he thought my issues would resolve on their own. That sounds really bad, doesn't it?"

"Hey, you're looking at someone who definitely could've benefitted from therapy from an early age, too, but I barely knew what it was until I went to rehab."

"At least you got there eventually. It's just, the idea of sitting in a room and telling a stranger all my issues makes me break out in hives. It feels self-indulgent, like people have bigger problems, you know?"

I looked at her affectionately. "Everything is relative, Ellen."

She exhaled heavily. "I'm a mess."

"A hot mess though," I said, nudging her with my elbow. "And hotness is all that really matters in life, right?"

She laughed. "You're a goof."

"And you're gorgeous, tell me something else. You've achieved so much with your books, but what else do you aspire to?"

Ellen took a moment to think about it. "This might not sound very original, but I'd love to go travelling. I haven't been on a holiday since I was eighteen."

I frowned. "Why not?"

She lifted a shoulder and pursed her lips, like she felt awkward or embarrassed. "I guess I don't really have anyone to go with, and I've always been too afraid of travelling alone. Nick backpacked across Asia all by himself. He's very fearless in that way. I feel like travelling will make me a better writer. If I could see the world, experience other cultures, it would help me understand people better, portray their emotions and motivations more realistically on the page."

"It's true that travel broadens the mind," I said. "But you shouldn't feel like you need someone to go with you. Then again, if you're not comfortable going alone, you shouldn't feel obliged to do that either. Sure, whenever I'm in the mood to get away, I just go. But like I always say, it's different strokes for different folks."

"Maybe I'll be brave enough someday."

I held her gaze. "I've no doubt you will."

A moment passed before she spoke again. "You're very good at giving advice, do you know that?"

"That's only because I've made so many mistakes."

She ran her finger through the sand, making a pretty swirl shape. I stared at her lips, wanting to kiss her. "Come here," I murmured and reached out to grab her chin.

She shifted out of reach. "I'm not kissing you with cider breath, Julian, go away."

I grinned deviously and came at her. "Oh, yes you are."

She squealed and rolled to the side. I crawled on top of her and laid a big, wet slobbery kiss on her lips.

"You're awful," she complained, unable to help her laugher.

I gazed down at her, my chest too full. "I'm the best and you know it."

Her expression softened as she whispered. "Yeah, I think you might be."

Twenty
Ellen

Parties were not an easy thing for me. As I got ready for Dad and Shayla's pre-wedding dinner, my nerves kicked in, just like they always did. I was going to have to see all my relatives, meet Shayla's, smile and make small talk all evening. After the book signing back in London, my 'interacting with people' reserves were almost dried up

I was just glad Julian would be with me. In this new world where I didn't dress up, but rather was brave enough to be myself, he was a comfort blanket I feared letting go of.

Last night, we got drunk on the beach, then came home and passed out in bed. I wasn't even disappointed that we didn't have sex, because it was the most fun I'd had in ages. Just the two of us, hanging out, talking and being silly together.

Again, the place in my heart that he'd claimed expanded.

Julian was so open and playful, so loving even though he'd grown up in a way that should've hardened him. I got the sense that his relationship with Rose, the way she loved him like he was her own flesh and blood, was the one thing that saved him from himself.

I put on the bright yellow cocktail dress and studied myself in the full-length mirror by my bed. I'd originally bought it for Elodie, but maybe she wasn't the only one who could pull it off. Maybe Julian was right, and Elodie was me just as much as I was Ellen.

I pinned my hair up in a loose bun, making an extra effort with my makeup. Julian emerged from the bathroom in a towel, having just showered. We spent most of the day lounging around and watching TV. It had been bliss.

"Cameron's picking us up soon, so you better hurry," I said as he came to stand behind me. I stood by the mirror, putting on my earrings. He bent and pressed a kiss to the hollow of my neck and a tremor went through me.

"Don't worry. I won't take long," he murmured, then went to get dressed. Sometimes even the way he spoke turned me on.

Julian really knew how to pull off a shirt and slacks combo. He was going formal tonight and my thighs clenched at the sight of him.

"Quit looking at me like that or we really will be late," he warned, eyes hot as they wandered over my dress. "You look amazing, by the way. Channelling Elodie are we?"

I smirked. "Maybe."

"Well, she looks good on you."

A horn honked outside, and I knew it was Cameron. He wasn't one for making the effort to get out and knock. I slipped on my heels when we reached the bottom of the stairs, then opened the front door. Cam's Volkswagen sat idling by the kerb, Nick in the passenger seat. I took a deep breath and held Julian's hand as we walked over and got inside.

"Swit-swoo, look at you all gussied up!" Nick exclaimed. "I think you're a good influence on her, Julian."

"I try my best."

"I'm Cameron," my other brother put in, eyeing Julian suspiciously through his overhead mirror.

"Hello, it's great to meet you," Julian nodded. Cameron only grunted in response then put the car into gear.

"Don't mind Mr. Congeniality over here. He's in a mood because Shayla's been trying to set him up with her niece," Nick said.

"It's a bit incestuous, if you ask me," Cam grumped, eyes on the road.

"You haven't even met her yet. She could look like Jessica Alba for all you know."

"She could also look like Ann Widdicombe. I'd rather not take the chance."

Nick rolled his eyes. "If she's her niece, then she's hardly going to be as old as Ann Widdicombe."

Cam blew out an irritated breath. "A young version of her then."

"I don't know," Julian put in. "Old Anny was kinda cute in her day. I bet she loves taking charge in the bedroom, too. Those conservatives are always a kinky sort."

Nick let out a loud laugh. "I like your boyfriend, Ellen. He's funny."

Cameron remained unimpressed as he focused back on driving. When we arrived at the hotel where the ceremony would take place tomorrow, Julian came around to my side of the car to help me out.

"And a gentleman, too," Nick commented with a wink. "I think this one's a keeper."

"What do you think?" Julian whispered in my ear. "Want to keep me?"

I swallowed thickly, not sure how to respond. I shivered when he pressed his hand to my lower back and guided me inside. A private dining room had been reserved, and Dad and Shayla stood by the door, welcoming everyone in.

Shayla wore a fitted burgundy dress that came to just over the knee, her dark hair styled in wavy curls. She was very attractive, not just for her age, but in general. Dad had done well for himself, but then again, so had she. My dad was always known as a catch around our town, but no woman had been able to turn his head until Shayla came along. She was ambitious and headstrong, perhaps a little vain, but also savvy. I figured she wasn't all bad, especially since she knew about my books and didn't tell anyone. She was loyal to Dad. If he asked her to keep a secret, she kept it. At least that was something.

She was a little taken aback when she saw me, since every other time we'd been together I wore baggy jeans and cardigans. "Ellen, you look beautiful. I hardly recognised you."

Dad frowned, seeming to nudge her a little. She coughed, realising how that sounded. "I mean, you've always been beautiful, but that dress is simply stunning on you." She came forward and kissed me on each cheek.

"Uh, thanks. I'd like you to meet Julian," I said.

Her eyes lit up when she saw him. Even though she was marrying my dad tomorrow, I didn't blame her. It was the effect Julian had on most women and Shayla was no different.

"Oh, yes, the boyfriend. Greg told me. I'm so happy to meet you, Julian," she said, giving him the same kisses on either cheek. She studied him as she withdrew, her expression thoughtful. "Do you know what? You look so familiar, have we met before?"

Something in my gut tightened. *Had* they met before? Since Shayla moved here from London, it was definitely possible.

"I don't believe so," Julian replied cordially. "I think I'd remember a face as lovely as yours."

She tittered in response, and we went to take our seats. Something about the incident niggled at me though. When we were seated, I leaned close to Julian. "What was all that about?"

He frowned and fiddled with his place setting. "I'm not sure. We might've crossed paths, but I don't recognise her."

"Oh. Well, you probably just remind her of someone."

"Probably," Julian agreed.

After that one speed bump, the rest of the evening went without a hitch. I managed to make small talk with my cousin, Chloe, who sat on the other side of me, while Julian chatted with Nick. I knew those two would get along.

When we got home, we had the house to ourselves, since Dad was staying at the hotel. He and Shayla were sleeping in separate rooms, for fear of bad luck, but my future stepmother didn't want to take the risk that he'd be late. Since we only lived a twenty-minute drive away, that wasn't very likely, but I got the impression she wanted everything to be perfect.

I stepped into my bedroom and Julian closed the door then came up behind me. He pulled my hair out of its bun, swept it over my shoulder then proceeded to pepper kisses along my neck. I sighed in pleasure and sank back into him. His arm wrapped around me, his hand pressing to the front of my stomach and bringing my bottom flush with his erection.

"I've wanted you all evening," he confessed, hand moving up. He pulled the front of my dress down and slipped his hand inside to fondle my breast. I arched my spine, circling my hips against his hard-on. He let out a deep, masculine groan then broke away.

I watched, breathless, as he pulled what appeared to be a blindfold from his bag. Next, he removed a small black box and presented it to me like a gift.

"For you," he said, mouth curving in a way that sent my pulse racing.

"What is it?" I asked, full of curiosity as I tore the box open. Inside was a bright pink dildo. I blinked, then glanced at him. He wore a sexy smile and I laughed.

"That is quite possibly the girliest dildo I've ever seen."

"I thought the inviting colour might make it less intimidating."

I stared at it, admittedly fascinated. "I've never used a sex toy before."

Julian's expression smouldered. "In that case, you're in for a treat."

He pushed me back onto the bed, pulled up my dress and yanked down my knickers. I was already wet when he flicked a switch and it started to buzz.

Well.

My throat went dry.

I squirmed when he settled between my legs and planted kisses along the inside of my thigh. I felt him press something into my hand and realised it was the dildo. He guided it to my sex; the vibration sparked through my nerve endings.

"Oh, my...*God,*" I breathed, undulating at the new sensation.

Julian took the blindfold and tied it around my head to cover my eyes. Everything went black, somehow heightening the feel of the dildo. He stripped me bare, kissing the tops of my breasts, my nipples, and my stomach. I felt his weight leave the bed, the swish of fabric as he undressed.

I continued to hold the dildo in place, but I didn't feel confident enough to move it. Even though I couldn't see him, Julian's gaze seared my skin. I knew he was watching me, drinking me in.

"Slide it inside," he gave a husky command.

My throat bobbed as I lowered the toy. I was so aroused it slipped right into me, and Julian emitted a raspy growl.

"You look incredible right now."

I moaned, instinctively moving it slowly in and out. Julian's weight returned to the bed. Softly, he pushed my hand away and took charge, pushing it in deeper, harder. My sighs filled the room as my head fell back. All I could hear were his masculine sounds of approval, all I could feel was him skilfully fucking me with the sex toy.

What new world was this?

It didn't even feel wrong to do this in my childhood bedroom. Everything with Julian felt right, so right it scared me. Emotions threatened to push to the surface when he pulled off the blindfold.

"This was a bad idea. I need to see your eyes," he said, taking my mouth in a passionate, hungry kiss. The dildo fell away when Julian pushed inside me. His hips moved in a hypnotic rhythm, hands moving between our bodies to rub my clit. I came quickly, harshly, and while he was still inside me.

My sex clenched around him and Julian spanked my thigh. His face was a picture of male need, as he pushed in and out, seeking his own release. "That's my girl."

The possession in his eyes hit me like a sledgehammer. It was only when he came that I realised he hadn't been wearing a condom. I gasped as the hot, silky feel of him filled me up. His body fell on mine, totally spent. Several moments of silence passed between us before he swore under his breath. He'd clearly come to the same realisation as I did.

I rubbed his back soothingly. "It's okay."

"I'm so fucking sorry, Ellen. I don't know what came over me."

My voice was gentle. "It's okay, I promise. I'm not on any contraception, but I can get the morning-after pill. It's not a big deal."

He moved away from me to sit on the edge of the bed, head in his hands, internally berating himself.

"It's not okay. It was reckless."

"Julian, nobody died. It was both our faults." I reached out to touch him, but he shook me off.

"Ellen, I'm a sex worker, do you understand what that means?"

All of a sudden, my gut dropped. I peered at him questioningly. "Surely, you get tested?"

"Yes, I do, and I'm clean, but you don't know that. You need to be more careful."

"Julian, you're not just some man I picked up off the street. I know you and I trust you."

"You shouldn't be so trusting."

"Why not? You're clean. I'm clean. There's nothing else to worry about."

He stood now, looking down at me with such conflict and contrition. "I never do that," he said shamefully. "When it comes to protection, I don't ever let my guard down."

I stood too and came to wrap my arms around his neck. "Well, we've been growing closer, more comfortable with one another. It's only natural that our guards would slip."

He sank into my hug and buried his face in my hair. I pulled him over to the bed, where we crawled under the covers. This time, he wrapped his arms around me, but he was quiet.

His silence gave me a bad feeling, but I tried not to dwell on it, and after a while, I fell asleep.

The next morning, I woke up and my bed was empty. For a moment I had a dreadful suspicion that Julian had gone, decided this arrangement was too much for him and left.

But then I heard the front door open and shut, and feet pad up the stairs. Julian was dressed in jeans and a T-shirt, his hair still damp from a shower.

"I went for a walk and got us breakfast. Come downstairs when you're ready. I bought coffee and croissants. We'll stop by the pharmacy after we eat and get you the morning-after pill."

I felt a little bashful when he spoke so casually, but then, there was no reason for embarrassment. We were both responsible adults, and we knew what had to be done. After breakfast and our trip to the pharmacy, I showered, did my hair and makeup and put on my pale pink chiffon dress. It was strapless with a sweetheart neckline and nipped in at the waist before fanning out into a swishy, A-line skirt. I loved it so much. It was neither an Elodie nor an Ellen outfit, but something new entirely. I'd bought it online only a week ago and was delighted when it arrived and fit perfectly.

I left my hair down and clipped it to the side. Julian wore a suit, and as always, he looked good enough to eat. I fiddled with my necklace.

"Here, let me," he said, and came to stand behind me. He took the thin gold chain, his knuckles brushing my collarbone as he clipped it in place. "There you go. Perfect."

He stared at me then, just...taking me in. He was smiling, but there was something sad in his eyes.

I reached up to stroke his jaw. "Are you all right?"

He exhaled a somewhat shaky breath. "Yes, weddings make me emotional, that's all."

I squeezed his shoulder. "Big softie."

In spite of Shayla's red colour scheme, the wedding ceremony was beautiful. The hotel was once a stately manor, and the reception room let out into the most gorgeous landscaped gardens. Julian and I sat at a table with Nick and Cameron, Shayla's niece, Katie, who was actually pretty cute, and Shayla's sister and her husband. They kept arguing over whether or not to call the babysitter and check in on the kids. I thought it was nice how they worried.

Dad and Shayla were at the head of the table, and I had to admit, they did seem pretty happy.

"Your tits look fucking fantastic in that dress," Julian whispered, and I shot him a warning glance. I didn't want either of my brothers to hear, and certainly not my dad. Some guests approached to give their congratulations to the happy couple.

"Well, I guess I owe you fifty pounds then," Nick sighed to Cameron.

For once, my grumpy brother looked pleased with himself. "Yes, you do. And I don't take checks."

"Why do you owe him money?" I asked quizzically.

Nick kept his voice low. "We made a bet on whether Shayla's ex-husband would show up to the ceremony at the very last minute and object to the wedding."

I laughed. "Why would he do that?"

"I don't know. I just liked the idea of it. The drama."

"Her ex-husband is an accountant. Accountants don't do drama," Cam said.

Julian and I shared a secret look. Accounting was my fake profession for Elodie, and she'd certainly not been the sort of woman to shy away from adventure or drama. "I don't know, maybe he has a wild side," I put in.

"Well, it appears he doesn't since he never showed up and now I'm out of pocket," Nick griped.

"It's your own fault for being so fanciful," said Cameron.

There was an announcement that food was about to be served and the guests chatting with Dad and Shayla went to take their seats. We were served gazpacho for a starter, and then for the main course, we had roast pheasant.

"Yay, tiny chickens," Nick grinned, and I rolled my eyes. He was such a big kid sometimes. I sensed someone's attention and glanced up. Shayla was eyeing me strangely and I couldn't tell why. Her gaze went to Julian, hardening somewhat, and a chill went through me.

Why was she looking at him like that?

Before I had time to analyse the thought, Shayla cleared her throat. "So, Julian, you never mentioned what you do for work."

I stiffened, growing defensive. "Why do you want to know?"

263

My dad did a double take at my snappish tone. Up until this point, the conversation had been nothing but cordial. "Ellen, don't talk to Shayla like that. She's only making conversation."

She's being a bitch, is what she's doing, I thought to myself, quickly putting two and two together. She'd recognised Julian yesterday. Obviously, she must know him from somewhere, must've remembered him and figured out his profession. Maybe one of her friends told her about him or introduced them at one of those fancy parties he attends.

"She's being nosy," I clipped, dropping my cutlery to my plate.

Julian's hand found my knee and gave a gentle squeeze. When I looked at him, his eyes beseeched me not to make a scene. There was also a sadness, the same I'd seen in him earlier, only now it had multiplied.

All of a sudden, I felt like I'd lost him.

I couldn't lose him.

"I'm not being nosy at all. In fact, I only ask out of concern for you, Ellen. You're my stepdaughter now, and I wouldn't like to see you being taken advantage of."

"Is there something I'm missing here?" Dad asked, looking between the two of us.

"Yeah, I second that," Nick added. "What's going on?" He placed a hand to the back of my chair as though taking my side, even though he didn't know what was happening. I loved him so much for that.

Shayla lifted a napkin and dabbed her mouth, keeping her voice low so that only those sitting at the table could hear. It was still far too many ears for my liking.

She turned to Dad, settling a hand on his arm. "Greg, remember last night when I thought I knew Julian from somewhere?" Dad nodded. "Well, now I've remembered and I'm gravely concerned."

Dad's brow furrowed, his hard stare resting on Julian. I stood from the table abruptly. "That's it. We're leaving. None of you can judge me, and certainly not you. You might know my dad, but you know nothing about me," I said in defence, eyeing Shayla harshly.

A fire lit in her gaze. "Ellen, this man is not your boyfriend. He's a paid escort. I know because a colleague of mine in London used to hire such men. She was widowed and lonely, but she had money. Often, I'd see her at parties with handsome young men on her arm. Several times she attended with Julian."

Dad's confusion turned to shock as his attention fell on me. "Ellen, is this true?"

"Please don't blame her, Greg. Your daughter is a very wealthy girl, and she lives all by herself in a big city. Personally, I'm surprised she hasn't been taken advantage of before now."

"Oh, shit, Els," Nick whispered, reaching out to squeeze my wrist.

After remaining silent, Julian finally spoke. "Mrs. Grant, I have never and would never take advantage of anyone. Whoever hires me does so of their own free will and there is absolutely no shame in it. I have no idea what you are trying to do here, but if you were so concerned for your new stepdaughter, then you might've considered taking her aside and speaking privately, instead of humiliating her in front of her family."

Shayla's eyes narrowed to slits. "Her family care about her. They have a right to know."

I blinked, tears suddenly filling my eyes. I couldn't handle how my dad was looking at me, couldn't handle the judgement. Julian was right, even if she thought she was doing the right thing, she'd humiliated me.

I turned and fled the room, running out into the gardens. I found a private spot behind a row of hedges and flopped onto the grass. Tears streamed down my face and I sobbed.

This was a new low for me.

How could everything go to hell so quickly?

"Ellen?" Julian called. "Ellen, where are you?"

"I'm here," I answered, a sob in my voice.

He rounded the hedge and knelt before me, taking both my hands in his. "Oh, darling, don't cry."

"I hate her. How could she do something so cruel?"

"Because she doesn't believe she's being cruel. She believes she's being righteous. She thinks I am a lowly cad out to exploit you."

"She couldn't be further from the truth," I sniffled. "You changed my life. I wasn't living until you came along."

Those sad hazel eyes met mine. "It's what I do. I try to help."

I blinked away my tears. "Why are you looking at me like that?"

He emitted a heavy breath and looked away a moment. When he looked back, his expression was full of remorse. "I'm very fond of you, Ellen."

I shook my head and let go of his hands. "Don't do this."

He caught my chin, forcing my eyes to his. "We were never meant to be forever, and look at you now. Like you said, you've changed, and it's beautiful to see."

A lump formed in my throat and I felt like I couldn't breathe. Everything inside me rebelled. He couldn't do this to me, not now. I wasn't ready for this to end.

"Please, Julian," I begged, sobbing again. "I need you. I need you so much."

He wiped away some of my tears. "You only think that because you're frightened. But my job is done, Ellen. You don't know it yet, but you're going to live such a life." His voice faltered a little at the end.

Hastily, I stood and pushed him away. "So that's all this was to you? A job?"

"Ellen, you know things between us weren't typical for me."

"Then why are you talking like they were?"

He ran a hand through his hair, frustrated. "Because if we continue any longer, I'll only hold you back. I'll only..." his words trailed off, his voice heavy with emotion. "I'll only break your heart."

I sucked in a painful breath, staring at him as I whispered, "Too late for that."

I turned and strode away. He didn't follow. I walked to the front of the hotel and climbed into a cab. I just wanted to go home, wrap myself up in my familiar childhood blankets, and wish the world away.

Because I didn't want to live in a world without Julian in it.

Twenty-One
Julian

I felt wretched. Utterly wretched.

The look in Ellen's eyes. The heartbreak written all over her face almost did me in.

I knew what she thought. She thought she loved me, but she was misguided. I wasn't a man to fall in love with. I was a man to be lusted after, and that was what she felt, mistaking it for something more.

With how I was becoming so attached to her, so possessive and protective, now was definitely the time to end it, before things got even more complicated. I couldn't risk hurting her worse further down the line. Because I felt so much for her, and I didn't trust myself not o self-sabotage, taking her down with me.

I walked all the way from the hotel into town. Finding a pub, I went inside, very tempted to order a drink. But I didn't. I knew if I allowed myself to sink that low there might not be any crawling back.

I was already torn in two.

Shayla had done the hard work for me, and yet, I wanted to hate her for it. But I couldn't. In her mind, she was doing the right thing, even though she went about it all the wrong way. I was growing too close to Ellen, closer than I'd ever grown to any client before. In my heart, I predicted this would happen, but I was foolish enough to dive in anyway.

I sat at the bar for an hour, wallowing. When I left, I walked along the beach until I reached Ellen's dad's house. It was almost two in the morning. I didn't want to wake her

268

up, but I needed to get my things and leave. Hopefully there would be a train along soon to take me back to London.

As I neared the porch, I saw my suitcase, packed and waiting for me. On top of it was a white envelope. It was thin, and before I even opened it, I suspected what was inside. For a moment, it felt like my heart ceased beating.

I felt sick.

Then I got angry because there was a cheque for ten thousand pounds inside. Ellen was paying me for my services and I'd never felt so fucking pissed off and self-hating at the same time. I'd left behind the shame for my work a long time ago, but that wasn't what I felt now. Now all I felt was empty, because I never should've agreed to sleep with her in the first place. And now I was standing with a check for ten grand in my hand and I didn't want a single penny of it.

Being with Ellen, getting to know her, none of it had been for financial gain. Every single second I spent with her was because I wanted to be there. Not because I was being paid. Not because it was a job. But because I was drawn to her in a way I'd never been drawn to anyone before.

This money, it felt more like a slap across the face. A bucket of ice cold water emptied over my head.

With a heavy heart, I left the envelope on the entry table, took my things and walked the short distance to the train station. I passed a group of women on their way home from the nightclubs.

"Hey, gorgeous! Wanna come with us?" one of them called.

I only shook my head. Not even the arms of another could soothe me now. I'd set Ellen free. Like one of her beloved birds, I'd trained her, and now she was ready for the wild. She didn't know it yet, but it was for the best. She'd find someone and be happy. I'd only disappoint her in the end.

When I reached the station, I had two hours to kill before the next departure to London. I found an empty bench and sat down. Like I always did when I needed to hear a friendly voice, I pulled out my phone and called Rose.

When she answered, I realised I'd woken her up. She sounded drowsy. "Julian, is everything all right?"

"No, it isn't."

"Oh, honey, what happened?"

I proceeded to recount the weekend's events. When I was done, Rose's voice was full of empathy. "Don't go back to London. Get on a plane. Come here," she said, and for the first time in a long time, some island solitude sounded like exactly what I needed.

We said our goodbyes and I left the station, ordering a cab on my phone. I was going to visit my best friend in the whole world, enjoy some peaceful quiet, and get my head on straight.

"Where's the nearest airport?" I asked the driver when my cab arrived.

"Exeter's about forty minutes away."

With an ache in my chest, I replied, "Perfect. Take me there."

Twenty-Two
Ellen

I woke up early the next morning after a measly three hours of sleep. I felt like I'd been hit by a truck. My eye sockets hurt from so much crying, and my muscles panged with exhaustion. After I left the wedding, I wrote a cheque and left it on the porch for Julian to find, alongside his suitcase.

I'd been angry. Foolish and bull-headed.

I went downstairs. His suitcase was gone, but the envelope had been left behind.

The regret that filled me was monumental.

I'd been so upset that I'd acted impulsively and irrationally. Yes, I technically owed Julian that money, but it was the wrong way to go about it. It was cold and heartless, mean-spirited, but the way he ended our relationship had been cold and heartless, too. Sure, he'd seemed regretful, miserable even, but he still did it. He must've felt what was happening between us. It couldn't have been all one-sided.

My stomach churned as I went into the living room and found my dad sitting on the couch. He looked tired, too, his hair ruffled, grey bags under his eyes. I felt terrible for ruining his wedding day. Well, maybe I didn't exactly ruin it, but I definitely made it less than perfect.

"D-dad. What are you doing here? I thought you had a flight to catch." He and Shayla were supposed to be spending two weeks in the Maldives for their honeymoon.

271

"It doesn't leave for a few more hours," he said and patted the space beside him. "Come here. We need to have a talk."

Exhaling heavily, I went and sat next to him. I still wore my dress from yesterday, only now it was crumpled and stained with snot and tears. I may have used it to wipe my face during my middle of the night cry-athon.

"Dad, I'm so sorry I ran off yesterday. I just couldn't face everyone after what Shayla said."

He wrapped his arm around me and pulled me in tight. His warmth was a comfort I hadn't known I needed.

"She shouldn't have said what she did. I already had a word with her about it."

I pulled back to look up at him in surprise. "You did?"

Dad let out a tired breath. "Shayla's a good woman, Ellen. She's good for me, and she is actually very fond of you, but believe it or not, tact is not her strong suit."

She was fond of me? This was news.

"I was so embarrassed by what she said, Dad. You must think I'm pathetic."

"Ellen, I would never think that. You're my only daughter and I love you."

I sniffed. "Yes, but...she made me sound like such a naïve idiot. Like a silly little girl being conned out of her money, when that couldn't be further from the truth. Julian and I started out as friends. Yes, he's an escort, but that doesn't..." I paused, took a deep breath. "That doesn't really have anything to do with what was between us. He's helped me more than you could ever know."

It was the truth. Whatever Julian and I had, it was real. No part of it was contrived, and there was nothing anyone could say to change that.

Or maybe I was just fooling myself. Maybe every woman he was with felt this way after he left them.

Dad pushed a strand of hair away from my face, his voice gentle. "Do you think I can't see that? I can see the change in you, Ellen. You're more confident than you've ever been."

Hearing him say that meant a lot. It meant that the way Julian made me feel wasn't all in my head. He really had helped me, even if he'd abandoned me in the end.

I blew my nose with a piece of tissue. "Yes, well, what Shayla said made Julian sound seedy, but I was a living a shell of a life before he came along. I couldn't talk to people. I could barely handle it when customers came into the bookshop to make a purchase. I've been this way my entire life. I thought I was condemned to always be like that until Julian showed me the strength hidden inside me."

Dad blinked, and it looked like he was holding back tears. In all my life, I'd only ever seen my father cry a handful of times, so to see that emotion in him now really did a number on me. He looked away, trying to get himself together.

"You remember what I was like as a kid?" I went on. "I couldn't talk to anyone, and when I did, I went into panic mode every time. Over the years it's gotten a little better, but not by much." I let out a joyless laugh. "I must've been born defective or something."

"Please don't talk about yourself like that, Ellen. You went through so much, losing your mother."

"But I don't even remember her. When I look at pictures, I might as well be looking at a stranger."

Dad fell silent and I studied him. He appeared to have something to say but was conflicted.

"Dad, what is it?"

He leaned forward and held his head in his hands, not replying. When he finally sat back, I got a chill down my spine, because there were horrors in his eyes, horrors and regrets and infinite sadness.

"I always told the three of you that your mother died in a car accident, because it was easier. There was no way to tell a child the truth. But then, as you grew older, it got even harder. I didn't want to explain why I lied, so I just went on allowing you to believe it."

Wait, what?

"You lied?" I asked in disbelief.

He looked miserable, but then, he seemed determined to see this through, to tell me the truth. My entire body tensed as if for a blow.

"I took Nick with me to work one Saturday, and your mother stayed home with you and Cameron. You were only a toddler, barely two years old, and Cameron was about to turn five. Three men broke into the house, intending to steal our valuables. I still don't know exactly what happened, but the police pieced it together."

He paused to draw breath, like the pain was still fresh. My heart pounded. I couldn't believe what I was hearing. All my life I'd known that certain facts were true, and now they were being flipped on their head.

When Dad spoke again, he took my hand in his. His warm palms were a soothing contrast to the awful story he told. "The police said your mother must've walked in on the thieves. One of them struck her on the head with a blunt object. They might not have intended to kill her, only incapacitate her, but the blow was fatal. It was hours before I got home with Nick and found you all. They'd tied Cameron up and locked him in the bathroom. He was shaken and traumatised, but he hadn't witnessed his mother's death, didn't really know had happened. But you..."

"But I?" I prompted, heart in my throat. I had a sick feeling I knew what was coming, but I daren't believe it.

"I found you on the floor, in the same room where your mother's body lay lifeless, crying your eyes out. Up until that day, you had started to speak. Your development was on a level with any other two-year-old. You were just starting to form sentences. But after... after you went quiet, never spoke. For a full year you were silent, only making a sound when something upset you and you cried. When you finally did start talking again, it was only to me, Cameron, or Nick. With anyone outside the family, you were mute until after you started school."

Tears rose to the surface. The very fact of who I was suddenly made sense after twenty-nine years of life. And Cameron, God, was this why he was so unhappy all the time? Were we still suffering from post-traumatic stress, even after all these years?

I stood and walked to the window, looking out at the view. I wrapped my arms around myself, feeling a chill, letting the facts my father had just revealed sink in. A vision of the break-in went through my head; Mum's fear, my terror, and poor Cameron being tied up.

"What about the men who did it? Did they catch them?"

Dad exhaled. "Yes, several months later they caught them after another robbery a few towns away. They went to prison. It was a small justice when compared with the fact I'd lost my wife, the mother of my children."

A tear fell down my cheek. "Oh, Dad."

He sucked in a breath. "It was a long time ago, but sometimes the memory is still so fresh."

I frowned sadly, then an awful thought struck. "Did it happen here?"

Dad rubbed a hand over his face. "No. I moved us away soon after your mum passed. It was too hard to stay in a place where such awful things had happened, and I…I feared someone might say something to you kids as you got older. Here, nobody knew us. It was a fresh start."

"Good." I was glad I hadn't grown up there, and that my dad had the means to move us away. Still, my brothers needed to know the truth, and it had to be Dad who told them.

"You need to tell Nick and Cam," I said quietly.

"I know, and I will when the time is right. I'm so sorry I never told you, Ellen. I've never been good at expressing my feelings, but I love you so much and I've only ever wanted what's best for you. In my foolishness, I thought the lie was better for you than the truth."

I turned to look at him. "Maybe it was better. I can't imagine what it would've been like having that knowledge at a young age. It could've messed me up even worse."

"You're not angry?"

My heart clenched at the vulnerability in his eyes. "Why would I be angry? None of what happened is your fault. You tried to protect us. You were alone in the world with three small children and you did what you thought was best."

"Ellen," Dad choked on my name, his eyes shiny with unshed tears.

I returned to the couch and wrapped my arms around him. We stayed like that for several minutes, just holding each other. Dad had always been my pal and confidante, but he usually just let me talk. Now he'd been the one to reveal things and I felt closer to him than I'd ever been before.

"This Julian, I don't know the full nature of your relationship, but I do know what a man looks like when he loves a woman, Ellen."

I drew away. "Don't say that, Dad. We've ended things, so telling me that only makes it hurt more."

"Do you love him?" he asked.

"I...I don't know. I feel like I do, but I don't know exactly what love is supposed to feel like."

"Is he the first person you want to see every morning, and the last you want to see at night? When you have news, is he the first person you want to tell?"

Yes, yes and yes.

Still, I shook my head. "I'm not sure. You're being very understanding about all this, by the way."

"Most of us, when we get to a certain age, we learn to stop judging people. You also want your children to be happy, no matter what. If he's what makes you happy, Ellen, then that's all I care about."

He didn't care about his profession?

Who was this open-minded man who talked freely about emotions, and what had he done with my stoic, awkward, manly man of a father?

"I don't know what's going to happen between us now," I said sadly.

Dad rubbed my shoulders. "I'm always here if you need me, Ellen. And you can stay for as long as you like if you're not ready to go back to London yet."

I arched an eyebrow. "I'm not sure Shayla will be too happy to have me hanging around."

"Shayla won't mind." Dad paused and sucked in a deep breath. "She's very sorry for how she acted yesterday."

277

"Yes, well, there's nothing any of us can do to change it now."

"She's outside in the car. She'd like to apologize in person, if you'll allow it."

Oh, hell. Shayla was the last person I wanted to see right now, but the fact she'd waited outside in the car for the past hour made me feel bad. Not much, but a little. Then again, she deserved some discomfort after what she put me through.

"I don't really want to see her, Dad."

"That's all right. You don't have to."

I looked at him and guilt ate at me. I didn't want him going off on his honeymoon with this hanging over him, so I relented, emitting a long breath. "Fine. I'll let her say her piece."

I followed Dad outside. Shayla looked anxious when she saw us emerge. Good.

She got out of the car and came right over to me, as though to give me a hug. I stood back, my posture defensive. We *definitely* weren't there yet. Not by a long shot.

"Oh, Ellen, I can't apologise enough for my behaviour yesterday. You must think me a horrible woman."

"I think you should've spoken to me privately. If you had, I would've been able to tell you that Julian had not taken advantage of me in any way. Whatever was between us, it was completely consensual and *my* own business as a grown, almost thirty-year-old woman."

"You're right. You're old enough to know your own mind. But I know how much your father cares for you. He worries about you living in London all by yourself. I just got a little carried away, thinking I was doing the right thing. I hope you'll find it in you to forgive me."

278

My expression was hard. "It's a bit early for forgiveness."

She sniffled. "Yes, I understand. Maybe we can work towards it over time."

I relented a little. "Maybe."

"I'd like that, Ellen. And thank you for coming and hearing me out."

I nodded, went to give Dad one last hug and wished him an enjoyable honeymoon.

After they left, I finally peeled off yesterday's dress and climbed into the shower. The hot water washed away some of my tension, but I still felt torn open on the inside. Even if I did love Julian, he didn't love me. Sure, he cared about me, but it wasn't the same.

The idea that we were done shot an arrow through my insides. Then there was the story of what really happened to Mum. I had this constant pain in my stomach over it, imagining how terrified she'd been, how quickly you could end a life. My entire being ached, and I just wanted to fast-forward to a time when I didn't feel this way anymore.

When I got out of the shower, I dried off and put on some clean pyjamas, planning to drown my sorrows in junk food and romcoms.

I'd just brought all my pillows and duvet down to the living room when the front door opened. Nick walked in, a paper bag in hand. "I'm here with breakfast, a sympathetic ear, and a shoulder to cry on. Any takers?"

I really did love him.

We sat and talked for hours. I told him everything, all about Elodie, and how I met Julian, the entire story of our relationship from beginning to end. Nick didn't judge, instead he seemed fascinated with it all. He'd always thought he was the adventurous one in our family, the one who took chances, threw caution to the wind. But it seemed I had a bit of an adventurous streak in me, too.

"I can't believe you hired a male escort, that's just so…anti-Ellen."

"Well, technically I didn't hire him, because no money was ever exchanged."

He chewed on his lip, and I sensed a confession coming on. "When I went to Amsterdam, I slept with a prostitute."

My eyes widened. "You did?"

Nick nodded. "It was pretty rough. I came away feeling bad about the woman, bad about wanting to pay for sex in the first place, just plain bad about everything. I ended up paying her double what I originally owed."

"Oh, Nick."

"I had to. It was clear she was only doing it because she didn't have another choice. But I don't think that's the case for everyone. From what you've told me of Julian, it sounds like his job is a personal choice. He actually gets something out of it."

"Yes, I think you're right," I said, feeling both forlorn and jealous. Jealous of all the women who were going to have him now that we were over.

"If that's true, then you just need to let him be who he is. You can't change people, Ellen. You can't make them want a white picket fence and a country cottage if they'd prefer a balcony with a city view."

"It just hurts. Letting him go hurts so bad, Nick," I said and dropped my head on his shoulder.

"I know, Els. But it'll get better, I promise. Time heals all wounds."

***

I stayed at Dad's for almost two weeks until he and Shayla were due back from their honeymoon. I told myself it was time to get back to reality. Bernice had been taking care of Skittles and Rainbow for me, and it was definitely time to relieve her of her duties. Besides, I missed my birds.

They didn't even know how lucky they were to have a partner for life, a little friend to be by your side for all your days.

During my stay at Dad's, I'd thrown myself into my book. I didn't check my emails, barely even looked at my phone. Instead, I wrote. Emotion had built up inside me and it needed an outlet. As such, the final *Sasha Orlando* book was turning out to be very tumultuous. All of my feelings these past two weeks became her feelings. I couldn't help it. Writing the story was like therapy.

From the start of the series, Sasha developed a close friendship with Toby, her boss at the newspaper. Over time, they started to have feelings for one another, but because they're both seeing other people, and also because it would be unprofessional, they keep their relationship platonic. I'd never originally planned for them to get together, but there was a large contingent of readers who shipped Sasha & Toby, and I wanted to finally give them their happy ending. I'd even written a sex scene. A real, detailed, unadulterated sex scene!

Anyway, it seemed that immersing myself in a fictional happily ever after helped me forget about the lack of one in my own life.

When I arrived at my house, Skittles and Rainbow went apeshit. I know it's hard to picture lovebirds going apeshit, but just picture them flying all over the place, tweeting like mental, nipping at my hair, and pooping on my shoulder.

I had to change my shirt afterward.

I steeled myself to finally check my emails and missed calls. There were several from Daniel, a couple of texts from Suze wondering where I was and to let her know I was okay asap, but nothing from Julian.

I shouldn't be mad at him for not trying to contact me, since I hadn't tried to contact him either, but it still stung. Things between us really were over and I needed to start accepting it. Getting my heart to accept it was half the battle.

My guilt over Suze ate away at me until finally, I decided to bite the bullet. I needed to come clean to her, and then she could decide whether or not she still wanted to be my friend. It was Monday, so I texted her back, apologising for the radio silence, and said I would meet her the next morning at the café.

Her response came not long after.

Suze: *Okay, but I want an explanation for why I haven't heard from you, lady!*

Damn, this wasn't going to be easy. But I had to be brave, otherwise I'd spend the rest of my life hiding, and I was sick of it, sick of keeping track of lies.

The following morning, I didn't put on a lick of makeup, no wig, or fancy outfit. No mask. Instead I wore jeans and a T-shirt, my hair pulled into a ponytail, glasses firmly in place.

I walked into the Polka Dot Café, a lump in my throat when I spotted Suze at our usual table. She scrolled on her phone and sipped a latte. My hands shook, and my pulse thrummed as I walked up to the table, pulled out a chair and sat. Suze's eyes flicked up from her phone.

"Sorry, but I'm waiting for someone."

"Suze, it's m-me," I stammered, staring her dead in the eye. *Not too much eye contact, Ellen. You don't want to come across like any more of a crazy person.*

She blinked, frowned, then shook her head. She stared at me for a long moment, taking in my hair and eyes, how different I looked but with Elodie's face.

"I...I'm not sure what's going on here," she said, clearly perplexed.

"I'm Elodie."

She was still openly staring at me. "Right."

"But my real name is actually Ellen," I said and scratched nervously at my wrist.

"Okaaay," she drew out the word as she let that sink in.

"You probably think I'm a complete nutjob."

"Um, I'm just a little...confused, I guess. Are you some kind of catfish?"

The lump in my throat hardened, because that's basically what I was. I just hadn't employed the internet to pretend to be someone else, I'd done it in real life. I couldn't tell if that was better or worse.

"In a sense, yes."

Suze looked out the window, head bobbing up and down. "Right," she said again.

A moment of awkward silence fell. I didn't know what else to say. Suze stood from the table. "This is a little weird, so, uh, I'm going to leave now."

I deflated at her departure. This had gone so badly. She'd already reached the door of the café when I jumped to my feet and went after her, stepping out into the street.

"Wait, let me explain. If you still don't want to know me after, then I'll leave you alone, I promise," I called out.

She was a few feet away when she stopped, turned around and walked back to me. "I guess it would be good to understand why you did this."

I sucked in a breath, nodding. "I want to tell you."

She blew out a breath and placed a hand on her hip. The awkwardness between us was palpable. I think it might've been better if she just got angry, at least that wouldn't feel so unbearable. "Well, should we go back inside?" she asked, eyebrows lifting.

I inhaled deeply. "I live not too far from here. If you want, we can go to my house and I'll explain everything."

Suze was hesitant. "I'm not sure going to your house is the best idea."

"True, but I promise I'm not some kind of serial killer. I just think if you see where I live, then you'll be able to better understand why I did this."

She stared at me for another long moment, seeming to conclude I wouldn't harm her. Besides, without my heels, she was a good few inches taller than me. And she worked out. If it came to it, Suze could definitely take me in a fight.

"Fine. You have twenty minutes and then I have to get back to work."

We started on the short walk to my house. "Thank you for giving me a chance."

She chewed her lip, glancing at me speculatively. "You better not blow it."

"I won't."

Suze folded her arms, her body language a little defensive. "So, why did you do it? What was in it for you?"

I swallowed, readying myself to explain. "This is going to sound bizarre, but the night we first met, I'd just won a makeover at a drag show. That's why I wasn't dressed as myself. I didn't go out with the intention of fooling you,

284

but we just got talking and I felt so much more confident to pretend. My real self would never go to a bar and befriend someone like you, Suze. My real self had problems leaving the house, if I'm being honest."

Something about what I said made her eyes soften. She looked like she felt a little sorry for me now. "So, you're what, an agoraphobe?"

"Not quite. I do leave the house. But I've always had issues interacting with strangers, and people in general. Being Elodie helped me break free of that. Your friendship meant a lot to me. I knew it was wrong to lie, but I selfishly didn't want to let you go." When I looked at her, my eyes were full of a thousand apologies.

She folded her arms, let them fall to her sides, then refolded them again. "This is all a lot to take in. You should've just told me who you really were. I still would've wanted to get to know you."

I wasn't so sure about that, but I didn't argue with her.

"I'm so sorry I did this to you. You didn't deserve to be lied to, but really, being your friend, seeing you every week, and talking with you brightened my day. You're so cool, Suze, and you're kind and talented and strong. You're the sort of person all women want as a best friend."

I stopped talking when we reached my place. Suze was silent as I pulled out my keys and slotted them in the door.

"You live here?" she asked, sounding surprised.

I nodded and led her inside. Her attention went to the mural I'd painted on the walls. She ran her hand over it and asked, "Did you do this?"

"Yes, I, um, have a lot of free time on my hands."

I walked into the kitchen and she followed, gasping when she saw Skittles and Rainbow in their pretty antique cage, the cherry blossom fanning out on the wall behind them. For a second, I saw my house through her eyes, and it was pretty magical. I'd put a lot of time into making it a haven, and it was certainly that.

"How can you afford all this?" she asked, and it was a valid question. This was London, and a highly sought-after neighbourhood at that. It didn't come cheap.

"I'm an author. I write books," I replied. It was one of the first times I'd offered the information freely and it felt good. I definitely wasn't the old Ellen anymore.

"You do? Which books?"

"Have you heard of the *Sasha Orlando* series?"

Suze blinked at me. "Yes, I, um, I have. I've never read them, but those books are everywhere. Wow, Elodie. I mean, uh, Ellen."

I swallowed and tugged on my sleeve, frowning as I confessed, "A lot of the stories I told you, they're actually from my books."

Her eyebrows jumped. "You made them up?"

"Yes. I want to apologise for that, too. For lying."

Suze looked around, then back to me. "I guess you get points for being inventive."

A moment of quiet fell before I asked, "Would you like some tea?"

She turned to me, seeming to surprise even herself when she replied, "Yes, I would like some."

I went to put the kettle on as she stepped up to the birdcage. "They're very pretty."

"Their names are Rainbow and Skittles. They're lovebirds," I said.

"How long have you had them?"

"Almost six years." I was so relieved that she was making conversation and not leaving and telling me where to stick my friendship.

"Ellen?"

"Yes?"

"Why are you coming clean about all this now?" She was clearly trying to understand my motivations.

I exhaled heavily. "I guess I just got sick of hiding. I don't want to pretend anymore."

"So, you want to start over?"

"If you'll allow it, yes. I'd like to be your friend as me. As Ellen."

A small smile shaped her mouth as she pulled out a chair. "In that case, you better start talking. I want to know everything, and leave nothing out." She paused as her eyes wandered around the room. "I have a feeling Ellen is a lot more interesting than Elodie ever was."

The relief that hit me was monumental. I hadn't realised just how much I'd wanted Suze's acceptance. She was one of the few friends I had in this world and losing her would've hurt.

So, I finished making the tea, sat down across from her and started to talk.

***

"I have big news," Daniel declared as soon as I picked up the phone. After Suze left, I finally got around to returning his calls.

"Oh? What kind of big news?"

"We've had another offer come in about purchasing the film rights for the *Sasha Orlando* series. And before you say no, just listen. I think you'll like this offer."

I had a feeling I already knew where the offer had come from. After meeting Damon Atwood at Julian's flat and hearing him speak so passionately about turning my books into films, I'd certainly been convinced he could do them justice. At the time, he had no clue he was talking to

287

the author herself, which only worked to convince me further.

"I'm sure you've heard of the actor, Damon Atwood," Daniel went on. "Well, he plans on making his directorial debut and—"

"Have your people draw up a contract and I'll take a look," I said, cutting him off.

"Wait, what?" I'd clearly surprised him. "Um, do you mean to say you're interested? Because I had a whole spiel ready and I definitely didn't think you'd agree so easily."

"Well, I've finally decided it's time for Sasha to meet the big screen, but I want to write the screenplay, or at least be a part of the team writing it. That's my only condition."

"In that case, I'll get right to work," Daniel replied. He sounded overjoyed, which was expected given the commission he was going to earn on this deal.

The following week I was working a shift at the bookshop when Rose walked in. Just the sight of her made my chest hurt, made me remember how much I missed and yearned for Julian. His absence in my life was marked, but I wasn't going to force myself on someone who didn't want to be with me.

"Hi, Ellen," she greeted with a wave then went to peruse the shelves.

"H-hello, Rose," I replied and endeavoured to concentrate on the magazine I was reading. It was no use though. I wanted to grab her and demand she tell me everything about Julian. I wanted to know if he missed me like I missed him. But then, what if he didn't? That knowledge would just make me feel worse.

A few minutes later she approached the counter with a copy of *The Catcher in the Rye*. "I know it's shameful, but I've never read it. Damon said I should. It's one of his favourites. Speaking of which, he's over the moon you've agreed to enter into talks about the film rights for *Sasha*."

I gave a small smile. "Well, I was very impressed when I heard him talk about it that time at…" I faltered before I could finish the sentence and her eyes softened. A few moments of quiet passed between us before she spoke.

"Julian has never been an easy person," she said, almost like a confession. "We've been each other's only family since we were kids, and well, I know him better than anyone."

"You don't have to—"

"I want to," she insisted. "I want you to hear this, because of all the women he's had, I've never seen him so miserable as he's been these last few weeks after leaving you."

He was miserable? A part of me rejoiced, but another part felt awful. I didn't ever want him to be sad, even though I really wanted him to miss me.

"Julian has always been full of light, despite a lot of suffering in his life. It's miraculous when you think about it. My mother passed away when I was still a teenager, and if it wasn't for Julian looking out and caring for me, I don't know where I might've ended up. We had nothing, and he resorted to selling his body to feed and clothe us. He took that bullet so I didn't have to, and as a result, I will always love him, no matter what."

The thought of the two of them being so helpless, with nowhere to turn, made my heart heavy.

"You might not realise it, but he's the most selfless person you will ever meet. Everything he does is for others. I've seen him change lives. He just has this way of influencing people. I'm sure you've felt it for yourself."

"Yes," I whispered. "He definitely changed me."

Her eyes grew glossy. "The thing is, you changed him, too."

I looked away, sniffling. "I'm not so sure about that."

"But you did. Do you know he's stopped working? Even before he ended things with you, he wasn't himself with any of his clients. He doesn't know it, and he'd probably deny it if asked, say it was passing infatuation, but he was falling in love with you, Ellen."

All at once, the air left my lungs. "Then why did he leave me?"

"Because he was frightened. You have to understand, Julian has always resigned himself to being unlovable, or to being loved temporarily. It's a crutch he uses so that he never has to invest in one person, never has to have his heart broken. His mother was a careless woman. She loved him in her own way, but she struggled with depression, so her love never really came across. In the years when Julian lived with her, she went from one partner to the next. She cheated on most of the people she was with, and that's all Julian ever saw. He never saw a loving, monogamous relationship. When he grew up, he took on the same behaviour, but he's not the same as his mum. He's not careless. If anything, he cares too much. He gives all of himself away and leaves nothing just for him."

"He said he thought it was for the best that we end things. That it would hurt at first, but in the long run I'd see he was right."

Rose's bright blue eyes turned sad. "He's pushing you away. I've tried to reason with him, but he won't listen. He's been staying with Damon and I on the island. We just got back to London last night."

"I don't know what to do, Rose. I..." my cheeks flushed as I swallowed. "I want to be with him, but he doesn't want to be with me. Or at least, that's what he's telling himself."

She reached out to squeeze my hand. "Julian doesn't respond well to being pressured. Give him time. I think he'll come around eventually. He's too smart not to."

I stared into her kind, caring eyes, so grateful that she'd come to talk to me. But the thing was, I deserved better than to wait around. I understood that Julian viewed himself a certain way, that he didn't believe he could be loved unconditionally, loved forever, but how could he not see that was how I felt for him? How could he be so wilfully blind?

I was torn in two over this.

One part of me yearned for Julian, was heartbroken for all the suffering he'd been through, but the other part was angry. Running away from love was the coward's route, and though he might need time, I wasn't going to hang about the house, pining and waiting for him to come looking for me.

For years I'd been trying to build up the courage to go travelling. I'd just submitted my book to my editor, so I now had the free time not to mention the funds to finally tick an item off my bucket list. I'd wasted so much time, entire decades of my life inside my room, making up stories but never experiencing life firsthand.

When I got home after my shift, I opened up my laptop, navigated to a travel website and started to make some plans.

Twenty-Three
Julian

Several months later

"**I want you** to come on board as a technical consultant for the film," Damon said as he lifted his cup of coffee.

I glanced up from the newspaper I was reading with breakfast and arched an eyebrow. "Pardon?"

"I keep forgetting that you still haven't read Ellen's books. The film is based on book one, *Good Girl, Bad Lady*, and the storyline revolves around Sasha writing an expose about male escorts. Your expertise would be extremely helpful."

"I'm aware of the storyline. If you hadn't noticed, Rose likes to discuss the series ad nauseam." My irritable countenance didn't put him off. I'd been a grumpy bastard for months now, and Rose and Damon were saints for putting up with me. I couldn't remember the last time I'd felt myself. I thought that being without Ellen would get easier with time, but so far it hadn't.

I'd not seen her since the day of her father's wedding. When I came home from Skye, I made sure to avoid the Polka Dot Café and the area near her house. I feared that if I saw her, I'd crack, get down on my knees and beg for her forgiveness, take any scraps she was willing to give.

Then, during a weak moment, I'd taken a stroll past the bookshop. When I spotted Bernice inside, I couldn't resist going in. I had no plan, other than a deep-seated need to see Ellen, make sure she was okay. I asked Bernice if she'd be on shift that day, but she only shook her head and informed me Ellen had taken a few months off to go travelling across

Europe. My heart sank at the news, but another, selfless part of me rejoiced. She'd finally built up the courage to go explore the world by herself.

"I'd like to get your real-life perspective," Damon went on, drawing me back to the conversation. "The story is told from Sasha's point of view, but I want to depict the experience of the escort she develops a relationship with in the most realistic way possible."

Real life had definitely mirrored fiction with that one.

"I'm not sure I'm right for that job," I replied and closed the paper. "And I'm sure Ellen would prefer it if I weren't hanging around the set."

"She's the one who suggested you," Damon said, and I blinked. *She had? Was she back from her travels?*

Everything inside of me thrilled at the idea of seeing her, and then immediately rebelled against it. My feelings for her were dangerous. I'd come too close to losing myself to her completely. As a recovering addict, the idea of being so vulnerable with another person was terrifying. If she rejected me, and inevitably she would eventually, it might send me straight back into the arms of my greatest love, heroin.

"She admitted that when she first wrote the book a number of years ago, she was young and new to publishing. She didn't do any real-life research, didn't talk to anyone within the profession. And like I said, since it's all from Sasha's perspective in the book, it works. But in the film, we're trying to show all viewpoints," Damon went on in an effort to convince me.

I frowned as I thought about it. "You're not just making this offer because you're sick of me moping around the flat?"

In truth, not only had I been grumpy for months, I also hadn't worked. I was at a point where I could afford to take some time off, but I definitely couldn't afford to do this indefinitely. I needed to start earning again. The problem was, my interactions with clients had been difficult at best. I'd tried, but like with Cathy after I'd started to grow close to Ellen, I couldn't bring myself to be intimate. All I thought about was Ellen, and how I wished I was kissing her, touching her, taking her into my arms.

Nobody else would do, and that's what terrified me. For so long I sought pleasure in many beds, now I only yearned for one.

"Julian, I don't exactly know any other male escorts. Besides, I don't want anyone else for this job but you. It's a great job opportunity, with a potential for similar jobs down the line. We've also just cast the lead role."

That piqued my curiosity. I wondered what A-lister they'd found to play Sasha. "Oh?"

Damon smiled. "Our old friend Alicia has agreed to play the lead."

Well. That was interesting. "And Rose has no objections?"

Back when they'd worked on the West End together, Alicia had eyes for Damon. In the end, she'd succumbed to *my* charms, but I still couldn't imagine Rose being thrilled about her coming back into their lives.

"Rose has known for a long time that I've no romantic inclinations towards Alicia. Besides, she's perfect for the role. We couldn't go with anyone else."

"And how has the rest of the casting been going? Rose mentioned the other week you were having some troubles."

Damon rubbed his jaw. "We haven't found the right person yet to play Toby, Sasha's boss at the magazine. We need someone who's good-looking, but older. Also, someone who isn't a huge star. Alicia needs to be the clear headliner."

I almost grinned. "Was that in her contract?"

Damon shot his eyes to the ceiling. "What do you think?"

I chuckled, and it was the first time I'd felt any sort of humour in who knew how long. It was just *so* Alicia to insist on being the main attraction. It was one of the things that had drawn me to her. When I thought of how Ellen was her opposite in every way, I wondered if maybe that had been my problem. I'd always gone for women like Alicia, women who were like me, perhaps subconsciously knowing they wouldn't fall for me. But Ellen...

"Well, what do you think?" Damon prodded, interrupting my thoughts.

I sighed. "Let me think about it."

He started to smile. "Great."

I wagged my finger at him. "Don't go getting too excited. I'm not agreeing to anything yet."

But really, I did need to work. It was only the thought of being around Ellen that made me hesitate. Then again, with her newfound confidence and travels, I'd be surprised if she hadn't moved on to someone else by now. Even thinking it made me want to lash out, but I kept the urge at bay. I drummed my fingers on the back of the chair to release some nervous energy when an idea struck. "How about having David audition for the Toby role?"

Damon appeared thoughtful as he rubbed his chin. "He just finished a stint in *Sweeney Todd*, right? Has he done any other acting?"

"Do music videos count?"

Now he laughed. "Not really, but give me his number and I'll get in touch. See if he's interested."

Later that day, I stood outside Montrose, the assisted living facility where my mother resided. It was an hour outside of London, but I still felt guilty for not visiting more often. It was just that these visits, they drained me. And then I felt guilty for feeling drained. It was a vicious cycle.

When I went inside, I was immediately welcomed by a smiling receptionist. A fresh vase of flowers sat on her desk, colourful and vibrant. Mum used to live in a much worse place than this, but once I started to earn enough money, I transferred her here. Sometimes I wondered if maybe it was a little *too* nice. She was comfortable here and didn't want to leave.

I guess there were worse ways to live. At least at Montrose, I knew she was being cared for. She was taking her meds, getting up every morning, socialising with the other residents. It was the best possible scenario.

On the outside world, Mum had been a wreck. In here, she had peace, a routine, predictability. It was the only way I knew to keep her safe.

When I reached her room, I stopped a moment to mentally prepare myself. I did this every time. Took a deep breath, steeled myself just in case she wasn't feeling well. And when Mum didn't feel well, she took it out on whoever was around her.

I knocked on the door and waited. A second later a quiet voice called, "Come in."

I stepped inside and found her sitting by the window, a word search on her lap. Her hair looked washed and her eyes bright. My tension eased. She was having a good day, thank Christ.

"Hi, Mum," I greeted and went to set the bag of goodies on the table. I always brought the same thing; gossip magazines, chocolate, and the expensive coffee pods she liked. Last Christmas, I'd gotten her a Nespresso machine and it was her new favourite thing. She said it tasted just like the stuff you got at fancy cafés.

"Your hair's grown longer," she commented, eyeing me with the tip of her pen in her mouth. She chewed on it a moment.

I ran my hand through my hair. She was right. It had gotten longer. "Definitely needs a cut."

She scoffed. "Bet you think you look like Jim Morrison."

"That's one person I've never been mistaken for, Mum."

"Hush, for a second. I'm trying to concentrate."

I shut my mouth and looked out the window while she circled a word she just found. Mum had a view of the courtyard garden. There was a woman sitting on a bench with a tiny dog on her lap.

"They let you have pets here?" I asked.

Mum rolled her eyes. "You talking about Maureen over there?" she said, eyeing the woman outside. I nodded. "Not everyone's allowed. You need to have perfect behaviour."

"And you don't?"

She huffed a sigh. "I could have a pet if I wanted, but I'm not interested. Maureen spends half the day picking up poo. And the stupid thing barks constantly. Does my head in."

"You never did like animals," I said in agreement.

She eyed me. "What's that supposed to mean?"

"Just that I never had a pet growing up."

297

"You survived, didn't you? Anyway, pets are overrated."

A silence fell, and Mum went back to her word search. I made us both some coffee and set a cup down in front of her. "Thanks," she said, eyeing me warily.

Mum saying thanks was a big deal. Most of the time she just accepted stuff without talking, like I owed her for the simple fact she brought me into the world.

I retook my seat and noticed her still watching me. "What's going on with you?" she questioned.

Quite like her thanks, Mum asking questions about me was also unusual. She knew what I did for a living, but since it paid for her life here at Montrose, she rarely mentioned it.

I decided to hell with it. I was going to answer honestly. Maybe it would shock her out of her indifference. "I think I might've fallen in love with someone."

Her brow ticked upward ever so slightly. "Other than yourself? I guess there's a first time for everything."

"Yes, Mum. I fell for someone other than myself. Big shocker."

Mum thought that because I bought expensive clothes, took care of myself, and lived a somewhat luxurious life that I was inherently vain and selfish. I think it suited her better than to accept the reality that I was sensitive, that I had feelings and could bleed just like everyone else.

Still, she appeared curious, her attention wandering over me, her word search forgotten. "Is she one of those women, the ones who pay money for you to chauffeur them around?"

'Chauffeur them around' was Mum's code for 'shag them senseless'.

"No, she isn't one of those women."

She was quiet, then said, "And how does she feel about you…you know, spreading it around like that?"

"I don't spread anything around."

She waved a hand through the air. "You know what I mean."

"She never judged me for what I do for a living, if that's what you're asking. But if you must know, I'm not doing that anymore anyway."

She sat a little straighter, probably because me not working equalled to her not having her expenses paid to live here. "Don't get your knickers in a twist. I can still afford to pay for this place."

Mum sniffed and folded her arms. "So, this woman, you gave up whoring yourself for her?"

Normally she wasn't so blunt. Mum had an infinite number of ways to describe prostitution without actually saying the words. "No, I didn't give it up for her, but I did give it up *because* of her."

Mum was quiet again. She appeared to be thinking, so I drank my coffee and let her think.

"Since you're here, telling me your woes, I'm guessing things didn't work out in the end."

My expression was solemn. "Unfortunately, when it comes to love I've inherited your bad luck."

She grunted and looked away. "More trouble than it's worth."

For once, she was right. Loving people *was* more trouble it was worth, and Mum was a shining example of that. I loved her to my detriment because she was my mum and I'd never get another. I loved her even though almost all of her decisions ended up hurting me.

"Julian," she said and I looked up. It wasn't often that she uttered my name.

"Yes, Mum?"

Her expression showed a rare hint of remorse. "You shouldn't listen to me. This woman, maybe she loves you back. Maybe you just need to take a chance. You don't want to end up like me. I hurt everyone who ever tried to love me, because I was hurt too many times myself, and now I'm all alone."

Was that what would happen? I'd end up exactly like Mum?

Her uncharacteristic show of emotion and vulnerability was jarring. I reached out and took her hand. For a second, she flinched, but then accepted my touch. "You're not alone. You have me."

Mum blinked, and I thought I saw a watery shine in her eyes. When she spoke, her voice was so quiet it was almost a whisper. "I don't deserve you."

"Too bad, you've got me."

She gave me a glimpse into just how grateful she was, how sorry she was for everything she put me through, all in one infinitely sad expression. Reaching out, she stroked my hair away from my face. "You're a good person, Julian. Too good. I know I give you shit all the time, but you don't deserve it. Sometimes my misery wants to make everyone else miserable, too."

"It's okay, I understand."

And I did. When I was a teenager, I started to suffer from the same depression as Mum. I knew what it was like to be a black hole and want to pull everyone down with me. But I was stronger than Mum and I fought it. I got it under control. It required constant upkeep, but it was the only way I kept from succumbing to darkness. I'd fallen once before, fallen so bad I almost killed myself with drugs. But I'd never go back to that. I couldn't.

"If you think she'll give you another shot, you should take it," Mum went on. "You don't get too many chances for love in this life. More often than not, it's unrequited. So, when it's real, you've got to grab hold of it."

I absorbed her words. I let them sink into me and embolden me. Because she was right. How often do we find connections like the one I shared with Ellen? Sometimes only once in a lifetime. Sometimes not even once.

I could take a chance on her, or I could continue to live in this liminal world where I've spent so many years existing. Giving myself to people, but then taking myself away just as quickly, always moving on for fear of getting too attached. Or I could try let someone love me, and love them in return.

I hadn't seen Ellen in months and I still thought about her every single day.

What was the point in yearning for someone like that when they were just around the corner, completely and totally within reach? Was it some form of sadism? Self-sabotage?

I was wrapped in my thoughts all the way home from my visit with Mum. While walking by a bookshop, I saw a display of the entire *Sasha Orlando* series, and it felt like a sign. On autopilot, I went inside, bought a copy of every single book and walked out with a heavy bag on my arm.

Halfway down the street, there was a teenage girl with a box of puppies. Living in the city, I'd come across countless people giving away puppies and kittens, and all other manner of baby animals on the street. Each time I'd taken a look at the cute little things and continued on my merry way. But not today. Today I stopped completely.

The girl's face was red as she handed a puppy off to a smiling couple. The sign over the box read: FREE PUPPIES. MY MUM IS MAKING ME GIVE THEM AWAY. ONLY TO GOOD, CARING HOMES.

Instantly, my heart went out to her.

"What breed are they?" I asked, peering down at the fawn coloured pups.

"Chihuahuas. I have to give them away because we don't have room in our flat," she replied, bereft.

"They're so tiny," I commented.

She nodded. "They don't need much space, just someone to care for them. They need a lot of love."

Feeling bold, I said, "I'll take one."

Sadly, she turned and picked one up. "This is Sheila. She's the bossiest of the litter, if you think you can handle that."

I smiled warmly. "I am partial to a bossy female."

She handed me the pup and I took her in my arms. Sheila was sleepy, and she immediately snuggled into me. For a second, I was a little boy again, the one whose Mum said no every time he begged for a pet.

"I think I love her already," I breathed.

"She'll get fluffier as she gets older," the girl said. "Her mum, Hilda, is my dog and she's really fluffy."

"I'll invest in some good lint rollers then," I said, unable to stop smiling.

When I arrived back at the flat, Damon sat in the living room, a laptop open in front of him and stacks of paper all around. He did a double take when he saw me.

"Uh, Julian, is that a dog?"

I flounced into the room, holding my new baby. "You can refer to her as Sheila."

Damon scratched his head. "Okay, but...you don't even have a garden."

"The balcony will do. And she can come with me every morning for a walk in the park. There was a girl out on the street giving them away. I had to take one."

Now he chuckled. "Well, don't tell Rose that. She'll be out trying to find the girl to get one for herself."

I saluted him as I headed for the kitchen to find a bowl to pour some water for Sheila. "By the way, I'll take that consulting job if it's still going," I said casually while I opened a cupboard.

"You will? That's great," Damon replied, and I smiled to myself.

By taking the job, it would put me in direct proximity to Ellen. And I had a new goal, one nobody could deter me from. I was going to win her back, claim her heart, and make her fall in love with me all over again.

Twenty-Four
Ellen

"Miss, can you sign for these, please?" the delivery guy asked as I answered the door. He held a giant bouquet of flowers.

It was early in the morning and a car would be arriving any minute to take me to Pinewood studios for the first day of filming. I'd been home a few weeks. My dad had been caring for Skittles and Rainbow while I was away, but I think they were glad to be settling back into their regular routine, and so was I. Although now I had to get used to a brand new one as the filming for the *Sasha Orlando* movie started in earnest.

Today I wore a dark blue tea dress with tiny hot air balloons printed all over, a black cardigan, purple tights, and mustard ballet flats. Ever since I said goodbye to Elodie, I'd slowly started to develop a new style, one that was all my own.

I finally found that little bit of confidence to let my inner girly girl fly free.

I still wondered if the outfit was "writery" enough, or if I should wear something more serious. While I was travelling, I'd collaborated via email and video chat with Levi Wilkins and Stacy Young, an award-winning screen-writing duo, to adapt *Good Girl, Bad Lady* for the big screen.

It had been both intimidating and exhilarating to work with such amazing writers, and I was more than a little excited about the first day of filming. I'd missed out on the read through due to nerves (yes, I was still a work in progress), but luckily Levi and Stacy were able to be there in my place. Now they were off working on their next project, so I would be the only writer on set during filming. Needless to say, I was shitting myself. Just a little bit.

Today, I'd meet the cast, and I was most nervous to see the actress who would play Sasha, Alicia Davidson. I saw videos of her auditions, but due to scheduling conflicts, we hadn't yet met in person.

And yes, I was also aware of the fact that she and Julian had been together in the past. I wasn't going to hold it against her, because Damon had been right, she completely embodied the character of Sasha and there was no way we could've gone with anyone else. Still, I was wary. What if she still had feelings for Julian? What if she discovered our relationship and held it against me?

"Sure, I can sign," I said, scribbling down my name on the electronic gizmo before taking the bouquet inside. I placed it on my kitchen table, studied the flowers a moment, then plucked out the card to see who they were from. A part of me wished they were from Julian, but I knew that would never happen. It had been months since we'd seen each other.

Dear Ellen,

My warmest congratulations on the film and best of luck with your first day on set.

Love,

Daniel

I chewed my lip, a little perplexed at how he signed off. *Love* was just so personal. It was how you spoke to family and people you were close to. Then again, our relationship had evolved. Nowadays, we met for coffee and chats, not only for business. I considered him a friend, but more and more he'd started to hint he was interested in me not just platonically.

I was flattered, and admittedly, it did feel exciting to have a man like Daniel be interested, but I was distracted. I thought about Julian all the time, even when I was strolling through the winding streets of Venice, boating across Lake Garda, or sunbathing on the pristine beaches of Southern France. I still felt that pang in my chest that he was no longer a part of my life.

Since my return, I've been meeting Suze at the Polka Dot on Tuesdays, just like before. Unlike before, Julian was never there. I felt his absence strongly. When I suggested to Damon that he offer Julian the technical consulting role, I may have had a hidden agenda. I'd been grasping at straws, but never in a million years did I expect him to take the job. He'd be around while we filmed, and the anticipation of seeing him was almost too much to handle.

When I arrived on set, my palms were sweaty. The first person I saw was David, and I was glad for a familiar face. He'd snagged the part of Toby, Sasha's boss, and I thought he was perfect for the role. I'd sat in on his audition, and it turned out he was actually a pretty good actor. I also had to explain the whole Elodie thing to him. It turned out, Julian never told him the truth about me, but he was pretty understanding. I got the feeling David was a hard man to shock.

"Ellen," he said, coming to walk alongside me. "Look at all this. It's exciting, isn't it," he said, gesturing to the dozens of crew members milling about. I'd never been on a film set before, so I felt like a duck out of water.

"Yep. Pretty exciting."

He gave my shoulder a soft squeeze. "Hey, don't be nervous. You've got this."

With that, he went, and I was alone. I stood there for a few seconds, unsure where I was supposed to go, when a runner appeared in front of me. "Hello, Miss Grant. I've been instructed to bring you to Mr. Atwood."

I exhaled in relief and followed her. Damon was standing in a replica of Sasha's bedroom. It was almost spooky how much it resembled what I'd created in my mind. There was the bright yellow lampshade on the nightstand, the poster of *The Breakfast Club*, Sasha's favourite film, on her wall.

"Okay, this is bizarre," I said as I approached.

"I know," Damon agreed. "The set designers have done an amazing job. By the way, there's someone who'd like to meet you."

He led me to a dressing room that read 'Alicia Davidson: Lead Actress' on the door. I sucked in a deep breath for courage while he knocked. A voice called for us to come in.

Alicia sat having her makeup done. She wore a dressing gown, her scarlet hair in hot rollers. With her bright eyes, full lips and curvy figure, she was the womanly ideal every girl wished she could be. I'd tried with Elodie and learned an important lesson; you don't need to be perfect or incredibly beautiful for people to accept you. You just need to be yourself.

I had more friends now than ever, and all because I'd started to accept myself. I understood my issues and worked every day to be braver, to push myself further than before.

Today was a clear example of that. The old me might've declined the invitation to come on set and be a part of the filming. She would've stayed home and fretted over it.

As soon as Alicia saw me, she gave a wide, friendly smile. "You must be Ellen. I've been dying to meet you in person."

Her makeup artist stood back as she came and embraced me in a hug. "I can't tell you how long I've waited for a role like this. Sasha is an icon and I'm beyond grateful that you chose me to portray her."

Well, it hadn't been just me, but I didn't bother to correct her. I was too much in awe of her presence. She definitely had that rare quality, that thing that made her stand out as a star. We were starkly different, and yet, we'd both been with Julian. In a weird way, that made me feel less intimidated, like we had something in common.

"It's so lovely to meet you," I squeaked. "I'm a big fan of everything you've been in."

"Oh stop, you don't have to say that."

Damon cleared his throat. "We're filming a scene with Sasha and Toby today. The one where she pitches the story about male escorts. You can stick with me if you'd like to sit in on it."

I nodded. "Yes, I'd like that."

Alicia gave me another hug. "Go on. I'll see you later. Maybe we can grab lunch sometime?"

Lunch with Alicia Davidson? I gulped. "Sure."

She beamed at me. "Okay, great."

When we neared the set of Toby's office, I saw a familiar face and my entire body stiffened. My heart thrummed, threatening to beat its way right out of my chest. I'd thought the time apart had made me stronger, that travelling had built my confidence, but as soon as I laid eyes on him, I was anxious as a school girl. Butterflies took charge of my insides, held me hostage.

Julian stood chatting to David, with what appeared to be a tiny dog under his arm, its fluffy tail wagging. *He had a dog now?* Maybe it belonged to someone else.

I swallowed back my nerves as I approached. "Hi again, David. Um, hello, Julian."

At the sound of my voice he turned, and for a second the air left me. I'd almost forgotten how beautiful he was. He'd cut his hair a little, but it was still long enough to grab hold of. His eyes sparkled as he gazed down at me. "Ellen," he breathed. "It's so good to see you."

His friendly demeanour caught me off guard. I'd worried he might be standoffish, cold, and aloof. But he was as warm and amiable as he'd ever been. There was an intensity behind it though. The way he stared at me, seeming to drink me in from head to toe. Pleasurable tingles skittered down my spine as I endeavoured not to melt under the fervour with which he took me in.

I tried to speak some words. Any words. It took great effort. "It's good to see you, too." *Heartbeat, please stop fluttering.* My attention went to the dog, its cute little eyes peering up at me. "Who's this?"

Julian gave her fluffy head a ruffle. "This is Sheila. She was penniless and living on the streets, begging fishmongers for scraps just to survive, so I took her in, spruced her up, and now she's living her best life."

"I thought you got her from some girl whose dog gave birth to a litter," David interjected.

"Hush, David, my story is far more interesting and dramatic," Julian scolded playfully. "I'm sure Ellen can appreciate that, being a writer and all." His handsome eyes seared me and I flushed.

How did he do that with just one look?

"Well, she's adorable." Swallow. Cough. Try to act natural. "H-how long have you had her?"

"Just a few weeks. She was a poop machine for a while there. It wasn't pretty. But now she's excreting less frequently, which is a relief to all involved. Rose has been helping me clean up. I'm pretty sure I owe her some sort of luxury hamper at this point to say thank you."

I gave a soft laugh, nervous flutters encapsulating me at his proximity. It was odd how we could spend so much time apart, yet chat like none of it ever even happened. Well, *he* could. I was having a little more trouble. "This is your first dog, right?"

He nodded. "It's been a learning curve. We've been on the outs a few times, but now we've come to an understanding."

"I'm glad to hear it."

We stared at each other for a long moment, while someone from wardrobe grabbed David. Julian didn't leave, instead he stayed and just…gazed at me. I swallowed tightly, eyes wandering over him, his angular jaw, bright hazel eyes, sculpted lips. I couldn't help it. He was just so freaking beautiful. I wasn't sure how I survived all this time not having his face to gaze at. His attention wandered from my eyes, down my nose, and to my mouth before rising back up again.

"I met Alicia," I said, breaking the intense moment. "She's very pretty."

"She is," Julian agreed. Even though I was the one to bring it up, his agreement made my chest burn. Just a little. "How were your travels?" he asked.

He knew I'd been away? "How did you—"

"I might have dropped into the bookshop hoping to see you," Julian confessed. "Bernice told me you'd taken some time off."

My chest thrummed. He'd come looking for me? That must've been a while ago if I'd been travelling at the time. Had he been hoping to rekindle? So many questions filled my head. I cleared my throat. "I'm actually not working there anymore. What with the travelling and all this film stuff, plus I've been doing more signings. I just don't have the time."

"Well, it's good to be busy," he said.

I nodded in agreement. "Yes, it is."

After a few moments of heavy silence, more people started to arrive on set. They were preparing to film the first scene between Alicia and David, so I went to take a seat close to Damon. Julian stood nearby, taking it all in. He put Sheila on the ground and she ran right up to me and hopped on my lap.

Julian chuckled. "She likes you. Queens always recognise other queens."

I flushed at the compliment and pet Sheila's head. *Why was he being so nice? And so flipping sexy intense?* I was going to have a heart attack if he didn't quit smouldering at me. It was like everything I'd hoped for had come true. Julian was looking at me like he remembered the intimacy we'd shared and wanted to relive every single moment.

Alicia appeared on set, flanked by several members of her team. She wore a pencil skirt and a tight blouse, her hair in a loose ponytail and her makeup done to perfection. She noticed Julian right away, her lips curving in a sultry grin.

"I heard you'd come on board. It's good to see you," she said as someone fixed the collar of her blouse.

311

My stomach twisted, witnessing their interaction. Everything inside of tensed and rebelled at the idea of them spending time together, possibly reuniting.

"You, too," Julian replied, but he didn't say more.

He stood a little closer to my chair and bent down to pet Sheila. "There's a good girl," he murmured lovingly, and I stiffened at his closeness. He was talking to the dog, not me, but still, the affection in his voice thrilled right through me.

There was a lot of technical stuff going on, with Damon giving directions to cast and crew. I sat back, absorbing it all. This really was a dream come through. For years I'd resisted movie offers, mostly because I knew there was no way I could be involved. Too many people. Too much pressure. And if I wasn't involved, then how could I ensure they didn't mess it up?

A part of me was still freaking out on the inside, but another part was handling her shit. I could do this now. I wouldn't allow myself another choice.

I glanced up at Julian. His attention was fixed on Damon as he exchanged a few words with Alicia. I stared at his profile, a pain in my chest, a pang of longing. He must've sensed me looking because his eyes flicked to mine. I blinked and looked away, too hot. I took off my cardigan, folded it and placed it on the side of my chair.

"Action," Damon called and suddenly they were filming.

I got excited for a whole other reason as Sasha (Alicia) walked into Toby's (David's) office and took a seat in front of his desk. I could've recited the lines from memory, since Levi, Stacy and I had spent many late nights editing and revising, trying to make the script absolutely perfect.

It didn't take long for me to fall into the scene, like I really was watching a movie. Well, it was more like a stage play, but it was enthralling nonetheless. It turned out Alicia and David had great chemistry.

"I told you, I can do more than write fluff pieces about the latest celebrity trend," said Sasha. "I want to explore something real, something that will hook readers in, make their hearts race."

"Fluff pieces are your job. That's what you signed up for," Toby replied stiffly.

"But I can be so much more than that I can make this column shine."

"You can make it shine by writing me an article about the pros and cons of dating apps."

Sasha folded her arms. "God, you really are a sauceless bastard sometimes."

Toby pushed his glasses up his nose, a deep indent forming between his eyebrows. "What did you just call me?"

Sasha stood, her expression defiant. "I called you a coward," she said, then turned and left the office.

I smiled to myself. They really brought the interaction I'd written between Sasha and her boss to life. The relationship between the two, the *will they or won't they*, was a huge driving force behind the series' popularity. I smiled thinking of how thrilled my readers would be when they finally got together in the last book.

Damon called for a break and I went to grab a coffee from the cafeteria. After being so close to Julian for the last hour, I needed some space. I was emptying a sugar sachet into my latte when somebody pinched me on the shoulder. I turned around and Alicia stood next to me.

"That was fun! I adore your writing. Sasha has some great lines. Sauceless bastard! I laughed so much when I first read that."

I gave a small smile. "Thanks. She's definitely a lot of fun to write."

"Hey, can I get a macchiato?" she asked the catering guy. I thought it was pretty down to earth of her to come order her own coffee. I always imagined big stars had a team of assistants to do that sort of stuff.

"Coming right up."

I heard a tiny bark and then saw Sheila running up to me, Julian chasing after her. He scooped her up before she could jump on me. "You've gained a new fan," he chuckled.

"I think she just likes having a warm lap to sit on during filming," I said and reached out to pet her.

"Oh, she's just darling," Alicia crooned, bending close and letting the dog lick her whole face. "My makeup artist is gonna give me hell for this, but I just can't resist doggy kisses," she continued on a chuckle, then glanced at Julian. "I may end up stealing her before the shoot wraps."

"I better keep an eye on you then," he replied.

Alicia waggled her eyebrows. "You better."

Julian turned to me, placing a hand on my shoulder for a second. The touch was warm, thrilling. His voice was low and intimate. "Can we talk later?"

My tummy flip-flopped. "Sure. I have a car taking me home at five if you want to share it?"

His expression heated. "I'd like that. See you then."

Alicia eyed him as he walked away, then looked at me. "Are you two…"

"No! No, we aren't. We're, um, neighbours," I said, rambling a little. It was a lie, but I didn't want her speculating.

"Oh, right. Well, Julian's an amazing guy. We actually used to have a thing, but it didn't work out."

"You did?" I said, hoping she'd keep talking. I was stupidly eager to have my heart broken with details of her and Julian's relationship.

She sighed. "He's incredible in bed, but he just wasn't what I was looking for relationship-wise, you know?"

"Oh, well, that's too bad."

She knocked back her macchiato in a few gulps. "Yep. Well, I better get back. They'll need to redo my makeup after little miss cutie pie licked my face off."

I nodded and waved her away, exhaling once she was gone. This shoot was going to be a lot more tumultuous than I anticipated. I remembered the flowers Daniel sent this morning and realised I hadn't yet sent a text to say thank you.

Ellen: *Thanks for the flowers. They're lovely :-)*

His response came quickly.

Daniel: *My pleasure. Are you free for dinner tonight? xxx.*

I frowned at the kisses, unsure how to reply. He definitely wanted more than friendship, but I just wasn't in a place to date anyone. Yes, it had been months since Julian and I were together, but I still had feelings for him. It wouldn't be fair to Daniel to start something when I was still getting over someone else. There was also the fact that he was my agent. We had a professional relationship and that complicated things.

Later on, I found Julian chatting with several members of the crew. I managed to catch his eye and he approached.

315

"I'm leaving now if you still want to have that talk."

"Of course, lead the way."

Julian opened the door of the car for me and I climbed inside. It was a town car, and the driver was wearing earphones, which made me feel more comfortable to chat. My heart still raced though. I had so much I wanted to say, so much I wanted to ask.

And I had absolutely no idea where to start.

Twenty-Five
Ellen

I fiddled with the sleeve of my cardigan. "So, um, how have you been?"

Julian tilted his head to me, his gaze running from the hem of my dress that reached just above the knee, all the way up to my mouth. I felt exposed. He laid me bare with nothing more than a glance.

Instinctively, I pushed my thighs together, and a low heat simmered between us. Perhaps having this conversation in the confines of a car wasn't my finest idea. Sheila settled in on the other side of Julian, curling up into a ball and closing her eyes. I sort of wished she was in the middle so that we'd have a little more space. As it was, we were right next to each other, and it made everything feel that much more amplified.

Julian's expression was devastatingly handsome yet sad. It made my heart go *whump*. "Do you want the honest answer or the airbrushed one?"

"The honest one?" My words came out sounding like a question.

Julian sat back, his head falling against the seat as he exhaled heavily. "In that case, I'll tell you, I've not been doing marvellously well, I'm afraid."

I didn't speak, only stared at him. I hadn't been doing marvellously well either, emotionally speaking, but I didn't tell him that. Not yet.

He levelled me with those ruinous hazel eyes, his lashes impossibly long and thick. "I've missed you, Ellen. More than you can imagine."

My voice was a whisper. "I've missed you, too."

His expression was wistful and a little melancholy. "Even when you were off on your solo travels?"

"Yes, Julian, even then."

Neither one of us spoke for a minute. The journey back to the city was going to take over an hour, maybe longer in evening traffic. And it was going to be pretty uncomfy if we had to sit in silence the whole time.

"I haven't worked in months." Julian's confession shocked me out of my thoughts.

I stared at him, taken aback. "You haven't?"

He shook his head. "It's been a struggle."

"But why?"

He shifted in place, his face contemplative as he appeared to decide how best to explain. "Since you, being intimate with other women has not been easy. In fact, I haven't felt the urge to be with anyone, and that's quite atypical for me. Typically, once I finish a relationship, I move on to the next. But even when we were still..." he paused to gesture between us. "You know, my relationship with clients had started to decline. You were all I could think about."

I frowned, feeling frustrated. "Why are you telling me all this?"

"You said you wanted honesty."

"Yes, but—" I made an aggravated hand gesture. "I don't know what I'm supposed to say. I don't know what you want from me."

"You don't have to say anything, Ellen, not if you don't want to. And all I want from you is—"

My phone chimed and I frowned in frustration. *Just finish the sentence, Julian, please, because I'm not brave enough to finish it for you.*

318

My eyes flickered back and forth between his when it chimed again. He arched an eyebrow. "Do you want to check that?"

I pulled out my phone and found two texts from Daniel.

Daniel: *So, dinner? I can make a reservation somewhere nice. xxx*

Daniel: *There's a table free at Celeste, but I need to give them an answer asap.*

When I looked up, Julian was reading the message over my shoulder. I slid my phone back in my bag. "It's not very polite to read other people's messages, you know."

Julian didn't beat around the bush, ignoring my statement when he asked, "Are you seeing Daniel?"

"That's none of your business."

"I know that, but I would still like to know if you are."

There was a flash of jealousy in his eyes. I scratched my neck, feeling like I might be coming out in a rash. "No, we aren't seeing each other. But he's started making…"

"Advances?"

I exhaled. "Yes, and I'm not sure how to respond. He's my agent. We have a professional relationship."

Julian's attention went from eyes to my lips and then back again. "Would you like to date him?"

My stomach twisted. "No?"

He gave a soft, affectionate chuckle, but there was sadness behind it. "You don't sound too sure about that."

"I'm just confused."

He reached out and touched my knee, his hand firm. I could feel his warmth even through my tights. "Don't let the pressure get to you. Do what *you* want to do, Ellen."

After all these months, the feel of his hand on me, even in such a small way, was drugging. I didn't want to go out

319

to dinner with Daniel, not when I was stuck in a car with Julian and he kept staring at me with those heart-breaking eyes of his.

I swallowed tightly. "I guess I'm still trying to figure that out."

Julian nodded and looked away, his face a picture of thoughtfulness. I cleared my throat, needing to change the subject.

"So, how does it feel to see Alicia again?"

I suspected he knew what I was up to when his eyebrow ticked ever so slightly upward. "It's always nice to see an old friend."

"Don't you mean old flame?" I nudged him with my shoulder, trying to lighten the mood but it sort of fell flat.

"What we had happened almost three years ago. Now I merely see her as a friend."

"She's so beautiful."

His lips twitched, a little of his sparkle returning. Did it please him to imagine I was jealous? Well, I was. Anyone would be, knowing the man they loved had once been with a Hollywood actress, renowned all over the world for her beauty.

The man *I* loved.

The thought was sobering, but it wasn't something I could ignore. If it weren't for the fact that he'd ended things, I might've been brave enough to take a chance. Confess how I felt right here and now. But he *had* been the one, and though he confessed to not being intimate with anyone else in months, I still wasn't one hundred percent clear where we stood. There was a niggling sense of doubt in the back of my mind.

What if he got cold feet again?

What if he just upped and decided he couldn't be with me a second time?

Julian's attention wandered over me once more and I shivered. "Beauty is in the eye of the beholder, Ellen."

I sucked in a breath and looked away. My phone rang with a call from Nick. I really was popular this evening. Turning away from Julian, I picked it up immediately.

"Hi, Nick, how are you?"

"Ellen," he said, sounding glum and I instantly knew why he was calling. My heart thudded. These past few months, I'd been waiting for this call. Waiting for the time when my dad would finally summon up the courage to tell my brothers the truth about what happened to Mum.

"Dad told you," I whispered.

He sounded like he'd been crying. And knowing my jolly, life and soul of the party brother had been crying made my stomach ache. I'd had months to come to terms with this, to accept what happened. For Nick, it was all fresh.

"Yes," Nick breathed.

"What about Cam?"

"Dad told us both together. Cam's angry, but he seems to have accepted it. You know him, he'll just keep all his feelings locked up. Can I...can I come stay with you for a little while? I need to get away."

"Of course. You can stay with me for as long as you need."

"I just have to pack a few things and see if Sharon will cover my shifts at the café. I should arrive later tonight."

"That's fine. I'll wait up. See you then."

I hung up and exhaled a breath. I had a feeling I wouldn't get much sleep tonight. Nick would want to stay up and talk things out. It was how he processed. Cameron was the opposite. Like Nick said, he kept everything locked tight until one day I feared he might implode.

"Is everything okay?" Julian asked.

I let my head fall back against the car seat. "It's just some family stuff."

"Want to talk about it?"

I glanced at him. I guess we did have some time to kill, and maybe it would be good for Julian to know what had happened to me. How it affected me in later life.

"It's pretty bleak."

His expression was wry. "I'm well acquainted with the dark."

I worried my lip, then finally replied, "After everything that went down at the wedding, my dad told me some stuff about my mum. She hadn't really died in a car accident." Julian was quiet while I spoke, listening intently. "She was actually the victim of a break in. I was there when it happened, witnessed the whole thing. I was only two years old at the time, and Dad said I became totally mute afterward. It was years before I started to talk again. I guess that's where all my fears stem from. I've started seeing a therapist, just once a month, but it's helping me sort through my feelings."

"Oh, Ellen," Julian murmured and without warning pulled me into his arms. "I can't imagine how it must feel to find all that out."

I sank into his embrace, not realising how much I needed it, how much I needed to tell him that. He stroked my arm up and down, his touch tender, soothing. "Dad told Nick and Cameron today. Nick's coming to stay with me for a little while. He needs some time to process."

I blinked away the tears that wanted to fall. They were half due to sadness for my brothers finally knowing the truth, and half due to the fact that I'd missed Julian so, so much. And being this close to him, it felt like all my cells were coming alive again.

I just wasn't sure if I was being foolishly hopeful. Maybe Julian was just being kind for the sake of working on the film together. But no, he wouldn't have told me all that stuff about giving up his work if he hadn't intended for me to draw certain conclusions.

"That day when we…when you ended things. I shouldn't have left you that money," I said.

"You don't need to apologise."

"Yes, I do. It was a horrible thing to do. It belittled what was between us and I hate that I acted in anger."

"You're not the only one who regrets their decisions that day," he replied and I turned my head to look at him. I saw the honesty in his eyes, the truth of his words. And I…

"I believe you," I whispered then rested my head on his shoulder.

Julian continued stroking my arm. He held me for the rest of the journey and I felt myself growing closer to him. It was so natural to just relax around him. Neither one of us spoke, not wanting to break the connection. When the car stopped outside my house, I was sad to leave him. I wanted to invite him inside, but I knew Nick would be arriving soon. And anyway, it would be a bad idea to rush things.

Despite my worries, I felt something happening between us. The way Julian was behaving around me felt like he was finally opening up to the possibility of us. To the idea of being with just one person.

He placed a chaste kiss on my cheek then helped me out of the car. When I went inside and closed the door behind me, I slid right down to the floor, where it felt like all my emotions had been scattered.

***

The next morning, I got a text on my phone from an unknown number.

Hey, Ellen. This is Alicia. We never had the chance to exchange numbers yesterday, but this is mine. I was wondering if you'd like to do lunch today?

I stared at the screen for a full minute, trying to figure out how to respond. My coffee was going cold where it sat on the kitchen counter.

"Who's Alicia?" Nick asked when he walked up behind me.

I shot him an annoyed glance. "Why does everyone think it's okay to read my messages over my shoulder?"

He raised his hands in the air. "Someone's feeling touchy."

I pursed my lips. "Sorry. I'm just a little tired this morning."

As predicted, Nick and I had been up until the wee hours talking, discussing our childhoods, all the unexplainable things about us that finally made sense. I'd texted Daniel and told him I couldn't go to dinner. I felt bad for saying no, but I didn't want to lead him on. It would be worse to give him false hope, especially with my feelings being all tangled up in Julian.

I eyed Nick. "The text is from Alicia Davidson."

My brother blinked at me. "The actress in your film? Are you two besties now?"

"Yes, the actress. And no, we aren't besties. But she's trying to befriend me. It's weird."

"Why is it weird?"

I dropped my gaze when I replied, "Because she and Julian used to be a thing."

"Oh, that is a little weird. And a little scandalous." He waggled his eyebrows.

"She didn't hire him. As far as I know, it was a real relationship."

"Ah, got ya. So, you think she's trying to scope out the competition?"

"No, that's the weird thing. I think she genuinely wants to be my friend."

"Well, that's great. Be her friend. I'll tag along to lunch if you need backup."

Now I rolled my eyes. "Oh, will you now?"

"Hey, redheads are Cam's thing. You know I prefer brunettes."

"Hmmm, true."

"So, can I come?"

"Well, I'm definitely not going alone. I need someone there to fill the silence in case I choke."

Nick grinned. "And I can chat for England. We're a match made in heaven."

His endlessly cheery demeanour, even in the face of Dad's revelation, drew a smile out of me. Nick accompanied me to the set that morning, and I had to admit, I was pretty excited for him to be there. I was proud of myself and I wanted to share that pride with my brother.

When we arrived, Nick went in search of a bathroom and I in search of coffee. Over in the cafeteria, I spotted Julian sitting at a table. Sheila was sprawled out on his lap, snoozing, while he held a book and sipped on a latte. I was a little distracted by how handsome he was, dressed down for once in jeans and a T-shirt. I didn't immediately notice just exactly *what* he was reading.

His attention was glued to *The Games We Play*, the eighth *Sasha Orlando* novel. Did that mean he'd read the entire series? The ninth and final book was set to release in a few short weeks.

Butterflies invaded my belly.

I wanted to know what he thought of the series, but I was also terrified. His opinion meant too much to me. The first book was all about male escorts, but my research had been limited, confined mostly to books and what I could find on the internet. Julian had real-life experience, which was one of the reasons why he was here on set to give advice.

I grabbed two cappuccinos before I approached Julian's table. "So, you finally gave in?"

He glanced up, his eyes dancing when he saw me, his lips curving into a pleased expression

"What can I say? I've been converted."

I opened my mouth, then closed it. I mean, if he'd made it through to book eight then he must at least be enjoying them. I sat down and took a sip of my coffee.

"Looks like you're almost done."

"Yep. Then I'll just have to wait until the last one releases." His smile was playful. "Unless you'd like to send me an advance copy. There have to be some perks to knowing the author, right?"

I fiddled with a sugar packet. "I could *possibly* do that." A pause as I met his gaze. "So, you like them?"

His smile grew wide. "Ellen, I adore them. You are a fantastic writer and Sasha's adventures are giving me life right now."

I felt myself flush. "Really?"

"Yes, really. Besides, I should've known I'd love them. I always was obsessed with Elodie's stories. It was the first thing that drew me to her—to you. I eavesdropped on yours and Suze's conversation before I ever turned around to see what you both looked like."

Hold up a second. He eavesdropped? This was news to me.

"You mean before you spilled your coffee on our table that time?"

Julian closed his book and placed it aside. "Darling, you had me entranced for weeks before we ever actually met."

My eyelashes fluttered. "So, you just…listened to our conversations?"

Julian nodded. "It was my favourite real-life soap opera. I should've known it was far too entertaining to be real. Plus, your stories always had a beginning, a middle, and an end. Real life isn't usually so neat."

How on earth had I not noticed him?

"That's…that's so…" I sputtered, not knowing what to say.

"Shady?" He chuckled. "I told you I have the face of a rapscallion. Sometimes my behaviour matches up."

A part of me was annoyed, while another part was flattered he'd noticed me long before I ever noticed him. Or at least, he'd noticed Elodie. In what universe does a man like Julian go undetected for so long? He should become like, a secret agent or something.

His voice was low when he leaned across the table to murmur, "You seem a little flustered, Ellen."

"I'm just trying to get my head around it."

"What's there to get your head around? I was drawn to you. It's simple."

I was locked in his gaze, unable to look away. Julian exhaled a sigh, as though smitten by the very fact we were staring into each other's eyes. He really was too much sometimes.

"There you are," came Nick's voice and I looked up as my brother walked towards us. His attention went from me to Julian, his eyes asking, *Am I interrupting something?*

I gave a very faint shake of my head, even though he *was* interrupting a little. He was interrupting me getting lost in the dreamy hazel depths of Julian's gaze.

"Well, I might see you later," I said, standing and handing Nick his coffee. I led him away and we walked around the set. I pointed out things of interest and he took it all in. I was glad for him not bringing up the fact that Julian was here. I'd mentioned to him last night that he'd come on board as a technical consultant, but I don't think Nick realised that meant he'd be around during filming.

We watched them shoot a scene between Alicia and Peter, the actor who was to play Ralph, the male escort character from the book. Then there was a short scene between Alicia and David. I got the sense that they were attracted to each other, just something in the way Alicia looked at him, and my mind started to wander. As a writer, you often drew inspiration from moments in real life.

"You're mean," Alicia said and swiped him on the shoulder.

"I'm just trying to give you a heads-up," said David. "If you sit in that position, Gary the cameraman will be able to see right up your skirt."

"Gary! Is this true?" Alicia exclaimed, and the cameraman's cheeks went bright red.

David chuckled and looked back to Alicia. "You see!"

"Oh, my God, I'm asking Vanessa in wardrobe to lengthen this skirt before our next scene."

When we broke for lunch, Alicia came right over. I introduced her to Nick and she led us to her private dressing room where her assistant had set up an array of food for us. We ate sushi and talked about some upcoming scenes.

"So, where are you two from originally?" Alicia asked as she brought a California roll to her mouth and took a bite.

"We're from Torquay. It's in Devon, on the coast," Nick replied. I loved how he wasn't intimidated or fazed by having lunch with a famous person. I personally had a little bit of training when Julian and I went to all those fancy parties. My brother was a fish out of water, but you'd never be able to tell.

"It's a beautiful place," I added. "We get a lot of tourists in the summer, but there are also quiet spots if you know your way around."

"It sounds lovely. Maybe I'll pay a visit before I fly back to the U.S."

"You'll want to wear a disguise if you do," Nick suggested. "The locals might go a little crazy if they find out you're in town."

"I'll keep that in mind," she said with a pretty, red-lipped smile.

"So, you and David seem to have great chemistry," I said, then amended. "Acting chemistry, I mean."

Alicia chuckled. "Well, it's not too hard to have chemistry with someone who looks like him, but it helps that he's actually a lovely person, too."

"I'm so pleased with how your scenes are turning out. You two really bring Toby and Sasha to life."

She preened at the compliment. "I'm glad to hear it."

When we finished up, Alicia walked us to the door of her dressing room. Just as we stepped out, Julian was walking by with Sheila. He had her on a leash this time with a little pink harness. It was adorable.

"There's my future baby." Alicia bent down to pet the dog. "I'm still deciding if I should risk jail time and just steal you," she whispered playfully as she ruffled Sheila's head.

Julian glanced at me. "Ellen."

I tugged on the handle of my handbag, remembering our car ride yesterday, how he'd held me. "Hey."

"Cute dog," Nick said, grinning.

Julian didn't take his eyes off me. "She is decidedly cute. Ellen, I've actually been looking for you. I was wondering if we could go over the afternoon scene together? I just had a few notes."

My throat tightened. "Sure." I turned to Nick. "Will you be okay for a while?"

"He can hang out with me and David. We're due to run lines in a couple of minutes," Alicia put in as she stood, her perceptive gaze travelling from me to Julian.

Before I knew it, Julian was leading me to a small rehearsal room down the hall from Alicia's dressing room. He opened the door and gestured for me to go inside. I stepped in, both exhilarated and nervous as hell to be alone with him yet again.

Twenty-Six
Julian

Ellen's shoulders were tense.

I followed her into the empty room and closed the door behind me. Sheila gave a little bark, since she had a thing about people closing doors. She really was a bossy little pup. I gave her a warning look and she piped down.

Ellen took a seat by the table, where I'd left a copy of the script. I hadn't just been making up an excuse to get her alone. I really did have notes about the scene, but now that I did have her all to myself, the urge to approach her from behind, push her hair to the side and kiss her neck was strong. She wore a loose jumper that fell over one shoulder, baring her soft, smooth skin. The exposed black strap of her bra was an enticement I struggled to resist.

She started turning pages, all business. "So, which part did you take issue with?"

I placed a hand on the back of her chair, and she shifted away slightly. I moved closer, allowing the tip of my thumb to briefly touch her shoulder. She sucked in a small, barely perceptible breath.

"Page sixty-five. The conversation between Sasha and Ralph." Ellen found the page and I reached across her to pick up a pen. If I wasn't mistaken, she trembled a little when I got close.

Again, I resisted the urge to touch her and underlined the part I thought she should consider changing. Sasha asks Ralph, the escort who has agreed to be anonymously interviewed for her column, if he ever sees a day when he'll retire and settle down. Ralph says no, it's not in his nature to be monogamous.

"I don't think Ralph should be so certain in his answer. In the books, it says he's thirty-five and has been working as an escort for twelve years. That's a long time. I think he might be a little jaded at this point in his career. I think he would be more open to trying out a different way of life, if the right lady came along. Maybe he doesn't want it outright, but I think it's something he would at least consider."

Ellen was quiet, listening to me speak as she made notes in the margins. "Are you speaking from personal experience?" she asked, her voice deceptively casual as she continued scribbling down notes.

"That is what I've been hired for, to give my personal opinion based on experience."

She was quiet again, then said, "So, you've felt jaded?"

"Isn't it obvious? I wouldn't have stopped working if I didn't feel that way."

"Any particular reason?"

I dragged a hand down my face. "There are a few."

Finally, she looked at me. "I'm sorry."

"What for?"

I saw her throat bob as she swallowed. "For not understanding your situation better. It must've been so jarring to have me come along and just expect you to..."

"Expect me to?"

She heaved a frustrated breath, appeared to steel herself. "Expect you to give your entire self to me, to make yourself so vulnerable when it's something you normally guard against."

I took the seat next to hers, grabbed her hands and shifted her so that she faced me. "Ellen, you didn't expect anything. You drew me in, yes, but I came willingly."

Her gaze dropped shyly to her lap. "And how do you feel about monogamy now that you aren't working as an escort anymore? Is it something you see yourself possibly being interested in?"

"Ellen, I—"

Her hopeful eyes flicked up. "Yes?"

I took a deep breath, levelled her with a firm look and decided to lay all my cards on the table. "A lifetime with just one person wouldn't feel like a life sentence if I got to spend it with you."

Her breath hitched, eyelashes fluttering. "I...that's very..."

"Romantic?"

Her voice was airy. "Yes, but, do you mean to say you want to be with me? You want us to try again?"

I brushed my thumb across the inside of her wrist and held her gaze. I made sure there was no way she could misinterpret my meaning when I replied, "Ellen, I would be the luckiest man on earth if you were to give me a second chance."

I saw the turmoil and uncertainty in her eyes. It was expected, since I'd given her enough reason not to trust me by breaking up with her.

"I don't want to rush," she whispered, a tremble in her voice.

I pulled her into my arms. "I would never rush you. Just know I'm here waiting for you, whenever you're ready."

She moved away, seeming to gather herself as she cleared her throat and quickly switched back to our original topic of conversation. "You're right about Ralph. In the film. He shouldn't be so closed off to the idea of monogamy. I'll make some changes to the dialogue and run them by Damon. Do you mind if I keep this copy of the script? I'll return it to you later today."

"Sure."

She stood, tucked the script into her bag and headed for the door. I reached out to halt her, lightly catching hold of her elbow. "Ellen."

She stilled and looked back at me. Her eyes were so big, so open, so guileless.

"Yes?"

"Really do think about it. Don't make any rash decisions. I know I have a lot to make up to you, but I'm not going anywhere. Like I said, whenever you're ready, I'll be here."

When she left, I felt like she took my heart right along with her.

***

Ellen

After informing Damon of the small changes to the script, I left the set early. I told Nick he could stay and hang out if he wanted, but he declined and came home with me anyway. I needed time to think about what Julian had said. Yes, I loved and adored him, but I worried about him getting cold feet again. What if he suddenly decided he didn't want to be with me anymore, just like he did after Dad's wedding?

I couldn't go through that again.

Suze's birthday was coming up, so I decided to immerse myself in some shopping to take my mind off things. I felt like I owed her an amazing gift after everything I'd put her through, which why I was browsing the handbags at Selfridges. I knew she was a fan of Marc Jacobs. I was trying to decide between several options when a familiar voice said, "Pardon my intrusion, but do I know you from somewhere?"

On the other side of the handbag display stood Warren Gold. He had several shopping bags on his arm, but unlike the last two times I'd met him, he wasn't accompanied by a lady friend. My chest thrummed at the sight of him, nerves fluttering in my belly. How on earth had he recognised me?

"Um, no, I don't think so," I said, dismissive, allowing my hair to fall across my face. Today I'd glammed myself up, wearing a bright red tea dress and more makeup than usual. I thought it might make me feel better, but so far it hadn't really worked. Anyway, I guess it meant my resemblance to Elodie was a little more pronounced than usual.

He came closer, eyes moving over me keenly. "Are you sure? You seem so familiar."

"You're mistaken."

A beat of silence fell, then, "Elodie? You're Julian's Elodie, aren't you?" Warren smiled widely when it finally hit him.

I refused to make eye contact, feigning preoccupation with the handbags as I let out an irritable sigh. "What do you want, Warren?"

"You *were* a client of his. I knew that old friend story smelled false. What's your kink? You like dressing up? Role play? Honestly, I don't know why. You're very pretty just as you are."

"I don't have a kink. Now, if you don't mind, I'm trying to shop."

He didn't take the hint. "Have you and Julian parted ways?"

"That's none of your business."

"I'll take that as a yes. You know, I haven't seen him around much lately. I thought maybe he'd found some lucky lady to settle down with, pop out a few kids."

I made a hostile noise in the back of my throat. This bloke really didn't know when to leave well alone.

"Then again," Warren went on. "I don't see that ever happening for Julian. Men like us, we don't settle down. Love is a foreign concept. Julian likes to fool himself that he's a romantic, but when it comes down to it, it's sex that matters most."

Even though I was trying my best to ignore him, his comment hit home. What if Julian was just fooling himself? What if the idea of a monogamous relationship was more appealing than the reality?

"If you're in the market for someone new, I really would love to take you out," Warren went on, his lascivious eyes slithering over me.

"No, thank you," I said and moved to walk away.

"If you're holding out for Julian, you're wasting your time. I can't count the number of women who've fallen for him. He left them with nothing but broken hearts. Don't be one of those women, Elodie."

I didn't reply, too many pent-up emotions clogged my throat. He placed a business card down on the table where the handbags were displayed then sauntered off. Needless to say, I didn't pick it up.

My encounter with Warren haunted me for the next two days. Every time I saw Julian, he had such expectancy in his eyes, waiting for my answer. I was too scared to give it to him. Warren had sown a seed of doubt that had spread roots deep in my psyche. Now I was questioning everything.

Three days after my encounter with Warren I was on set, texting with Nick. There was a break in filming and most people had gone to get food. I sat down on the chair next to Damon's.

My brother had gone home to Torquay, and I always missed him when he left after a visit. Some days I felt like convincing him to move to London and live in my spare room, that way I wouldn't feel so alone all the time.

My heart longed for Julian, pined for him, but I feared him pulling away. Going through that rejection again would be torture.

"I'm feeling a little down," a voice said, and I looked up, frowning when there was nobody there. It took me a second to realise the voice came from the monitor in front of me. Damon and Julian were on the set of Sasha's living room. Damon looked to be fiddling with the curtains, trying to fix the folds so that they were all even, while Julian lounged on the sofa, looking crestfallen.

"I thought you were enjoying the job," Damon replied.

"I am, much more so than I expected but..." he trailed off.

"You're having a hard time being around Ellen?" Damon guessed, and I sucked in a breath. I knew I shouldn't be listening to this, but I was glued to the seat.

"Yes," Julian went on. "She's been distant. I laid my cards on the table for her, made it clear I wanted to try again. She said she needed time, but that was three days ago."

Damon scoffed. "Three days is hardly a lifetime."

"It is when you love someone."

Time stood still. *Had I just heard him correctly?* My body filled with a thousand tiny butterflies flapping their incessant wings. For a second, it felt like my heart ceased

337

beating. Like the world had been flipped on its axis. Hearing Julian say he loved me so casually, like he'd known it for a long time, set my entire being alight. A thrilling rush of adrenaline raced through me.

Damon shook his head. "You obviously don't see what I see."

Julian perked up. "What do you see?"

"That the woman is head over heels for you."

"You're just saying that."

"Believe what you want, but I'm telling the truth."

Julian went quiet, thoughtful. "I'm so in love with her, Damon, but I think I screwed everything up by breaking things off. I'm not sure she can forgive me for that. Maybe she shouldn't."

I stared at the screen, took in Julian's beautiful, sad face, and all I wanted to do was run to him, take him in my arms, and kiss all his pain away. All of a sudden, Warren's poisonous words had no meaning. They were nothing, not when I could see the stark, honest yearning radiating from Julian's very being.

Damon spoke then. "Why shouldn't she? Rose says she's never seen you like this over a woman. If what you have with Ellen is a once in a lifetime thing, then I don't think you can do anything else but tell her that."

"I have told her."

"Did you though? Sometimes you speak in riddles. Did you actually tell her you love her?"

Julian huffed a breath. "Not in so many words."

"Then tell her."

Before I could hear what Julian said next, I was up from my seat. I left my things behind, my phone and handbag, too determined to get to him. When I reached the set, I was completely breathless. Julian and Damon looked up as I braced myself against the fake door frame.

Julian's brows drew together as he stood. "Ellen, is everything all right?"

I shook my head. "No, it isn't."

I didn't give him time to reply. Instead I ran to him, threw my arms around his neck and planted my lips on his. I felt his shock in his sharp intake of breath. I kissed him with such force, with everything I had inside me. At first, he kissed me softly, unsure, but as the initial shock faded, his body responded. His arms came around my waist, tightening, and my spine arched instinctively, my breasts pushing against him.

He let out a groan, his tongue sliding along my tongue. We only broke apart when Damon cleared his throat.

"Uh, I'll give you both a moment."

Damon left, and Julian pressed his forehead to mine, his breathing choppy. "What was that for?"

I bit my lip, a wave of shyness hitting me. That kiss was one of the most forward, brave moves I'd ever made. My gaze went to the cameras. "One of the cameramen left the monitors on."

He stared at me a moment, putting two and two together, before his lips curved into a sinful smile. "Well, aren't you sneaky."

"I heard what you said," I blurted.

Julian tilted his head, eyes flickering between mine. "How much did you hear?"

I swallowed the thick lump that had formed in my throat. "All the most important bits."

"Such as?" he prodded.

My voice lowered to a whisper. "That you love me."

He exhaled, looking at me like he was taking all of me in. He reached out and tucked a strand of hair behind my ear, his fingertips warm on my skin. "I have loved you for quite some time, Ellen."

"Then why didn't you tell me?"

"Because I feared you might not say it back. I feared the consequences of loving someone when my entire life I've avoided it."

His words swept me up, like a tidal wave.

A moment passed. I was too shell-shocked to speak. Julian massaged the back of my neck, like it was a natural instinct to touch me, soothe me. His voice was gentle, cajoling. "And now it seems my fears are coming true."

"What? No! I love you. I love you, too," I babbled.

Julian's chuckle was full of affection. "I do believe your kiss told me that just a moment ago."

I tried to focus on breathing. "The kiss, right. The kiss."

His eyes were tender now. "Is there anything else you'd like to tell me?"

I bobbed my head foolishly. "Yes, that I want to be with you."

"Be with me, then," he purred and caught my lips in a kiss. This one was slower, more intentionally seductive than the last. Julian drank me in, his tongue circling mine. My brain was a scramble of lust and heat when he captured all my hair in his hand and pushed it aside so that he could lick and suck at my neck.

"Come with me," he said, taking my hand and dragging me behind the set, where there were no cameras lurking. Quick as a flash he pushed me up against the wall and kissed me like it had been a thousand years instead of a few months.

I moaned when he pressed his erection against my belly. His movements became frenzied, his need for me evident in his desperation to get as close as possible. One hand moulded my breast over my top, while the other reached down to slide beneath my skirt. He fingered the lace of my underwear softly before he pushed past the barrier and stroked my aching clit.

I gasped into the kiss, hands pawing open his shirt, so I could feel his skin. I needed him now more than ever. Anyone could come along, but I was lost in the moment, too far gone to care. Overcome with the need to see him come apart, I grabbed both his hands, stopping them in their exploration. I turned us so that he was the one with his back to the wall, then lowered to my knees.

"I've wanted to do this for a really long time," I whispered, hands shaking as I reached for his fly.

His Adam's apple bobbed in his throat as he gazed down at me, murmuring a raspy, "*Ellen.*"

I pulled his cock from his pants, maintaining eye contact as I pressed my lips to his tip. In all the research I'd done about blow jobs, one thing seemed to be key; eye contact was a big turn on. It seemed to work when Julian swore under his breath, his chest rising and falling rapidly. He reached down to stroke my cheek and I took him into my mouth.

"Jesus," he growled quietly, his head falling back against the wall.

I licked his tip, then swirled my tongue around the head. This made his eyes roll back and a series of swearwords fell from his mouth. I loved watching him, adored the reactions I could elicit.

When I took as much of his cock into my mouth as I could, he undulated. I moved my mouth up and down, building up a rhythm, enjoying the noises that came from him. They were unlike his usual noises during sex, somehow more strained and needful. He reached down again and stroked my hair away from my face, his fingers caressing my cheek and jaw.

"You're so beautiful, Ellen. You look incredible right now."

I moaned and cupped his balls. Another tip I learned online which appeared to work. Julian grunted, his voice breathless. "Are you sure you've never done this before?"

I chuckled as I sucked him and that seemed to drive him even more wild.

"Fuck, I'm nearly there," he rasped right before he came.

I was in a daze, hardly believing I just took charge like that. "I need you," I breathed, and Julian swore.

"I don't have a condom."

"That's okay, I'm on the pill now." After the last time, I made it a priority.

He eyes darkened as he pulled me up to stand. Lighting quick he flipped me around, shoved up my skirt, yanked down my knickers and pushed inside me. I was surprised he could go again so quickly, but then, Julian had always been insatiable and he hadn't had sex for months.

We were skin to skin and it felt amazing. He fucked me fast, his thrusts hard and desperate. I bit down on my lip to keep from screaming. In the background, I could hear the cast and crew returning from lunch.

"Crap," I said past a moan.

Julian sucked my earlobe into his mouth. "You're a dirty little thing once you get going, aren't you," he whispered then nipped me with his teeth.

I stifled a yelp. His hand went under my top, sliding down the cup of my bra to squeeze my breast. I sighed when he pinched my nipple right at the same time he fucked me deep.

His hand moved down my body, under my skirt to circle my clit. His movements matched the speed of his thrusts, and when I came on his fingers and cock, I couldn't help the loud moan that escaped me.

"Perfect," Julian purred, his voice husky in my ear. He pulled at my chin, turning my mouth to his for a kiss. I felt like goo, soft and malleable.

When we heard footsteps approach, we scrambled to right ourselves. We managed to make ourselves decent just in time before a crew member walked by carrying equipment. He barely spared us a second glance as he continued on his way.

Julian made a soft noise of satisfaction as he wrapped his arms around me. "These last months have been dreadful. The worst of my life. I'm never letting you go again."

His words spread a warmth across my chest and I sank into his hug. When I pulled away slightly to look up at him, he was gazing down at me with such fondness and love, I felt like I might burst. This morning I'd still been so unsure, but as soon as I heard him speak on that monitor, as soon as I saw the look of sheer longing on his face, the sound of agony in his voice, I knew he was being true. He didn't want to hurt me again, and so long as I gave him a second chance, he'd do everything in his power not to, and that was good enough for me.

"I love you so much, Julian. You have my heart now. Please be careful with it."

He took my hand and placed it over his chest. "Don't you know? You were in here from the very beginning. If I hurt you, I hurt both of us. And I would rather die than be without you again."

I blinked several times as his heartfelt words sank in. I was going to be brave and take a chance at happiness. And I believed him completely.

I no longer felt alone in the world. Julian was the other part of me now. We were in this together, and I wouldn't have it any other way.

Epilogue
Julian

One year later

The flashing lights were somewhat blinding. In all my years escorting and socialising, I'd never actually walked a red carpet.

Ellen and I emerged from a town car, stepping out into a frenzied, exhilarating atmosphere of anticipation. Fans and members of the press had gathered outside the theatre for the premiere of *Good Girl, Bad Lady*. Ellen and I linked arms as we prepared to enter the fray.

"Deep breaths in and out," I soothed as I led her toward the start of the red carpet.

She nodded and inhaled, visibly nervous. "Deep breaths. Okay."

I smiled and pressed a kiss to her cheek, nuzzling a little before I pulled away. "You've got this, Ellen."

Tonight, she wore a long champagne coloured gown that Suze had designed especially for her. A plus side to having a fashion designer as your BFF. I considered sending her a thank you note. The dress swept over Ellen's curves, hugging her in all the right places.

I looked forward to later, when I could slide it off her perfect body.

Damon and Rose were just ahead of us. Rose stood off to the side with Damon's PR agent, while the newly minted director answered questions from eager journalists. Over the last few years, he'd gotten much better at interacting with the press. I remembered when he and Rose first met, he was stiff and awkward whenever he was being interviewed.

"Damon cuts a fine figure in that suit," Ellen commented, and I levelled her with a playful scowl.

"I'm the only be-suited gentleman you should be admiring tonight."

She gave a flirtatious grin. "Just keeping you on your toes."

I thought of how much she'd changed over the last year. Before, Ellen had a panic attack every time she had to talk to a stranger. Now, she was out and about most days, whether it was for business meetings or attending various book events, she was a veritable social butterfly. It was incredibly gratifying to see her shine.

And I was a lucky bastard.

After over a year, I'd surprised myself with how suited I was to monogamy. Just like there were positives to being single, there were many positives to being in a relationship, too. I adored having a partner, someone to share all aspects of my life with. Someone to come home to, because Ellen was my home now. I never felt the urge to stray, to seek comfort with another. In Ellen, I found what I hadn't realised I'd been looking for. My heart had been searching for her all this time, I just hadn't known it.

After several months and much discussion, we'd decided to move in together. I'd grown frustrated switching between my flat and her house, and since she had the bigger place, we agreed that was where we would live. I did say I was an evolved modern gentleman. I could handle the fact that my partner earned significantly more than me.

I may have had quite a lucrative career as an escort, but I couldn't compete with the likes of E.S. Grant.

Speaking of careers, I found a new and engaging calling in film and TV. It turned out there was a certain need for technical consultants with my particular variety of experience. It was fast-paced and exciting, and I was currently consulting on the set of a television show that featured a call girl.

Ellen and I moved along the barricade. Lots of people had brought books for her to sign. After about twenty minutes, we finally made it to the press section.

To our left, a journalist called out, "Miss Grant! Miss Grant!"

Unlike the actors attending the premiere, Ellen didn't have a PR agent to field requests. It might be something for her to consider, seeing as her books had become even more popular since the movie started getting promoted.

Seeing her apprehension, I placed my hand to the small of her back and whispered in her ear, "Picture them all naked, perhaps?"

She arched an eyebrow. "Sometimes I wonder if you have a secret desire to become a naturist. You have a startling preoccupation with nudity."

I slid my thumb over the inside of her wrist. "Only yours, and mine. Preferably together."

A satisfying shudder went through her and she gave a breathy giggle. We reached the journalist, a blonde woman with an asymmetrical bob. "Miss Grant, you look fantastic tonight. How does it feel to finally see your story on the big screen?"

Ellen opened her mouth, closed it, then opened it again. Like I'd coached her, she took a deep breath in and out, then finally replied, "Well, I haven't actually seen it, but I'm pretty excited. I feel incredibly fortunate that all this has happened. Few books see their films actually come to fruition."

"Very true! Do you know anything about a sequel? Has it been given the green light?"

She laughed. "Slow down, nobody's even seen the first one yet."

I beamed at her, unable to help the pride I felt. She might've been a little tongue-tied to begin with, but now she was taking it in stride.

"And what about the lead actors? Are the rumours true that they're dating?"

Ever since filming began, gossip surrounded Alicia and David, and whether or not they were seeing each other. David told me it was all false, and that he and Alicia were merely friends.

"I have no idea," Ellen replied. "You'll have to ask them that."

The woman affected a disappointed pout and then there was a flurry of activity as another car arrived. Almost to contradict my previous thought, the door opened and David emerged, followed by Alicia. If I wasn't mistaken, they both looked a little rosy-cheeked. Had they just…?

Alicia took David's arm and they strode forward to greet the fans, sign posters, and pose for selfies.

I glanced at Ellen and saw she was just as intrigued as I was, though the fact that they arrived together didn't necessarily mean anything. Co-stars arrived at premieres together all the time. Still, this wouldn't help the rumours.

As David and Alicia passed us by, I caught hold of my friend's elbow. "Something you'd like to tell me?" I asked curiously.

David shook his head, though I did catch a hint of coyness. "Nothing at all, Julian."

That sneaky bastard.

I knew the look of a man who was getting laid. Though honestly, if Alicia made David happy, then that was good enough for me.

Ellen and I entered the cinema and I quickly procured her a glass of wine. She took it gratefully.

"That was crazy."

I smiled with affection. "Better get used to it."

We made our way inside. There was to be a short question and answer session before the film started. I stood off to the side as Ellen took a seat on stage next to Damon. Also present were David and Alicia, and two other members of the cast, Peter and Anna. The host introduced everyone and asked Damon several questions to start; *why did he choose this particular film for his directorial debut, how had the characters spoken to him.* Alicia and David shared a few funny anecdotes from the set, while Peter and Anna expressed how lucky they felt to be involved.

Ellen spoke of her apprehension about having her book adapted for film. Her voice was clear and concise, confident even. I knew it took a lot for her to speak in front of hundreds of people, but with all the signings she'd done she was definitely getting used to it. She told the host how Damon was the only one she trusted with her baby, and that his vision truly captured her.

The host opened up questions to the room and lots of hands shot up, naturally. He pointed to a woman with brown hair. She stood, and an usher presented her with a microphone.

"Hi, everyone. My question is for David and Alicia. Are the rumours true that you're a couple?"

The two shared a glance, then Alicia replied, "The rumours are false. We're just friends."

349

There was a sound of audible disappointment from the audience, which gave me a chuckle. Everybody liked to get invested in a good showmance. I suspected that if they were seeing each other, they were keeping it under wraps. The next question came from a diminutive woman in the middle row.

"My question is actually about the storyline in the books. I'd like to ask E.S. if she originally intended for Toby and Sasha to get together in the end, or if it just happened naturally over the course of the series?"

Ellen sat forward, smiling at the woman who was clearly a big fan. "No, actually. That wasn't my original intention. After all, Sasha had a number of love affairs with various characters in earlier books, but over time it started to become clear to me that she had feelings for Toby. In the end, he was the one to steal her heart. It all happened very organically."

"Thank you," the woman replied and sat.

Ellen's eyes met mine. In some ways, I was Sasha and she was Toby. For years, Ellen had been writing about us and she didn't even know it.

The session ended and she walked off stage. I took her in my arms, hugging her tight. "You did great. I love you so much."

"I love you, too," she said, whispering her lips across my neck and sending a jolt of awareness directly to my crotch.

I took her hand and led her to our seats. "Just you wait until I get you home."

We sat and I kept our hands linked together. She laid her head on my shoulder just as the opening scene began…

A smartly dressed Sasha hurries through the streets of London when it starts to rain. The fat drops threaten to ruin her outfit, so she buys a paper from a newsstand and uses it to shield from the downpour. When she finally reaches the office building, she dumps the paper in a trash can. She shakes herself off, takes a deep breath and strides toward the reception desk.

"Hi, I'm Sasha Orlando. I'm here to interview with Toby Richards."

The receptionist looks her up and down. "Right this way, Miss Orlando."

END.

About the Author

L.H. Cosway lives in Dublin, Ireland. Her inspiration to write comes from music. Her favourite things in life include writing stories, vintage clothing, dark cabaret music, food, musical comedy, and of course, books. She thinks that imperfect people are the most interesting kind. They tell the best stories.

Find L.H. Cosway online!

www.lhcoswayauthor.com
www.facebook.com/LHCosway
www.twitter.com/LHCosway
www.instagram.com/l.h.cosway

L.H. Cosway's *HEARTS* Series

Praise for *Six of Hearts* (Book #1)

"This book was sexy. Man was it hot! Cosway writes sexual tension so that it practically sizzles off the page." - A. Meredith Walters, New York Times & USA Today Bestselling Author.

"Six of Hearts is a book that will absorb you with its electric and all-consuming atmosphere." - Lucia, Reading is my Breathing.

"There is so much "swoonage" in these pages that romance readers will want to hold this book close and not let go." - Katie, Babbling About Books.

Praise for *Hearts of Fire* (Book #2)

"This story holds so much intensity and it's just blazing hot. It created an inferno of emotions inside me." - Patrycja, Smokin' Hot Book Blog.

"I think this is my very favorite LH Cosway romance to date. Absolutely gorgeous." - Angela, Fiction Vixen.

"Okay we just fell in love. Complete and utter beautiful book love. You know the kind of love where you just don't want a book to finish. You try and make it last; you want the world to pause as you read and you want the story to go on and on because you're not ready to let it go." - Jenny & Gitte, Totally Booked.

Praise for _King of Hearts_ (Book #3)

"Addictive. Consuming. Witty. Heartbreaking. Brilliant-- King of Hearts is one of my favourite reads of 2015!" - Samantha Young, New York Times, USA Today and Wall Street Journal bestselling author.

"I was looking for a superb read, and somehow I stumbled across an epic one," - Natasha is a Book Junkie.

"5+++++++ Breathtaking stars! Outstanding. Incredible. Epic. Overwhelmingly romantic and poignant. There's book love and in this case there's BOOK LOVE."- Jenny & Gitte, Totally Booked.

Praise for _Hearts of Blue_ (Book #4)

"From its compelling characters, to the competent prose that holds us rapt cover to cover, this is a book I could not put down." - Natasha is a Book Junkie.

"Devoured it in one sitting. Sexy, witty, and fresh. Their love was not meant to be, their love should never work, but Lee and Karla can't deny what burns so deep and strong in their hearts. Confidently a TRSoR recommendation and fave!"- The Rock Stars of Romance.

"WOW!!! It's hard to find words right now, I don't think the word LOVE even makes justice or can even describe how much I adored this novel. Karla handcuffed my senses and Lee stole my heart."- Dee, Wrapped Up In Reading

Praise for *Thief of Hearts* (Book #5)

"This is easily one of our favorite romances by L.H. Cosway. We were consumed by the brilliant slow-burn and smoldering student/teacher forbidden storyline with layers of uncontainable, explosive raw emotions and genuine heart." – The Rock Stars of Romance.

"I was in love with this couple and was championing their relationship from the start." – I Love Book Love

"One of my fave reads of this year. Mind-blowing and thrilling, let this story sweep you off your feet!" – Aaly and the Books.

Books by L.H. Cosway

Contemporary Romance
Painted Faces
Killer Queen
The Nature of Cruelty
Still Life with Strings
Showmance

The Hearts Series
Six of Hearts (#1)
Hearts of Fire (#2)
King of Hearts (#3)
Hearts of Blue (#4)
Thief of Hearts (#5)
Cross My Heart (#5.75)
Hearts on Air (#6)

The Cracks Duet
A Crack in Everything (#1)
How the Light Gets In (#2)

The Rugby Series with Penny Reid
The Hooker & the Hermit (#1)
The Player & the Pixie (#2)
The Cad & the Co-ed (#3)
The Varlet & the Voyeur (#4)

Urban Fantasy
Tegan's Blood (The Ultimate Power Series #1)
Tegan's Return (The Ultimate Power Series #2)
Tegan's Magic (The Ultimate Power Series #3)
Tegan's Power (The Ultimate Power Series #4)

Made in the USA
Middletown, DE
15 August 2018